THE

DARK SHORE

ALSO BY KEVIN EMERSON:

THE LOST CODE: BOOK ONE OF THE ATLANTEANS

THE
DARK SHORE

BOOK TWO OF THE ATLANTEANS

KEVIN EMERSON

KATHERINE TEGEN BOOKS
An Imprint of HarperCollins Publishers

Katherine Tegen Books is an imprint of HarperCollins Publishers.

The Dark Shore: Book Two of the Atlanteans

Library of Congress Cataloging-in-Publication Data
Emerson, Kevin.
    The dark shore : book two of The Atlanteans / Kevin Emerson.
— 1st ed.
        p.   cm. — (The Atlanteans ; bk. 2)
    Summary: On the run from EdenWest, Owen, Lilly, and Leech
cross North American deserts seeking Atlantis and find a third
Atlantean, the wild child Seven, who is goddess of the Heliad-7 death
cult in Yucatan.
    ISBN 978-0-06-206282-6 (hardcover bdgs)
    [1. Science fiction.   2. Identity—Fiction.   3. Goddesses—
Fiction.   4. Environmental degradation—Fiction.   5. Atlantis
(Legendary place)—Fiction.   6. Yucatán (Mexico : State)—
Fiction.   7. Mexico—Fiction.]   I. Title.
PZ7.E5853Atl 2013   2012029923
[Fic]—dc23   CIP
                                                          AC

Typography by Torborg Davern
13 14 15 16 17   LP/RRDH   10 9 8 7 6 5 4 3 2 1
❖
First Edition

For Bryan, who would make a great partner when roaming future wastelands in an ancient flying machine

After the fracture and the flood
The masters and their magic consumed by the
    ravenous earth
There was a journey
Through aeons of dark, as the world healed
The refugees seeking a new home but lost, so lost
And when the seas calmed and the land quieted
And the stars could bear to watch once more
The memory descended in ships of blue light
To rise again
Hoping this time to reach the heights of the masters
Without resurrecting their horrors.

PART I

Call: *Listen! Listen for the song!*
Response: *Where has that sweet music gone?*
Call: *She's gone with the river, gone with the trees,*
Response: *Gone and left us on our knees.*

Call: *Listen! Listen! What's that you hear?*
Response: *The wind of change, the drum of fear.*
Call: *Hear our footsteps, hear our hearts,*
Response: *Is this the end, or just the start?*
—TRADITIONAL GREAT RISE MIGRATION CHANT

These bones are old, older than you know,
You remember me like yesterday,
But that was years ago.
—THE TRILOBYTES, "SONG FOR THE CRYO"

1

IT WAS DAWN WHEN WE DESCENDED OVER THE FIRST city of the dead: Gambler's Falls, in what had once been South Dakota, at the western reach of the Great Mississippi Desert. We'd flown over other towns during the long night. They'd all looked the same: ghostly geometric sketches in moonlight, the buildings intact, the cars in orderly lines along streets or neatly parked in driveways. You could almost imagine the people still sleeping peacefully, except for the dark streetlights, the open car hoods and gas tanks, and on everything, the thick crust of blown sand.

What made Gambler's Falls different was the wall.

And the corpse.

We were dropping out of a vacant blue sky. The sun had just risen behind us, orange and fiery, and though the wind on my face was still the hollow cold of night, I could already feel the lethal heat on my back. Lilly was asleep, curled beside me. Leech sat in the front of the triangular craft.

We'd been going for fourteen hours since escaping from

EdenWest, and we needed a place to hide from the sunlight and EdenCorp. I'd spotted a narrow canyon on the far side of town that might work.

As we lowered, I cast a glance behind us, looking for any sign of Paul's forces, but as it had all night, the horizon kept its secrets. At first, I'd thought that Eden would be right on our tail, but Leech and I had discussed it and figured that actually it would take Paul some time to get a team together to come after us. His hover copters would need modifications for the real sun, and fuel and supplies. They were probably on their way by now, but we had a head start, and I figured we could afford a few hours of rest.

"You sure we have time for this?" Leech asked skeptically as we flew over the outskirts of town. "We're already so far off the bearing."

"I've got to sleep," I said. It had been more than twenty-four hours since I'd slept at all, and days since I'd had anything more than a few meager hours. "Otherwise, there's no way I'm going to get us to your marker."

As the night had gone on, this had become the latest tension between me and Leech. He'd been sketching maps, and, using the lines we'd seen etched in the top of Mount Aasgard back in EdenWest, he'd come up with a bearing that pointed southwest. Leech believed that this bearing would take us to some kind of Atlantean marker, the next stop on our way to the Heart of the Terra, the place we had to get to before Paul.

I trusted Leech's idea. He was the Mariner. It was his job to plot our course, and my job as the Aeronaut to get us there. But instead of following Leech's bearing, I had been flying due west, toward Yellowstone Hub, where I was from. All through the night, Leech had noted that we were getting farther off course and adding to our time. My point was that going to Hub made more sense as a first move, because we knew we had my dad there, and we could get supplies to stock up for the longer journey.

"I get that you need your beauty sleep," said Leech begrudgingly, "but— Whoa . . ." He leaned over the side of the craft. "Check that out."

I looked down and in the shadows between buildings, I saw the wall. It was maybe ten meters tall, an uneven pile of stacked furniture, sandbags, bricks, and chunks of concrete, all stitched together with barbed wire and telephone lines. Its spine was lined with jagged shards of glass. It undulated like a serpent through the streets, past the overturned, blackened hulks of cars and trucks, the spills of furniture and trash, and sometimes right through collapsed buildings.

"Dude, look out!" Leech shouted.

I'd gotten distracted by the scene, my exhausted brain in slow motion, and now we were too low. Directly in front of us, the wall crested to a high point. Perched at the top was a cockeyed lookout tower, a square wooden platform with a blue plastic tarp over it. The tarp had been shredded by wind, but the aluminum poles were still standing, including the one sticking up through the middle.

That was where the body was.

I slammed down on the pedals in the floor of the craft. The vortex engine, a black triangle of polished stone with swirling blue light in the center, hummed at a higher pitch. Its glow increased and I felt a teeth-rattling vibration as the antigravity propulsion kicked in. We leaped skyward, barely clearing the body.

Lilly jolted awake. "What happened?" She pulled up on my shoulder.

"Dead guy," Leech reported.

Lilly craned back to see. "Jesus," she muttered.

"I don't think Jesus was involved," said Leech.

The body was mostly bones, with some stretches of cooked, leathery skin still spanning joints. A few tatters of brown clothing fluttered in the breeze.

"There are more," said Leech. He pointed to a heap of brown bones and clothing at the rubble-strewn base of the wall. "Looks like they were trying to get in."

"What do you think *they* were, warnings?" Lilly was looking over my shoulder at the tallest building in town. It was brick, and about twelve stories. Incomplete letters on its side suggested it had been a bank. Brilliant sunbeams silhouetted skeletons, one displayed in each window.

A decorative border had also been constructed around the roof that gave the building a castlelike appearance, only these miniature battlements were actually stacks of skulls. Lots of skulls.

"I would take those as warnings," I said.

"Looks like that's what they were trying to protect." Leech pointed in the other direction.

The wall made a rough circle through the town, and at its center, just beyond the downtown blocks, stood an enormous building, a giant expanse of flat, sand-covered roof. A tall sign beside it, white with faded blue letters, read:

WALMART SUPERPLUS GAMBLER'S FALLS

"I used to go to one of those, back before I was cryoed," said Leech. "It had pretty much everything. It makes sense that they defended it."

There was another body strapped to the flagpole outside the front entrance, and all the glass doors had been covered with plywood. The body looked similarly leather skinned and old.

I banked the craft and headed out of town, toward the canyon I'd seen.

"What happened here?" Lilly asked quietly, watching the streets slide by. Most of the buildings and houses were flattened. A few beams and remnants of walls stuck up from the sand, along with the skeletal stalks of scorched trees.

She'd been asleep all night, except for one period where she'd stirred, whimpering softly to herself. The one word I'd been able to make out was "Anna." She'd said it in a despairing way that took me right back to the secret lab beneath Camp Eden, where Lilly had found her best friend pried open and turned into a cruel science experiment, one that had been done in search of the Atlantean code that we had inside us. The image of Anna, of her ribs and her organs, the tubes, and her wide, terrified eyes . . . I couldn't shake it.

"Like," Lilly added, "who were these people?" I remembered her wondering about this very thing back on the raft at camp: Thousands of years from now, what would future beings think about this lost society of the twenty-first century, this *us*? Of course, on the raft, she'd been talking about an empty swimming pool in her old backyard in Las Vegas. Here we were talking about a massacre.

Maybe this was more than Lilly had bargained for. It was definitely more bleak and violent than anything I'd seen back at Yellowstone Hub, but I had at least heard tales of the things that happened out in the wild lands.

"Holdouts, probably," said Leech. "That's what they were called back in the Rise."

"Yeah," I agreed, suppressing a flash of annoyance. Even though we were out of Eden and back in my part of the world, Leech still liked to act like he was the expert on everything. But he was right in this case, so I let it go.

This whole part of the continent had once been fertile cropland, but during the middle of the Great Rise, the river system dried up. It had been one of the cruel jokes of climate change. The warmer the atmosphere got, the more water vapor it could hold, and so even though the oceans were rising, the land was drying out.

There had been time for people to evacuate, but not many places left for them to go. Aside from the lucky few who could buy their way into EdenWest, the other options had been grim. A family could either head for the coast and pack onto a tanker bound for the employee prefectures of Coke-Sahel, or make the migration north to the Borderlands of the Habitable Zone, where visas into the American-Canadian Federation were already rare and disease and crime were common.

"Instead of leaving," Leech explained to Lilly, "they fortified, and tried to make a go of it, like at Hub or Dallas Beach. Those groups sometimes can get support from the ACF."

"Most of them fail, though," I said, "from plague or infighting or starvation. Sometimes all three."

"Mmm," said Lilly, still gazing at the wreckage below.

She shook her head and leaned into me. The warm press of her melted through the chill of the long night.

"Hi," I said, glancing over. She was huddled in my LoRad pullover, her long, dark hair matted from sleeping. Her eyes were as clear and breathtaking as ever, sky blue with tendrils of pearl white. A curvy pattern of pale lines snaked down her almond-colored cheek, indentations from using her red waterproof bag as a pillow. I reached over and traced one of the lines in a slow S from her eye to her chin. "Funny sleep marks," I said.

She smiled and kissed my cheek, her nose pushing into

my cheekbone. I felt her eyelashes on my temple. The sensation was already something familiar. Even though it had only been two days since our first kiss, I had this feeling of knowing every detail of it, her lips, her breath, how it smelled a little salty—and I couldn't imagine that I had ever not known that. Each kiss was like a dust storm across my mind, wiping everything else out.

But then she pulled away sharply. "Ow," she groaned. She rubbed at her neck, at the slim red lines of her gills.

"What's up?" I asked.

"They're really sore," she said, scratching lightly. "They feel dry."

"Mine used to feel that way before I'd come down to the lake at night," I said, "like they needed water." There was barely any trace left of my gills. Not even two days since they had stopped working, and now it was almost like they'd never been. Another in a series of changes so complete that I could barely remember what had been before. Had I really swum for hours in the dark of Lake Eden? Had I really felt at home in the pressure and cold of water, felt stronger there than on land even? And now air was my home. Instead of water currents, I reacted to wind speeds. Instead of the pressures of different depths, it was the tension of sails against the breeze.

Lilly ran a finger over the faded lines on my neck. It caused only a faint echo. "I can barely see them." She frowned and turned away.

"Hey," I said, wanting to reach for her shoulder, but the

morning thermal breeze was picking up, so I had to keep both my sore arms on the sail lines. Ever since my gills had faded, things had been different between us. Not bad, just . . . off. I'd lost my gills because I was an Atlantean, one of the Three. Leech was, too, but Lilly . . .

It didn't seem likely. Her gills hadn't faded like Leech's and mine had. She'd also lied about seeing the siren, except Leech hadn't seen her either, so that didn't prove anything.

I still didn't know why I'd seen the siren. I wondered if maybe it was because the skull beneath Eden had been mine. Maybe that was also the reason my gills had come and gone so quickly. Leech's had probably faded because of prolonged contact. He'd been around my skull for years, working in the underground temple right above it. Maybe being here in the craft with my skull would be enough to make Lilly's gills fade. . . .

Or maybe she just wasn't one of us. And if that turned out to be the case, what did that mean for the rest of our journey? It had already crossed my mind that there might come a time when I could go and she could not, where the difference in our destinies would separate us. Maybe she felt that, too, like a cloud over us, despite the relentlessly clear sky. Thinking about it caused a cold squeeze of adrenaline in my gut.

"It will be okay," I said. I didn't know if I meant the pain in her gills, or us, or even the unknown that lay ahead of us. Either way, I worried that I was lying.

Lilly sighed. "Yeah." She rubbed at her gills again. Her

gaze stayed distant, like she didn't quite believe it, either.

The sun was getting hotter by the minute, making my skin itch even through the heavy sweatshirt I was wearing. It was a product of EdenWest, though, with no UV Rad protection, and out here, it wouldn't be enough. We'd spent a few hours in the late afternoon sun the day before, and I already had a sore feeling on my scalp, and worrisome pink blotches on my legs and hands.

"How about we rest inside that Walmart?" asked Leech, gazing behind us. "Then we could check it for supplies."

"There's nowhere to hide the ship," I said. "I think that canyon will be safer, and, besides, ten more hours and we can be at Hub. We just have to hold out a little longer."

"Yeah, but I'm hungry now," said Leech. "And what makes you think your dad can even help us?"

"Who else can we go to?" I asked. Our only other option for supplies seemed to be tracking down a Nomad pod, but we had no idea where to find one, and Leech still liked to go on about how they were savages, even though Lilly and I knew otherwise. Before finally succumbing to sleep last night, Lilly had scanned the gamma link for the Nomad Free Signal but hadn't found it.

Leech had a good point about my dad, though. Because really, it was hard to imagine what his reaction would be to my story:

Hey, Dad, listen. I know I only left for Camp Eden last week but I'm back and some things have . . . changed. And now I need help getting supplies without alerting anyone that we're here because, oh, did I mention we're on the run from the EdenCorp? They want me because I'm a genetic descendant of the ancient Atlanteans, one who can help them find the Brocha de Dioses—sorry, Paintbrush of the Gods—which is ancient technology that can reverse the course of climate change. You know, save the world.

No, I know, saving the world sounds great! But there's one problem: we don't trust Paul and his board of directors and their Project Elysium, because they did a bunch of terrible things to our friends, not to mention how they've been running the search for Atlantis and us Atlanteans in secret for over fifty years. I know, right? If their reason was really as simple as saving the planet and the population, why would they be keeping it such a massive secret? Yes, that is pretty suspicious.

What? Oh, right, What exactly is MY plan. We're going to find the Paintbrush of the Gods ourselves and then decide what should be done. No matter what, we'll protect it from EdenCorp.

This craft? It's mine. I know, cool, right? Yes, I can fly it. How? I learned from a dead kid named Lük, whose consciousness—well, technically his Qi-An life force—was trapped inside a crystal skull.

So . . . does all that sound good? Okay, great! Now, we just need a bunch of food, a tent, and some other supplies, and then I need you to go ahead and let me fly off into the sunset with no word of where I'm going . . .

Just like Mom did.

I probably wouldn't add that last line. But even without it, how exactly was Dad going to react? When I tried to picture it, I could only imagine him freaking out.

And even if, somehow, he thought this all sounded fine—that it was perfectly okay for me to fly off to who knows where while being pursued by EdenCorp—then what? I was assuming that my dad, who had trouble with the two flights of steps up from the cavern promenade to our apartment because of his breathing issues, who could barely cheer on the Helsinki Island soccer team without breaking into wicked phlegm-filled coughs, was going to be able to ferry us supplies without collapsing?

Not likely.

But I hadn't mentioned all this to Leech. I didn't want to give him any more ammunition to add to his argument for bypassing Hub and heading southwest. Maybe going to Hub was dumb, but I couldn't help wanting to go.

And it was more than just supplies: I also really wanted to see Dad. The feeling surprised me. We weren't all that close, and yet as last night had passed, the feeling had come on strong. So much had happened in the last week, from drowning to my Atlantean awakening to our escape. All of it played in my mind like some brightly colored and impossible dream, and it was like, What had my life even been like back at Hub? It felt so distant, which was ridiculous because I could clearly remember the quiet nights on the couch with Dad, the lonely days walking to school and sitting more silent than not among my little class, the dank subterranean light, the smell of sulfur and rock. It was all right there in my mind . . . and yet it seemed like there was a gulf, a vast space, between that old version of me and this new one. And while new Owen, with a purpose, with Lilly, was definitely a big improvement on who I used to be, I also couldn't help feeling unstuck somehow, like I had left my old reality and was floating outside it now, slightly out of sync with time and space.

I fiddled with the leather bracelet that I'd made back at camp. Crude stamps spelled out *Dad*, followed by a coarse etching of what, at the time, I'd thought was just a funky symbol for Camp Aasgard, but that I now knew was an Atlantean symbol, maybe for Atlantis itself.

It was the old me and the new. And so maybe I just wanted some concrete connection between the two, like before I could go be this crazy thing, this Aeronaut, I needed to make sure I was still old Owen, too. A week ago, I wouldn't have imagined wanting that, but now I found that I did.

All of which was why I said to Leech, "You haven't *lost* your bearing, have you?"

"Of course not," he replied.

"So after Yellowstone, we'll correct our course."

Leech gave me a weird look: less annoyed, more serious. "Look, I just think it's wasting precious time." He almost sounded worried.

"Well," said Lilly, "I vote with Owen. So deal with it." She started rubbing her back. "It's getting hot, fast. Is that where we're headed?"

"Yeah." We were coming up on the small canyon. It was narrow and curvy, its walls striped in every shade of brown.

"Looks homey," Leech muttered.

"It's concealed," I said. "That's the point."

On its bank was what had likely been a park. There was a wide expanse of cracked pavement, a flat area with picnic tables awash in drifts of sand, the skeleton of a playground poking out. Beside it, the canyon opened into a wide mouth, like there had been a waterfall. Below that was an empty scoop of land; maybe it had been a pond. Kids had probably gone swimming there, way back when.

But as we passed over the park, we saw that now the dry pond was something very different.

"Aww, man!" said Leech.

"Uh . . ." Lilly breathed, sounding nauseated.

The dry depression was piled with bodies.

2

THERE WERE TOO MANY BLACKENED BONES TO
count, hundreds of people, all dumped one atop the next,
the entire pile burned. A deep set of ruts, tire tracks that
no water had ever come to wash away, led to an enormous
dump truck parked back beside the city wall.

"Plague, you think?" asked Leech.

"Probably flu," I said. "It always hit bad in places with
close quarters. Maybe RP two."

"What?" Lilly asked.

"Rise pandemic two," I said. "People called it red tide.
One of the symptoms was busted blood vessels across a vic-
tim's face. I was little when it happened, and we got lucky
out at Hub. There were only about ten cases and they got
them quarantined in time."

"Red tide?" said Leech, like he thought that was a stupid idea.

"Well, what do you think it was, then?"

Leech peered at me for a second, then just shrugged.

"Doesn't matter. Whatever it was, it probably took out most of the town, but I bet that was just the beginning. There's a thing, population trauma syndrome, where survivors of pandemics lose their grip on reality. Maybe that's when they started building battlements out of skulls and hanging bodies on sticks."

"Is there a thing with boys knowing so many details about plagues and death?" Lilly asked.

"It's interesting," I said.

"Agreed," said Leech, and we actually shared a rare almost-grin.

"They shouldn't be contagious anymore, after baking in the sun for years," I said, bringing the craft down over the bodies. I noticed now that there were no skulls. They'd all been put to use back in town.

Lilly spoke quietly as she peered down at the tangle of limbs. "Why should we save this world, when things like this can happen?"

I shrugged, but didn't reply. She had a point, but again I was surprised by her tone. Of everyone back at camp, Lilly had been the one most passionate about taking action to make things better.

"We should just keep going," Leech muttered. "I'm not going to be able to rest with those things nearby."

"I gotta sleep," I said. "I'll get as far from them as I can."

I brought the craft over the dry falls and into the mouth of the narrow canyon. We floated through shady curves.

The riverbed was a strip of light sand, boulders here and there. The rock walls looked like they'd been smoothed by hands.

"Okay, now we give this a try," I said. I pressed the pedals all the way back, and we touched down gently on the sand. I watched the vortex dim. We'd already lost the thermal balloon in our escape from Eden. If the vortex went completely out, the craft would be useless.

I closed my eyes and drifted inward, a sensation like falling backward into water, until the outside world disappeared. I felt the hum of the nearby crystal skull, which was tucked in Lilly's bag.

Around me was the setting I'd seen before: a stark gray beach along a crystal-blue alpine lake, surrounded by steep, snowcapped mountains. Behind me was the Atlantean city, in a fjord that, according to Paul, was in Greenland, a city that would also be their last outpost. Its narrow spires reached for the high clouds. The flat roof of its tall central pyramid was lit with pale white globes.

You're sure this will work? I asked Lük, who sat cross-legged nearby, coiling sail lines. He was my age, both ancient looking and strangely like me, our genes linked but separated by hundreds of generations.

Both our craft were tied to stakes in the sand. They drifted in the water, little waves making plunking sounds against their wooden hulls. There were no other students around.

He spoke. *A charge to the mercury vortex engine should*

last you a couple thousand kilometers under smooth flying conditions. It uses nearly no power when idle.

Okay, good, I said. *At some point, we're going to need to construct a new thermal.*

Lük closed his eyes for a moment, thinking. A shadow crossed his face.

What? I asked.

He looked around, frowning. *We will need to reconnect with the skull to access that information. It should . . . it should be here, but it's not.*

Huh, okay, I said. He was still peering at me. *What?* I asked again.

I'm not sure, said Lük. *I am noticing other gaps in information. I believe the skull should have created a more complete melding between us. We should convene again.*

Okay, after I get some rest we can have another skull session.

I swam back up to the surface and took my feet off the pedals. The vortex dimmed to the faintest glow I'd seen so far, but it stayed lit, emitting a low hum.

"We're good," I said, grabbing the black backpack that Dr. Maria left behind with us. Lilly hauled her bag out and we all retreated to a spot near the wall, deep in the safety of shadows where the rippled sand was fine and soft. As I dropped down to my knees, I felt my entire body shutting down.

Lilly spread out her blanket. We sat in a triangle and I pulled out two of the remaining soymeal bars from Dr.

Maria's pack, along with a single water bottle. We had only one more bar, a package of synth veggie crisps, and no more water.

I tore open the wrappers and started breaking the dirt-brown bars into chunks. "Two thirds each," I said.

As I handed two bits toward Leech, I thought of the moment in the predator-prey game when he hadn't given me the food credits, when I'd pushed him and we'd started a fight that we'd never finished. We locked eyes now, and I wondered what we would do with that unresolved hate, now that we were partners. He raised his eyebrows and took the two pieces, like he was acknowledging what I felt, too: we might annoy each other, but we were also a long way from those identities we'd still been pretending to have in the Preserve.

The few bites of pasty bar only made me more hungry. I opened the water bottle and took a single sip before passing it around.

"You know," said Leech as we ate, "given that most everybody in this town seems to have died suddenly and terribly, there might actually be some supplies left over in that Walmart."

"We're not going in there," I said. "If you were from out here and knew the protocol for red tide, you'd know that it can be carried by mice and roaches, which are bound to be in there, especially if there's old food lying around."

"Listen to the brain," said Leech.

"I am, actually."

Leech laughed to himself. "Red tide . . . Sorry, I can only listen to it for so long."

"What do you know?" I said. "You were cryoed for what, thirty years—"

"Forty-seven and a half," said Leech. He stopped laughing.

"Right. Out here, this is my world."

"As far as you know," said Leech. He shoved his soymeal bites in his mouth, then got up and started trudging down the canyon, kicking sand. "I'll take first watch."

"I do know!" I called after him, and immediately hated how defensive I sounded. I reminded myself that I was at least his equal.

Leech waved a hand over his shoulder. "Whatever. Boys' room is this way." He disappeared around the corner, but not far enough that we couldn't hear him relieving himself.

"Nice." Lilly groaned.

"I can't believe we're stuck with him." I said. I lay back on the sand, lacing my fingers behind my head and staring at the curving rock above us and the slim river of visible sky. The sand smelled like it had been washed. A low layer of cool air hovered over it. I felt my eyelids getting heavy, my legs turning to cement.

There was a light sound of static from beside me. Lilly had pulled out her computer pad. She was running her finger back and forth, causing a warbling hiss of empty gamma link frequencies as she scanned for the Free Signal again. When we'd left Eden, we'd had Paul's phone, but it had self-destructed when Lilly tried to use it, like we'd seen Aaron's do. She'd thrown it overboard.

Lilly sensed me looking. "Get some sleep."

"Right." I wanted to talk with her more, but sleep pulled me down. I drifted beneath the static from the computer, back through a dark night's journey, through the open air vent, back into the TruSky of EdenWest, past the hover copters, down to the lab and bodies we'd seen, down into the dark green water with its ghostly blue siren, and finally into black sleep.

For a while.

Owen.

I swam up from dark depths, the siren's call beckoning. I was back in the lake and I had gills again, fluttering magically. The shimmering blue form floated before me.

Who are you? I asked her, like I had the last time I'd seen her, in the skull chamber beneath Eden.

And just like last time, the siren didn't answer, only turned and wriggled off into the murk.

I tried to swim after her, but my surroundings began to change. Water was replaced by walls: the dingy metal panels of our apartment back at Hub. I was suddenly much younger, in my bed wrapped in blankets and cowering against the wall.

"Owen, they're here. Want to go see?" Mom stood over

me, her cowboy hat on. It was the night that the Three-Year Fire reached Yellowstone. She held out her hand, but I didn't want to go because I felt certain about something: *going out to see the fires makes her leave.* Yet I was getting up anyway, just like I had in real life.

Why was I back here? The second time I'd closed my eyes in two days, and both times I found myself reliving this same night. Once again we headed up and outside to the ledge on the caldera wall, to watch the pyrocumulus clouds sail overhead like the warships of a conquering army, to watch the herd of flames plunge over the rim, with me trying to be brave because my mom was enjoying the show, and yet inside feeling so scared, so vulnerable, certain that if my mother knew what I was feeling, it would make her leave us.

But then, unlike that actual night, light began to bloom around me. Suddenly, it was the next morning, the sky gray, the world a dead wash of ash around the black skeletons of trees. The ash was smooth, erasing the lines and contours of the world. A canvas to start again. Gray flakes of it still fell from the sky, just like over the Atlantean city where Lük and I first met.

The world smelled sour like burned wood and electricity. Everything swam in heat and there were spots of glowing red cinder here and there. And . . .

Someone was screaming. A girl. I couldn't tell if this was a memory, too, or a new dream reality. All I knew was that I had to reach her, had to hurry, so I turned and jumped off the ledge. I floated down over the burnscape, arms out, soaring.

I landed on my knees in the ash, a fine powder, still warm. It clung to my arms, chalked my hands, smudged my jeans.

Nearby, a tree carcass popped and hissed, its cinder jaws gleaming red.

Owen.

I looked up and there she was.

Not the siren.

A girl. She was young, with deep red hair that fell to her shoulders and quartz white skin, translucent like

—like the skull—

and reflecting the color of the ash. The ash and the skin nearly the same. Something was wrong with her. Maybe an illness.

If it gets worse, she will leave.

The girl gazed at me with enormous brown eyes and a kind of brokenhearted expression, her eyes so serious, her mouth so small. She wore LoRad pajamas decorated with smiling green frogs. . . . How old? Three? And what was her name? I felt like I knew it. Had known it at some point. It was something I was *supposed* to know. I could almost envision the blank spot where that information should have been, but it was lost to me. She held a toy crocodile, its velvety tail hanging down and making little swipes in the gray . . .

And she was starting to sink into the ash. Inch by inch,

up her pajamas as if she were being erased.

I have to save her. That I knew for sure. I was worried about her, *terrified*, only the ash felt like mud, resisting me . . . and my legs were suddenly weak and useless, like my dream was at the mercy of technicians, laughing mischievously as they changed the rules.

Wait! I kept trying to run, but my legs churned, and I sank, too, down into the ash which was now also the sky and water, and I was drowning, like in the lake all over again. The black trees floated in the murk, their branches like sickly veins twisting through the gray, and I couldn't find the girl—

O-wen.

I thrashed around. Up. Down. Which was which? Who was calling me—siren or little girl?

Except this voice sounded different. I saw a glowing form again, but it wasn't the siren. This was a rectangle of light, and there seemed to be a face floating in it.

All at once my mind woke up enough to stash the dream props back in their closet, to attach gravity and time and space to the real. Ash became water became air. I felt the hard sand against my cheek, the oven-hot air of midday.

The light was the computer pad, lying next to Lilly, who was asleep on her side.

I sat up and saw a face on the pad.

"Ahh, there you are."

Paul's face.

3

PAUL GAZED UP AS IF FROM A WINDOW IN THE SAND. His tinted glasses were on, his expression calm. Other than an inky bruise on the side of his head—the spot where Lilly had slammed him with the skull—he looked like he always did: a mystery, only he wasn't a mystery to me anymore. I'd seen his electric circuit board eyes—the bionic implants— and so his stillness now just made me think of an android, cold and calculating.

"Enjoying your trip?" he asked.

I picked up the pad, feeling around its edges for an off switch, but I couldn't find one. This must have been some older model; Lilly had said that her parents had left it to her when she was cryoed.

"Owen, look at me."

I kept fiddling.

"Owen, my boy . . ."

"Shut up!" I shouted, holding the pad at arm's length, as if he might reach right through and grab me.

"Okay, don't get so worked up," said Paul. "I just want

to talk before you make a mistake."

I looked at him. "Mistake?" My whole body was shaking. "My only mistake was not realizing what you were sooner."

"Oh, come on," said Paul. "Have you and your pals made me out to be a villain or a monster? That kind of thing? Because I think if you really reflected on our conversation in the temple, you'd realize that I am the best ally you three could have."

"I remember the temple," I said. "When I didn't agree to join you, you tried to hook me up to the skull like I was another one of your test subjects."

"Well, let's be clear about that." Paul smiled. "You were my *prize* test subject. You hold the key to saving humanity, and I can help you unlock it."

"Stop!" I felt a surge of hate like a wave breaking inside me. "Just shut up!"

"Owen?" Lilly rolled over, eyes blinking open. When she saw Paul, she lurched up. "Turn it off! If they're transmitting to this pad that means they can track our location."

Paul glanced in Lilly's direction and smiled. "I always liked Miss Ishani's instincts. Owen, please don't let her kill this chat before I've had a chance to warn you."

"Give me that." Lilly grabbed the pad.

"It's about your father. About your home. You can't go there."

"Good-bye, jerk," Lilly said, tapping quickly to reveal a side menu on the screen.

"Hold on." I caught her wrist.

"Owen," Lilly urged, "anything he says is a lie."

"On the contrary," said Paul, "remember what I told you, Owen: I've never lied to you."

I knew Lilly was right, and yet, based on what Paul had just said, I also knew that he'd guessed we would head for Hub, which meant that they could try to intercept us there. Maybe if I let him say whatever manipulative speech he had planned, we could break it down and figure out their strategy for catching us. If there was one thing I hadn't liked during the past night, it was looking back at an empty horizon and wondering where Eden was.

I took hold of the pad. For a second, I thought Lilly might not let go. But she did.

"Fine," I said. "What."

"Thank you," said Paul. "Now listen carefully. This morning, EdenWest sent a message over the gamma link to all major federation intelligence and news agencies stating that three suspects had escaped from EdenWest. Detailed descriptions of you all were included in this statement, as well as of your craft." He stopped.

I knew what question he wanted me to ask. "Suspects?"

"Indeed. Three suspects wanted in connection with the murders of EdenWest's head of security and communications coordinator."

I tried to hide my surprise, but Paul saw it, and it made him smile.

"Yes, that's right. Because let's think through what

really happened yesterday, Owen. Photos of Cartier, dead from the arrow wound, were circulated, as well as surveillance footage of you pushing Aaron to his death from your craft."

"He survived that fall!" I countered. "I saw him come up."

"That's funny," said Paul. "He doesn't surface in the footage. And there were many eyewitnesses when his body washed ashore on the Camp Eden beach this morning during polar bear swim."

I wanted to reply, but I was knotting up, heart racing, breath getting short. And I could tell that Paul was enjoying this. So I stayed quiet, trying to give him nothing.

"Right now," said Paul, "law enforcement in every major city-state has your profile and knows that Eden is offering a substantial reward for your return. And that includes Yellowstone Hub. So, you may want to skip your little homecoming."

"Turn it off," said Lilly. "That's enough of *him*."

"Not quite," said Paul. "You'll want to hear this part, Miss Ishani. I also wanted to let you know that we captured your coconspirators as they tried to escape. Evan, Marco, and Aliah have proven quite . . . useful for rounding out the intelligence profiles we sent out about you."

Lilly couldn't hide her expression either. "You're lying," she said.

"Is that him?" I turned to see Leech hurrying around the corner.

"And I found *this* interesting," Paul continued. "After Evan had been interrogated, and just before I cut open his chest and hooked him up in my lab—"

Lilly threw her hands over her mouth, trying to hide a gasp.

Paul's smile grew. "I asked him if he wanted me to tell you anything, Lilly, I mean since you two have such *history*. And he said, with tears in his eyes, I kid you not, that he would never forget that night in the boathouse."

"Shut up, liar!" Lilly reached over my hands and stabbed at the glass with a shaking finger, opening the menu again.

"Owen, think about it," said Paul. "You don't have any options. So just sit tight and wait for us to arrive. I promise you I'm willing to forgive yesterday's squabble."

"Hey!" Leech shouted, running toward us. "Hey, you!" He was pointing at the pad.

Paul's head twitched like he may have heard Leech. "You're the *one*, Owen," he said, "the one who can lead us to Atlantis. And like I told you, I want to follow you. But you can't do it alone, especially not as a fugitive."

"Go to hell," I said to him.

Paul frowned. "Owen. Really. There's more I could tell you. More you *should* know. I'm keeping things from you for your safety, but, trust me, you do not want to make this journey without me."

Lilly reached the gamma link menu.

"I'll even give you time to let the other two escape if you want. They don't matter to me, Owen. Only you. *The*

Three is a myth. You are all that matters."

"Bye!" said Lilly.

"I'm coming for you, either way."

Lilly's finger was descending toward the Disconnect button when Leech snatched the pad out of our hands.

"I matter too, you ass lesion!" he screamed at the screen, then he twisted and hurled the computer. It twirled across the canyon.

"Hey!" I shouted.

"What are you DOING?" Lilly echoed.

The pad smashed against the far wall and fell to the sand, broken glass pattering around it.

Leech just stared after it, his face red, shoulders heaving up and down. "They can track us with that."

Lilly jumped up and ran to the wreckage. "That's why I was disconnecting it, you idiot!" She slid onto her knees and started picking up the pieces.

"Disconnecting it isn't enough," said Leech. The sight of Paul seemed to have gotten to him even more than it had rattled me. He looked so different from the cocky kid I'd known in Eden. His hands were shaking, fingers fluttering. He caught me noticing and made fists. "If they hacked into that pad, that means they have the unique network ID it creates when it connects to the gamma link. They could reverse link to the pad anywhere and determine its location."

"Gamma link is only identifiable when it's connected,"

I said, remembering what I'd heard about data hackers back at Hub.

Leech rolled his eyes. "Maybe where *you* come from," he said. "How do you think he appeared on it just now? Lilly, didn't you disconnect the link before you went to sleep?"

"Yes," Lilly muttered.

Leech looked at me. I thought I'd see his slopey, know-it-all grin, but instead he had a serious expression, like he really wanted me to understand where he was coming from. "See?"

"Fine."

"Besides," he added, "we have Aaron's subnet pad."

Lilly thrust the broken parts down on the sand. She got up and stomped over to Leech, glaring down at him. She was a good ten centimeters taller. "Yeah, but then we need a subnet connection. And where are we going to find one of those out *here*?"

Leech just shrugged.

Lilly spun away. "That's what I thought." She threw herself down on the blanket.

A silence passed over us. There was only the gentle shush of wind slipping along the contours of the canyon. The sight of Paul had shattered the slight sense of safety I'd been feeling and reminded me of what we were running from, and what would happen if we were caught.

I glanced at Leech, wondering about his behavior.

It was one thing to not want Paul to track us, but Leech had seemed so furious at the sight of him. Maybe it was because of Paul's comments about me being the only one who mattered. What could he have meant by that? Leech was just as important. Maybe Leech was still wounded by Paul's betrayal. Paul probably knew those comments would upset Leech, just like his comments about Evan had been designed to upset Lilly.

She stared off into space, biting her lip. The thought of Evan cut open like Anna had been . . . no matter how I felt about him, he didn't deserve that. No one did, and . . .

"It was our fault," said Lilly.

"Yeah," I agreed. The thought sunk deep into me. Evan and Marco and Aliah had saved us from Paul. If it wasn't for them, we'd be in that lab, and now they were paying for it.

And of course that would torment Lilly. I thought about going over and trying to do something supportive, like rub her shoulder, but I found myself hesitating. I couldn't stop thinking about the other thing Paul had said: a night in the boathouse. . . . What had that been? Lilly had his T-shirt in her bag. . . .

I hated how the thought of them burned me. I needed to just deal. They hadn't even been going out anymore when I showed up. But maybe it also felt like more evidence that our connection was no longer the same—or worse, that it had never even been what I'd thought it was in the first place. After all, she'd lied to me about seeing the siren.

All of these thoughts crowded in my head, spinning wildly and feeding off one another. Maybe that had been Paul's plan. If so, it had worked. Lilly, Evan, Paul's cryptic comments about me, and on top of all that, now we couldn't go to Hub. And Dad was going to hear these allegations against me. What would he think of his son, the escapee and accused murderer? Would he be brought in for questioning?

Paul had cut us off from the world, given us nowhere to go that was safe. It all felt like too much, but I tried to push through the storm of doubt and focus.

"If he hacked into the pad," I said slowly like I had to pull each word out of a giant, tangled heap, "then doesn't that mean he knows our location right now?"

"Yeah," said Lilly absently.

"And that means we need to get moving." I looked at Leech. "Looks like you get your wish."

Leech nodded seriously. I was glad to see he didn't want to gloat. "So, the bearing then?"

"Yeah."

"I don't get it," said Lilly. She'd snapped out of her trance. "If he knows where we are, why not just come get us? Why did he contact us first? It's almost like he's giving us a head start."

"He probably wants to see what we'll do," I said.

"We're still his lab rats," muttered Leech, "even outside Eden."

"So, what? . . . He's just toying with us?" said Lilly. She sounded defeated again.

"No," I said, feeling a surge of resolve. "He doesn't have us yet." I turned to Leech. "Where do we go?"

Leech pulled his little black sketchbook from the waistband of his shorts, along with Aaron's subnet computer pad, which he'd been hanging on to all night. "I made some new sketches while you were asleep," he said, kneeling down and opening the notebook.

I joined him. Lilly hesitated for a minute. I saw her reach up and rub at her gills, wincing. Finally she crawled over beside us.

"Check it out." Leech pointed at a map drawn across two pages. "Things aren't quite to scale here, but"—he pointed to a circle with a plus sign in the top right corner—"that's EdenWest, and we're about here." He indicated a small dot, then moved his finger along a dotted line that left EdenWest and ran diagonally over the landscape toward the far corner into the triangles of a mountain range. It ended at a little star. "That's the bearing, and that's the marker."

"I still don't get how you are seeing these maps," I said, "when we haven't found your skull yet."

"I've been thinking about that," said Leech. "I think, since the Atlanteans couldn't know which skull we'd find first, they put a little bit of the information for me in all of them, you know, so we could get on course. That's what allowed me to use the map room in Eden. And those maps I could see pointed to this place." He indicated the star in the mountains.

I looked at the map and felt like something didn't line up. Leech had drawn a compass rose in the top left. This was what was disorienting me. The compass was at a cockeyed angle. I pointed to it. "You've been saying that our bearing needs to be southwest. But doesn't this compass mean that we're supposed to go south instead of southwest?"

This question seemed to excite Leech. "Okay, right, it would, *if* those were the true compass directions, but see that's the thing that I, well, that *we* figured out back in the navigation room in Eden. The maps that I see in my head, they're oriented different. My north, is that way," he said, extending his arm in the same direction as on the compass he'd drawn, "but really, actual north is that way." He ticked his arm to the left like the hand of a clock.

"So," said Lilly, "you have the wrong north in your head."

"Not wrong," said Leech, "just old. From about ten thousand years ago, during the Atlantean time."

"So you're saying the North Pole moved?"

"Well, it moves all the time, historically. Sometimes the poles even flip. But something bigger than that happened between the Atlantean time and now. It's not so much that the pole moved as I think the *land*, the whole crust of the earth, moved. A lot. I think it was because of the Paint-brush. Point is, any map we find has to be recalibrated based on where things are now. That's part of what makes the Atlantean sites so hard to find."

"You never struck me as a big nerd," said Lilly, and

though her tone was still sullen, there was a slight gleam in her eyes finally.

Leech smiled at this.

"How far is it to the marker?" I asked.

Leech ran his finger along the line. "A thousand kilometers, give or take."

I did the calculations in my head. "That's like seventeen flying hours. We should have just enough power in the vortex to make it." I looked up toward the top of the canyon, at the sun angling down the walls. "It'll be light for a few more hours. We'll be easy to spot. And we're gonna fry out there."

"May be more dangerous to stay," said Lilly.

"Yeah," I said, getting to my feet. "Let's go."

We threw our bags in the craft and climbed aboard.

"Here." Lilly passed around her bottle of NoRad. We covered our faces and arms and legs, feeling it tingle as it sank in. We saved some for later, and I hoped it would be enough.

The vortex was still swirling, humming softly. I pressed on the pedals and we began to rise.

"Watch the walls," I said to Leech. There was no wind down here, so the sails were useless. He leaned out and pushed off whenever we drifted close to the side.

We rose slowly out of the canyon. As the skull battlements on the bank building appeared, I watched for Paul's forces.

"See anything?" I asked.

"Nope," said Leech.

"Nada," said Lilly.

"Okay." I brought us up into the full heat of the late afternoon sun. A lot of good our escape would be if we all got Rad poisoning. I checked the wind: beneath thermal gusts, there was a steady breeze at about five knots.

My feet flexed, but I didn't start us moving. As if it sensed my pause, my stomach rumbled again. I wondered if it had been loud enough to hear, and found Leech looking at me.

"Seventeen hours is a long time," he said, "especially on one bottle of water."

I sighed. "Seventeen at best."

Leech glanced back toward town. "This could really be our best chance for supplies."

"There might be something else on the way," I said immediately, feeling the urge to go, to run, and maybe also not wanting to give in to Leech, but I reminded myself that we had to be past that kind of thinking if we were going to survive out here. And he was right. We'd already flown six hundred kilometers, and over all that land, this was the only place we'd seen that might possibly have supplies.

I gazed at the Walmart, feeling a surge of worry.

"It's probably worth checking out," said Lilly.

"Yeah." I yanked on the sail lines and we banked around. We were a few hundred yards away when there was a flash of light. The Walmart SuperPlus sign, standing high above the vacant parking lot, was flickering to life. A weak light, barely visible in the afternoon sun, only a few of the bulbs inside the cracked plastic working, but still: on.

I slowed the craft. "You all saw that," I said.

"Generator?" Leech asked.

I looked around for the gleam of a wind turbine somewhere nearby.

"There," said Lilly, pointing at the roof. "Underneath the sand: solar shingles. Enough are exposed to make a charge."

"It just turned five o'clock," said Leech, checking the computer. "The sign's probably just old tech on a timer. And, if there's power to run the sign, there could still be power in the freezer cases and stuff."

These were realistic possibilities, but I couldn't help mentioning, "Or there could be people."

"What are the odds?" said Leech.

"Fine. We'd just better be fast," I said, and ignoring the ringing of my nerves, I brought us down toward the store.

4

I KEPT A WIDE BERTH AROUND THE FLAGPOLE BODY.
The plywood covering the front doors and windows seemed
intact and formidable, so I looked for another entrance.
There was a little doorway sticking up near the center of
the roof. I landed on the sand beside it.

I hopped out beside Lilly and we checked the warped
metal door. "Locked," I said, jiggling the handle. "It
doesn't look too strong though . . ." I shook it back and
forth harder.

"Here, let me." Lilly pulled me back and delivered a
vicious kick. The door smacked open, yawning inward on
one hinge.

"Nice," I said, turning to smile at Lilly, but she'd
already headed back to the craft. I stepped into the doorway. "Stairway into darkness," I reported. I started down,
but Lilly grabbed my arm again.

She'd gotten her knife, the one she'd taken from a
Nomad body back in Eden. "You should stay," she said.

"We can't leave the ship unguarded. We'd be screwed without it, and you're the only one who can fly it."

"Makes sense," Leech agreed, joining her.

"You're staying, too," she said to Leech. "You're the two who have to get to Atlantis." She slipped the knife in her belt. "I'm the expendable one."

"Hey," I started, "we don't know that for sure—"

"Don't," said Lilly. She rubbed at her gills, grimacing. "I'll scout it out and come back with a report." She started down the stairs.

Leech gave me a slight nod and started after her.

When Lilly turned, he said, "I'm gonna watch your back."

"I don't need—"

Leech brushed past her. "Okay, you watch mine. Going in there alone is stupid and you know it."

Lilly grabbed Leech by the shoulder and stepped in front of him. "Fine, but you follow me."

Leech fell into step behind her. As he turned and started down the next set of stairs, he looked up at me. I nodded, knowing he actually meant it as a kind of pact between us this time, rather than as a challenge.

Their footsteps slapped on the concrete stairs. The sound faded away, and then I was alone with the hollow afternoon wind, waterless, bracing my skin with grains of sand.

I kicked at the side of the ship, hating that Lilly was

down in the dark, and it wasn't me that was with her. I thought about going down anyway, but she was right. If anything happened to the ship, we were goners. But still . . . I wondered if I was even on her mind right now, or if it was just Evan. I knew that wasn't fair of me, probably wasn't even true, but I couldn't help it.

The sun beat down on me. I thought to stand in the shade of the doorway, but first I walked around the perimeter of the roof, scanning the horizon. The distant stone hills were still, but I couldn't shake the feeling that Eden was out there somewhere, that they were watching. I looked down the streets leading away in right angles, each ending at a section of the wall, half-expecting to see gold-visored peace forces lunging over the jagged battlements.

I passed close to the front of the store, and paused to look at the body on the flagpole. It had been lashed to the pole with thick purple ropes, like the kind of cord you'd use for cave diving or mountain climbing. There were two big awkward knots, one at the waist and one at the neck, and the body was slumped over to the side. It was dressed in a white shirt and pants. There were stains on it, patches of burned reds and black, but overall the clothing and the body seemed to be in better shape than the one we'd seen on the wall. Maybe this one wasn't quite as old.

I thought of what Lilly had said, this morning: *Why should we save this world, when things like this can happen?* I wondered what would lead people to do this.

Madness, I guessed. I remembered hearing stories of massacres, mass suicides and genocides as resources dried up. There had been some weird stuff, too, about when Eden-South fell to the Heliad-7 cult, rumors of human sacrifice and even cannibalism, but I never paid too much attention to the news programs my dad would have on in the mornings. Other than the sports, most of the news was just dark and depressing.

I figured these bodies were supposed to be warnings. And what had become of the people who'd killed this person? Had they left? Died themselves? Or were they still here, somewhere? Probably not, given the state of things. But I still felt my nerves humming, and wanted to get moving.

Beware the horrors.

I flinched. The voice had come from beside me. There was no one there . . . Wait, there was. An impression, faint, flickering, like a smudge of the light. Now I could see her: the primitive face, the short figure, her skin cast in a blue shimmer, hair black, dress maroon. She wore a necklace with a tiger carved out of soapstone, her waist and forehead adorned by strings of hammered copper and turquoise, ruby, and jade.

The siren.

"You," I said. "You still exist."

She shimmered like a projection, her amber eyes overlaying the horizon. *I have existed since the beginning. And I would visit you more, but it takes a great effort to reach you,* she said, *even briefly.*

"I mean you're still in my head, or whatever."

Not in your head. She raised a finger and pointed at me. The finger neared my chest and flicked through my shirt and skin. I felt a light burning there. *In you.*

"What does that mean?"

The siren just turned back to the body on the flagpole. I followed her gaze. "Do you know who did this?"

It is a sign, she said. *A warning.*

"From who?"

"Who" does not matter. "When" is the key. It is the way of things that each cycle comes to an end; order and intention dissolve; Qi and An become estranged, their harmony lost. This discord unleashes horrors. But it is also the way of things that balance returns, and the cycle starts anew.

"You aren't making sense," I said. Then I wondered if the siren might get mad at that, but I was tired of hearing all these cryptic statements.

Yet when she looked at me again she seemed to smile. *When the music of the Terra is lost, they create gods to give voice to the darkness. But these gods know only what humans know. What is of this earth cannot control it, and thus the horrors are unleashed.*

Her voice grew louder in my mind, crowding out my other senses. *You must beware the gods and their horrors.*

The words burned into my brain, and I thought, *I will.*

I felt a moment of weightless being, and then realized my eyes were closed. I had become totally still. I'd even stopped breathing. I opened my eyes. The siren was gone.

The moment of stillness seemed to have brushed away a layer of static, as if my senses had been cleaned. As the world bled back in, I felt the breeze between the hairs of my arms, felt the sharp, probing heat of the sun on my head. I smelled the dry baked earth, but something else too. Something slightly sour and metallic . . .

And there was a noise. A low hum that I hadn't noticed before. Droning, with an occasional dip in pitch. It got louder as a gust of wind billowed against my face. The smell got stronger too. Coming from ahead of me.

I peered at the body, and stepped closer to the edge of the roof. As I neared, I saw a blurry movement around the limbs. The drone increased. Another waft of acrid odor hit me. I knew the sound now, and saw the source.

What I had thought were black stains were flies. Thousands of flies. They were whirling in orbit around the corpse. Its arms and legs were alive with their crawling, a rippling layer of black bodies and vibrating wings.

Tiny flashes caught my eye. Little movements, not the flies, but instead glints of light that seemed to fall away from the body toward the ground.

I peered over the edge of the roof, all the way to the concrete. There was a shimmery light at the base of the flagpole. It was different from the flat light of sun on sand.

This was a reflection on liquid. Water? No, beneath the surface sheen, the substance was too dark, too opaque.

I took a deep breath and had a hard time filling my lungs around my galloping heart. I looked back up. Saw a flash and followed another little light trail. It was the reflection off a droplet. It plinked into the puddle below.

A puddle of blood.

And even though I knew exactly what this meant, everything it meant—it was hitting me like blows to the chest—I just kept standing there staring. . . .

Blood means it's fresh. Fresh means someone just put it there, new since this morning. . . . Someone who's still—

Until a piercing scream tore me loose.

Lilly.

The scream ended in a distant metallic crash.

I spun and sprinted for the door.

5

I THREW MYSELF DOWN THE FIRST FLIGHT OF STAIRS, legs moving too fast, losing control and slamming into the cement wall. I spun and headed down the next flight, this time grabbing the rail, taking two steps at a time. The light from the doorway above began to fade. On the third flight, the darkness total, my ankle buckled. Pain surged up my leg.

I limped to the open door at the bottom of the stairs. Faint light spilled in. I caught my breath and ducked out. The stairwell I'd come down was part of a column in the center of the store. There were a couple small lights on in the ceiling. A little more light seeped in around the seams of the plywood on the front doors, but gloomy shadows hung within the maze of aisles in all directions.

I heard a sharp smacking sound, something metal hitting the tiled floor. And then a rush like whispers. I ducked out and started toward it.

I reached a main aisle. Many of the shelves were bare,

but then sections like art supplies or dishware looked so full and orderly it was as if the store had just closed for the evening. I passed rows of smashed glass cases, some empty, others still full of now valueless things like perfume and nail polish. In the clothing section, the overturned racks looked like carcasses, their skeletal limbs sticking up, left-over clothes like skin bunched and folded.

Many of the electronics had been spared, things like retinal-fit cameras that you slung over your eye. The small, sleek designs looked newer than things I'd seen at Hub. At first it surprised me that they were still here but then again there'd be no way to recharge batteries, and also probably little desire to record this world for posterity.

I spied another object that would be worthless to most people but that we happened to need: a reader for the video sheet we'd printed in Dr. Maria's lab. I tore open the plastic package and slipped the thin, cylindrical device in my pocket.

Up ahead there was an eerie blue glow. A sign read GROCERY. I heard a hum. Leech had been right: at least some of the freezer cases seemed to be on.

I wanted to call out to Leech and Lilly, but I couldn't risk revealing myself until I knew what was going on. There was another muffled sound, and then a sharp crack behind me. I ducked into a side aisle. My heart beat so furiously I worried that someone would hear it.

A noise grew, metallic and jangling, like a machine

rolling, along with the rhythmic slapping of feet.

"Careful!" someone whispered.

Now I heard laughter.

Lilly sped by. She was kneeling inside a four-wheeled cart made of blue plastic, being pushed by Leech. He got to full speed and jumped up so that his feet were on the back of the cart.

"Woo!" he shouted.

"Look out!" Lilly warned.

They flew by me and there was a huge crash. I saw that they'd collided with a shelf at the end of an aisle, scattering a display of lamps.

Lilly and Leech cracked up, Leech in sandpapery chuckles and Lilly in big, high giggles. I'd never heard her laugh like that before. She got out of the cart. "Okay, that was too fast. Your turn."

I wanted to scream. But I hung back out of sight for another second because I also had a sudden, deflating feeling. Lilly was actually enjoying herself, so different from how she'd been all day, and I hated that it didn't include me. I fought off an urge to just turn and head back up to the craft, and ran over to them. "Hey!" I whispered. "What are you doing? You're supposed to be hurrying."

"We were hurrying," said Lilly between breaths, her smile fading, like here was no-fun Owen. "That's why we were going fast. It just happened to also be fun," she added, looking absently into the space near my shoulder and rubbing at her neck.

"Well, what about supplies?" I asked.

"We got supplies," said Leech, motioning to the cart.

I saw a strange collection of items: a fuzzy pink blanket and pillow set, decorated with rainbows and horses, a dust-coated clear plastic case labeled BOCCIE, with colored balls inside, and even a box of white holiday lights. "What's all this?"

"They were supposed to be some comforts for our palatial flying machine," said Lilly.

"Don't worry, Dad, we got some food," said Leech, his obnoxious camp voice returning. "What was left of it, anyway." He held up one can of stew and a box of dry millet noodles. "Which is why we were *hurrying* to the freezers."

"Fine," I hissed, hating how Leech had called me Dad. Actually, I sounded more like my mom, the way she always used to get with us when we'd get too loud in the common kitchen. "But we need to get out of here, now."

"Why are you whispering?" Lilly asked.

"Because there's someone here!"

This made Lilly whisper too. "What?"

"No there's not—" Leech began.

"The body!" I hissed. "On the flagpole. It's fresh. Flies, blood, all of it."

They both started glancing around.

"We should still check the freezers," whispered Leech. "It's worth the risk if there's food there. Come on."

"We don't have time," I said.

"We haven't run into anyone down here *yet*," Leech reasoned. "Whoever put up that body might be in some other part of town. Or maybe they don't even know how to get in here. I mean, we used the roof."

"Leech is right," said Lilly. "We should at least check those cases."

"It will only take a minute," Leech added. "And I'd rather not starve out there."

"Fine," I said. "Quickly."

Leech started pushing the cart, its wheels clattering. I grabbed the side. "That's too loud."

He nodded and we left the cart, jogging quietly up the aisle, heads darting back and forth at each intersection.

We reached the first aisle of tall glass cases. They were dark, some of the doors hanging open. Packages had spilled out in spots, crushed and crumbled, sometimes coated in a dark layer of dried mold.

The next set of cases was lit in blue. The air tingled with electricity and the scent of moisture. The cases to our right were totally empty, the glass clear, but the set to our left was clouded with condensation and splintery patterns of ice crystals.

We checked the first one. Frozen food boxes were stacked top to bottom. There were box meals, things I'd never heard of like NegaFat, Skinny!Skinny!, and a ridiculous line called Ms. Martina's Pre-Rise Kitchen, showing a plump woman in an apron inviting you toward a warmly lit oven, like she wanted to stuff you inside and cook you. There were other things, too. Rice waffles, juice concentrate inserts for HydraPak water bottles in more flavors than I'd ever seen . . .

"Oooh man," said Leech. He popped open the next door down, releasing a cascade of cold fog. He yanked out a small round container. "Ice cream. Greenland Pastures creamery." He yanked off the lid, shoved his finger in, and devoured a large scoop of dark chocolate. "Mmm . . . tastes kinda old, but not bad."

Lilly reached past Leech and grabbed a box of frozen burritos. She ripped open the box, pulled one out, and held it to her gills. The cold made her close her eyes and her mouth momentarily settled into a relaxed line.

"Someone's definitely been here," said Leech. "Most of this stuff is relatively new. They had Greenland Pastures in EdenWest."

"Then let's be fast," I said.

Lilly stepped past Leech and peered at the third case down. It was frosted opaque. She yanked on the handle. The door popped open in a hiss. Lilly stumbled back, then waved at the icy fog. "We should just get a day or two's worth, whatever seems like it will keep best since it's gonna thaw—GAH!"

Lilly launched backward, slamming into the far glass doors with a thud. She slid down, her eyes transfixed. She glanced at me. Went to say something but didn't. Couldn't.

The door swung back and forth, its old hinges creaking. Leech peered inside. "Okay . . ."

I looked in.

There was a body stuffed in the freezer case. A man, middle-aged. His skin was icy blue, his eyes frosted shut, hair and beard prickly with crystals, and his body contorted to fit into the rectangular space. He was dressed in a pure white jumpsuit, zippered up the front. Unlike the body outside, he hadn't yet been soiled by blood or sand or flies. There was something smooth and solid in his mouth.

"Is that wax?" Lilly had gotten up and joined me. "It's like a seal. You can see his teeth on the other side."

Leech popped open the next door down. "Here's another." He moved to the last door of the aisle. "Annnd, a third."

I saw a woman's face, and another man. White jumpsuits, eyes closed, mouths sealed. I felt my nerves ratcheting tighter. Bodies on poles, in freezers. Real people being used as signs, stored like meat . . .

"What's that symbol on their outfits?" Leech asked.

A voice from behind us answered, "It is the sign of the daughter of the sun."

They'd come up on us without a sound. A man and a woman, maybe in their fifties. The man was tall and thin with wispy white hair, angular features, and green eyes. The woman was shorter, square shaped, her black hair streaked with gray. They were both dressed in floor-length crimson robes held closed by black belts. The robes had the same symbol as the jumpsuits, embroidered in gold. They wore black-strapped sandals. I had seen outfits like these before. They were kind of like what the Atlanteans wore in my first vision, the one where I'd seen the Three having their throats slit.

These two were definitely products of this world though, not that ancient one. Their faces were tanned and spotted with freckles and black moles. The man had a coin-sized purplish mark on his temple: a Rad lesion. They both looked like they'd spent significant time in the sun without any kind of protection. The woman was smiling, and I could see that she was missing a few teeth, her gums dotted with brown here and there.

"Who are you?" Lilly pointed her knife at them.

"I'm Harvey," said the man, "and this is my life partner, Lucinda. I know the bodies are a bit alarming, but they are only meant to serve as warnings to potential thieves or scavengers."

"And each of the volunteers knew that his discarded

vessel might be used for this purpose," Lucinda added. She was smiling warmly at us.

Lilly glanced back at the cases. "Did you just call them volunteers?"

Lucinda nodded. "Yes, their divine essence has been liberated in accordance with official Heliad-Seven custom."

"Right," said Leech, as if he understood what they were talking about. "So did you guys come up from Desenna?"

"Yes," said Harvey. He held up his right hand, palm out to us, fingers slightly spread. So did Lucinda. And there was something weird about their fingers. . . .

"Are you both missing your pinkies?" Lilly asked.

"A sacrifice of the flesh," said Harvey, smiling, "for the body is only a shell, a temporary home for the divine inside, which is eternal."

"Oooh-kay," said Leech under his breath. I saw him balling his hands into fists. Lilly flexed her fingers around her knife.

Harvey lowered his hand. "Please forgive us for taking so long to greet you. You took us by surprise and we wanted to make preparations for the occasion."

"What are you doing here?" Lilly asked.

"We are the caretakers of this monitoring station," said Harvey. "We were sent here to listen for word."

"Word about what?" I asked.

"Why, about you," said Lucinda. "About the Three." She looked at Lilly. "You can put the knife away, sweetie.

Nomad, isn't it? From the team that attempted to rescue you."

"Yeah," said Lilly, but she kept the knife trained on them.

"You know about that?" I asked.

"Of course we do, Owen." And he knew my name. "That Nomad strike team was working in conjunction with the Benevolent Mother and Desenna. We helped to monitor the operation. Don't let these things surprise you. You're going to have to get used to your importance. After that operation went awry, we never dreamed we'd be so lucky as to actually get to meet you. But then we heard the news of your escape, and imagine our surprise this morning when we saw a blue light coming from the East, right at dawn, just like in the Epics!"

"It was like a dream," said Lucinda. She blinked, and I thought I saw tears.

"We reported your passing," said Harvey, "and hung a fresh totem outside, so that Chaac might bring you luck on your journey. Then, we just started packing up to go, you know? Mission accomplished. The Three on their way! But lo and behold, then there were sounds on the roof and in you came."

"'And the Memory descended in ships of blue light,'" said Lucinda dreamily. "We are blessed." She was looking at us like we were holotech stars, standing there bouncing in place, making her earrings and bracelets jangle. She fiddled nervously at a necklace: a silver chain with a small black pendant at the end.

"What?" Leech asked.

"Oh, sorry," Lucinda mumbled.

"She's talking about the Epics of the Three," said Harvey. "You know, 'Three guardians of the memory of the first people,' and so forth."

"I've heard that part," I said, "but not that other thing you said."

"No, of course not," said Lucinda. "No one's heard *all* of the Epics. But there is a passage of it inscribed in the walls of the Atlantean temple near Desenna."

"There's a temple at Desenna," I said, checking this off in my head. "What's that one like?"

"Well, we've never been inside," said Harvey. "No one has except the Benevolent Mother and her team, and of course the daughter, Heliad, she who can speak to the mind made of crystal."

"Wait," I said, "there's a girl in Desenna who can communicate with a crystal skull?"

"Yes, Heliad. The Daughter of the Sun," said Harvey. "She has the memory of the first people."

"Got it," I said, and felt a little fall inside at hearing this. I glanced at Lilly, but she didn't meet my gaze. The Nomads had mentioned a skull in the south and a girl, but I had still hoped that the third Atlantean might be Lilly. This pretty much made it official that she wasn't. Lilly didn't react. It was like she'd known all along.

"What else does this passage from the Epics say?" Leech asked.

"It talks first about the journey of the Atlanteans," said Harvey, "after the flood that destroyed their civilization. The people tried to rebuild, but they had lost so much that the Atlantean society never recovered to its prior heights. Eventually, it evolved into other civilizations: Sumerian, Egyptian, Chinese, Olmec, which in turn evolved into others, and so on until now."

Some of this sounded familiar from what Lük had told me in the skull.

"And that's just the beginning," said Harvey. "There's—"

"Harvey . . ." Lucinda tugged on his arm. "These kids must be starving." She smiled kindly at us. "Aren't you?"

"Kinda, yeah," I admitted.

"Of course," said Harvey. "Sorry. Luce is right. We have so much to tell you, but not on empty stomachs. Will you join us?"

"We're kind of in a hurry," I said. "Eden is coming."

"Yes, I'm sure they are," said Harvey, "but, like I said, this is a monitoring station. We have sensors in place. If anyone gets within thirty kilometers of this place, we'll know and can get out of here. I'll show you the readouts. This way." Harvey took Lucinda's hand and they started down the aisle.

Lilly and Leech and I turned to one another.

"They don't seem dangerous," I said.

"Paul didn't seem dangerous, either," muttered Leech.

"On the one hand . . ." said Lilly, and she flashed a look at the bodies in the freezers, "but on the other hand, you two are gods in their religion. Plus . . ." She rubbed her stomach, "Hungry. And they have information."

My stomach wanted to trust them, too. And "If the third Atlantean is in Desenna," I said, "we're probably going to need to go there."

Leech sighed. "If I vote no, I'll get outvoted again, so . . ." He started after them.

I glanced back at the frozen bodies, at the food, and took a deep breath. "Here we go," I said to Lilly, and we followed the robed figures down the dark hall.

6

HARVEY AND LUCINDA LED US FAR DOWN THE STORE, Lucinda pushing our cart, until we reached an open area beneath a sign that read HOUSEWARES. They had cleared everything to the sides, and created a makeshift apartment with walls made of boxes and stacked furniture. A standing lamp with an amber shade cast warm light over two couches, a pair of recliner chairs, and a monitor screen, all arranged to form a square with a plush blue carpet and a glass coffee table in the center. Behind that was a bed, a few tables that were serving as a kitchen area, and a desk covered in primitive-looking computer equipment.

"Have a seat," said Lucinda.

We sat down, all three of us on the same spongy couch, instinctively staying close as a unit. I immediately fixated on the coffee table. It was covered with brightly colored plates of food. There were little round things that seemed to be meatballs, tiny puffs of a flaky pastry, fried rolls, and chunks of a bright yellow fruit.

"Some of it's been here a few years," said Lucinda. "A few things for decades, but it's all still good. Kroger and the major food companies developed some amazing preservatives during the Rise. Almost like they knew people would be storing stuff for long periods!"

I tried one of the pastry puffs. The warm, flaky outside collapsed around a gooey, tangy center. There was some kind of meat in there.

"That's real Arctic soft-shell crab from the 2050s," said Harvey, "after the Arctic Sea became ice free and before the anoxic tides killed all the sea life there."

He placed a little square device on the table. It had a grid with a glowing white dot in the center. "This is a reading from the proximity sensors. The white dot is us. If anything else shows up on this screen, then we can worry. This is how we knew you were arriving.

"Now, back to the food. We've got something fresh, too." He moved over to a waist-high, black structure, opened the lid, and turned a dial. There was a *thwump* of air and a quick lick of flames burst inside it. Some kind of grill, connected to a round white tank. He tied on a flower-printed apron, then pulled foil off a plate. A tangy smell tingled my nostrils. Harvey began slapping sticks lined with chunks of pink meat onto the grill. As each landed, it released a loud hiss and a burst of steam. He closed the lid.

"Drinks?" Lucinda put three glass bottles in front of us, a tan liquid inside. The glass was beaded with condensation.

"It's horchata. Made with Mother's new rice strains that can survive in our saline soil, and sweetened with agave. You'll like it." She sat down on the opposite couch, looking at us expectantly.

I took a sip. It was creamy, dusted with spice. It put all that fake-tasting bug juice at camp to shame. "It's good," I said.

"I'm glad you like it." Lucinda smiled warmly. Her free hand was fiddling with her pendant again. I wondered if we made her nervous. "Here, while you're waiting . . ." She picked up a slim black remote control and turned on the monitor.

The screen blared to life, showing the Northern News Network. A female newscaster in a black suit stood on a bustling, modern street. Glassy buildings filled the skyline. Tiny trolley cars slid by on rails. People strolled by in suits, all well-trimmed, carrying handbags and briefcases and all holding silver sunbrellas over their heads.

"—are here in Helsinki Island for the second day of the Northern Federation summit."

I had the same feeling I always got when seeing a glimpse of life up in the Habitable Zone. It looked so easy, so *vital*. Like if you lived there, life would feel like it had a point. That wasn't always the case at Hub. Helsinki didn't look like an Eden city; there weren't SensaStreets or people out water-skiing, living a life oblivious of the real world, but still . . . It looked nice: living on the surface, going to a school with actual windows.

"Today, the N-Fed will be turning to EdenCorp's request for the easing of trade tariffs with Southern Oceania. As we've reported before, one of the key issues is that EdenCorp will not reveal why exactly they are pouring all these resources into the region."

"I'm sure Eden will tell them," said Leech sarcastically. He sounded like he was thinking the same thing as me: Was this something that had to do with Project Elysium?

"Also up today, the N-Fed will consider the American-Canadian Federation's call for increased sanctions against the city-state of Desenna due to what they describe as 'barbaric' practices. For more we go live to the Borderlands."

The picture cut to a man standing among an endless sea of tents and tarps, with stark-looking people huddled in groups beneath every triangle of shade.

"The situation here is getting worse. Despite the continuing spread of Supermycin-resistant cholera-D, many refugees are refusing the vaccine and instead

choosing the Live Bright philosophy of Heliad-Seven.
In response, the ACF is asking for new bandwidth
sanctions and trade embargoes against Desenna."

I heard sniffing beside me, and turned to see Lilly's eyes watering.

"What?" I asked.

"I hate thinking of my parents there," she said, "knowing they spent the last days of their lives in that hell."

"Barbaric," Lucinda scoffed. She switched off the screen. "I can assure you, Heliad-Seven isn't anything of the sort."

I wondered how that could be true, considering the body outside, and the *volunteers* in the fridge.

Harvey opened the grill again and a plume of smoke leaped up into the rafters. He pulled the kebabs off and brought them over.

He was halfway to us when there was a distant, heavy thud from above. I glanced up toward the ceiling shadows. Had that come from the roof?

Harvey saw me looking up. "Don't worry, that's just the air-conditioning system," he said, rolling his eyes as he returned and put the plate of sizzling meat on the table. "It hasn't worked right in years, clipping on and off now and then, but you know, nobody out here really knows how that old tech works anymore."

"Okay," I said, "I'm just jumpy."

"Of course, but you don't need to worry. Look . . ." Harvey pointed at the monitor. There were no disturbances, just our white dot.

I nodded at this, and, hearing no more sounds from above, found that my worry was no match for the magnetic pull of the sizzling meat before us.

"You've probably never had tapir," said Lucinda. "It's wonderful."

"That's like a tropical pig," said Leech, "right?"

"Yes," said Harvey. "You know, they are extinct in nearly all their original habitat, but Mother has been able to breed this species for resilience and Desenna has its own stock now."

"This Mother of yours seems to have it all figured out," said Lilly.

"She is inspiring in that way," said Lucinda.

It smelled salty and sweet. Saliva flooded over my tongue, as if the technicians were throwing valves wide-open.

"Go ahead," said Harvey.

We each took a kebab. I pressed my teeth against the seared flesh. It cracked open, and tangy juices filled my mouth. It was the best thing I'd tasted, maybe ever.

"Wow," I said. Leech hummed in agreement.

"And you don't have to worry," Harvey said with a laugh, "I know there are those nasty rumors, but we are most definitely not serving you *people* or anything."

My mouth froze. I almost spit out my bite.

"Nnn," Lilly moaned softly beside me.

I forced myself to swallow. "We hadn't been thinking that," I said weakly.

"Good," said Lucinda. "All that nonsense couldn't be further from the truth. We're nothing like how these Gambler's Falls people ended up."

"What happened here?" Lilly asked around another bite.

"Well, they did okay for a few years after the great American exodus," said Harvey. "The ACF thought they were too small to recognize, so they pledged themselves to Heliad and started getting support from Desenna. But then pandemic wiped them out."

"Was it red tide?" I asked.

"Oh no," said Lucinda. "I think it was one of the later ones. Red tide was pandemic two, wasn't it?"

Harvey nodded. "I think this was six."

"Told you," Leech said to me.

"Six?" I asked, ignoring him. "I haven't even heard of three, four, and five. Were they small?"

"Three and five were small, other flu variants," said Harvey, "like six, I think. But pandemic four was brutal."

"Black blood," said Leech.

"What's that?" I asked. I was surprised I hadn't heard of these. Then again, if they hadn't reached Hub, I wouldn't have much reason to know about them.

"A form of septicemic plague that affected the white blood cells," said Harvey. "One of the late stage symptoms was the veins turning black. That was a nasty one."

"That's gross." I was surprised to feel a wave of nausea. Normally this kind of talk didn't bother me. Maybe I had just eaten too fast.

"It was a nasty business here, at the end," said Harvey. "People went a little crazy . . . but thus there were supplies left behind and the power still worked, so we chose this spot as a monitoring station. Which brings us back to the present." Harvey slapped his hands together and rubbed them. "It is just amazing that you made it out of Eden."

"I guess," I said. I tried a meatball and washed it down with more horchata.

"Do you know where you're headed next?" Lucinda asked.

"We're still figuring it out," said Leech immediately. That was smart, I realized, not giving away the few things we knew. For as nice as these people seemed, we still didn't know who we could trust for sure.

"You're certainly in a heap of danger," said Harvey, "which is why we have a message to give you from Mother." He produced a small piece of paper and cleared his throat formally. "'On behalf of the people of Heliad-Seven, the Benevolent Mother would like to invite you to Desenna, where you will be reunited with your sister of memory. In addition, Mother can offer you protection from Eden's forces and all the support you need to complete your journey. We have a Nomad pod on the way right now, who can escort you safely to the city.'"

"This is so exciting!" said Lucinda. "First Heliad returns, and now the Three are reunited! All is just as Mother predicted!"

"What do you mean by 'predicted'?" Leech asked. He turned to Lilly and me. "Their 'Mother' used to be Eden-South's version of Paul. She led an overthrow from inside."

"A revolution," said Harvey. "The first liberation."

It worried me to hear this. Their Benevolent Mother might not be a part of Eden now, but she had been. Did that mean that on some level, she was like Paul?

"For years, the Benevolent Mother foretold the return of Tona's daughter," Lucinda explained. "Tona is the sun deity. Mother said that when the daughter of the sun returned, she would be the direct connection to the first people, whose ways we emulate, based on Mother's transla-tion of the ancient texts inside the Atlantean temple. We all looked forward to her return, and yet, after a decade, hope had begun to fade. Then just as all was seeming lost . . . there she was! We all gathered on the beach and watched as she swam up from the depths, emerging from the sea in a flowing white dress, the beautiful Heliad among us. And we have rejoiced ever since."

"That was something," said Harvey, closing his eyes, smiling. He put a hand on his chest and inhaled deeply through his nose.

I could barely follow all this. I thought that the Heliad-7

cult was only a few years old, but clearly they'd been around awhile before they overthrew EdenSouth.

"Why was all seeming lost?" Lilly asked. "I mean, Heliad is the most popular religion outside the Habitable Zone and the Edens, isn't it?"

"Well, yes," said Lucinda, a shadow crossing her face, "but there was a seed of doubt. A rumor . . ."

"A heresy is more like it," Harvey added, his face puckering like he'd eaten something spoiled.

"You see," said Lucinda, "people began to fear that, instead of the gods returning, as Mother predicted, they were in fact *leaving*. A rumor began to spread that the gods had forsaken earth, and that the end-times had come. This was in spite of the teachings of the Benevolent Mother, in spite of the magic she could show us, and her prophecy of Heliad's return."

It's understandable in an age like this," said Harvey. "People have a right to fear for our future. I mean, you see what we've done to this planet. Is it so hard to believe that humanity has been forsaken, that the gods have had enough? Even in Desenna, the Rise may be over, but living is hard and only gets worse. There is more hope now that Heliad has returned, and now that the Three have come . . . but still, even *we* have thought, from time to time, that who could blame the gods for leaving, to start somewhere new?"

Harvey and Lucinda shared a wide-eyed glance, Harvey

rubbing his hands together, Lucinda fidgeting with her pendant.

"That's why we wondered . . ." Lucinda began, speaking in a hushed tone, but then, she shook her head. "I can't."

Harvey rubbed her leg supportively. "What Luce was going to say was, we were wondering, since you've been in Eden . . ." He swallowed hard, and continued in a fearful whisper, "Do you, by chance, know of the Ascending Stars?"

I glanced over at Lilly and Leech. Their looks matched my thought. "The what?"

"The Ascending Stars," said Harvey, still quiet. "The lights that rise from earth into the ethers of space. People claim to have seen them. There are rumors from the south of lights that leave in the night."

"You mean like satellite launches or something?" asked Lilly.

"No," said Lucinda. "They're not from any of the countries that control space launch. These are from remote spots, places thought to be uninhabited."

"It's these sightings," said Harvey, "that fueled the legend of the gods departing. In Desenna, the people who spread these rumors say the stars are ascending from Tulana, the resting place of the souls where the gods dwell. Of course, Tulana is just myth. Still, people believe . . . and until Heliad returned, it was this rumor of the Ascending Stars that threatened to bring down Desenna."

"I've never heard of any of that," I said. Lilly and Leech motioned in agreement.

Harvey sighed. "Some believe they're connected to Eden somehow, a part of Project Elysium. We thought you might know." He sounded disappointed.

"Nope," I said. "Do *you* guys know anything about Project Elysium?"

Harvey shrugged. "We know that it is secretive, and that it is Eden's plan to create a new paradise after their domes fail. This is the standard theory. And we know that seeking Atlantis is part of their plan."

Harvey paused and looked to Lucinda. They both seemed to be growing more nervous as we talked.

"We know of many people," Harvey continued, "who wish they could be part of Eden's plans, even in Desenna, though to say so would be treason."

"You mean be part of the shiny new paradise," said Leech.

"Yes," said Lucinda. "That would be nice." She sounded like she might be one of the "many."

A silence passed between us. Lucinda fiddled with her necklace, rubbing her thumb over the top of the pendant. I caught a better glimpse of it and saw a design on it, like three raised circles. She and Harvey both stared into space. It seemed like more than just worry between them. There was sadness, too. I wondered, had they lost children to the pandemics? Had the plastics cancer made them unable to have kids at all? Had their loved ones died too soon? There were so many possible causes for a person's sadness in this world.

At the same time, in the pause, I started to become aware of a clock ticking inside me. These people had not turned out to be a danger; in fact, in these last few minutes I'd actually felt almost safe. Food was helping that. It was the first time in days that my guard had been down, but Paul was still out there, coming for us.

Another deep thud echoed above us. Still blank. I thought of what Harvey had said about air-conditioning. I remembered the sound of air warping ducts when the heat came on out at Hub. Those booms were hollow and empty. These sounded heavier. I glanced at the sensor again. "Nothing on there?" I asked.

Harvey seemed to snap out of some daydream. He looked down at it. "Nope."

Still, I couldn't help worrying about the craft. Had I tied the sails off? If one of them caught the wind, the craft could blow into the wall or over the edge.

"We should probably get moving," I said.

"Going?" said Harvey. "Oh, but, well, what about our offer from the Benevolent Mother?" Harvey checked his watch. "The Nomad pod should be here in just about fifteen minutes. Why don't you just stay and finish eating?"

"Um . . ." I said. I turned to Lilly and Leech, wishing I could read their minds. Lilly shrugged slightly.

"It's a great invitation," Leech said, eyeing me, again like he was checking that we were on the same page, "but we had a prior plan, and so we need a minute to talk about it, you know, just *us*." He started to stand.

"Yeah," I agreed. This was more good thinking by Leech. "We've had a long few days, so maybe we'll just head up to the roof and talk it over, and then we'll let you know?"

"Oh," said Harvey, "I mean . . ." He shared another worried glance with Lucinda, almost like he was trying to send her mental messages. "I guess a few minutes would be . . . fine?"

I wondered if they'd be in trouble with this Benevolent Mother if we were to leave, if failing to convince us was the kind of thing that could get you packed in a freezer.

Lucinda nodded at Harvey, and turned back to us. "Sure, of course." Her voice had started to shake, matching the fidgeting of her hands. She glanced down, seeming to study the black pendant as it flipped between her fingers. "That should be okay. Just, um . . ." she said, "remind me again, which one of you is, is not, you know, one of the . . ."

"You mean not an Atlantean?" Lilly pointed her thumb at herself. "That would be me. Why?"

I hated hearing her say that. But something about what Lucinda had just asked struck me as odd. *Remind me again . . .* Had she actually asked about that before? I didn't remember it. Maybe that was just her nerves, or she misspoke.

There was a clicking sound. Something tiny and plastic.

It took me a second to find the source: Lucinda's pendant. I wondered if she'd broken it in all her nervous fidgeting. She was staring at Lilly, saw me gazing at her, then her eyes flicked away almost like she'd been caught.

"Excuse me." She lurched up from her seat, but her movement was erratic. Her knee slammed the table, and our bottles toppled over. Horchata splattered everywhere. "Oh dear!"

My bottle rolled off the table and landed on the carpet. I reached down to grab it, some random polite instinct kicking in, triggered by nerves, and I caught a glimpse under the coffee table. I noticed a pair of shoes in the shadows. They were only in the corner of my eye for a second, but that was enough time to see that they were sneakers. . . .

Small sneakers with bright pink ponies on them . . .

Too small.

I popped up, glancing over at Lucinda's big, square feet in their bulky sandals.

"What is it?" Harvey asked, but his eyes widened like he knew what I'd just realized.

"Nothing," I said. I tugged Lilly's elbow and started to stand. "Just that we should go have that talk." I tried to sound calm, but I was speaking fast. "So, we'll be right back."

Except I had no intention of us ever coming back down here, or waiting for the Nomads to arrive, because now I knew:

There was someone else here. Someone who owned those sneakers, who Harvey and Lucinda had kept secret from us. Someone small. A daughter maybe . . . and those bumps up on the roof—

"Whoa!" shouted Leech, jumping up.

Lilly yanked me back down to the couch. I turned to see her collapsing, her eyes flipping back in her head, and through terrible hacking sounds, white foam bubbling out of her mouth.

7

"LILLY!" I GRABBED HER BY THE SHOULDERS. HER entire body convulsed, her fingers a blur of twitches, eyes gritted closed, the white foam dribbling over her lips, across her cheeks and chin.

"What's happening?" Leech asked.

"Okay, that's—that's just a dose, so . . ."

I looked up to see Harvey on his feet, aiming a two-pronged grilling fork at us. Lucinda had a serrated kitchen knife in one hand, and in the other, she had her finger on that necklace.

"What did you do?" I asked, my voice vibrating from Lilly's spasms. She was calming though, and I heard a breath fight its way down her frothing throat.

"I released a dose of the neurotoxin that you all ingested." Lucinda's eyes flicked to the bottles of horchata. "It's sap, from the curare tree, contained in nanocapsules. It was an insurance policy in case you refused to cooper- ate." She held out her necklace. "One button for each of you. I press it, and y-you get poisoned." She glared at us, but I saw the knife shaking in her hand.

"Now, you two," Harvey motioned with his fork. His hands and voice were trembling, too. "You carry her and we head to the roof together. And if we go now, then Luce doesn't hurt your girl anymore."

"So what," said Leech, "you're forcing us to go to Desenna? We were—"

"We're not taking you to Desenna!" Harvey snapped. "We're trading you in for passage on the Ascending Stars. That's our deal."

"Deal?" I asked.

"With EdenCorp," said Harvey.

"We're sorry," said Lucinda. "We really are, but, w-we have our reasons." She slid her finger back over the pendant. "Now pick her up and move!"

I locked eyes with Leech, trying to read his gaze. We were not going back to Eden. Could we take these two on our own? I glanced down at the hilt of the knife in Lilly's belt. But one move and Lucinda could poison us.

Leech started to bend over. "You take her legs," he said.

"Um, okay . . ." Maybe he was thinking we should wait until we were on the stairs. That would be a good spot to try to get that necklace, dark and tight quarters.

"Luce, get our bags," said Harvey.

Out of the corner of my eye, I saw Lucinda turn and rummage behind the recliners. She hoisted two stuffed hiking backpacks over her shoulders.

I worked on grabbing Lilly's legs, my arms wrapping around the stubbly skin of her calves. I glanced up and saw Leech bent over Lilly, but then he quickly scooped some of the white foam from around her mouth, and rubbed it over his own lips and chin. His eyes met mine, dead serious, his face slathered with the foam. I was about to ask him what he was doing when he lurched up.

"Uhh," he moaned, clutching at his stomach. He started to shake and made a spray of Lilly's foam with his lips.

"Hey!" Harvey looked frantically to Lucinda. "Luce! Turn it off! You dosed the boy by mistake!"

"What?" Lucinda dropped the bags and started fumbling at her necklace. "I don't—I didn't—"

"Aaaaa—" Leech made a convincing choking sound and staggered back. He slammed into our shopping cart, then spun around and lurched over it, making more retching noises.

"Turn it off!" Harvey shouted.

"I'm trying!"

I pulled Lilly up to a sitting position, to get her arm around my shoulders.

Leech reared up from the shopping cart, spinning back around, his eyes fierce. He cocked his arm back, a dark green object in his hand. One of the boccie balls. He uttered a guttural howl and hurled it.

The ball struck Lucinda in the sternum. There was a

brutal thud and she crumpled to the floor, making a hollow sucking sound and grabbing at her chest.

"Luce!" Harvey's eyes went wide and he seemed frozen in place. He never saw the second boccie ball coming. If Leech's aim had been better, it might have killed him, but the ball glanced off the side of his head, making his eyes roll. He careened backward into the gas grill, sending it crashing to the floor, then staggered forward and fell through the coffee table in an explosion of glass.

There was a *thwump!* of air and light. Flames leaped free and raced across the carpet.

"Get the necklace!" Leech shouted. He saw me glancing at Lilly. "I got her."

I darted around the coffee table to where Lucinda was flailing on the ground like a tortoise on its back. Her attempts to breathe made a dry, wheezing whistle. Her eyes were wide, hands clutching at her chest, her mouth gaping for air like a fish out of water.

I dropped down on my knees beside her and felt a moment of indecision and I hated myself for that, but I also couldn't keep away the feeling that this woman needed help, that she'd been injured badly—

"Acchht! Acchht!" I spun around to see Leech on the couch, bending over Lilly, who was convulsing again. He had his hands by her face. Her arms were beating at his back.

"What are you doing?" I shouted, but he didn't answer.

I turned back to Lucinda and flailed at the loose folds of her clothes and the moist, flabby skin beneath, blistered with lesions. Finally, my fingers hooked around the neck-lace chain. I yanked on it, and the pull of the chain hauled Lucinda up by the neck for a second before it snapped and her head thudded back to the floor.

Flickering caught my eye and I saw flames quickly side-stepping along the box-and-furniture walls.

I shoved the necklace in my pocket and stumbled to Leech and Lilly. Just as I got there, Lilly doubled over and vomited all over her own legs and mine, a swirl of white foam and brown liquid thick with still-recognizable chunks of pastry and tapir meat.

Leech turned away from her and stood up, breathing hard. "Okay, now me." He looked up at the ceiling, took a deep breath, then started shoving two fingers down his throat.

I understood, now. He was trying to get the neurotoxin out. Leech bent over and vomited dark brown, lumpy fluid. There was no white foam, as his capsules hadn't yet been activated.

"Your turn," Leech said hoarsely. He started to cough. Smoke was clouding the air around us.

"Never done it before . . ." I looked up to the ceiling and put my fingers in my mouth. Where did you press? I had no idea I—

Weight crushed against my back and white-hot pain

tore into my shoulder. Harvey growled as he tackled me and crushed me to the floor.

"You bastards!" He roared into my ear, his breath hot against my cheek. "We have to do this for Ripley! Otherwise I'd kill you, I swear to Tona—"

"Get off!"

Harvey was cut short by a thick thud. His weight left me. I flipped over to see Leech wielding another boccie ball.

Harvey careened sideways. Fresh blood seeped down from his hairline. He wiped at it, his eyes darting this way and that like they were out of sync with each other.

"You think you can use me?" Leech shouted at him, spit flying, his voice shredded from vomiting. In the weird angles of light cast by the fallen lamp and the flames, he looked insane, a wild creature. "You think you can use us?" He lunged and tackled Harvey.

I staggered to my feet and saw Leech straddle Harvey's body. "Want to trade us like meat?" Leech shouted. "You think we're worth nothing?"

"Nnn," Harvey moaned weakly.

Leech's hand rose high over his head. The boccie ball, already shiny with liquid from its last attack, glistened in the lamplight.

"Leech, don't!" I shouted.

Leech's arm hurtled earthward.

There was this awful sound, like something damp and fibrous cracking. I heard a patter as droplets splattered against surfaces, and then a horrid, soft moan oozed through the darkness.

I stood frozen, knees shaking. My shoulder burned. I saw the grilling fork on the ground, covered in my blood.

Leech stood up over Harvey. His shoulders were heaving with hard breaths, his head dropped. He turned and staggered back toward us, his blood-soaked weapon in hand.

"Uhhh," Lilly moaned, sitting up. She wiped at her face. "Yuk."

I could barely think. We needed to get out of here. I looked to the smoky ceiling and started shoving my fingers down my throat. They grazed against the back of my tongue, the weird smooth-but-hard of my throat, and the fingers felt foreign there, wrong, scraping and blocking. I fought the urge to pull them back out and pushed farther, gagged, gagged more, and then my insides finally convulsed and I doubled over and thick, mealy soup poured out onto the shards of what had been the coffee table. Squishy sour chunks clogged my nostrils and I coughed and heaved again and again. I looked down at the mess of spatter and for a moment had the dumbest thought, feeling guilty that I'd ruined the food. . . . It was like my brain wanted to think about anything other than all the awful reality around me.

"Quick," said Leech, low and lethal, "before Eden comes."

The fire had spread to the carpet, licking toward us, and

I heard sharp cracks as it stampeded hungrily through the store.

Leech stalked over to the shopping cart, loaded his arms with the noodles, the can of stew, the pink blanket and pillow. The boccie ball was still tight in his fist.

I turned and held out my hand to Lilly. "Can you stand?"

"Yeah," she croaked. She pushed up from the couch, wobbled, and grabbed my shoulder. The touch caused a fresh surge of pain. "Sorry," she said when I flinched.

"It's fine."

Thick smoke wrapped around us. As we turned to go, I heard a weak moan from Lucinda. *Don't feel sorry for them*, I thought. *They were going to give you to Paul.*

"Come on!" Leech shouted from ahead.

We ran through the clouds to the center of the store. Lilly and I were leaning on each other, hobbling along. I was seeing spots in my vision, and my body felt so tired, so empty. The rancid odor of vomit lingered with us.

We staggered up the stairs, leaning against the railings. Rounding the last flight, we saw the rectangle of pure blue sky. Leech hurried through. Lilly and I made our way up and out into the light, only to run right into Leech's back.

"Shit," he said.

We looked ahead.

The craft was gone.

"Aw no." I ran forward anyway, looking around wildly. The roof was empty.

"Where did it go?" Leech shouted.

"No, no, we should have *known*!" I said. "I should have . . ." I scanned the horizon, but there was nothing.

Smoke was beginning to seep out of cracks and vents, obscuring the view. I ran for the edge of the roof. Maybe whoever had taken the craft had tried to fly it, and crashed. . . .

Then I heard a humming sound above us.

I looked up and barely had time to dive out of the way as the craft careened out of the sky on a steep angle. I hit the ground just before the ship landed with a tearing slam. It skidded across the roof, spinning half around and slamming into the low wall at the edge.

I jumped up and stumbled toward it. It looked empty.

A head popped up. A girl with frizzed-out blond hair. She was younger than us, maybe eleven or twelve, with a curveless body and bony arms sticking out from a teal tank top. Her shoulders were seared red from the sun. She looked around, dazed.

"Hey!" I could see already that one of the sails had come untied, and the mast looked bent.

She saw me and started looking frantically in all directions.

"Ripley!"

I turned and saw Lucinda at the top of the stairs. She had Harvey draped across her shoulder. Smoke poured out of the door behind her.

"Mom!" the girl shouted.

"Run, Ripley!" Lucinda wheezed, her voice gurgling. "They're murderers!"

"No!" I pushed my weak legs, sprinting for the craft. Ripley saw me and screamed, her eyes wide, pupils adrift in seas of white.

"Please, no!" Behind me, Lucinda had dropped to her knees, sobbing, Harvey sprawled on the roof beside her.

"Don't!" Lilly was grabbing Leech's shoulder and keeping him from another attack.

"Ripley, RUN!" Lucinda screamed.

I had just reached the edge of the craft, could hear Ripley's whimpering breaths, when her feet slammed the pedals. The craft lurched upward. I threw my arms over the side just as it whacked me in the jaw. I nearly lost my grip but managed to hang on.

We hurtled upward in an arc, town far below us. The sails caught, then luffed again, and we were thrown into a wicked spin.

"I don't know how it works!" Ripley screamed, through sobs.

I struggled to throw my leg over the side, but the spin was too strong. "Press back on the left pedal!" I shouted.

Ripley stabbed at the pedals. The spin relented for a second, and I was able to drag myself into the craft.

I got to my knees but fell into her. "Get off me!" she screamed. I felt something hot and wet through my shirt and I finally got a good look at Ripley. Her face, her arms, every inch of skin was covered in tiny, oozing spots, little red holes with yellowish pus dribbling out. I could see the squirming white lines under the skin. Heat worm, a parasite that thrived in polluted water supplies. There was a treatment for it, but it was impossible to get down here. I remembered a couple cases in Hub, but I'd never seen anything like this. Ripley's skin was literally alive with the wavelike pulsations of worms burrowing through her. They were probably in her muscle tissue, by now, an advanced state. Eventually they would start eating through her organs, her bones, her brain.

This was why Harvey and Lucinda were trading us to Eden: for the chance to save their daughter.

Ripley slapped at me. Her feet hit the pedals again and we were thrust into a steep dive. The sails caught and wrenched us into a spin worse than the first.

"Daddy, help!" Ripley screamed.

I tried to flip back inside my head and find Lük, thinking, *I need to pull out of a dive!* but I couldn't find the Atlantean city. Everything was a blur.

"Get out of the way!" I gripped her bony shoulders and tried to push her toward the front of the craft.

"Leave me alone!" She wailed through snot and tears, and as I blocked her blows I saw the white smudges of worms leaking out of her nostrils and tear ducts. She writhed like a snared animal, her fists flying at me.

I held her firm. "Let me fly!" I shouted. With the world blurring around us, my gaze locked with her wide, young, worm-scribbled eyes—

And something happened. It was like reality slipped, or like there were two things in my mind at once. This Ripley girl in front of me screaming as we spun . . . but then over her appeared that strange, gray ghost girl with the red hair and frog pajamas from my dream. She was screaming and crying, too, writhing, terrified in my grip. And I was trying to pull her up, but once again she was sinking into ash, and there was heat and burning and . . .

And then there was more. I saw the Atlantean city, the training lake, Lük standing by his craft. "Ready for another test ride?" he asked through a whipping wind. This layered on the others, so that the gray sky of Lük's world was also the ash and the spin and Ripley's screams.

It was all too much, and I felt tearing in my head, like thoughts were pulling away from their scaffolding.

"You can use the—" Lük began but then his voice cut out. The Atlantean lake suddenly disappeared from my mind as if it had been switched off.

There was a squealing scream. I had lost my grip on Ripley, and the force of our spin had yanked her out of the craft. She clung to the side.

Sinking girl in the ash. Falling girl in the craft. Which was which?

I threw myself forward and tried to narrow my mind

down to a single line of thought: *Grab the girl! Save the craft! Don't die!* My hand found her moist, wormy forearm and pulled her in, dropping her to the floor.

Images slid again . . . burns on the girl in the ash, her breathing wrecked—

I gritted my teeth and tried to press in on my brain, fix everything in place. . . . *You are in the craft. Over Gambler's Falls. Get up. Get up!*

I opened my eyes and flailed around in the blurring spin until I got hold of the sail lines.

How do I stop this spin? I tried to shout to Lük, but there was no answer. And no time.

I got into my seat, feet to the pedals. Had to figure this out. I felt the force of the spin, and backed off the thrust. Waited for the winds to catch a sail . . . There. I hauled it in and let the other sail billow out. The wind yanked us forward, and we made a curving arc that finally took us out of the spiral.

I banked around, and headed back. I tried to straighten the craft, but the bent mast was dragging us sideways. I was able to compensate but had to work harder to keep the ship straight.

Ahead, smoke rose from all corners of the Walmart. In the craft, Ripley lay curled on the floor, whimpering.

I dropped back to the roof. The ship thumped awkwardly, stopping after a light bounce.

Lilly and Leech were just standing there, looking

stunned by everything. They walked toward me. Lilly wobbled like she could barely stay up. Her face was gray.

"Ripley!" Lucinda staggered toward us, Harvey still lying on the roof. Her hands were covered in his blood. She wiped her hair out of her eyes, leaving blood smears across her cheek, down her nose and mouth.

Ripley dragged herself up, her body shuddering. I heard her teeth chattering, a mix of fear and the fever that was probably scorching her insides.

"I'm sorry," I said to Ripley. I hadn't even thought through what I was saying or why. "You can come with us, if you want. We can try to get you help—"

"I hope you burn in the glare of Tona!" she screamed, worm-clogged spit flying, and she lurched away, toppling out of the craft and then getting up and running for her mother. In my mind, I saw another flash of the girl in the ash. My head ached. What had happened to me up there?

"We need to move," said Lilly, watching the horizon warily. Her knees hit the side of the craft and she pitched forward, dumping supplies onto the floor. Then she started to stagger in, but stopped. Her eyes darted around the craft. "Where's my bag?"

A single glance and I knew: her red waterproof bag was gone. I also noticed that two of the three clay pot heat cells were gone. Dr. Maria's black backpack was still there, wedged against the side.

"Crap," I said. "During the spin . . . We can look for it. Come on."

Leech hopped inside. "We don't have time—"

"Yes, we do," said Lilly, and even with the pain and fatigue in her voice, it was clear there was no arguing with her.

I hit the pedals and we lifted away from the roof, the ship now flying with a shudder, like a limp. As we rose, I looked back at the single form of Lucinda and Ripley, kneeling, clutched in an embrace beside Harvey. Clouds of black smoke erased them from my sight.

"We're leaving them to die," I said, the thought hollowing me out even further. "If it's not the fire, it's going to be Desenna for the betrayal, or Eden for failing to keep us here. And the girl's got heat worm so bad that she'll probably be dead soon, anyway."

I looked over at Leech. He was watching them, too, but his eyes were narrowed, his face spotted with Harvey's blood. "That's their problem," he said quietly.

I checked the horizon as we rose. Still no copters. To the west, the sun had tired to orange and was lowering through the cloudless sky.

I leveled off and started to make wide circles over town. The vortex responded more slowly to my movements. Its blue had dimmed.

"There," said Lilly after a few minutes.

We lowered to a dry plot of land in front of a house, one in a row of skeletons on what had once been a residential street. Lilly's bag was lying there on the hardpan of dirt and fossilized grass. She grabbed it and we lifted off and I headed southwest on Leech's bearing as fast as we could go.

Lilly checked the contents of the bag. All the items were still inside, but I had known from the jangling sound the moment she'd picked it up that my crystal skull, my connection to Lük and the Aeronaut's knowledge, had shattered.

8

"THAT WAY" LEECH SAID, POINTING OFF STARBOARD after checking the first stars that appeared in the twilight. There had only been four other words spoken between us in the hours since Gambler's Falls.

"How are you?" I'd asked Lilly, as she put a bandage from Dr. Maria's medical kit on my shoulder. We'd also found a bright pink Rad burn on my scalp, which had started to blister, and was smoldering more with each minute.

"Fine," she'd replied, but she hadn't sounded it, her voice hoarse like it had been rubbed with sandpaper.

She was curled beside me in the craft now, her head on the pink pillow, her blanket over her. One hand cradled her sore stomach, the other rubbed at her gills.

"Did you hear me?" Leech asked.

"Yes," I muttered. I was slowly getting the hang of compensating for the bent mast, but the wind gusts had strengthened once the sun went down, hot gusts that seemed to be fleeing back to space, and the whole craft creaked ominously as I fought to keep it on course. My arms were trembling with fatigue, and my empty stomach, wasn't helping.

"I don't know if it's the nanocapsules that are still in my gut or your flying," Leech said, now holding his stomach, too, "but I am going to lose whatever I've got left in here."

"I'm working on it," I said quietly and had to resist the urge to bank the craft hard enough for him to accidentally fall out, or at least hit the side hard. I also resisted saying that the craft wouldn't have been damaged if Ripley hadn't panicked, and Ripley might not have panicked if Lucinda hadn't appeared screaming, holding her bloody father . . . bloody because of Leech. But I had enough of a battle on my hands just keeping us in the sky.

Because of the damage, I was also having to push the vortex engine harder to keep us at speed. I estimated that we'd slowed to about forty kilometers an hour, and I didn't dare go any slower. The engine's light was growing dim. Under this strain, it wasn't going to get us to the marker.

I'd tried to find Lük in my head, but he was gone. The mountain lake was still there, but its surface was still, windless. There were no boats, no students around, the city perfectly silent. The whole scene was like a program that had been paused.

I held the sail lines in one hand and reached into Lilly's bag, moving my fingers gingerly, until I found a sharp edge.

I pulled out a half-moon shard of broken skull the size of my hand. The crystal was cold, heavy, and dark. Blurry reflections of the stars twinkled faintly in it, but that was all. Its white glow, all its memory, was gone.

No more tips, no more training. If I was going to keep us flying, I'd have to do it on my own. And it was a lonely, hollow feeling, like something that had been lit up and glowing warmly in my mind was now shut off. Screens gone black, the technicians staring at their consoles blankly . . .

No, no more technicians. They were gone, too. Needed to be. They'd been a nice idea, a way to deal with that feeling of not knowing myself, of not being in control, but now I knew how much was up to me. I still couldn't control the forces against me or what change my Atlantean DNA would reveal next, but I was the only one in charge of how I would deal with it. Like right now: I was keeping this craft in the air, not Lük, not technicians. Just me. I had to do these things, believe in my powers, or we were going to end up back in Eden. Owen, boy from Hub, descendant of Atlantis, one of the Three who had to defend it against Paul. That was who I was and I had to *be* it.

And the weak groan from beside me was another part of this: I had to take care of Lilly, like she'd taken care of me when my gills had failed. I'd brought her out here, even after she told me to leave her, and so she was my responsibility, but it was more than that. I wanted to be responsible for her. To her. Looking at her lying beside me, hurting, I didn't care about her past with Evan. I didn't even care that she'd lied about the siren. None of it mattered. I couldn't let it.

I wanted to show her what I could do. I wanted us to get through this and have each other, whatever that meant. I'd only known her a little over a week, but from a dream of finding a little archipelago somewhere to just waking up tomorrow, I had no vision of the future that didn't include her. It was like she'd said back on her island, *like we were already past all that*. Past uncertainty and doubt, past worry about trust. We just *knew* each other. I'd thought when I first met her on the dock that I loved her, but that thought had been stupid, because now I knew that I actually did, and it was a deeper, almost scary feeling. I had an urge to wake her and tell her all this . . . but I let her sleep and focused on flying.

I took one more look at the skull shard and threw it out into the black.

Lilly stirred a half hour later. "You should eat," I said. Flying had gotten a little easier, the gusts dying down to empty desert cold. I could spare a free hand, and passed her the stew can we'd gotten.

Lilly looked at the can warily. "I don't think I want to put anything in there right now," she said, her voice leathery.

"It's been a few hours since the poison. I think we're in the clear."

Lilly considered this, then took the can. She whittled at the seam with her knife, the dimming blue glow of the vortex on her lips and nose. As she did, she asked, "What was that, back there?"

I glanced over my shoulder for what seemed like the millionth time, but all I saw were stars down to no stars where the earth began, and a faint silver aura of approaching moonlight.

I wondered if Leech would offer any answers, but he didn't. He was sitting at the front of the craft, chewing on dry noodles, making sucking sounds as he softened them with saliva. He was hunched over, sketching. I'd noticed that when he drew, he seemed barely aware of anything else. I wondered how he could be just working after what he'd done. The memory of him raising that boccie ball, smacking it down, the wet crunch of skull . . .

"Well," I said, "I think all that stuff about Heliad and Desenna is true."

"That the third Atlantean is there," said Lilly. "A girl. Your *sister of memory*."

"Sounds like it," I said.

"Which means we need to go there," said Lilly. She didn't sound thrilled.

"Unless we can find some other way to contact her."

"We should still go to the marker first," said Leech. So he had been listening. "It's important."

"As important as the third Atlantean?" I didn't really mean that question to sound antagonistic, but it did.

"Kinda, yeah," said Leech. "That's where my maps run out. I can't see anything past it. I think we need to go there for me to know what comes next."

"Fine," I said. "That was the plan anyway."

Leech leaned back over his sketchbook.

"And that family," Lilly continued, "they were going to turn us in to Eden over those Ascending Stars they were talking about?"

"And to get help for the girl's heat worm," I said. "Eden probably offered to treat her."

"Huh," said Lilly. "If they did, it was a lie. The Edens haven't been able to get medications like that from the Northern Federation for years. I heard on the Free Signal that relations are bad because Eden won't reveal what Project Elysium is."

"It probably wouldn't have mattered in her case, anyway." I pictured Ripley's worm-filled eyes again and felt my stomach tremble. And thinking of her reminded me of the girl from my dream, standing there in the ash. The image seemed distant now, but at the moment in the craft, it had been so real feeling. I didn't remember ever having an episode like that before. Maybe it was a side effect of my whole system reorganizing itself, a kind of discharge in my brain, like the ionization lightning inside Eden.

"Hey," said Lilly. She rubbed my arm. "You just left for a minute."

"It's nothing." I found myself looking into her eyes, and

for a second I felt totally connected to her again, as close as we'd been on Tiger Lilly Island, when she'd shoved the brownie in my mouth and I'd felt my first raindrops. Those moments had seemed like things from another life for the last two days, until just now. My thought from earlier returned. I felt a warm rush, and almost wanted to tell her—

But then she looked away, rubbing at her gills. "I just can't get all those horrible images out of my head."

Horrors. That reminded me: "I saw the siren again."

"You did?" Lilly asked.

"Yeah. This afternoon on the roof, right before I came in to find you guys. She said to *beware the gods and their horrors*."

"And what did your special ghost girlfriend mean by that?" Leech asked.

"Not really sure. I was looking at the body on the flagpole. The only gods we've heard about are part of Heliad-Seven. I've been wondering if she was warning us about Desenna."

"If she's even real," said Leech. "But we probably should be worried about Desenna. I mean, those people chopped off their *fingers*. And who knows how voluntary their volunteers even are? Plus, for being members of Heliad-Seven, those three back there were trying pretty hard to get into Eden instead."

"Gods," said Lilly. "That's what they were saying the Ascending Stars were, too. Gods leaving us. Freakin' people and their gods. My parents were Hindu. A lot of good anybody's gods did during the Rise."

"Well," I said, "what could the Ascending Stars really be, then?"

"Maybe this will tell us." Lilly put aside the stew can and reached down to Dr. Maria's backpack. She pulled out the video sheet and unrolled it. It was a paper-sized rectangle, flexible and translucent and crisscrossed with intricate threads of circuitry. Looking at it now, I felt a burst of nerves. What would we find out? I almost didn't want to know.

I handed her the reader device. It had a narrow slot across its top that the edge of the sheet fit into. Lilly clicked the sheet into place, and the reader began to hum, sending a charge up through the circuitry, lighting it in ghostly white. The light was not unlike the skull: two vessels of information, thousands of years apart. The light matrix bled together, solidifying into a shimmering square that seemed to hover just above the page. Words appeared:

PE QUARTERLY REPORT TO EDEN BOARD

They dissolved and there was Paul's face. I felt my skin crawling at the sight of him. "Members of the board," he said, "by now you've seen the various numerical data. So here is a summary of where Project Elysium stands."

9

HE WAS SITTING AT HIS DESK BACK IN CAMP EDEN, glasses on. His face looked smooth, like maybe he'd put on makeup for the occasion. And that was weird, but again, here was further proof that even Paul had someone to impress: the board of directors, who'd looked in at me from a video screen back in the skull chamber like I was some fancy new piece of technology.

"So, this is from before we escaped," said Lilly.

"Before we were caught, even," I added.

"As you all know," Paul began, "we are firmly on schedule in phase three of the four-part project plan. Here is an update on each component:"

A graphic replaced Paul, white words on a red background, a basic bulleted list:

EdenHome
- Climatization
- Transit
- Fusion Mining

Paul spoke over the list: "Basic climate systems are up and functioning normally at EdenHome. Our preliminary modeling of the likely effect of the Paintbrush of the Gods indicates that full climate restoration should be completed within a few months of activation. So, our overall time line remains intact.

"The transit plan to EdenHome is currently at seventy-five percent. This is five percent behind schedule, but our recent covert action, Operation Reclaim, has been a success and should help get us back on track. Otherwise, fleet construction is nearly complete, and transit from the Edens to the docks at Egress is ready and on standby.

"Finally, as I know you're quite aware, uranium mining is proceeding ahead of schedule."

Paul appeared again for a moment. "I hope the mining dust isn't interfering with visibility on the driving range," he said, smiling slightly.

"You're so funny," Lilly cracked at the screen.

I imagined the wrinkly old board of directors, men of power and money, standing around serenely playing golf, on green grass, wearing hats, while the rest of the world baked. I hated them even more.

Another graphic appeared:

Brocha De Dioses

- Salvage Team Update
- Status of Subjects

"Teams Alpha through Delta have been following map information obtained from the research at each Eden complex, and cross-referencing it with the maps we obtained from Test Subject One."

"Hey, that's me," Leech said sarcastically.

"He called me Subject Two," I said.

Paul continued: "Satellite imaging has led to some new excavations, but so far we do not know the precise location of the Heart of the Terra, where the Paintbrush of the Gods is hidden. We still believe that it will be the capital Atlantean city, and we have found more evidence to point to my initial theory as to that city's location, but for the moment we are still operating covertly, so as not to arouse suspicion in the global community.

"Here at EdenWest, we continue to monitor the progress of Test Subjects One through Eleven, with subjects One, Two, and Five showing the most progress. We remain suspicious of the claims from Desenna of an Atlantean among them, based on the data sets we had from Eden-South before it fell, but obviously there is a time gap that is unaccounted for, and so it is possible that dear Dr. Keller has discovered a new subject."

"Is Dr. Keller the Benevolent Mother?" Lilly asked.

"Yep," said Leech.

"We are receiving regular reports from our operatives within Desenna," Paul said. "As far as we can tell, for the moment at least, Heliad-Seven remains no great threat.

"Based on that assumption, we have sent operatives into Coke-Sahel to determine if the recent rumors there are true, but it is too soon to tell."

I glanced at Leech. "Did Paul ever say anything to you about Heliad-Seven?"

Leech clicked his tongue. "Not really. We did talk about EdenSouth, though." It sounded like there was more to that story.

The next slide appeared:

Egress
- Northern Federation
- Selectees

"To this point," said Paul, "our operatives in the Northern Federation report that, while there have been rumors about our preparations, no one has realized our true aims, outside of wild speculations by the usual gamma link fringe broadcasters in the Nomad Alliance. We remain confident that no one takes these claims seriously, but just in case, an added benefit of Operation Reclaim should be the silencing of that element.

"The preparations at Egress continue on schedule. As you are no doubt aware, we have notified all selectees that the departure command is imminent. All have agreed to enhanced monitoring during this final stage, so that we can maintain absolute secrecy, which as you know will be of the utmost importance."

Paul appeared again. "It won't be long now, gentlemen. I'm sure you're as anxious as I am to shed these claustrophobic confines and stretch out into the new future. I'd love to come up and present this report in person, but I am just on the cusp of a fascinating discovery here at camp and need to monitor things closely over the next twenty-four hours. I may be getting in touch again with some important news. . . . Until then." The screen went black.

"I suppose I'm the fascinating discovery," I said. I was glad to have Paul's face out of my sight.

"Yeah," said Leech quietly. "I think that video was right before he came and pulled me from a dodgeball game and hooked me up to your skull for ten hours."

"That must have been bad," I said.

Leech didn't look up. "You think?" He kept drawing.

It was obvious to me now how much anger and hurt were festering right below the surface in someone who I'd first thought was just an arrogant bully. Leech's sneer was really a mask over pain, pain that made him obnoxious and sometimes violent. And I found myself actually wanting to know more. I realized this was a moment to try to connect with him, but I still didn't quite know how to talk to him. I especially didn't want to set him off, since seeing what his anger could lead to.

"I bet his next report doesn't sound so chipper,"

said Lilly, "after we escaped."

"Knowing Paul," I said, "he probably found some way to gloss it over." I thought about what we'd just heard. "It's weird. Paul asked me if I wanted to save the human race. But if setting off the Paintbrush was going to help everyone, why not just tell the Northern Federation countries what they were up to?"

"Well, maybe because the people in the north don't have it that bad," said Lilly. "What if the Paintbrush caused the Arctic to go back to being an inhospitable ice field? Then all the people in the Northern Federation would have to move south, and it would be chaos all over again. They'd probably like to stay right where they are, and they're the ones with big militaries."

I remembered the vision inside the skull, when I'd first met Lük, of the ash-filled sky and the stormy ocean. "Paul said he thinks it can be improved with modern technology, but maybe they're keeping the Paintbrush a secret because it's going to devastate the planet before it heals it. Maybe this EdenHome place is set up to weather the storm and keep Eden's people safe."

"Not even all their people," said Lilly. "When Paul said you could help save humanity, he only really meant the selectees. The elite of the elite. Everyone else in the Edens is probably getting left behind along with the rest of the world."

"What a surprise," I said, "Eden choosing who gets to

survive and who gets to die."

I thought of the kids at camp, like Beaker and Bunsen, Xane, Mina. "We should have warned them," I said. "Nobody at camp knows what's coming. And I doubt they're selectees."

"We didn't exactly have time," said Lilly.

"I wonder who Test Subject Five is?" said Leech.

"Paul said there were eleven total," said Lilly. "Could be any of those bodies we saw in the lab. Anna . . . Could be me or Evan, Marco, Aliah . . ." She blinked at tears.

"Paul might have been lying," I said, "about Evan. They might have escaped. He's lied about so many other things."

"Maybe," said Lilly.

A silence passed over us. The winds had calmed and the moon had risen, a swollen yellow disk. We flew for a while. Lilly fiddled with things. Leech drew.

Something cold touched my lips. I flinched, then saw it was the stew can, its top gouged open. "Have some," said Lilly. She pressed it against my mouth and tilted it up. Cool, congealed chunks slid onto my tongue: mushy meat, slick potatoes, gelatinous broth, decades old, but it was so salty and so much better than nothing. As I gulped down a few bites, I felt my mouth exploding with saliva, and I craved water, but we'd agreed to try to make it through the night without using any more of our last bottle.

I pushed the can away before it was gone. "You have the rest," I said.

Lilly shook her head, and her hand returned to her gills. "I tried a few bites, but my throat is too sore to eat." She held it out toward Leech. "You?"

"No thanks," said Leech, crunching another dry noodle.

Lilly held the can back to my mouth and I sucked down what was left. When I was done, she held it in front of her and looked it over. She made a little laughing sound. "You guys remember recycling?" she asked.

"Yeah," said Leech with a chuckle. "That was hilarious."

"We still do that out at Hub," I said.

Leech sighed at this, shaking his head. I was going to ask why, but Lilly was going on.

"Do your part to save the planet," she said in a mocking official voice, "that was the whole thing with recycling, right? And, like, back in Vegas in the fifties, we had to compost our food scraps and only flush the toilet when it was absolutely nasty. . . ."

"We had urine recycling," said Leech. "So gross."

I realized that Leech had never talked about where he was from.

"Yeah, us, too," said Lilly. "They said you couldn't taste it, but I swear sometimes it was kind of sour and chalky."

"Yuck," said Leech.

"And it's just like, you look back on it," said Lilly, "and . . . what was the point? We did all that stuff, trying to be environmentally conscious, and in the end it didn't do a damn thing to save the earth. My family were big believers, recycling all our cans, reusing everything, even taking the UV light baths, and then some power plant would run for ten minutes and pump out more carbon dioxide than we could ever save, and everything would be screwed anyway. It was such a waste."

I was surprised to hear something so cynical from Lilly. This was not like the girl from the raft. It seemed like everything since then had worn away at her sense of hope. "You had to do something, though, right?" I said.

"Yeah but"—Lilly had started tearing at the skin around her fingernails, like she did when her thoughts got serious—"what we should have done was headed north sooner, or at least gotten the hell out of places like Vegas, and listened to the warnings the planet was clearly giving us from the start. I remember all the politicians talking about how we could stop the Great Rise, how we were just around the corner from some policy or invention or whatever that would slow it down, but those were lies. It was all already in motion, you know? We'd been wrecking things for hundreds of years already, thinking that we could just act however we wanted and God would take care of us. And by the time people started waking up to the dangers, it was way too late. Nature had already made up its mind."

"Yeah, but that's because we basically are nature," said Leech.

"What's that mean?" said Lilly.

"I mean we're a part of nature," said Leech. "We're not separate from it. The Great Rise was going to happen, same as everything else. Us warming the planet is no different from an elephant knocking down all the trees and making a savanna. It's just life doing its thing."

"We killed all the elephants," said Lilly, "and practically every other animal."

"Yeah, but that's still just nature, too. It's not like we came here from outer space. Nature made us. It's not wrong, it's just success. Survival of the fittest. Human beats elephant, or whale or any other extinct creature."

"Except that *success* ended up killing off over half the human race," I said. "We spoiled our own planet."

"Not spoiled, just changed. Same thing every other animal does," said Leech. "Take a disease or termites or something. They eat and multiply until there're no more victims and they're drowning in their own feces, and then they die off, and the ones that are left evolve."

"And the cycle starts anew," I said, remembering what the siren had said.

"Huh?" said Leech.

"Nothing."

"So it's okay for humans to just die out," Lilly continued.

"*Okay* isn't part of it," said Leech. "It just is. Dinosaurs rise and fall. Humans rise and fall. Maybe next it will be rats or roaches or some intelligent plant. Point is, it's all nature."

I was surprised by this. Another thing I hadn't expected from Leech was this kind of thinking about the world. And I also remembered where I'd heard it before. "Paul talked like that."

"Yeah," said Leech. "He called it natureism. He may be a jerk, but the idea makes sense."

"And so do you agree that it should justify him doing whatever he wants?" asked Lilly.

"I'm not sure what I believe," said Leech quietly. "Not anymore." He returned to his drawing.

Lilly turned to me. "What do you think?"

"Um." I wasn't sure. "I think the thing about nature has a point. I mean, our brains evolved out of the same muck as every other thing that's ever lived."

"Great," muttered Lilly, "you boys are useless. Maybe Paul's right, then. Maybe this is all just 'natural.' So in that case, who cares about anything?"

"Come on," I said, "maybe there *is* a reason for, like, recycling and all that: but it's not to stop the world from changing. It seems like the world is going to change no matter what, whether humans cause it or something else. But . . . I think just because you're part of nature doesn't mean you get to do whatever you want. It's like, you might have your own bedroom, and you can do whatever you want in it, but if you trash it too much, you can't live in it anymore. Or something."

"I like it, O," said Lilly, and I finally thought I saw a spark in her eyes. "Do unto others as you would do to your bedroom. Bedroomism."

I smiled. It felt good to be talking, spinning ideas by blue light, free in the dark, like we had on the raft. It was also the first time in days that Lilly had used her old nickname for me. "Also," I went on, "if you mess up the bedroom too fast, you end up breaking things, or in this case killing people. So sure, maybe on a million-year scale, the death of a few billion people doesn't actually matter, but on a personal scale, part of being human is morality, and it's wrong to kill another person. So maybe that's where you draw the line." I couldn't help glancing at Leech as I said this, remembering the boccie balls, but he was drawing intently.

"So our creed is Thou Shalt Not Kill nor Muss Thy Bedroom," said Lilly. "And so it was." She considered the can in her hand. "That said, don't suppose we're going to find a recycling center out here." She tossed the can over the side of the craft.

"I hope you two can live with yourselves when that can murders some poor little mouse down there," said Leech.

"I like it better when you're drawing quie—" Lilly was stopped by a violent cough. It grew, sharpening, and after a minute she was doubled over. I put my hand on the middle of her back, felt her rib cage convulsing.

"Yikes," said Leech.

Lilly's coughs made the whole craft shake. She lost her breath, and they became these dry stuck sounds, like there was nowhere deeper to go. Her body kept hitching . . . finally a long, slow breath sucked in and fell out.

I rubbed her back slowly. She got more breaths in. I ran my hand up to her shoulders, but then I pulled away. Something felt wet by her neck. I found smears of blood on my palm. I pushed her hair aside. "Your gills," I said quietly. The slits were swollen with blood.

She touched them, looked at her fingers, and nodded, but she didn't say anything. She just leaned back on the pink pillow, curled up, and closed her eyes. I put the blanket over her.

We flew on. A few hours later, Leech tucked himself in the front of the craft and dozed off. The moon was high now, just past full, its light much brighter than the vortex.

I watched the stars, adjusted for the winds, and tried not to think about anything: the long nightmare day we'd had, Lilly's condition, Project Elysium, what we might find tomorrow, or the fact that we were nearly out of water. It all felt like too much, and I had an urge to just stop, and yet there was no stopping. Our only answer was to keep moving.

Sometime later, we passed over a small city, a forest of silent towers of steel, brick, and glass; a grid of still streets; and miles of dusty suburbs, appendages connected by highway arteries. For a moment, I thought I saw a light down there and brought us up higher.

A couple hours after that, as I fought exhaustion and sleep phantoms, I started to see white shapes on the ground. They were large, oblong, like the bellies of huge creatures, lying at odd angles. Most were pointed at one end, flat at the back. . . .

Boats. A marina on what had probably once been a lake. Masts stuck up like the horns of the long dead narwhals. Masts might mean sails, and sails could be used to make a new thermal balloon. Judging by how dim the vortex was, we were going to need one, soon.

I brought us down near the docks, between two concrete buildings. As I placed the craft on the cracked pavement, Lilly and Leech both stirred but didn't wake.

I wanted to search for a sail now, but I couldn't fight the exhaustion. I curled up on the floor near Lilly, thought about getting under the blanket with her, of how she'd held me through the night when my gills were changing, but I didn't feel quite sure. So I moved close but not touching, my head on the bench. I stared into the mellow blue swirl of the vortex and let it pull down my eyelids.

I dropped into dreamless sleep until near dawn, when

my eyes fluttered open to bright sky. Lilly was still asleep beside me. Her face looked dangerously red, and there was a fine mist of sweat on her forehead.

I raised my head to see that Leech was gone, and the vortex was dark.

10

I TRIED TO STAND BUT FELL BACK UNDER A WAVE OF bright spots and pain. It took a minute to fade. Everything hurt. My head felt squeezed, like my brain had dried up and pulled away from the inside of my skull. My eyes were sticking at the seams, and blinking didn't help. My mouth felt like dry cloth.

I managed to get up. I checked my shoulder. It was sore and stiff. A brownish stain had seeped through the bandage covering my grilling fork wound.

We were in a triangle of shade, but the sun was creeping down into this space between the two buildings. The air had that electric feel of buzzing molecules, the world heating up, and the craft wasn't moving again until we either made a thermal balloon or magically summoned lightning from the sky.

I pulled out our last water bottle, took a few sips, and fought the urge to drink it all.

I gently shook Lilly's shoulder. Her breaths were short

and raspy, her gills dry, cracked, red canyons with flaky rims, surrounded by brown crusts of blood and vomit. The surrounding skin was red and hot with infection.

"Lilly," I said quietly.

"Nnn." She flinched, batting at my hand. Her eyes slowly opened. They were bloodshot.

"Hey. We need to move."

She nodded and slowly sat up, rubbing at her head. I passed her the water bottle. She took a few sips, but winced as she swallowed. "I don't think there's any part of me that doesn't hurt." Her voice was little more than a croak. "Where's Leech?"

"I don't know. Maybe looking for supplies."

Lilly rummaged into her bag. "Here," she said, holding out her bottle of NoRad.

"Thanks." I squeezed a blob into my hands and passed it back to her. I covered my legs, neck, face, and hands with the purple slick, and then also reached under my clothes to cover my shoulders. I rubbed it gently over my scalp, the burn there igniting at the touch. My fingers came away with sickly pink pus. "This isn't going to be enough to protect us."

"No . . . ow," Lilly moaned. She'd been trying to get the NoRad near her gills.

"I think they're getting infected," I said. I fished into Dr. Maria's backpack and pulled out the medical kit. There were three little packets of AntiBac.

Lilly tilted her head and pulled her tangled hair out of the way. I squeezed out a dab of the clear ointment and carefully pressed it onto the first gill line. She winced.

"I'm sorry," I said, being as gentle as I could.

"It's okay," said Lilly. "Just get it on there."

But I realized that I hadn't just been apologizing for my touch. There was more on my mind to say. "No, I mean sorry for all this. For everything I've put you through."

Lilly eyed me sideways. "What's that supposed to mean?"

"Well, I mean, just . . ." I finished one set of gills, pushed her chin with my finger, and started on the other. "Because it's my fault. All this stuff that's happened to you, because of me . . ."

Lilly flinched away like I was a spider. "Because of you."

"No, well, I mean, yeah, since you're not one of the Atlanteans . . . I just, I don't know, feel bad . . ." I trailed off because it seemed like every word I said was making her eyes darken and her mouth tighten further.

"I'll finish." She snatched the AntiBac from my fingers.

"What?"

"You think this is about you. . . ."

I tried to figure out what I'd said wrong. "Well, no . . . but, I mean all this has happened because me and Leech are part of the Three and—"

Lilly threw the packet at me. "This was my choice, Owen! I chose to help you and come with you."

"I didn't mean that you didn't have a choice, just that, you told me to leave you up at the Eye, but I didn't, and now—"

"I was trying to save you!" Lilly shouted. "I *wanted* to go with you, to be here, but at the time it looked like there was no other way, and— Whatever." She got out of the craft on wobbly legs. "Even if I *only* have these stupid gills, even if I only have *some* of the super-special DNA that you have, that doesn't mean I'm not connected to it. And that's, uh! That's not even why I'm here! I can't believe you don't get that!" She threw her hands up and stalked off.

"Lilly, wait." I got up, but my legs were like jelly. I sat back down, white spots clouding my vision. I heard Lilly's footsteps trudge away across the sand.

I sat there for a few minutes, head spinning, a salty, metallic taste in my mouth, and wondered what I'd said wrong. Lilly had been so down since we'd left Eden, so why wouldn't I feel sorry about that?

I tried standing up again, and made my way out from between the buildings. I passed a collapsed deck and piles of round tables and shredded umbrellas. The early morning sun scalded my cheek. I felt my sweat evaporating instantly.

Ahead, the land sloped down steadily, first as bone-white sand, then as stripes of brown and red rock, down and down to the boulder-strewn low point of a long-dry lake. The docks were the floating kind, like back at camp. They lay on the sand, kinked in crooked S shapes like the spines of ancient dinosaurs. The boats were leaning over, piled against one another. Others were scattered out on the sand, tied to buoys, their sand-crusted hulls facing skyward.

"Lilly!" I called. I hopped onto the nearest deck, the old planks creaking, and hurried into the shadows between the boats. The thermal breezes whistled between them, clattering loose rope lines.

I heard serrated coughs up ahead, and found Lilly hanging down from the chrome railing of a sailboat. She dropped to the sand, a rolled-up sail under her arm, and knelt in the shade beneath the hull. She started rolling it out. The sail was blue and red, made of thin nylon.

"I'm gonna need scissors and twine," she said.

"Okay, but what did I say back—"

"Later. This now." She coughed again.

"I don't know how we're going to design a thermal without Lük's help," I said.

"My mom taught me how to sew," said Lilly, spreading out the sail. "I know—how very pre-Rise of me, right? But she was into making her own saris for us. And she taught me basic stitches. So, hey, I can actually be useful!"

She set to work, measuring and punching holes with her knife like I wasn't even there.

I walked back up the dock, surveying the boats, wondering which to search for supplies—

Until I heard a low sound. A voice. Close by. I took a

few steps back. . . . It was coming from up inside a tall, cockeyed yacht. The boat's giant black propeller was at my waist height. There was a sneaker tread in the sand on one of the blades.

It sounded like Leech. Talking to someone.

I climbed up to the deck as quietly as I could. A sliding glass door was half open. I peered inside. Leech sat on a little couch in a small cabin with dark wood walls, hunched over the subnet computer, talking quietly to it. The screen was lit but I couldn't tell with what. It seemed unlikely that there was a subnet connection here, but still . . . I turned my ear closer—but my shifting weight made the floor creak. Leech's eyes snapped up.

I ducked back but I knew he'd seen me, so I stepped in. There stuffy air had a dry, baked smell. Leech had already turned the computer off.

"What are you doing?" I asked.

Leech made his classic squint. "What do you mean?"

My nerves were ringing, and I hated how Leech inspired that feeling in me. "I heard you talking," I said.

Leech stood. "Yeah, well, I talk to myself when I'm bored. I was just looking for food, but everything's picked clean." He started toward the door.

I stepped in front of him. "I saw you talking into the pad. Who were you talking to?"

Leech stopped inches from me. "You know, just because we're all *brothers on a quest* now doesn't mean that I forgot what happened in the Preserve. I still owe you."

"Who were you talking to?" I said, my heart pounding. "Was it Paul? You're still working with him—"

Leech was on me before I could react. He grabbed me by the neck and threw me down. I toppled over a little coffee table that was bolted to the floor, and I felt a bell-ringing pain in my leg. I landed with my back on the couch, legs on the table, and butt sunk down to the floor. There was a gash on my shin, blood flowing out.

Leech just glared at me. I saw that his hand had lowered to his waist, where a long section of green plastic netting hung from his belt. Cradled inside the netting was the boccie ball, still crusted in dark smears. Now he could swing it.

"Like it?" said Leech. "Lilly's got a knife, you've got a ship. I figured I needed something, too." He pointed to my cut. "We're even for the Preserve. But if you think that I would talk to Paul, that I would—I don't know what you're thinking—rat us out, to *him*, after everything he did . . . you're crazy."

We glared at each other for a second. I wondered if I believed him. Then he looked toward the door. "Where's Lilly?"

I pulled myself up. "Making a new thermal. She needs twine and scissors."

"Well," said Leech, "let's find some." He moved into the galley area.

I watched him for a second, wanting to press him again

or to just take off without him. But neither was an option.

I headed down a small staircase and found myself in a triangular bedroom at the bow of the ship. There was one big bed and a set of bunk beds, some little family's hideaway from the world. Parents, two kids. They'd all slept here, out on the water, listening to the waves hitting against the boat. Were any of them still alive? Most likely not. What had they done when the Rise hit? Migrated north? Succumbed to disease? Tried to get into an Eden? I thought of Harvey and Lucinda, back on that Walmart roof, the desperate measures they'd taken to try to save their child.

And it hit me that for every one of these skeleton boats, there had been a family, and for every abandoned house in every empty town we'd flown over . . . hundreds, thousands, millions into the billions, all over the earth. They weren't just numbers, they'd been lives, each one with bunk beds and special sheets and they took vacations, had dreams, maybe even missions they were on, and they'd all been alive and they were all gone now. It was staggering to try to think about.

We searched three boats and found scissors and a few different thicknesses of rope. No water or food anywhere. Leech also collected knives, and by the time we returned to Lilly, he had four in his belt.

Lilly was resting beside the fabric, her face dangerously red, her hands shaking.

"Let me help," I said. "It's going to need an opening in

the base for the heat—"

Lilly glanced darkly at me. "Please go do something else."

"Right." I started up the dock.

I heard footsteps, and Leech joined me. "She doesn't want my help either."

We returned to the craft without speaking. It was still in the shade, barely. I untied the one remaining clay pot and twisted it into grooves on the top of the vortex. Then I knelt beside the little silver wheel on the side of the craft. It had cups for catching water, to make it spin. Slim copper-colored arms, an alloy that hadn't turned green in thousands of years, connected the wheels to the hull. When the wheels spun fast enough, they'd make a charge to spark the heat cell.

I tried spinning the wheel with my palm, but I couldn't get it going very fast before my hand was throbbing.

"That's obviously not going to work," said Leech. He was leaning against the wall in the shade, watching.

"That's really helpful," I replied, and tried again.

I heard him sigh. "Try this." He knelt on the other side of the craft and pulled off his sneaker. He slipped it over his hand, and started hitting the wheel with the sole.

"Good idea," I admitted, and tried it, too. It worked great.

My arm quickly got sore, and I became aware of the foul odor that was wafting off the two of us, but soon the wheel began to hum, and finally there was a white spark. A tiny jet of flame burst from the copper nozzle atop the heat cell. I twisted it down to a low, blue simmer.

"Nice work," I said to Leech. My head was swimming, and when I tried to stand, my legs buckled again.

"Come on." Leech gave me a hand. "Let's head back to that yacht."

We stumbled down the dock, the sun blinding now, told Lilly where we'd be, and then climbed into the oven-hot cabin. We opened the windows, slapping away the crust of sand, but the breeze barely helped.

I lay on the couch. Leech on the floor.

"Florida," he said after a while.

"What?"

"That's where I grew up, at Inland Haven. Paul found me there when I was eleven."

I'd heard of Florida. It was one of the first parts of the United States to submerge.

"Inland Haven was the last high ground in the state," said Leech. "The first pandemic hit when I was ten. Killed my mom, bunch of relatives. Paul found me after that. Eden was matching their Atlantean samples against the international genetic database. He told me pretty straight up what he thought we were, and that we had a chance to be the key to saving the world."

"You mean 'we,' like us?"

"No. Me and my brother, Isaac. The genes run in

families, you know."

"Sure," I said. "I just hadn't really thought about it. I don't have a sibling."

"Yeah, well . . ." Leech sighed. "Paul offered to take us both to Camp Aasgard. This was, like, 2038, so EdenWest wasn't built yet, but they'd found the temple and were doing research there. Not long after we got there, I got the gills, very first case, and Paul said that he wanted to freeze us until they could build the right facilities and find the other Atlanteans. He said it would take decades, maybe longer, and that by the time we woke up, our families would probably be dead."

"That's tough," I said.

"It was just what I wanted to hear."

"Really?"

Leech exhaled hard. "Let's just say my dad didn't adjust well to life after Mom was gone. He was never the perfect dad candidate to begin with, not in his DNA, I guess. And he would get mad. Mad with his fists and . . . other things.

"One time Isaac got the end of a metal spatula. He had partial hearing loss after that. So we took Paul's deal. He felt more like a father to me than my own. Someone who thought I mattered, who I thought cared. Except, when you came along, that changed."

"Sorry," I said.

"Whatever. I should have seen it coming," he said. "Paul

always told me when there was a new test subject, like you, or the other CITs. Kids with potential. I didn't know about that lab you found, where Anna was, but I knew the rest. I felt like his second-in-command. But I wasn't anything to him except an ingredient. Something to be collected and measured and used."

"What happened to your brother?" I asked.

"When I woke up from Cryo, Paul said that they thought his DNA was a better match for an Atlantean temple at another facility."

"Did Paul tell you where they sent him?"

"EdenSouth," said Leech. "He was in Cryo there when the Heliad-Seven uprising happened. Communications have been cut off ever since. Nobody knows what happened to the Cryos. They could be dead, still frozen, woken up. Probably dead."

"But he could be alive," I said.

Leech shrugged. "What are the chances? EdenSouth was destroyed—that's what they say anyway. The cryo systems probably were, too."

"Or maybe they woke him up, and now he's in Desenna."

Leech shrugged again. "Sure." He didn't sound like he believed it. "So you asked me what I was doing before. . . . I was recording messages for Isaac. It's like a journal. Just in case . . . in case I find him. It's probably stupid. I just want him to know how I've been."

Hearing this awakened that urge in me to get in touch

with my dad again, to make sure he knew I was alive, where I was. It hadn't been decades, like between Leech and his brother, but it still felt like a long time. "Sorry," I said to Leech, "for thinking, you know . . ."

"It's okay. I get it. I haven't given you a ton of reasons to trust me."

"No," I said. "You know, just because Paul didn't want you to tell me I might be an Atlantean, that didn't mean you had to be a jerk to me at camp."

"Don't forget that you were also completely annoying," said Leech. "All mopey and wimpy. But, yeah, I should have known by how Paul acted when you showed up. When I think about it, it just makes me so angry, I can barely stand it."

I noticed that his hands were shaking. He had them by his sides, and now crossed his arms.

"That's not the anger," he said quietly.

"What is it?"

"Cryogenic sickness," said Leech. "The procedure got perfected in the later decades, but the cryo program was only experimental when we went under."

"That sucks," I said.

"Yeah, and it's getting worse. They had some treatments back at Eden, but . . ." He grabbed the shaking wrist, squeezing it.

I looked at Leech and thought that it was amazing how wrong I'd been about him. Then again, he hadn't made it easy.

A question came to my lips. I hesitated, but then asked it. "Do you think you killed that guy back there? Harvey?"

"I don't know," said Leech quietly. "I wasn't *trying* to kill him, but . . . I wasn't trying *not* to either. Anyway, who cares if I did? He was just another one trying to use us." He looked at me. "You know what Eden will do to us after they find the Paintbrush, don't you?"

I hadn't thought about that. "What do you mean?"

"I mean, once they've gotten what they need from us . . . it won't be like what you saw in the lab, with Anna and the others."

Now I understood. "You mean they'll kill us," I said.

"And it won't even be a thought," said Leech. "We may be a vital part of Project Elysium, but we're not part of whatever comes after that. We're going to have to do whatever it takes if we want to survive this. If people die . . . better them than me."

I looked at the knives in his belt. "Can I have one of those?"

"Sure." He handed me a serrated knife with a white handle.

I ran my fingers over it. "I don't know if I could kill someone," I said honestly, "if it ever came to that." I hated admitting it.

"Yeah, well, great," said Leech. "I better not die because of that."

We lay there silent. I dozed off. Lilly came in later. I

started to make room on the couch, but she headed for the bedroom.

We waited until late afternoon, lying still and silent in the coffin of heat.

"We should go," I said, "if we want to make the marker by morning."

We trudged back to the craft through wicked winds, sand pelting our faces.

Lilly handed me the thermal, and I spread it over the craft. "You did a good job with this," I said. The air hole was nearly exactly the size of the previous one.

Lilly didn't answer, just slumped into the craft and pulled her blanket over her to shield herself from the sun.

When the balloon was full, I got in, bumping Lilly's side by accident. She popped out of the blanket and unleashed a terrible wave of coughs. When she pulled her hand away from her mouth, there was blood on her palm. I saw fresh red trickling from her gills, too. She lay back and pulled the blanket over her again.

We rose into the golden late-day heat. The hot winds whipped, the craft harder to control with the natural sway of the thermal, and my already sore arms burned. When I turned around to check the heat-melted horizon, the pain made me cry out. More spots in my eyes.

"Save your strength," said Leech. "Don't you get it? They're not coming."

"What do you mean?" I asked, and yet I'd been thinking the same thing.

"Why should they?" said Leech. "We're going to lead Paul where he wants to go anyway, right? So why not just watch and wait until we get there?"

I hated this thought, felt it fraying the weak thread of resolve I had left. "You make it sound like we haven't escaped at all."

"I know." Leech started sketching.

I flew on, trying to think of some way to fight this new yawning sense of doubt. I kept checking the horizon, but it remained empty of answers.

11

DESOLATE. THE MOUNTAIN LAKE WHERE I HAD trained with Lük was still, the Atlantean city dark. The morning light flat, the sun unmoving, as if the world had been frozen.

Then it changed . . . to the ash-covered moonscape outside the caves at Hub after the fire. I was standing among the dead trees. They looked like skeletal animals about to come alive, to bend down with brittle creaks and spear me with their blackened skewers.

"Owen!" I turned to see Mom up on the ledges, hands to her mouth. "Owen!" She sounded desperate. Terrified.

"Psst."

Then it was dark, a single light throwing shadows. I sat up from blankets and looked across a little bedroom. Parents sleeping in a bed against the triangular far wall. I was up in a top bunk. Was this Hub? No, I was in that yacht back at the dry lake. The voice had come from below.

I looked over the edge of my bed to see a small face

looking up at me. "Owen, let's go see." A young boy with wide gleaming eyes.

"Isaac, no," I said to him. "Mom said stay here. Besides, Leech would be mad."

"I want to see the snow," said Isaac, with the kind of expectation that you'd feel about presents on Christmas morning. He was wearing frog pajamas. He had Leech's field of freckles spreading across his small, curved nose.

"It's not snow," I whispered. "It's ash, and it might still be hot."

"I want to see."

I checked Mom and Dad. They were still asleep. Dad's breathing was already labored at night, even this long ago. The bedroom was the yacht, but it was also Hub, my brain blending the two places. *It's my job to keep an eye on him*, I thought. But then the door was flapping open and little Isaac was gone, except now he had long, red hair. . . .

A hand shook me. I opened my eyes to the stars, and the whispers of the dream took flight on the breeze.

I was curled up in the front of the craft. Leech had woken me, and was sitting back down, his face lit by the dim orange glow of the battery flame. I'd given him a basic flying lesson at sunset. He'd picked it up okay, well enough to keep us in a straight line.

"What time is it?" I asked.

"One," said Leech. "I'm getting tired. You should take over."

Just after dark, we'd drunk most of the last water bottle, unable to hold out any longer, and shared the final package of synth veggie crisps. We still had a single soymeal bar, and we were chewing our way through the last of the dry noodles, but it was getting hard to dissolve them when our mouths were so dry.

We'd decided no more stops until the marker, unless we found some sign of an outpost or supplies. At the marker . . . after the marker . . . what would happen then? And yet, given our condition, it didn't seem worth spending any extra energy thinking about. We'd all gotten Rad burns over the afternoon, pink blistery swatches of skin. I had one on my shoulder beneath my sweatshirt. Leech's leg had a long strip, the center of which had shaded to brown. Lilly had an oozing spot on her cheek. I thought the cold night air would bring relief, but they just kept burning.

I got up, every muscle brittle, and traded places with Leech. Lilly was still asleep, her face pale, her lips purplish, her neck a worry of red and brown.

"Did she wake up at all?" I asked Leech as he lay down in the front of the craft, pulling the pink blanket over him.

"No. You both just moaned a lot."

I started to focus on the wind, trying to find just the right angle to get maximum speed, but then I felt Leech's eyes on me. "What?"

"You said my brother's name in your sleep."

"Sorry," I said.

"Don't be sorry, it's just weird. Tell me what you were dreaming about."

I tried to remember. "I don't know, really. I've been having this weird dream about back at Hub, around the time of the Three-Year Fire. Did you hear about that, living in Eden?"

"Yeah," said Leech. "I heard about it."

"Anyway, it was that, but then in the dream I was on that boat we found today, and your brother was there and it was like he was my brother or something. And then it turned back into this other dream I keep having where I'm outside the morning after the fire, in the ash, and there's this girl sinking into the ash. . . . I don't know . . . just dream stuff, I guess."

"You have weird dreams often?" Leech asked. I felt like he was studying me.

"I don't know, not really that I remember." I tried to think back. During camp, I'd been in a perpetually underslept haze. Maybe there had been some dreams about the siren and dark water, but that was about it. And before that . . . I couldn't really pick any out. Again, trying to think about my life at Hub, little more than a week ago, seemed like trying to peer through a foggy window. "I guess just recently," I said. "I figured with everything we've been through, a few weird dreams aren't too surprising. Why?"

Leech didn't answer. I heard him breathe in like he was about to say something.

Before he did, a bright flash caught both our eyes. It had come from the west, somewhere between us and the Rockies, whose distant moonlit peaks were now just visible. More flashes followed, a bunch in rapid succession.

The booms began to arrive, shaking the craft.

"Lightning rain?" Leech asked.

"I don't think so." Their quick attack reminded me of that explosion back in Eden, when the Nomads had bombed the doors as a diversion. "More like fighting."

The flashes grew brighter, the booms deeper. They were coming from a valley a few kilometers away.

Something tore through the air above us. A high-pitched, fast-moving sound. We looked up and saw a shadow shape skimming by, only visible as a glint of moonlight.

"Holy crap, that's a drone fighter," said Leech. It was lost to the darkness, but then twin beams of fire lit the sky from its likely trajectory, hurtling dashes of light that arced and disappeared into the valley.

And then the biggest explosion yet.

Another jet screamed overhead. More fire in the distance. I lowered us, and angled farther south.

"Hey, I want to see what's going on up there," Leech urged.

"Me too, but I don't want to be seen . . . or shot down."

Something in the craft began to beep.

"Whoa." Leech twisted around and grabbed the subnet computer pad. A green light was flashing on its top. He pressed a button and the sound stopped, the screen lighting.

"What's up?" said Lilly groggily. She sounded like someone had coated her vocal cords in glue and sand.

"We just hit a subnet zone," said Leech.

More booms and blast concussions pummeled the craft.

"And that?" Lilly sat up and peered toward the flashing lights.

"We're not sure. Hold these," I said, passing the sail lines to Lilly. I turned to Leech. "Let me see the pad for a second."

"Why?" Leech asked, but he handed it over.

I tapped the pad and found the video chat icon. "I'm calling my dad." I scrolled through headings for locations and found Yellowstone Hub.

"Don't," said Leech. "Eden will be monitoring that."

"I don't care." That feeling was back, like I needed to connect, and this might be my only chance. "Don't worry," I said. "I have an idea."

I found a menu of Hub numbers, and scrolled through links for the offices at the geothermal plant. I wasn't sure what day it was . . . but there was a good chance Dad was at work, especially without me around. Also, if Eden was expecting me to call him, they'd more likely be monitoring our home number.

I hit connect. A small horizontal bar filled and emptied, over and over. A message appeared, reading: *Video connection unavailable.* Then there was a beeping and a click as someone picked up the line.

"Hello?" The connection was uneven, broken by static and choppy cuts.

"Hi!" I shouted. "I'm trying to reach Darren Parker."

When the connection was solid, there were lots of sounds, grinding and humming, the workings of the geothermal station. It sounded bad, worse than I remembered even during the times when Dad would have to pull all-night shifts.

"Hello?" the male voice asked again.

"Is Darren Parker on shift tonight?"

"Da—you sa—? What was th—la—me?"

"His name is Darren Parker," I said slowly. "I—I'm not sure he's working tonight but this is his son, Owen, and I need to get him a message."

"—arker?"

"Darren Parker."

I heard voices, like whoever I was on the line with was talking to someone nearby. "—You think? Transfer him over to— What should I tell him, then?"

"They're going to rat us out," Leech warned.

But I had to keep pressing. "If he's not there, can I leave him a message?"

"Listen, kid, that's going to be tough b—"

The pad suddenly exploded with a shrieking high-pitched whine.

—EASE DO NOT FIRE! WE ARE A REGISTERED

NOMAD POD! I REPEAT: PLEASE DO NOT FIRE! WE ARE NOT RESPONSIBLE FOR THE CHEYENNE DEPOT RAIDS! WE ARE A REGISTERED NOMAD POD NUMBER SIX EIGHTY-SEVEN BRAVO. I REPEAT . . ."

"That's an emergency all-band broadcast," said Leech.

"There," said Lilly.

We could finally see up into the wide valley, awash in the flicker of flames and the bright darts of gun and rocket fire. A collection of vehicles snaked across the valley floor, following a sand-swept road toward us. I could see the canted angles of sailcarts and a trainlike conglomeration of electric wagons. Behind them to the north, an encampment burned. Tents in flames, flapping like fire birds in the breeze. Silhouettes scrambling in chaos.

Three heavy transport helicopters hovered, seeming to float in the night sky as if it were water. They took fire from Nomads positioned on the steep rocky sides of the valley. The copters retaliated with raining streams of ammunition.

"That's definitely ACF weaponry," said Leech. "Full-scale assault force."

A bright light arced out from the hillside and clipped one of the transport helicopters. Smoke plumed from its side, and it dove away from the fight, ditching on the valley floor.

"I REPEAT: WE ARE NOT RESPONSIBLE FOR THE CHEYENNE DEPOT RAIDS. WE ARE A

REGISTERED NOMAD POD. PLEASE, IT WASN'T US! THERE ARE UNARMED FAMILIES DOWN HERE! YOU—"

Another drone fighter screamed overhead and new rockets pummeled the hillside. The explosions roared, the flames joining one another and creating a momentary firestorm that dissolved into a wall of smoke. The broadcast cut to static. The sounds of gunfire slowed to an occasional pop.

I turned us farther south. Before we moved beyond the valley and the battle passed out of view, we saw one of the helicopters facing down the front of the fleeing caravan, destroying the first sailcart and then lowering its fat belly to the ground as the other vehicles ground to a halt.

Then we were back in darkness, the echoes of a few final gun bursts at our backs.

I thought of the Nomads we'd met back at Eden. Unlikely that Robard, who'd led the rescue operation, was among this group, but it would be others like them, ragtag tribes trying to carve out an existence with minimal supplies.

"Subnet signal is gone," said Leech, surveying the computer pad. "The pod must have had a mobile zone, but . . . no more pod."

"What is Cheyenne Depot?" asked Lilly.

"No idea," said Leech.

"I think it's military," I said. That sounded right. "Maybe a jump base for ACF troops."

"Those savages must have hit something pretty dear to the good ol' Federation to earn a beat-down like that, especially this far south of the border," said Leech.

"Whatever they did—" Lilly paused, coughing violently, "getting slaughtered was not an appropriate response."

I kept us moving, feeling tight. It wasn't just the slaughter. I'd missed my chance to talk to Dad. And that made the hum of worry increase. I didn't even know why it was so vital to me. It wasn't like I'd even contacted him from camp, but I couldn't shake the feeling.

We flew on through empty dark, silent except for Lilly's pained coughs.

12

FIRST LIGHT PAINTED THE HIGH GRAY PEAKS OF THE
Rockies all around us. I'd been steadily increasing our
altitude, up into thinner, colder air. The winds funneled
between the peaks, shooting down the valleys. I had to tack
back and forth, fighting them as we climbed.

I'd seen pictures of how these naked brown mountains
had once looked: wearing skirts of trees, even blankets of
snow, with glaciers like pendants at their throats. All of that
was gone, now. They were just jutting stone peaks and valley
floors of rubble. Some sickly yellow grasses had found niches
to live on. As we climbed, following the arterial branches of
mountain valleys like veins back to a heart, I saw the switch-
back trails of pronghorn, and even a sorry bone-bellied trio
digging their hoofs at a scree slope, making little clinking
sounds like someone sweeping up broken glass.

"Left," said Leech. The sun was maybe a half hour from
rising. A few stars still shone. Leech had been orienting to
an orange star that he said was Venus. He kept checking his

sketches. "Okay, we follow that valley southwest up to that saddle." He pointed to a shallow V high above. "And over that, I think we've got it." He checked his latest sketch. "There's going to be a plateau, maybe with a canyon. It's so weird . . ." he added. "I feel like I've been here before." Leech tapped his pen against the paper. "Still can't see what's beyond this, though."

Lilly coughed weakly. Her forehead glistened with sweat, and the fiery red around her gills had spread like a collar around her neck.

I increased our height again. There was a giant rock face in front of us, and I had to put us in a spiral to climb over it. We rose to parallel with the highest peaks now, the wide, blue dawn world falling away from us in every direction. The horizon seemed forever in the distance. The air was thin, brittle. I was taking deeper breaths but getting less out of them.

We lifted up into the saddle and entered an amphitheater surrounded by five jagged peaks. The basin in between them was a gentle bowl, sloping down to a V-shaped notch.

"There," said Leech, pointing down.

A little canyon zigzagged through the basin, not much more than a crack in the shell of the earth. It began as a funnel-like rock fall, then followed the slope of the basin.

I brought us down. "I can't fly in there," I said. The canyon was barely ten meters wide, and without the precision of the vortex, I'd never be able to manage it.

"We hike in, then, I guess," said Leech.

I turned the flame down to nearly off, and we settled toward the rocky slope. I landed in the shadow of the nearest peak, hoping it would keep the sun off Lilly.

"Lilly," I said quietly. "We'll be back. Just keep resting."

"Nnn." The sound was so fragile.

I turned back to Leech. He was looking at Lilly with something like actual concern. "I know," he said like he was reading my thoughts. "We have to hurry."

"Yeah."

Leech gathered his sketchbook, the computer pad, and his boccie ball weapon. I slid the white-handled kitchen knife into a loop in my shorts. We hopped out and crossed a naked slope of loose scree that yawned down into the canyon entrance. Here and there, spiky white plants clung to the slope, like cacti but with felty fingers. As we neared the rock fall, something skittered across the broken pieces, making me jump. I spied a gray lizard, about the size of my hand, with white stripes. It paused, sizing us up, then darted out of sight.

We skidded down the rock fall, and dropped into cool shadows, climbing down between large boulders. The canyon leveled out into a smooth, curving hallway. The air smelled slightly sweet. Beneath a few of the overhangs of rock I saw actual splotches of moss, and a couple little bursts of green plants.

We walked for about a hundred meters. There started to

be paintings on the walls, petroglyphs of wispy curved figures like you'd find on some rocks up near Hub, drawn by Native Americans. I saw hunters running, animals, shapes like birds, all sketched in burned reds and blacks.

The walls beneath the paintings started to get uneven, and now there were carvings. The paintings covered these in spots, as if the carvings were older. They were square designs with symbols inside, arranged like tiles. They were weathered, the corners smoothed or chipped and some whole sections crumbled away, but I could make out snakes, birds, spiders, and then some other shapes like stars and wild faces with long rectangular eyes and hooked noses, wide mouths, with bared teeth. There was something like a mammoth, and one like a big cat sitting on top of a turtle.

My eye caught one that made me pause: a figure that seemed to be a woman, floating above the ground. Angled lines burst out of the center of her chest that reminded me of light rays, and I felt a strange certainty that this was my siren.

We rounded a bend and the space to either side widened, the canyon top still just a narrow squiggle of light high above, but the walls arcing out beneath so that we were standing in a kind of domed underground space. To our right, one hemisphere arced over a deep hole lined with stones that were striped as if there'd once been water. To the left . . .

"Dude," said Leech.

The left half of the space was filled by a small city of stone. Rectangular buildings, two or three stories high and built from soft-looking tan blocks stretched right up until they just met the ceiling. Some had ladders extending up their sides. They had small windows. There was a circular building in the center.

"It looks like Anasazi," I said, remembering the photos from history books at school. "Maybe a thousand years old."

They were so still, so silent that I could hear a faint rush in my ears, maybe my blood. And there was something about that silence, that space, that almost made me feel like there was someone here. Some ancient presence, as if years in the thousands were really just seconds ticking by. It gave me a dizzying feeling of being infinite and incredibly small at the same time. Like I was everything and nothing.

"I feel weird," Leech whispered.

"Me, too," I replied. "What's yours like?"

"There's this pulling," he said, "like I've got a magnet inside me."

I remembered that feeling from beneath Eden. "Follow it."

Leech nodded. I noticed that his legs were twitching, and then a fast-vibrating shudder ran up his torso and made him close his eyes.

"I felt nervous, too," I said, hoping it would make him

feel better, "when I was being drawn to open the skull chamber."

Leech glared at me. "I'm not nervous," he spat. "It's the cryo sickness." His voice quavered as he said it. "Damn . . ." I saw him shake again. He flexed his hands into tight fists, like he was trying to control it. "Guuuh!" he growled, and jumped up and down a couple times. "Okay, I'm fine. Let's go." He was still trembling as he moved ahead.

We climbed up an initial rock wall and crossed a narrow ledge in front of the first buildings. I peered through small doors, into shadowy rooms. There were items inside, pottery and wood structures, all of it neatly arranged, as if the people might be back at any time. It reminded me of the towns we'd flown over, like museum exhibits. At some point, maybe because of water, too, these people had walked away into history.

We climbed a series of creaky ladders and edged across a narrow ledge, our backs against the bricks, facing out at the cavern. "These people were either really small or spiders," said Leech. We reached the rounded center building. "We're going in here."

There were no doors, so I boosted him up the side and he scrambled to the top. "This is it," he said. He reached down and helped me up.

A ladder led through a round opening into darkness. We climbed down and found ourselves in a shadowy room. There was a blackened fire pit in the middle, and the sides were cluttered with pottery. Blankets hung on the walls, striped designs in faded shades of red and brown and white.

"You think we're the first people who've been here since the Anasazi left?" asked Leech.

"It seems like it." The feeling of time being vast and yet also instant, increased.

Leech was looking around. "So now what?"

I peered through the gloom. "There." I pointed at the blanket hanging on the wall behind Leech. It was striped, but there was a hexagonal white patch right in the center, and woven into this space was a more geometric version of the Atlantis symbol I'd seen before.

"Hey," said Leech, "that thing." He stepped over and pulled the blanket aside. "Ahh . . . crap."

I ducked and peered around him. Inset in the wall was a little triangular vestibule with another thing I'd seen before: a depression in the shape of a hand, full of tiny white spikes.

"Your turn, Mariner," I said to him.

I heard Leech take a deep breath. "It better be mine this time," he said, flexing his hand.

"It will be," I said.

He placed his shaking palm in the depression and pressed down. "Oww . . ." he moaned. He held it for a few seconds, breathing hard, then jerked his hand free. We watched drops of his blood drip down the delicate spikes. "Nothing's happening," he said.

"It takes a second," I said. The blood reached the base of the spikes and began to slip into the creases around them.

The rock around us rumbled. Dust clouded our vision. There was a grinding sound like of stone gears, and a section of the wall began to rise. It slid up into the ceiling and then there was silence. Leech pulled the computer pad from his waist and illuminated the screen. He took a deep breath and ducked through.

The weak light outlined a small circular room. There was a waist-high pedestal in the center. I had been wondering if we would find Leech's skull, but instead we saw some kind of instrument perched there, gleaming like metal.

Leech moved quickly toward it. "Yes," he said.

"What is that?" I asked, stepping beside him. The instrument shone as if it were new. It was made of that untarnished copper like on the craft. It had a central cylinder surrounded by four metal arcs, like protractors, two horizontal and two vertical. On each arc was a little slider adorned with a red crystal.

"It's like a sextant, I think, but with more to it." Leech carefully grasped the instrument. He twisted it gently, and with a click it popped free. At the same time, there was a sharp crack and the pedestal crumbled away into tiny blocks that clattered across the floor.

Standing where the pedestal had been was a black obsidian ball, like we'd seen in the map room back in Eden. Leech put his hand to it. A faint red light began to glow inside, like a demon eye slowly opening. As it grew it turned from red to yellow to white, bright enough to make us squint. Pinpricks of light began to shoot out of it.

A map of the night sky appeared on the rounded walls around us. There was a black outline along the base of the wall. It looked like it was supposed to be land, with white, snowcapped peaks. As the light grew, the stars became uncountable. The Milky Way arced overhead. The painting put us in a high place, the world falling away in all directions, like we were on a mountaintop. All the stars were white, except a giant, golden star and a smaller, reddish star.

"Mars and Venus," said Leech. "Here, put your hand on the globe."

I did, and the globe stayed lit as he pulled his hands away and took the sextant back. "Okay, these two dials with the crystals are for orienting to Mars and Venus. And then, this one is to correct for polar shift . . ." He put the sextant to his eye, looked at Venus, looked at Mars, then moved slowly around, angling it up and down. "And this last dial is . . . yes, okay, got it."

"What?"

"It corrects for precession."

"For what?"

"Precession of the equinoxes," said Leech. "The earth isn't perfectly round, and so its axis moves over time, around in a circle of its own. It takes, like, 26,000 years to go around, and that makes the exact placement of the stars in the sky change. This map is from Atlantean time, something like ten thousand years ago, and so that's—" Leech tapped his temple—"about a one hundred thirty-eight degree difference." He fiddled with the dials. "If I correct for that, I can see the night sky as they did."

"Okay," I said, "that's one of the nerdiest things I've ever heard."

Leech grinned. "You probably mean that as some kind of compliment."

"Yeah."

"Here." He handed me the sextant and pulled his notebook from his pocket. "If we correct for the 'when' of this map, then we can figure out the 'where.'" He started sketching.

"The where?" I asked.

"This view isn't from these mountains where we are now," said Leech, gazing around. "It's somewhere else. The place we need to get to . . . Damn!"

I saw him shake his hand violently. He closed his eyes and took a deep breath.

"You can do it," I said to him.

"Tch," he muttered, but didn't add anything sarcastic. "Wherever this location is, it's where we need to go next. The one thing I can already tell is that it's south. Way south, from where we are now, anyway. I'll sketch the basics, then I can figure it out on the way."

"Do you think it's where the Paintbrush is located?" I asked.

"More likely my skull." He drew for another few minutes, while I gazed at the ancient sky. "Okay, got it." He stuffed away his notebook and stood. I handed him back the instrument. "This is awesome," he said. He held the sextant like it was a favorite toy. "Finally." It was the happiest I'd ever heard him.

I took my hand from the globe. It began to dim. Soon we were back in darkness.

We ducked back out to the Anasazi room, and climbed out of the canyon. As I hauled myself up the boulders, the white spots and headache returned and I gasped for breath in the high altitude, body squeezed dry of moisture, and so, so hungry.

Finally, we emerged in the daylight. The sun had just crested the ridge of the basin. I craned my neck the moment we were at the top, checking the craft, half expecting it to be gone again. But it was there, still in the shade, and I could see Lilly's hunched form inside.

I took a step toward it and was startled by a flash of movement nearby. I paused, looking for another lizard, and swooned a little, my head pounding, my vision swimming.

Then I heard a sound on the wind . . . low-pitched, vibrating. I winced, trying to push back the curtain of headache. The sound was coming from more than one direction, reflecting around the mountaintops, sharpening into something that was undeniably electric. . . .

"Come on!" I shouted to Leech and tried to get my rubbery legs going on the rock scree.

But the ground began to move.

Soldiers popped up from where they'd been lying in wait behind rocks. Rifles trained on us. They were on all sides, in light gray uniforms, wearing white Rad deflector masks with amber-tinted eyepieces. A group appeared by the craft. One of them grabbed Lilly, unconscious, yanking her up by her armpits, as three hover copters rose above the mountain walls.

"Hello, boys."

13

"MY SINCEREST CONGRATULATIONS TO YOU FOR finding this place and retrieving the radial sextant. Another myth come to life."

Paul's voice was being broadcast. I found the source; one of the troops was holding out a little black speaker device, as if these troops were robots and Paul their puppet master.

And maybe he was mine, too, because it was so obvious now how stupid we'd been. Leech had been right. Paul had watched and waited, letting us lead the way and collecting the necessary tool to get to Atlantis. All the energy, all the pain, all the suffering and blood seemed meaningless because here we were now, caught.

"You know what amazes me?" Paul asked, as if we were all here to have a philosophical conversation. "The Atlanteans knew to design that device to correct for precession and polar shift ten thousand years ago, which begs the question: How long were they navigating the planet before that?

The implications are astounding, but we'll have plenty of time to discuss it on the way. There's food and water waiting for you in the copters, and we have a long distance to cover." I thought I could hear his smile.

"You'll have to kill me," Leech muttered. He took a step back, edging his way down the trail into the canyon, clutching the sextant tight to his chest.

Paul sighed, a whoosh over his microphone. "Fine," he said. "Take the shot. We don't need him."

The soldier nearest to us dropped to a knee and raised his rifle.

"No!" Leech shouted and stumbled backward, but he tripped, his body betrayed maybe by his cryo sickness, our dehydration, or from the shock of having Paul call his bluff so casually.

I wanted to move—to do something—

There was a flash—

But it wasn't from the soldier's gun. It wasn't from the ground at all. Or the copters.

A searing jolt of energy vibrated through my body, burning my feet and blinding me. When I looked up, that soldier who'd trained his gun and the bunch closest to him were . . . gone. No, not gone but lying flat on the ground, and not all of them remained. The entire area had been charred into a black twist of melted rock with some vaguely human forms fused to it, all hissing and smoking.

Everyone looked around wildly.

Then the lightning struck again. This time I saw it: a pure white beam of energy streaking through the cloudless sky, as if hurled by a furious god. It incinerated a group of soldiers to my right. Another beam took out one of the hover copters in a spectacular explosion. It fell to earth in streams of flaming shrapnel.

The soldiers scattered, some taking up defensive stances, pointing their rifles skyward but not knowing what to aim at. Others just ran. More lightning bolts rained down. The air heated up with a smell of burned fabric, melted rock, and frying meat.

All I knew was that someone was helping us and that we had to move. "Come on!" I shouted to Leech.

We raced for the craft. My head exploded with stars and fresh waves of pain. My leg muscles felt stuck, no more elastic left. Even my cramp was igniting, twisting tight. But I kept moving as lightning rained to earth around us.

The two soldiers who'd been holding Lilly had dropped her to run for cover. She was slumped over the side. I jumped into the craft, and dragged her back in.

Another flash struck, then another.

Sound had lost meaning. The two remaining hover copters buzzed like frantic insects. Soldiers were shouting, some barking orders, others in panic. A few who'd been near the blasts, scalded but not killed, screamed in pain. Rifles fired uselessly into the sky. And everywhere was the hiss and crackle of scorched earth and flesh.

I heard a grunt and turned to see a soldier grabbing Leech's arm. Leech made a kind of guttural scream, beyond words. His free hand swung his boccie ball sling. It slammed the soldier in the shoulder. The blow loosened his grip and Leech spun, his face savage, and swung again.

I didn't see the impact because an arm closed around my throat. The tattered gray sleeve was half-melted to blistered skin. *They were going to shoot Leech,* I thought, my hand fumbling for the knife in my belt, *and they'll kill me, too, once they're done with me and Leech is right I have to*—my fingers clasped around the knife handle—*I have to fight! It is them or me.* I felt a flood of adrenaline. A red shroud of static and tightness fell over me and I wrenched against the soldier's grip, twisted my body away, and shoved the knife around my side. I felt it hit, fight resistance, then pop through clothing and skin. The soldier roared in pain as I shook him free, the bloody knife in my hand—

The bloody, dripping knife in my hand—

The soldier stumbled back, blood staining the side of his abdomen and I was getting us out of here. I reached wildly, spinning the burner to full power. The widening flame caught the side of my palm, but I gritted my teeth against the pain and kept moving.

Leech jumped in, cradling the sextant under one arm, his weapon in the other. I saw his attacker staggering to his feet but grabbing at his face, where Leech's second swing had crushed his nose and eye socket.

The craft started to rise.

"Faster!" Leech shouted.

"I'm working on it!"

The craft lurched. Black-gloved hands grabbed the side and yanked us down. I swung the knife, raking the blade across the fingers, and felt the vibrating of metal across bone and the soldier shrieked and the hands let go and we were up.

I didn't think, just threw the knife down inside the craft and tried to calculate the winds swirling around in this basin, tried to keep my throbbing head clear.

We rose out of the smoke of smoldering copter wreckage and burned bodies, and I caught a strong gust of wind. It was funneling south, following the trail of the canyon through the narrow notch. That was our best way out. I banked around and we lunged forward, the sails filling, my dead sore arms feeling like they would yank out of their sockets.

"What's happening?" Lilly croaked. "Eden?"

"Just stay down," I said, trying to sound calm. "It's okay."

Leech was watching behind us. "We need to go faster!"

I looked back and saw the two hover copters dropping into swerving pursuit behind us. Another lightning blast rained down, narrowly missing one of them.

I jammed uselessly at the pedals. "This is all we have!" Without the vortex, there was no way we could outrun them.

Two sharp cracks and then tearing pops. I looked up to see that bullets had punctured the thermal. More metallic cracks. Bullets tore through the sails. The wind began to howl through the holes, and we started to slow.

And suddenly I understood that this was all they had to do, and they would have us.

"Do something!" Leech shouted.

"I can't!"

More bullets tore at the thermal, and now the wind clawed at the openings, pulling the flaps wide. We slowed. We sank.

With our momentum we might still be able to make the notch . . . but we were dropping fast. I banked back and forth, trying to make us a smaller target. More bullets caught the underside of the craft, splintering through and barely missing Lilly and me. The craft started to shudder. Those shots had chipped the keel. We shimmied to the right, losing my course toward the notch, heading instead for the rock face beside it. And that was if we didn't plummet to the basin floor first.

"It's not going to work!" I shouted.

A muffled electronic voice suddenly screeched from nearby.

Leech pulled out the subnet computer.

"This is Heliad Tactical. Come in. Over?"

Leech stabbed frantically at the screen. "Yes! This is us!"

"Owen!" said a voice. "My name is Arlo. I'm at the command center in Desenna. We have you on gamma visual and are prepared to provide you with a power charge for your vortex engine. Don't worry, it will be smaller than the attack bursts we're using on Eden."

Power charge . . . it was hard for my brain to keep up. He meant the lightning. "Okay!" I shouted. "What do I need to do?"

"We have a lock on your position, so I just need you to take a straight line bearing and hold yourself as steady as you can. Let us know when you're stable and we'll deliver the charge."

"What is he talking about?" Leech asked.

"We're about to get struck by lightning again," I said. But keeping the craft straight was going to be tough. We were wobbling, listing, and still losing altitude. The holes in the thermal had widened, and the sails didn't have the same responsiveness with their damage.

I straightened us as best I could. "Okay!" I shouted but as soon as I did, we bounced to the side, rocking back and forth.

"Wait—" but I felt a tingling through my body, and white lightning tore down through the front starboard side of the craft, sending wood chunks flying, igniting part of the hull in flames, and sending us pitching violently downward.

"Did that do it?" asked Arlo.

"No, we need another!"

More bullets tore at the sails. There was a wicked

explosion as lightning found one of the copters behind us, but the last one bobbed and weaved and stayed in pursuit.

I fought to get us straight. It was even harder now. One of the sail lines slipped out of my sweaty hand. My arms were so tired. "Grab that!" I shouted to Leech. "Come back here and haul it this way!" I pointed with my chin.

Leech flailed for the line as another round of bullets tore at us. One of the three lines holding the thermal snapped. The other two strained. If we lost the balloon, we'd be in a free fall to the rocks below.

The craft shook, and Leech tumbled into me and then got up and yanked the sail line. There was a moment of straight flight—

"Now!" I shouted.

Energy burst from the sky. It was corralled by the mast, which lit up red hot as the charge siphoned through it. But unlike back in Eden, the mast was damaged now, and the energy traveled wildly down it, ribbons of light flashing out. One of these tore into the thermal balloon, which burst into flames.

Just then I remembered what would happen next. "Watch out—" but the ceramic heat cell exploded. I heard shards digging into wood and clanging off the mast. I turned my head, bracing for the sting, but only felt it on my leg. I turned back and saw that the cell had been jostled loose by the energy, and its debris had all flown off the starboard side. I'd been spared, and so had Lilly—

But not Leech. He was slumped over, head buried in his arms, his skin flecked with blood. And he'd lost hold of his sail line, leaving us to yaw back toward the notch wall. . . .

I finally heard the high-pitched whine of the mercury vortex coming back to life, spinning its beautiful blue. The leftover chunks of heat cell were falling into it and melting in swirls of white fire.

The thermal balloon was in flames. I tore at the one singed line that was still holding its fiery remnants. My fingers burned, but the charred rope unraveled and disintegrated. The balloon leaped free, flapping away behind us, a fiery demon that the final copter had to swerve violently to avoid.

I slammed my feet against the pedals and the vortex engine screamed. The force of the acceleration shoved me back. But we were still headed toward the wall beside the notch.

"Give me your line!" I shouted to Leech, but he wasn't moving. I shoved my hand down between his chest and arms, grabbing for the rope.

The wall was closing. My fingers found the rope, yanked it out, angled the sail. . . .

We hurtled through the notch, the hull just scraping the rocks, and out of the alpine basin at howling speed.

I looked back and saw the last copter lunge out of the gap but then veer off sharply, heading back to the basin.

Another lightning burst barely missed it, exploding into the rocky cliffs. I watched the copter leave and understood: Just as back at EdenWest, they couldn't shoot us down with the vortex engine going, or the fall would kill us. Disabling the thermal balloon and causing our slow descent into their clutches had been their only option. And for now, Paul still needed us alive, didn't he? Except he'd been about to shoot Leech . . . Maybe he'd been bluffing. Either way, it seemed that, at least for the moment, we'd escaped again.

I grabbed a blanket and patted out the flames on the charred side of the craft. Then I flew down a wide valley, sweeping toward the distant desert wastelands.

"Looks like you're clear," said Arlo. The computer was lying on the floor. "If you can set a course southeast at sixty degrees, we can rendezvous with you."

"Hold on a sec!" I called. Rendezvous with Heliad . . . Did we even want that? I looked to Leech. His head was still buried. "Hey," I said, shaking him by the shoulder.

He grunted something unintelligible and slapped my hand away. As he did, I saw the blood on his forearm.

"You okay?" I asked.

Leech slowly lifted his head and moved his hands away. It was possible, amid the blood and shredded skin and the shards of battery sticking out, that one of his eyes was still there, a flickering of white in the red.

But the other . . . it was only a mess of blood and flesh.

"I can't see," he whispered. His hands were fumbling around. One of them closed on the sextant, clutching it tight, and yet, it was useless to him like this, and we were useless without our Mariner.

Unless . . .

"Okay," I called to the computer pad. "We're coming. I can't set a precise bearing, but I can head southeast or close enough."

"Lie down," I said to Leech. "I'll get us to Heliad."

"Dangerous . . ." he mumbled . . . "We don't . . ."

"I know," I said. I looked from him to Lilly, passed out, infected. "But we're gone if we don't."

Leech nodded slightly. "It hurts." He collapsed to the floor of the craft, his arms over his eyes.

"We'll be waiting at the Houston docks," said Arlo. "Biggest cluster of lights on the horizon. You can't miss it."

"Got it."

"We've stored a cache of water and food for you, about fifty kilometers out from your current position. You'll hit an old interstate, and there will be a rest area with a gas station. On the roof of that station, in the northwest corner."

"We're gonna need medical help," I said.

"Don't worry. We're dispatching a full team. Dr. Keller is overseeing it personally. We'll be en route momentarily. See you soon, Owen."

The computer went dark.

I angled us southeast and pressed the vortex pedal to the floor. We left the mountains, back into the desert heat. The craft bucked and vibrated, stumbling on the air, as broken and beaten as the rest of us, but at least with the vortex we had speed again.

A half hour later, I put us down on the roof of the dusty service station and retrieved a thick silver cooler bag tucked in the corner. I fed water gingerly through Lilly's cracked lips. I helped Leech get a bottle down. When I took my own swigs of the frosty liquid, I nearly gagged on its completeness, its cold life.

There was fruit in the bag: something green and oblong. I cleaned my knife of Eden blood; tried not to remember that feeling, that sound; and then sliced through the green rind—resisting like skin—to find an airy, sweet orange flesh inside.

"Papaya." Leech groaned as he tried it, holding a piece in one hand and the sextant still in a death grip in the other. He was shaking all over. The blood on his eyes had begun to dry, making plates of thick, black crust. I wondered if he would ever be able to see again.

There were crackers, a round of cheese. I had to remind myself to go slow. Let the fruit settle and save the rest for later.

As I ate, I glanced over the wall of the service station, to where whoever had delivered this bag had also hung a fresh corpse from the roof above the empty gas pumps. A pool of blood beneath it. Another warning: Beware of Heliad . . .

And that was where we were going.

I took off again, across the wastelands toward the coast. We flew in silence, the merciless sun beating down on us. I covered Leech and Lilly completely with our two blankets, then hunched as deep as I could into my sweatshirt, but there was going to be no relief from the radiation. The burning intensified on my shoulders, my scalp. My legs began to sear. Pain grew and folded in on itself, my body too overwhelmed to even register it. And all the while I tried to think of nothing, to just stare through the daze of hurt and headache and the blinding light, muscles cramped and locked into place, and fly, fly toward the horizon, hoping I could get us there. . . .

To a land that inspired tales of blood, volunteers willing to die in service of a sun goddess, who was one of us. A cult that had overthrown an Eden, that had wielded lightning from the sky and smote down Paul's forces . . .

And it was that thought, later, as the sun mercifully set and the stars rose, that made me realize why the closer we got to Houston, to safety and healing for Lilly, to help for Leech, and a meeting with our third companion, the tighter and louder a nervous hum whined inside me.

I had once thought Paul and Eden had acted like gods. The siren had warned me to beware the gods and their horrors. Now we were willingly putting ourselves in the clutches of another deity, the Benevolent Mother of Heliad-7. Both wielded death, Eden in secret labs, Heliad out in the bright sun. And both wanted us. But while I knew all too well what Paul had planned for us, I had no idea what lay in store for us on this next dark shore.

PART II

Be at peace. Let yourself glow unbridled.
You have played your part; now we celebrate your release.
And as we set you free, know that you will be divine,
Divine in your freedom, a conqueror of fear.
—FROM THE DEATH RITE OF HELIAD-7

14

IT WAS NEARING DAWN WHEN I SAW THE LIGHTS OF
Houston glimmering on the horizon. All night, we'd flown
through cold and silence, Leech and Lilly lying still except
for one waking, when we all ate cheese and bread, barely
speaking. Lilly only managed a couple of bites.

In those last hours, I thought about almost nothing, my
brain in a kind of half-conscious daze, my body shaking
from the pain of the rad burns. I kept the stars in their same
position in my view, kept the blue of the vortex at its bright-
est, and just covered kilometers, getting as far as I could
from all the horrors we had seen in the last three days.

Houston had a small working electrical grid. A few pale
lights glowed in the buildings close to the new coast. Where
the power didn't reach, fires flickered in skyscraper windows, in alleyways, a world of silhouettes and shadows.

The air had become humid, a strange wet feeling
against your skin, far stickier than Eden. The sky had
turned purple and gray, the horizon layered with folds of

misty clouds, a soft blur like everything had been smudged. Beneath it was the rippled expanse of the sea, its surface showing a mirrorlike version of the sky. The swells made little flashes. Nearer, white scribbles formed on the tops of breaking waves. They crashed to shore, against heaping piles of debris, the remains of the homes and buildings that had once covered the miles from here to the pre-Rise coast. Offshore, I could see the occasional remnant of a building sticking out of the water. There was a sour smell and taste of salt and a gentle rushing sound.

I had never seen the ocean before. Only pictures. It seemed so mysterious, shrouded and secretive, and while I was glad to see it, to know we'd made it here, the sight also caused a steady tremor inside me, a great feeling of the unknown, something like I'd felt in the Anasazi city, a sense that I was a very small being in a very large world.

There were three long wooden docks at the water's edge. On the middle one, two torches began to wave in semicircular patterns. A signal, bringing us in.

I flew out over the water and made a wide arc back to the dock. The torch waver was standing beside a tall ship. It was wide and square, floating on two skinny hulls. Above each hull was a mast, though I saw no sails furled, no booms at all. Crew members moved on and off it in lines, busily loading and unloading supplies.

I put us on the dock with a little thud, and finally let go of the sail lines. I could barely straighten my fingers.

They were curled in clawlike grips. My palms were striped red and white. I had blisters that had popped open, leaked blood, then scabbed over, only to tear open again.

"Where are we?" Leech asked quietly, still lying with his arm over his eyes.

"The docks in Houston," I said. I turned to Lilly and rubbed her shoulder. "Lilly, we made it."

She didn't respond. I saw the movement of her breathing beneath the blanket, my only indication that she was still with us.

"Welcome," said the man who'd waved us in. He snuffed his torches out in a metal bucket of water and laid them down on the dock. When he stood, he raised his right hand, the fingers spread, his pinkie gone. "I'm Arlo, captain of the *Solara*, and assistant to Dr. Keller. You must be Owen."

He was tall and lean, with scattered curly black hair and stony features. He wore small, round glasses, and had a short beard. His skin was bronzed, red on his nose. There were dark patches of overexposure by his scalp, on his ear. He wore a collared shirt that might have once been white, jeans, and work boots that were unlaced. He looked like someone who'd spent his youth in libraries and classrooms, and the second half of his life hard at work outside, but also like a time traveler from an age before being outside had been dangerous.

"Hi," I said.

"We're glad to see that you made it here in one piece,"

said Arlo. "It sounds like you've had quite a few days."

"Yeah," I said.

Arlo looked at Lilly and Leech. "We'll get them taken care of." He called over his shoulder, "Serena! We need the medics!"

"Got it." A young woman with short hair and a black robelike shirt and pants hurried up the gangway to the ship.

I got to my feet, my legs aching and threatening to buckle underneath me.

"Here." Arlo grabbed my arm and helped me step out.

"Thanks." He reached for our bags and I saw that he had an intricate tattoo across the back of his neck. It looked like a bird. Its face was square and menacing.

Cloudy dawn light was beginning to reflect on the buildings. I saw now that there were decorations hung on the sides of many of the structures, metal sculptures that looked like square, angry faces with hooked noses. One was a giant version of that bird on Arlo's tattoo. It looked like a vulture, and was perched on top of a church steeple, its rectangular wings outstretched, as if to signify that this was Heliad's domain.

"That's Chaac," said Arlo, following my gaze, "our guardian spirit."

Serena returned with three others, a woman and two men. They wore black uniforms with red bands around their left arms.

"What happened to them?" Serena asked. Two of the medics were lifting Lilly and placing her on a stretcher. The other helped Leech stand.

"We're all dehydrated," I said, "probably Rad poisoning, too. Leech got hit with shrapnel during our escape. Lilly was attacked with a curare neurotoxin, but we got her to vomit it out."

"Curare? There's sure to be some residual amount in her bloodstream," said Serena. She looked me over, and produced a metal tube, squeezing a bright blue jelly onto her palm. "This will help your Rad burns." She dabbed it gently on. "We can do more after you rest."

"Look at her neck," said one of the medics, lifting Lilly's chin.

"Those are her gills," I said.

Glances flickered around the group. "Gills?" Arlo asked.

"Yeah," I said. "It's part of what happened to us, in Eden."

A voice spoke from nearby. "Don't worry, Serena. We were expecting it."

Arlo looked to the gangway and then straightened and shouted, "All Witness the Benevolent Mother!"

She was slim, tall, wearing a long black coat over a LoRad pullover, jeans and high black boots. She had mostly gray hair with streaks of coal. She walked briskly and yet looked, at first glance, more like someone from EdenCorp or Hub's governing council than the leader of a religion.

"Owen, I'm Victoria Keller." She stopped in front of me and stuck out her hand. We shook, her skin cool, her hand bony but not at all frail. "It's an honor to meet you," she said. "I have heard a lot about you."

"Hi," I said. "Thanks for saving us, back there."

"The least we could do." She smiled, looking me over, and I remembered something Dr. Maria had said back in Eden, up on the cliffs: Keller was as crazy as Paul. . . .

Yet, unlike Paul, Victoria's hazel eyes were lively and bright. Her gaze was intense, too, like if she was looking at you, it was for a reason. "I am so sorry about your encounter in Gambler's Falls. Those traitors that tried to turn you in to Eden . . ." Victoria sighed to the sky. "Thinking about them really upsets me. You must know, we just had no idea what they were up to."

"Okay," I replied, not knowing what else to say.

"Anyway, I'm glad we were able to help yesterday. Did you like our version of lightning rains?"

"What was that?"

"Power of Tona," she said. "Actually, it comes from high-altitude attack drones. We bought them from the People's Corporation of China. Normally I wouldn't tell someone that. As far as my people are concerned, it's part of the magic of Heliad, though I think they know the truth on some level, and yet still find my explanation more enjoyable. But you and I are going to need to talk frankly about a good number of things, so best to start now."

"Should we bring them to the infirmary?" Serena asked Victoria.

"Right away," said Victoria. "Owen, you can board with me, if you'd like. Ready?"

"Sure."

"I'll take your bags to your quarters," said Arlo.

"What's going to happen to this?" I pointed to the craft.

"We'll load it onto the deck," said Victoria. "Arlo, see to that, will you?"

"Of course."

"Excellent. Spread the word that we'll be departing as soon as possible." She started back toward the gangway. "We're not expecting Paul to try another attack right away, but I'd like to keep moving in order to minimize our exposure."

I followed Victoria toward the gangway, passing between two lines of people. On my left was the supply line. A steady stream of items were being unloaded from the hull of the ship: crates of bananas and long bean pods, and two cages with hulking black animals inside that I figured were the tapir that Harvey and Lucinda had talked about. On my right was a line of people with bags over their shoulders or beside them.

The man in front stepped up to a small table where two more black-robed women sat. He held out his right hand, placing it on the table. I noticed it was shaking. There was a small device, a narrow rectangle with a large razor blade at the top, and a half circle depression at its base. The man slid his pinkie into the depression.

The medic reached around and buckled a strap over his wrist. "Ready?"

The man nodded.

The medic placed her hand atop the device, then slammed down. There was a sick crunching sound. The second medic took the severed pinkie in a white cloth, then leaned in and cauterized the wound with a small, gun-shaped torch.

The strap was unbuckled and the first woman taped a bandage over the stump of finger. "Live bright," she said kindly. The man nodded and moved on up the gangway, breathing fast. The next person in line, a woman, clutching herself by the elbows, stepped nervously forward.

I turned, feeling woozy, and found that Victoria had stopped just short of the gangway. She took no notice of the finger removals but was instead facing the supply line.

"Is this her?" Victoria asked.

A girl was approaching. Two men escorted her, each with a hand on a shoulder. They nodded.

"You're Aralene." Victoria's voice became soft, motherly.

The girl stared into space. Her wrists were bound with a white cloth. She was skinny, her face hollow. She wore a tattered LoRad pullover and jeans, her hair greasy and matted. She was too thin, bony angles beneath her clothes. She had deep black circles under her eyes, a purple bruise across her cheek. And to either side of the white bandage on her wrists I could see black, scabbed-over lines. Cuts.

I heard her mumbling to herself: "I will be the magic, the divine inside me, I am the divine, I am . . ."

"Aralene," Victoria said again.

The girl stopped speaking. Her eyes slowly tracked up to Victoria.

"Hello, young lady."

"Hi," said Aralene, mouse quiet.

Victoria reached out and put two fingers against her forehead. "There's nothing more to fear," she said. "You're with Heliad now. We'll help you to live bright. No more darkness."

Aralene nodded, like she was convincing herself. "The divine inside me."

"Yes," said Victoria. "The divine inside you. It's still there. We're going to set you free."

Aralene smiled, but then her mouth scrunched and her eyes broke, tears spilling out. She whispered, "Thank you."

Victoria took the dirty, frail girl and embraced her, rubbing the back of her head. Then she stepped away and held her at arm's length. "Live bright," she said.

Aralene nodded again. "Live bright." She turned and continued into the lower deck of the ship, resuming her chant. "I am the magic, I have the divine inside me . . ."

Victoria turned to me. "It's a hard time to live in the world," she said as we started up the gangway.

"Did she try to kill herself?" I asked.

"Yes." Victoria glanced out at Houston. "I feel compelled

to help. I began my career in psychiatry in the ACF back in the fifties. Did you know that, pre-Rise, in the good old days of prosperity, the rate of suicides in the world was around one in ten thousand people? And for every one, there were another ten who attempted it. That might not sound like a lot until you remember that back then there were ten billion people. That's more than a million suicides, and more than ten million attempts. Those rates actually went down during the Rise, as people's survival instincts kicked in, but now, in the aftermath, it's much higher. Some estimates are one in two thousand. But you know as well as I do: There's not a lot of hope out there, is there?"

"No." I remembered suicides at Hub. Cave fever was what we called it. People couldn't take the constant dark, the fear, the sense that things were never going to get better.

"It's nice of you to take that girl in, to treat her," I said.

Victoria glanced at me. "We'll see what you think when we get to Desenna. But I will say this: I don't know what you may have heard about Heliad-Seven, but we have far lower rates of clinical depression and mental illness than any other citizenry on this tattered planet. People like poor Aralene there, they come to us for help. It's the least we can do."

"Oh," I said. "People up north say things, I guess."

"I've heard. Death cult, cannibalism, all kinds of things. But I assure you, while we are a unique society, we're nothing like those savage portrayals. At the end of the day, we're simply a people trying to find the best way to live given the circumstances around us. Not that much different from any other religion, really."

It sounded sensible. Victoria certainly didn't seem like the crazed leader of a death cult. "The hung-up bodies are pretty gruesome," I noted.

"Certainly," said Victoria. "That's the point. One thing I've learned is that, though we may not really be violent and scary, it is sometimes beneficial to *appear* as if we are, in order to keep our people and resources safe."

We reached the wide main deck. There was a raised aft section, where the control consoles were positioned under a silver canopy. I saw Leech and Lilly being taken downstairs to the lower deck. Victoria led me to the bow, where we leaned on a metal railing. I noticed that she still had both her pinkies.

Down on the dock, Arlo and two other men were attaching ropes to my craft. A crane began lifting it.

I heard a strange high-pitched call and watched a gray-and-white bird glide by, past the docks and over the heaps of broken wood and debris on the beach. It landed there with others.

"That's a seagull," said Victoria. "One of nature's heartiest birds. None of our destructive ways could harm them."

I looked out in front of the ship, at the gray sea rolling slowly. I felt disoriented just looking at it, seeing such a wide area move in such a way. I saw, too, that the water was murky, almost rubber looking, its surface a rainbow swirl of oil and chemicals. An infected ocean. The sky had lightened enough that I thought the sun must be up, and yet the horizon was still a misty blur of blues, grays, and whites. I could feel the moisture all around me, almost like tiny fingers holding me up.

"Your first time seeing the sea, I take it?" asked Victoria.

"Yeah," I said.

"It used to be a source of great poetry," she said, "but when it rose up and swallowed the coasts like some unthinking monster, people learned to fear it. I still think it's beautiful."

"Last call to board!" Arlo called below. There was a thud as my craft landed on the deck behind us.

"That's quite a machine," said Victoria. "I've only ever seen the etchings of Atlantean airships that we found in EdenNorth. It is amazing. That antigravity engine is technology that we can't even comprehend, and yet it predates everything we know."

"You've been to EdenNorth?" I asked.

"Of course," said Victoria. "You may already know that back before I was the Benevolent Mother, I was director of EdenSouth. Paul's equivalent. Well, I should say I had the same position as Paul. I do not wish to be considered similar to him in any other way."

"That's good," I said, but the idea still made me nervous.

"Don't worry, Owen," said Victoria. "I'm not working with Eden. They'd love nothing more than to take me down. But more important, I'm nothing like them. We'll have more time to discuss this once we get back to Desenna, but you should know that it is my number one goal to see that Paul and his Project Elysium do not succeed. So you can rest easy." She patted my back. "I need to go see to things as we depart. When you want to go to your quarters, ask anyone to fetch Arlo."

"Okay," I said. "And thanks again."

Victoria smiled, and unlike so many smiles I had endured from Paul, this one seemed real, kind. "You bet." She strode back toward the center of the deck, calling out to people as she went.

I watched her go and felt like, for the moment, we had reached a safe port.

The deck became crowded, a din of people shouting and hurrying back and forth. The crew was lean but tough looking, lots of tangled hair, beards on the men, dreadlocks here and there. I could see sunburns on the lighter-skinned people, and on everyone there was a look of exposure, including the dark discolorations of Rad lesions. A couple of the older-looking crew members were missing patches of hair. They called to one another in harsh voices, lots of foul language. Keller's people couldn't have been more different from Paul's in Eden. They were different from what I'd known at Hub, too. These people seemed to have no fear of the world, and they had the scars on their skin to prove it.

"All ahead!" I heard Arlo call from the aft deck.

I felt a rumble in my feet and the ship began to pull away from the dock. The twin hulls extended out like blades into the water. For the first few hundred meters, debris thunked against the sides: rotted chunks of walls, posts and beams and trash, soggy and bloated from the sea.

Then we were out into the open water, the color still grayish and oily, with an acrid twinge of burned gas. We began to rock slowly up and down over long swells, and I found myself gripping the railing, and feeling like I'd lost track of my center of balance.

The warm wind stung my face, and I kept licking my dry lips, tasting the salt. The foggy cloud cover burned off, and the sun began to sear through a white, hazy sky. I had to squint to see. The buildings of Houston slipped out of sight behind us. Ahead, the horizon stretched vast and distant. I thought of my old idea, about swimming off to find some hidden corner of ocean with Lilly, and realized that I had not considered how great and empty the ocean really was.

"Deploy the solar sail," Arlo called.

A large, golden sheet unfurled overhead, spun between the two masts. A crew member snared its triangular point and brought it back to a pole on the aft deck, clipping it into place so that a giant, shimmering triangle had been created above us. The fabric was somewhat transparent with golden threads and provided some shade from the sun.

But even in the relative shade, the heat had become liquid. I felt myself getting light-headed, and turned to look for Arlo. A crew member pointed me to him, up on the aft deck.

He led me down a narrow flight of stairs, into a skinny hallway, and to a little cabin. There was a bunk bed and a hammock in the triangular space. A small table beneath a porthole held a pitcher of water and a bowl of fruit and crackers. I downed a glass of water and had a few crackers before I finally lay down on the bottom bunk.

The bed was broken in, and I sagged into the middle of it. I fell asleep almost instantly and had no dreams I remembered, just dark and finally rest.

15

I WOKE UP SOMETIME IN THE MIDDLE OF THE DAY. Out the window I saw only brownish, oily sea and pale blue sky with high feathery clouds.

Everything felt sore. My arms and shoulder were locked up, my legs rubbery, but that might have been the steady rise and fall of the world around me. I thought about just lying back down, but wanted to see how Lilly and Leech were.

I found a bathroom outside our cabin. It had a sink with a little pump faucet. I washed my hands and face. So much dirt came off, along with black flakes of dried blood. Washing made a cut sting on my cheek that I'd forgotten I even had. I traced the little line back toward my ear. When had I gotten that? Then I remembered: from the first time we'd lit the vortex engine, escaping Eden. I should have remembered that back in the mountains, then I could have warned Leech before it was too late.

I examined the cut in the mirror and the Rad burns on

my scalp, arms, and a new one on my left shoulder. The skin was shriveling to brown, sickly pink pus oozing, but that blue gel had eased the pain. Back at Hub, I used to worry about getting hurt, the idea of cuts and bruises. Now I had more than I could keep track of.

I headed back up the narrow hall, asked around, and found my way to the infirmary. It was a cramped room: one center aisle with narrow cots against the walls. Lilly and Leech were lying across from each other.

"Hey there." Serena came over to me as I entered. "Your friends are settled in. I've got their fluid levels up and have started treating their wounds. You have any sore spots?"

"A wound on my shoulder," I said. "The Rad burns are feeling better."

"Let's take a look." Serena sat me down on a bed. I peeled my shirt off gingerly. "First things first," she said. "Let me check your vitals." She started to put a blood pressure cuff on my arm, and I noticed that she had black-painted fingernails. It seemed like an odd coincidence, a little thing, but still . . . "The doctor at Camp Eden had nails like that," I said.

"Maria," said Serena. She blinked, tears forming.

"You knew her?" I asked.

"I did," said Serena. "We were friends. We trained in Desenna together." She sighed. "Were you there when she died?"

"Yeah," I said. "She was trying to draw attention away

from us. And she gave us supplies. If it hadn't been for her, we probably wouldn't have made it out of Eden."

Serena sniffled. "She was tough. She was the first to volunteer for that position, to go undercover. She knew how dangerous it was."

"She cared about me," I said. I hadn't had a chance to think about Maria since we'd left. It made me tight inside. I pictured her up on that ladder, firing at those copters, only to be riddled with bullets.

"Well," said Serena, "you were worth it. That's what they're saying in Desenna, anyway."

"I don't know about that," I said, "but thanks."

Serena taped a bandage to my shoulder, then applied more blue gel to my burns. "Infection's not too bad, and I've seen way worse Rad burns. You don't seem to be feeling any Rad poisoning, so you should be okay." She smiled at me. "Thanks for telling me about Maria. She lives on in your mission."

I felt a little weight settle inside. First the CITs, now Dr. Maria . . . The list of people who made sacrifices for us was growing. It made me wonder if I was up for it, if I could hope to honor them, but is also made our mission more important. This wasn't just about me, or even the three of us, anymore.

As Serena moved to another part of the room, I went over to Lilly's bed and sat on the edge. She stirred. Her neck was wrapped in bandages that looked moist. A bag of fluid hung beside the bed, a tube leading to her arm. She looked like I had, I supposed, after I'd drowned. They'd washed her face, and in spite of the dark circles under her eyes and the cut on her chin, she looked beautiful and delicate, clean in that angelic way like the very first time I'd seen her on the Eden docks. I felt an ache inside.

"Hey," I said. I took her hand. "It's Owen."

"Hey," she whispered faintly.

"She shouldn't talk much," said Serena from nearby.

"Sorry," I said. "Keep resting."

"We are floating . . ." she said softly.

"Yeah, we're on a boat, heading to Desenna."

"No," she said, and her lips spread into a faint smile, "we're floating on music. Do you hear it?" Her head began to rock back and forth, like she was hearing a melody.

"I . . ." She must not have been totally awake. "Just rest," I said.

"It's beautiful," Lilly whispered. "Someone's singing such a pretty song . . ." and then her face went blank as she drifted back into sleep.

"She keeps talking about that music." I turned to see Leech sitting up. His left eye was covered with bandages. His right eye was barely visible beneath swelling and redness, but at least you could tell that it was still there. He had the sextant on a thin rope around his neck.

I went over to him. "She's just out of it, I think. How are you?"

"They gave me some stuff for the pain, but . . . I'm not a navigator if I can't see."

"Your eyes will heal," I said.

"Tch," Leech scoffed. "Maybe one. Eventually. What's funny is that if we were still in Eden, I could get a bionic replacement, just like Paul. And it was leaving there that made this happen. That's some twisted luck."

"Qi-An," I said.

"What?"

"That's the Atlantean idea of the balance of all things. It has something to do with harmony."

Leech shrugged. "Great. Well, I don't know if this is Qi or An, or what, but either way, it stinks." He gazed toward a porthole. "Any idea what happens when we get to Desenna?"

"Not really. I talked to Keller a little. She seems nice. I think we're safe, for the moment."

"I wonder when that moment will end. . . ." Leech lay back, closing his eye. As he did so, his face clenched and I saw his hands shaking again. He seemed to sense me watching, and he said, "Yeah, that's getting worse, too."

"Sorry," I said. "Rest up."

"Sure," said Leech.

I left the infirmary, thinking I'd go up to the deck, but as I walked down the hall, I stumbled. The up and down of the water was making me feel woozy again. Plus, I was still exhausted, so I headed back to our room and lay down.

I tried eating a few bites of banana but it just made me queasy, and I fell asleep again.

This time, there were dreams.

They began in the infirmary on the *Solara*, only I was a patient. Lilly was there to see me. She and my dad were standing together, hands clasped, gazing at me, fear in their eyes.

"What?" I asked them. I looked down to see that my arms were striped with black, as if someone had drawn the lines of my veins on me. Except my skin was gray, translucent, the black veins beneath. I knew this: black blood, pandemic four, like Harvey and Lucinda and Leech had talked about. I knew, too, in the dream, that the black veins were late stage. Terminal.

"All we can do now is see what's in here." Paul appeared on the other side of the bed, glasses off, eyes clicking electronically. He reached down with a blue-gloved hand and sank his fingers into my flesh. It didn't hurt. I watched his whole hand disappear into my torso, and realized he was reaching in through my hernia scar, his arm sinking up to the elbow. The lump of his probing hand moved around my abdomen, the skin stretching. I could feel his fingers among my organs.

But now there was another sensation. On my cheek. Something old, ancient to me, a light pressure and movement. A thumb making a circle, clockwise on the skin of my cheek. "It'll be okay, honey."

I turned and found my mom sitting beside me, leaning close. Her eyes were wet, her mouth trembling, and I knew the feeling of that circle, knew it so well. . . .

"We'll be together again," she said. "I promise."

"Here we go." Paul's hand moved up, jostling around my lungs, and then there was a bolt of pain as he grabbed my heart.

"Just gotta shut this thing down," Paul said.

He squeezed, suppressing the beats—

I bolted up out of bed. My hand went to my hernia scar, and I felt a faint throb there, as if the dream had somehow reawakened that old injury. I was breathing hard and felt a coating of sweat all over me. My hands were shaking. What was with these dreams?

I got some water. Outside, the sky had cooled, the sea now purple and silver. Seeing my dad in the dream made me think of contacting him. I wondered if they had a gamma link on the ship. I headed up to the deck to ask, and to see where we were.

The sun had begun to set, growing bloated, an orange oval dropping into veils of gray mist. Beams of orange, pink, and purple reflected on high feathery clouds and over the slick surface of the gelatinous water.

I spotted Arlo standing with two others by my craft. One of the men was inside it, lit by the glow of the vortex engine. He was wearing a welding mask and holding a blowtorch to the kinked spot in the mast. I walked over.

"Hey, Owen," said Arlo. "We've been checking the damage to your craft here. We can patch the sails easy, and then it looks like the primary problem is the bend in the mast. We're getting that straightened so you're back in flying shape for tonight."

"Tonight?"

"Victoria will explain," said Arlo. "Actually, I'm supposed to take you to her."

We left the two men working on the mast and climbed up to the aft deck, where Victoria was standing by the navigation consoles. The solar sail had been furled, and we were moving slowly.

"Hi, Owen," said Victoria. "Did you get some rest?"

"I did," I said, though I felt more disjointed than rested. "I was wondering if you had a gamma link. I wanted to get in touch with my dad."

"That would be nice," said Victoria with a sigh, "but I'm afraid we don't. The Northern Federation blocks us from using the gamma network. It's one of their many sanctions against me. On rare occasions we are able to hack our way on, but that's about it. For the most part, it's really a blessing for the people of Desenna, but in this case I'm sorry it leaves you out of touch. I'll let you know if we are able to establish a connection." She pointed ahead. "For the moment, though, you'll want to see this."

There was land in the distance now, a black undulating

coastline beyond the purple sea.

"Take it nice and slow," said Victoria. The man beside her watched a monitor and slid little bars on the screen up and down. It showed a view of the underwater topography. Most of it was squiggly contour lines, but we were also nearing a series of uniform, geometric shapes.

"Tide's low," said Victoria, "so I wanted to bring you in by the scenic route." She pointed off to the starboard side. "Here lie the temples of the ancient kings."

The sun had sunk into the cloud folds, and the world cooled to lavender and blue hues. I scanned the gloom and then I saw a large, rectangular shape jutting up out of the water. It was skinny and long, maybe fifty meters, with curved ends. Chunks of it were missing. Most of it looked gray, but spots here and there seemed to still have a slight bit of faded golden color.

"You have to see the other side to get my joke," Victoria added.

We skimmed past the structure and I looked back. Giant metal letters in a script font stretched across the wall, reading:

HOTEL MAYAN GOLD

"Is it a beach resort?" I asked.

"Yes, they used to call this part of the Yucatán the Mayan Riviera. It was one beautiful resort after the next, for miles, places for the pleasure of people with too much money and time, and too little soul. They would come here to get fat and sedate their lives away. The kings of the pre-Rise world. Many of their descendants probably live in the Edens now."

Off to port, waves slapped against the skeleton of another building with a few remnants of grass roof.

"Even before this place went under, the hurricanes that were hitting it were really something. Furious storms. Now we get a monsoon season with long heavy rains that cause terrible flooding. All that rain from the dry parts of the world has to fall somewhere, I guess. Okay, here comes the best one."

A structure grew out of the mist and shadows. It was pyramid shaped, built of giant stone blocks. A huge sign stood on top, letters held aloft on metal girders. They'd probably once been brightly lit but were now covered in decades of bird droppings:

THE ATLANTEAN

"From what I've read," said Victoria, "that place had a whole sunken city theme, with rooms that had windows into aquariums, a scandalous mermaid show, a mall that had a swimming pool path through it. That kind of thing. Such decadence."

We passed a few more sunken structures. Some were acting as breakers for flotsam. At one point, an entire house was hooked cockeyed on a building top.

"South of here," said Victoria, "there's this place that used to be an ecotourism park. You'd go there and do things like look at animals and ride on zip lines. Imagine that: The same people who sank themselves in the Great Rise also had 'eco' tourism. I love the idea of people flying a few thousand kilometers in airplanes to ride on zip lines over caged and sedated animals and then eat burgers and ice-cream cones, all the while patting themselves on the backs for doing something eco-friendly."

In the distance I started to see a hazy corona of light in the gathering dark.

"There's home," said Victoria. "Now, to go put my face on for the people. I warn you, Owen, you're in for a little shock on our arrival tonight. I'll be putting on a bit of a show. I'm hoping that you'll be part of it."

"What do you want us to do?" I asked.

"Well, it's easy, actually. After we dock, I'd just like you to fly yourself and the other Atlanteans into Desenna and meet me atop the temple of Tulana. That probably sounds a little odd, but it fits with the mythology that we've created about your return."

"I know, the Epics of the Three. Your . . . those people in Gambler's Falls told me."

"Right." A look of distaste came over Victoria. "Well, that was one truth that they told you, anyway. My people are anticipating your return. This is a big moment for them, but, that said, I don't want you to think that I've brought you here just to use you as a puppet."

I hadn't thought of that, though now that she mentioned it, wasn't she?

"I mean, I am," Victoria confirmed, "in a sense. I guess what I'm saying is that this is where we begin to enter into our frank relationship. I want to help you and I want you to help me. It will make more sense after tonight, but this first move is a bit of a leap of faith on your part. Would you be willing to do that, and then we'll take it from there?"

I wasn't sure what to make of this. On the one hand, I didn't want to be a pawn in someone else's game. I'd gotten enough of that to last me a lifetime with Paul. And I remembered what the siren had said to me back in the skull chamber, about seeing both sides of something. Here was that question again: What would Victoria do if I said no?

But on the other hand, the way Victoria was presenting this made it seem, while not harmless, worth trying. She had saved us from Paul. It seemed like I owed her this.

"Okay," I said.

"Excellent." Victoria smiled. "Arlo will fill you in when we dock. And I will see you in about a half hour's time. And just remember to have an open mind about what you see. The people of Desenna are a free people. I don't force any of this. Can you do that for me?"

"Sure." I wondered what she meant by *this*.

Victoria turned to Arlo. "And make sure *she* does what she's told."

"I will," said Arlo.

Victoria climbed down the ladder and headed below deck.

The lights ahead had grown. I could make out a ridge of land, a bluff made of jagged black volcanic rock, with large buildings perched on top. They were lit by a few soft yellow floodlights and then torches that lined the roofs. The structures I could see seemed to be crafted of big stone blocks, and at the center was a giant pyramid with a flat roof. Though there were torches glowing around its perimeter rather than ghostly white lights, there was no denying its similarity to the one I'd seen in my visions with Lük, where the original Three had been sacrificed.

Beyond it, there was a general glow of light and haze, as if there was much more city that we couldn't see.

We arrived at docks at the base of the bluff. Crew members hurried around, throwing and securing lines. A staircase crisscrossed the black cliff up to stone buildings perched on its edge and a wide balcony where a line of silhouettes watched our arrival.

"Okay," said Arlo. "Let's head down to your ship."

Serena arrived at the craft just as we did, guiding Leech by the arm. "Here we are," she said to him.

"Hey," I said to Leech.

He turned toward my voice. "So, I hear you agreed

for us to be part of the big show." He didn't sound happy about it.

"Yeah." I looked around. "I'm not sure we have a choice, but I think it's okay. Where's Lilly?"

"Oh," said Serena, "Ms. Keller said it was only you two. I thought she wasn't . . . um . . ."

"Right," I said. "No, she's not."

"Everybody ready?" Victoria had reemerged. Her hair was up on her head now, wrapped tight. She'd traded her black coat and boots for a long crimson robe with gold trim, and was surrounded by an entourage of assistants in simple white robes.

"Yes," said Arlo. He checked his watch. "Just waiting on . . ."

"I'm here!"

There was a commotion over by the gangway. Someone was coming up, and the crew seemed very concerned with getting out of the way.

A girl breezed up onto the deck. She was taller than me, and wearing a long shimmering silver coat that stretched down to her black boots. She had blond hair tied into a braid that hung down over her shoulder. She strode toward us and there was something immediate about her presence, as if she thought she owned any room she was in.

"Hey, kids," she said, stopping beside us. She was chewing gum. "How's it hangin'?"

None of us replied.

The girl kept chewing. Her jade eyes flicking up and down, looking us over. "So, Mom, this is really them?"

Victoria stopped at the top of the gangway. "It's really them, and they've been through more than you've known in your lifetime, so I'd give it a rest." Victoria looked at me. "This is Heliad. And I'm not really her mother." She turned and headed off the ship.

"You're everyone's mother!" Heliad called after her. "The Benevolent and Wise! Chooser of Fates! The lead lemming into oblivion!" Heliad turned back to us, grinning. "She hates when I get on her case like that. So . . ." She stepped past me toward the craft. "How do I fly it?"

"Fly it?" I couldn't keep up. On the one hand, I felt like I already hated her, the way she was so full of herself and thought she could say whatever she wanted. I could feel the vibe from her: coming right at you, almost daring you to try to stand on equal footing. It was the kind of personality that always knocked me off guard, and I hated feeling like I was slipping back toward the old me, unsure of what to do or say.

At the same time, there was something exhilarating about her that I couldn't deny. The way she dominated my senses, smelling like flowers and some sort of citrus, her figure and movements instantly magnetic, and I didn't even want to be noticing these things but it was like the technicians were back, flipping switches and announcing: "We've got an attractive female coming in fast!"

And then even more than that was a strange feeling like I *knew* her. Obviously I didn't, but I had a sensation like I'd seen her before, and it was an old feeling, like I knew her from the past, the Atlantean past. Put it all together, and I felt stuck in place.

"Hey, slow down, sundrop," said Leech, who luck-ily was not having the same problem. Maybe because he couldn't see her. "Owen flies." I wondered how Leech could do that: slip back into that cocky, unimpressed persona like he'd had at camp. Especially now that I knew him better and knew the kind of life he'd had, the dark feelings he felt. I wished I could be more like him in moments like this.

Heliad eyed me. "Does he?"

"He's an amazing pilot, actually," said Arlo. "He's escaped from Eden's forces twice."

I was surprised to hear this assessment of my flying. I hadn't thought of myself as amazing. More like, surviving.

But I could go with that, and Heliad seemed impressed. "Well, by all means, you fly, then." She turned to Leech. "And what do you do? Make obnoxious comments?"

"I navigate," said Leech, but then he touched the ban-dage over his eye. "Well, I did."

She looked Leech up and down. "And they call you Leech. I won't ask. But you guys can call me Seven. Heliad is a ridiculous name. Has something to do with ancient Greeks or whatever. But, honestly, Mom just cherry-picked all this religious business anyway."

"Seven . . ." Arlo cautioned.

"What?" She rolled her eyes. "Come on, Arly, you know it's true. Heliad is the daughter of the god Helios," she said to me and Leech. "Seven refers to the seventh sun of Aztec history; Tulana is just a rip-off of Tollan, also Mesoamerican, and Chaac used to be a rain god, but she thought a vulture would be better; and then Desenna—do you know where she came up with that gem?" She didn't wait for anyone to answer. "It was the name of her lab partner back in grad school, I kid you not."

We were all just standing there listening, and Seven smiled, enjoying it. "So, here we are." She pointed at each of us. "Owen the Aeronaut, Leech the Mariner, and me, the mystical speaker to the Atlantean soul, or something like that." She thrust out her hand, palm facing down. "Hands in, team!" She grabbed Leech's hand and moved it on top of hers.

I hadn't even moved my hand toward her when she said, "On three . . . one, two . . . Atlanteans!" She threw her hand up in the air, then looked at me and laughed. "I never wait for three. Sorry. That was corny."

"Kinda," I managed to say.

I caught a movement out of the corner of my eye, and saw two medics approaching the gangway with Lilly on a stretcher.

"Hold on." I headed toward her.

"Who's that?" Seven asked behind me.

"Lilly," I said over my shoulder. I reached the stretcher and rubbed Lilly's hand. "Hey."

Lilly's eyes flickered half-open.

"How you doing?" I asked.

"Just listening to the music . . ." Her voice was a thin string of a whisper. "Do . . ." She trailed off, her lips making dry sounds. I leaned closer to her. "Do you hear it yet?" she asked.

"No," I said, "not really."

"It's like the most beautiful song," she said, and then she smiled and didn't say any more.

I ran a finger across her cheek, which she didn't seem to notice, and I felt a surge of worry for her. I also felt a pang of guilt for letting Seven affect me like she had.

"I'll find you later," I said. Lilly didn't reply, just sort of hummed to herself. They took her down the gangway and I returned to the craft.

"So, what's the deal?" Seven asked, looking over my shoulder. "There are only supposed to be three Atlanteans." Her smile had faded just a bit.

"She's Owen's girlfriend," said Leech.

This made Seven light up. "Ooh! Owen the swashbuckler, saving the damsel and bringing her along."

"No, not really like that . . ." I said.

"She's hot." Seven held up her palm. "Give me five. Flyboy snagged a hottie."

I started to lift my hand, but then stopped myself.

"She's part of the team," I said.

Seven raised her eyebrows. "Well, I think I might be jealous."

"I'm barfing," said Leech, pretending to wipe at his mouth. "Did I just barf? I can't see."

"Okay," said Arlo. "You guys should probably get going. Owen, you're going to fly just slightly east and then hold your position. You'll hear a horn, and that's when you come in over the city. Make for Tulana. It's the big pyramid, you can't miss it. Land just to the left of where the Benevolent Mother will be sitting."

"Got it."

"Time for the show," said Seven. She unzipped her coat and started slipping it off, revealing mostly bare shoulders and a flowing white dress. Her neck and wrists were adorned with golden jewelry. She produced a sparkling tiara from her coat pocket and placed it on her head, then tossed the coat in the craft and did a little curtsy. "Like it? Official uniform: Daughter of the Sun." She gazed at me. "It's okay—you can check me out."

"It looks good," I said, keeping my eyes on hers. And it wasn't easy, fighting the instinct . . .

"Ugh." Seven sighed. "So chivalrous!"

"I'll check you out," said Leech, "but I'd need to use my hands."

"Mmm, I think I'm starting to understand your nickname." Seven stepped into the craft.

Leech felt for the side and climbed in after her. "Is that the outfit you swam out of the ocean in?" he asked. Again, I was amazed how he could keep the cool banter going.

"The same," said Seven, grinning. "Except when it's wet, it gets kinda see-through."

"Thank you so much for that," said Leech.

I stepped in, but Seven was sitting where I needed to be. "That's where I sit," I stumbled, "to fly." Every sentence coming out of my mouth sounded so slow and stupid!

She scooted over barely far enough for me to sit, our hips jostling. I reached for the sail lines and found her staring at me with her jewel-like eyes and a wide grin. "Will you teach me? Pretty please? I'm good with knots and ropes."

"Maybe later," I said, and I wondered honestly how I was going to handle this.

"Okay," said Arlo, stepping back from the craft. "We'll see you inside."

Suddenly Seven was right by my ear. "Relax, flyboy." Her tone had completely changed. "This is just a show: See the princess dance and flirt."

"Oh," I said. "That's . . . you know, good to know."

"You're part of the royalty now, too," Seven said like a co-conspirator, "and here are the first two rules. One, if people want you to be a god, be one, even when you feel like an imposter inside. Two, if rule one makes you feel like you might die, remember: It could be worse. You could be like everyone else. So, play the game, everyone's happy, and we get out of here." She leaned away and became a goddess again. "Woo!" she shouted. "Let's do this!"

I powered up the vortex and curled away from the boat, out over the black water. The sky was nearly dark, a smattering of stars out, smudged by the damp air.

I brought us up to level with the buildings on the bluff and headed east like Arlo had said. We rose more, and I could see the grid of streets inside the city. I moved into position and hovered there. The roar of a crowd echoed in the distance.

"This is cool," said Seven. It sounded more like the whispered, real version of her than the goddess.

Finally I felt like I could respond with my guard down. "Yeah," I said. "Flying is one of the cool parts."

Before us was a high wall atop sea cliffs, the toothy silhouette of dwellings on the other side. Below, waves crashed against the rocks. At regular intervals on the wall were torches. And in the gaps between those, bodies hung down over the side of the wall. In the dark I couldn't tell how old they were, just that there were lots of them, stretching in both directions. It was a big city. A long wall. How many bodies did it take?

And I wondered again if we really wanted to do this. Here we were, on the dark shore of Heliad-7, our last chance to turn and run. . . .

But where would we go? We needed Leech's eyes. And besides, Lilly was already inside.

A low, long horn sounded.

"Ready?" I said.

"You bet," said Seven.

"Whatever," said Leech. "Tell me what it looks like."

I pressed the pedals, and we flew into Desenna.

16

WE FLEW OVER THE WALL AND ABOVE A WIDE AVE-
nue of low concrete buildings with tin roofs. The street was
dark. All the light was up ahead.

Arlo's men had done good work on the mast. The craft
was still a little unstable with the damage to the keel and
the hull, but it was definitely better.

I spotted the central pyramid, a massive structure rising
above everything else, so much like the one from my skull
dream. Victoria must have re-created it from what she'd
seen in EdenNorth. Wide staircases climbed its front and
sides. The back merged into a long square building that
abutted the cliff. In front of the pyramid was a wide plaza
filled with thousands of people and surrounded by ornately
carved buildings, some with columns and spires. It felt
like we'd flown through a time warp into the ancient past,
except for the giant video screens that were mounted on the
sides of the pyramid, so that the crowd could see what was
happening up top.

The buildings beneath us now were a few stories high, with wooden porches built on them. There were people on the roofs, all looking up at us and pointing and waving.

"Rule number three," said Seven, leaning out over the craft, "always wave to the minions. They lap it up."

"How many rules are there?" Leech asked.

"I don't know," said Seven. "I'm just making them up as we go."

We soared into the main plaza, hundreds of meters wide, and as we did, there was an explosion of sound, wild cheering, the crowd throwing up their hands, waving signs, blowing horns. The sound and the sight gave me chills.

"Is that as many people as I think it is?" Leech asked.

"Yeah," I said quietly.

"Woo!" Seven shouted, waving enthusiastically. "Now *this* is an entrance. Love us, you suckers!" she said.

The crowd was a frenzy of movement and sound. As we came closer, I could hear that there was a story being told. An amplified voice boomed through the plaza. It sounded like Spanish but not quite. Colored lights flickered and changed around the base of the pyramid. One made an outline of a giant serpent, another a turtle. They moved like waves washing over the stones. Images of fire and storms flashed over the video screens.

There was a hot blast of wind and a sizzle of electricity. A spear of lightning hurtled down and struck a metal pole at the back of the flat pyramid top. Bursts of flames ignited on building tops all around the plaza, coordinated with the strike.

The wind bucked the craft, and I fought to get us back on track. "What was that?"

"Part of the spectacle," said Seven, sounding bored. "This is the creation myth of Heliad-Seven. How the waters rose and the earth was thrown into darkness—that's the Great Rise—and the people were tricked into living in a false reality inside a dome. But then the Benevolent Mother heard the voices of the ancients and led everyone into the light. And when she did, the goddess Heliad was sent to earth by Tona as a show of faith. And she—that's me—was a harbinger that the Three would return, to bring harmony to humanity."

"So, we're part of the big story," said Leech.

"We're the *stars*," said Seven, "but, don't forget: Victoria is the director."

I flew us straight on and over the pyramid, then put us into a wide arcing turn, circling back out over the whole crowd, causing a huge roar from the people, before finally bringing us down on the wide, flat pyramid top, between glowing torches.

Across from us, Victoria sat in a giant golden chair, her assistants flanking her, only she wasn't Victoria anymore. In addition to her crimson robe, her face was completely painted a vibrant jade green. Her hands, too. Gold rings adorned her fingers, and atop her head was a fan-shaped headdress that I guessed was supposed to represent the sun. The jade face gave the whites of her eyes an unsettling glow. Seven had called her the director . . . and for the first time since meeting her, I worried about what she really was.

We stepped out of the craft, and a giant man, built like a stack of boulders, motioned us toward the front of the platform. He wore a crimson robe, too. His hair was cut close above his heavy brow. In his hand was a giant black knife. It looked like it was made of obsidian, its blade hand chiseled into rough serrations. He fell in step behind us and I remembered the dream I'd first had from the skull: the three dressed in white, their throats being slit. . . . What exactly were we playing out here?

"Howdy, Mica," said Seven to the large man. She didn't seem concerned.

"Miss Seven," Mica replied beneath the din. He gave her a formal nod.

We stood in a line and faced the sea of wild, cheering people, the ocean wind at our backs.

Mica raised his hands high over his head, and a wave of quiet swept over them all. It was eerie how quickly it happened, leaving an echoing silence in its place, as if the crowd were a single organism.

The silence held. . . .

"And the memory descended," called Victoria, her voice being amplified into the plaza, "in ships of blue light!"

The crowd exploded. I could pick out individual people

jumping, hugging one another. The air sparkled with confetti.

Mica's hands rose again. Silence.

I felt a brush of hair and found Seven by my ear. "This could go on awhile."

"Fear not that the gods depart!" Victoria called. "Fear not the rumor of Ascending Stars! For the gods have heard our call! The gods have come home to us! And we shall live again in harmony as the ancients did! We shall live free in the light!"

This must have been some kind of cue, because all at once the thousands shouted in reply:

"LIVE BRIGHT!"

Seven was by my ear again. "Good little fanatics, aren't they?" she said quietly. I glanced at Mica, standing a couple of feet behind us. He eyed Seven disapprovingly, but then looked away.

"The three have returned to complete their prophecy!" Victoria boomed. She really did sound convincing, a leader of the masses. "The three will heal the Heart!"

More cheering. Mica's hands. Silence.

"To make this journey, the Three will need to feed of the divine!"

"THE DIVINE IN US ALL!" the crowd replied. In the wake of this statement I heard weeping and sighs, little mouselike echoes in the giant space below.

"The divine burns within us! It is our gift, our treasure.

It is ours to give! We live bright in the world's glory, we do not fear, and then we give our divine back to the gods so that the cycle may continue!"

"WE GIVE THE DIVINE!"

A sound began to resonate throughout the plaza. At first, I thought it was a machine, but then I recognized that it was a human noise. The crowd below was making a sort of unison moan, an *mmmm* sound. The single note had a thousand layers and sounded like a million insects, or some kind of primeval tone, the sound of nature or creation itself.

"Mmmmmmmmmm . . ." they droned.

"Get ready for the fireworks," said Seven.

And now I heard a new voice from behind us. "The divine in me, the divine in me, I give . . . I give . . ."

"Dude," said Leech, "what is happening?"

I turned, thinking that I recognized that voice. Two women in crimson were leading a girl onto the pyramid top, a girl all in white. *Like the skull vision*, I thought again, but then I saw that the girl wasn't wearing robes but instead one of the pure white jumpsuits that I'd seen in the freezers in Gambler's Falls, with the Heliad symbol on the breast. A volunteer.

And I knew her. Aralene. The suicidal girl from the docks in Houston. She had been cleaned, her hair now radiant. Her face was painted a sparkling silver, so that she seemed to glitter like a robot, only with dark red lips and purple around her eyes. The women were guiding her but she wasn't fighting it. Her eyes were wide, and her arms crossed, her wrists no longer bound. She rubbed her biceps, kind of like she was cold, only slower, and with more force.

She shuffled forward, bare feet on the stones, as if in a trance. "I am the divine, I am the divine," she repeated, and I saw that she was smiling, her eyes wide. More than just wide, her irises were darting around to the sky and the crowd, like the world was a surprise and a wonder, almost as if she could see some magic that the rest of us couldn't.

As she moved to the center of the platform, I saw that something had been wheeled out. It was a short square of stone, a meter wide. It had leather cuffs on the sides, and a depression in the middle.

And, yes, I knew what this was, and yet my brain couldn't quite accept it. *People like poor Aralene there, they come to us for help,* Victoria had said. *It's the least we can do.*

Below, the droning grew louder. "MMMMMMMMM-MMM . . . ," its pitch rising.

"I will be divine, the divine is inside me . . ." Aralene's gaze darted about, like she was monitoring the arcs and dips of phantoms in the air around us. Her hands rubbed faster on her arms. Her head twitched, her chest heaving.

They led her to the short stone pedestal and turned her back to it, her profile to the crowd. Her eyes were spinning wild now, like her eyeballs had become unstuck in their sockets. Her smile had grown openmouthed. It didn't look right, it didn't look sane. . . .

And they gently laid her down on her back on the pedestal. She was still rubbing at her arms, but now the crimson-robed women grasped her wrists, held them down at her sides, and buckled them into the cuffs.

"MMMMMMMMMMMM . . ."

Victoria stood.

Mica stepped around to Aralene's side, so that he was facing the audience.

"The divine inside us is ours to give!" called Victoria. "No one can stop us from being free, in whatever form we desire! We are free people! We are free souls!"

"MMMMMMMM . . ."

Mica's hands rose, and he was holding the enormous knife, and I could see how crude and serrated its edges were. The blade was pointed down over Aralene's chest. This would not be an orderly incision like Anna's. There would be no electrodes and pumps.

"I am the divine!" Aralene was screaming now, her voice tattered and her face wild, and I couldn't tell if it was happiness or terror or some of both. The women held her, one at her shoulders and one at her legs.

"She thinks she wants this," said Seven. "Maybe she does. Either way . . ."

I stared at Aralene, chanting over and over, eyes spinning. "I am the divine!"

"We give the divine freely!"

"MMMMMM . . ."

I felt Seven's hand slip into mine and squeeze. I glanced at her. "Get ready," she said, her eyes dead serious. I didn't squeeze back, but I also didn't pull my hand away.

"MMMMMM . . . RAH!" The crowd went silent.

The knife plunged.

There was a crunch of bone, a sound of tearing.

Aralene screaming—but it died out.

Mica, bent over, his elbow and shoulder working up and down . . . sawing. . . .

Her body, convulsing.

I can't watch this, I can't. . . .

It was the lab beneath Eden. But instead of being hidden underground, we were atop a building, open to the world.

With an audience.

How could this be happening?

The knife did its work . . . Mica's hand fishing inside, working its way into the body . . .

"MMMMMMMMMM . . . RAH!" the crowd pulsed again.

The hand grabbing . . .

No. You can't do this to a person.

This had to be wrong. How could this not be wrong?

Finally, Mica was standing, his hand emerging.

When he held it up, blood dripping down his arm and the organ glinting in the light, the crowd erupted in ecstatic cheers, and a frenzy of wild leaping and dancing, as if they fed on this, on the blood, on the death.

Victoria stood and moved to the body. The body of a girl. Her name had been Aralene, a sad girl from Texas, who needed help . . . now open to the sky. A girl no longer.

The two assistants unshackled the wrists and carried the limp body away.

Mica placed her heart in the depression of the bowl.

Victoria placed her hand atop it. She lifted her hand and opened her palm, painted in blood.

And I began to fall over. In the last few days I had seen things I had never imagined, things I had never dared fear, but this . . .

Beware the gods and their horrors.

Beware this.

17

WHITE SPOTS GREW IN MY EYES . . . LOSING TRACK of my feet . . .

Seven gripped my hand tighter and leaned her shoulder against mine. "It's okay, flyboy," she said softly in my ear. "I told you to get ready. Remember, it's just a show. All of it."

"That wasn't a show," I whispered back. "It was a girl dying."

"It was that, too," said Seven.

"All hail the Three!" Victoria called. And I found her eyes squarely on me.

I looked away.

The crowd exploded one more time, and then it was over. Below in the plaza, drums began to beat through a din of excited voices.

"Come on," said Seven. Everyone was proceeding off the platform, down a back staircase. It led through a hall with stone walls that had no ceiling and was instead open to the night sky. As we walked, I felt a salty sea breeze across my face, such a simple feeling of life, and I took a deep breath. I had to find my composure, had to figure out what we had gotten ourselves into, and yet I couldn't find space to think around the memories of what I'd just seen.

We came to a stop at the bottom of the steps. Victoria was leading the small procession, and she had stepped to the wall. I watched her press her palm firmly against one of the smooth, symmetrical blocks. She held it there, then pulled it away and moved on.

As we walked past, I saw that she had made a handprint in blood. All down this entire hallway, each block had a similar print of a red hand. There were hundreds.

We passed through double doors made of glass. The next hallway still had stone walls, but the floor was made of brown tiles, and there was a modern ceiling with white lights.

Victoria stopped at a door and turned to Mica. "Take them to my chambers," she said. "I'll be up shortly."

She and her assistants passed through the door. Mica turned to us. "This way."

We followed the hallway to its end and started up a staircase that curved, its spiral getting tighter, as if we were in a tower. I walked behind Mica's hulking frame. He smelled like sweat and something sour, and I wondered if it was Aralene's blood. Behind me, Leech was leaning on Seven's arm as a guide. No one spoke as we wound our way up.

We reached a thick metal door, and Mica led us into a round room with stone walls and a wood floor. Cool damp air, tinged with smoke, rushed through four wide, curving, open-air windows that nearly made a complete circle around the room. In the center was an antique-looking wooden desk, with two leather chairs in front of it. I knew where I'd seen a setup almost exactly like it: Paul's office.

Outside, Desenna glittered in night light, a world of fire and smoke and a commotion of voices, of vibrant life in the tropical dark. The main pyramid was off to our right. Behind us was the black of the sea. To the front and south, the city stretched away in a flickering grid. There seemed to be electrical power for maybe a half a kilometer and then just firelight after that.

"She'll be up shortly," said Mica, and he left us.

I walked to the wall and leaned out, looking at the city.

"Um . . ." It was Leech. Seven had led him to the window. "I think I'm glad I couldn't see what just happened."

"Yeah," I said. I looked at Seven. "So, are we in any danger of that happening to us?"

She shook her head. "Nah, that's just the show for the masses. It keeps them happy."

"Happy," I said, still in disbelief. "That girl . . . her face. It was like she was excited to be there. Like she wanted to be killed."

"She was drugged," said Seven.

"Are you serious?" I asked.

"Doped up and chopped up," said Seven, "just the way the Good Mother likes it."

"That's not entirely accurate." Victoria strode in, back in her black coat and boots, her skin its natural color. The faintest trace of the jade green remained around one eye socket. It was as if that person onstage had been someone else entirely. "All volunteers are given something we call Shine. It's made from psilocybin and opium. It frees their minds of fear and numbs the pain of the liberation."

"So they don't know what's happening?" I asked.

"In the very end, no. But before that, they know what they have chosen," said Victoria. "You saw that girl in Houston today."

"Her name was Aralene," I said, feeling like it was important, like we owed her that.

"I know what her name was," said Victoria. "And I know that Aralene knew what she was doing. The medication simply helped her to be at peace with the choice. Obviously, no matter what a person's wishes, the body is a simple machine and it will try to avoid being killed, but the body doesn't always know what's best. It wants to preserve its genes, at whatever cost, but that doesn't mean that those particular genes are worth preserving."

I thought Victoria was sounding a lot like Paul. "How can you make a choice like that for someone?" I asked.

"I don't make the choice, Owen," Victoria replied, a note of frustration in her voice. "I didn't make that girl suicidal. The world does that. Nature does that."

"Bad Nature," said Seven like she was scolding a dog.

Victoria noted the uncertainty on my face. "I told you," she said, "that you would have to take a couple things on faith, until we had a chance for more frank conversation."

I shrugged. "So?" I didn't know what else to say. I was one part frustrated, one part afraid to say anything that could lead to the other end of that black knife.

"Look," said Victoria, "Aralene had tried to kill herself three times. Things aren't like they used to be. Unless you're lucky enough to live in the Federation, or in an Eden, there are no psychiatrists or counselors or mood-enhancing pharmaceuticals anymore. But that said, even a hundred years ago, when that girl could have been put on depression medication and given endless therapy sessions, she might have lived, but what kind of life would that have been?"

"Okay," I said. I could see her point . . . maybe, but I was still a long way from feeling like that equated with what we'd just seen.

"Aralene wanted to die," Victoria continued. "Well, she probably wanted to be happy, but that wasn't in the cards for her. Depression is medical. It's chemical. It's not her *fault*. It's just how she was built, part of nature's trial and error. So, I believe that if she wished to end her suffering, then she should be allowed to, and that choice should be given honor. Rather than have her bleed herself in a dark corner of the world and die alone, why not celebrate that divine spark inside her, as we deliver it back to nature, energy given back to the great cycle, toward a better future?

And in the process, give glory to thousands of people, who will celebrate her?"

"You mean cheer as she's cut open," I said. "How is that *glory*? Even if she wanted to die, to have all those people thrilling in it? How is that right?"

"Fair point," said Victoria, "but that's the one thing that *is* still like it used to be. People need spectacle. People need magic. People need to believe in something. And if you look at human history, people also need blood.

"Often, in a successful society, these needs coincide. Look at all the wars in human history, and tell me one that wasn't fought over bloodlust. There was always another way, but it never mattered in the end. Wars, genocides, witch hunts . . . There is something inside the human creature that *needs* the killing, the blood, to thrive, to feel unity.

"Now," said Victoria, "I don't have the weaponry to start a war with anyone. I can't even provide my people with simple entertainments like television, due to the sanctions. But what I do have is a population with no access to advanced medical care. Do you know the sickness and sadness we see? And there's nothing to be done. We can't operate on people's metastasized cancers. We can't cure their Rad cataracts. We can't vaccinate against the plagues, and we certainly can't help them when they're suffering from severe depression."

"So you've convinced them to die," I said.

"What I have convinced them of is that life is short and

brutal, but it can still have glory. In this new world, we can hide inside a dome or underground or inside layers of Rad protection, trying desperately to live as long as we can, or we can live bright, and when our time comes, we can return boldly to nature, by the knife. We all die someday, Owen, and out here, on the edge of the world, our own death is one of the only things we can control. We can wither, be eaten away by virus or sadness. Or we can be our own masters."

"How many people have you killed?" I asked.

"Liberated," Seven chimed in.

Victoria sighed. "Personally, only the handprints you saw. The ceremonial event like tonight is not how most people choose to go. I would never make someone hobbled by the measles five or late stage melanoma show himself on a stage. In those cases, we prefer a quiet infirmary ceremony. Seven's seen these: She administers the death rites. They are quite lovely."

"Yeah, my favorite part of the day," said Seven sarcastically.

"We only need a few public displays to keep the people engaged and help remind them that we're fragile, that during our short stay together, we need to be kind to one another and have community."

"That's weird logic," I said. "Community out of killing."

"Not really," said Victoria. "It's a powerful thing, what they feel on a night like tonight. It's human, it's animal, it's divine. We remember that we are part of nature. We sacrifice to save the many, to ensure resources for the healthy and young, so that the species may advance. It's scary, but isn't it also brave?

"The Great Rise was humanity's fault. We killed more than half our species by being selfish. We stretched the ecosystem like a rubber band, and then it snapped back. This has happened over and over in history, the rise and fall, since the Atlanteans. This time, I say let's try something different and stay in balance. Back to being part of nature, not trying to master it. Don't you see how that's dignified? It's not war criminals and thieves that we're marching up here and killing—"

"You just kill them in the basement of the courthouse," said Seven.

Victoria shrugged. "True. No resources to spare for a jail, after all. But when it comes to the volunteers, we take our turn, until nature takes us. And we are helping selection. The more of us live and die, the more generations, the more chances there are that one day, a child will come along who no longer feels the burn of the sun or suffers the Rad effects, and then humanity will adapt to this future. It is possible that the next rise of humanity doesn't include this version of us at all, but rather the next one."

"Seems kinda hopeless in the meantime," said Leech. "Knowing you're doomed to die young."

"No one has to be here," said Victoria. "When I led us

out of EdenSouth, many people made their way to other parts of the world. That's fine. But people choose to be here because their eyes are open. They see the reality of this world, and they'd rather face it head-on."

"But," I said, "in EdenSouth, you had all those resources you're missing now: medical facilities, sun protection. So why revolt?"

Victoria's eyes seemed to light up as I was saying this. "It's simple, Owen. Because EdenSouth was a lie."

"You mean the fake sun and the fake sky and everything."

"All of that, sure," said Victoria, "but I mean the real lie, the entire premise of the Edens." She moved across the room to her desk. "Here's my question to you," she said as she unlocked the top drawer. "What is the purpose of the Eden domes?"

"Which one?" Leech asked. "The one they say publicly or Project Elysium?"

Victoria rooted around in her desk. "Tell me both."

"Well," I said, "I guess what they say is that the domes are supposed to be a safe place to live."

"For people who can afford it," Leech added.

"But their real purpose is to learn about Atlantis," I said, "and to find the Paintbrush of the Gods before their domes fail."

"And why would they do that?" Victoria asked. She'd found whatever she was looking for in her desk, and was moving around to us again.

"Well, to save their people—"

Victoria cut me off. "And *that's* the lie, right there. Or at least, part of it." She stepped in front of us and held up a small, black cylinder. She flicked a switch on it, and a purple light shone from one end. "They don't want to save all of their people," she said.

She held out her right hand, palm up, and aimed the light at her pinkie finger, the one everyone else in Desenna was missing. The light pierced through her skin like an X-ray, through the flesh and muscles. In that circle of light we could see all the way to the bones. They were outlined in shimmery purple.

And on the middle bone of Victoria's pinkie, we could see a series of black lines.

"What's she doing?" asked Leech.

"Showing us the bar code on her finger bone," I said.

"It's an access code given each selectee by EdenCorp," said Victoria.

"The only ones who will actually be saved," I added.

"Yes," Victoria agreed, "and in all of EdenSouth, population two hundred and fifty thousand, take a guess how many selectees there were?"

"Just you?" said Leech.

"Hah." Victoria chuckled. "No, three hundred. A hair over point one percent."

Victoria flicked the light off and moved to the window. She swept a hand over Desenna. "All these people," she said, "they were never part of Eden's plan." Her voice quieted. "I couldn't live with it. So I told them, showed them the dome integrity data . . . and we made a different choice."

My initial horror at the sacrifice had faded, and now I didn't know what I felt. One part fear, one part awe.

"That's pretty bad ass," Leech said. He seemed to be firmly on the positive side.

"Yeah, Superhero Mom," said Seven, though this time with less sarcasm than before.

"Everybody chops off their pinkies to show . . . unity?" I asked.

"Precisely."

"But you didn't chop off yours."

Victoria smiled. "If I had, I wouldn't have been able to show you this now, would I? A leader needs to be prepared for all possibilities. Now, you're probably wondering where you fit in. . . ."

As she continued, I thought about what she'd just said. It didn't seem like a complete answer.

"For Paul," Victoria was saying, "you're a means to an end. Here, you are a different kind of hope. You've heard of the Epics of the Three."

"Yeah."

"There's a piece of it in the temple below EdenSouth. I'll show you when we go there tomorrow. I used it to create a mythology, about the Three, and how you would someday return. I had a feeling you would, after I discovered that we had a very likely candidate in EdenSouth's cryo facilities, our lovely Seven."

"Lucky me," Seven said.

"Always so grateful," said Victoria. "In my revolt, we took out most of Eden's technology, but I kept the cryo containment facility intact."

"Wait," said Leech, "you did?"

I thought he'd tell her about Isaac, but when Victoria asked him, "Yes, why?" he answered, "Just curious." Here was Leech, holding his cards again. His instincts had been right in Gambler's Falls.

"I introduced the prophecy of Heliad returning to earth someday," Victoria continued, "then I waited awhile after the revolt, until we'd built most of Desenna, and people were getting restless for something new. Then I woke up Seven and she found the skull, and that really got the people excited. It gave them hope in a force larger than themselves. That a better life would await the future generations. You two are the second part of that."

"How are we going to bring a better life for your people?" I asked.

"You already have," said Victoria. "It doesn't matter what you do from here on out. Just by actually arriving, and being connected to the ancient myths, you are real proof of the massive forces at work in life. It creates a sense of oneness, like we're connected to something larger, something divine. You'd be surprised how far that goes."

I thought of Harvey and Lucinda and Ripley. It hadn't

gone far enough for them. I wondered if there were others here who felt like they had: who would give us over to Paul if they had the chance. "So nobody here cares if we find the Paintbrush of the Gods or not?" I asked.

"What they care about is what I care about: that we stop Paul and his project from finding it and using it to save only his precious selectees. To that end, I am committed to helping you. Which is the other reason I brought you here."

There was a knock on the door.

"Sorry," said Victoria. "Mica knows not to disturb me unless it's important. Yes!"

Mica stepped in.

"Sorry, Mother," he said, using stage names again. "We have a visitor that I . . ." He gave Victoria a weird look. "Can I see you outside?"

"Okay," said Victoria uncertainly. "I'll be right back." She stepped out.

The three of us were silent for a minute, the conversation sinking in. I looked at Seven, who was by the window gazing out at the city. "So, can we trust her?"

Seven shrugged. "You can trust that she's telling the truth. I've been around her awhile and I am pretty certain that she really believes in all this business. She believes in us."

"I'm still waiting for the catch," said Leech.

"You don't think human sacrifice is a catch?" I said.

Leech didn't answer and the door opened. Victoria

entered and her eyes leveled on me. "Owen," she said, "we have . . . an unexpected visitor."

Mica stepped in, and then a woman. She had long, brown hair with gray streaks, held back by brightly colored barrettes. She wore a bright blue dress and had a frilly scarf around her neck. She was trembling, her hands fiddling with each other.

And inside, with no warning, I felt something slip and give way, like a floor falling through.

I knew this woman.

Her eyes looked wet. I knew this was how they'd always looked.

The chasm opened, and up from it flew memories, fluttering bat wings all around me, like from the cave depths beneath Hub at sunset . . . but no.

There was no way.

My brain had to be playing more tricks. . . .

"Owen?" she said softly.

"Mom?"

18

I STARTED TOWARD HER. THERE WAS NO WAY, AND yet with every step I became more certain that after eight years and so many questions and hurt thoughts and all the silence . . .

"Owen, honey!"

There she was in front of me and she looked the same, or older—she must have looked older, more lines on her face, her skin tanned and leathery compared to the pale subterranean complexion I remembered—but it was still her eyes, brown and wet. I used to think that she always looked like she'd either just been crying, or she was just about to. But they were also bright and wide, always showing exactly what she felt. That was something I remembered, too, that my mother, Nina, had never been able to hide what she felt, even when it was something I didn't want to know.

I threw my arms around her.

I remembered her taller, but we were the same height now, with the years that had passed. Now her chin buried in my shoulder, her frame smaller than mine, almost like I was the grown-up. Her hands rubbed up and down my back. And with my face in her hair I smelled her and that scent ignited inside me a deep feeling, wriggling like a fish being reeled up from somewhere down at the base of my spine, a feeling of familiarity that nearly made me cry. I knew this smell, this salty, powdery scent. It was Hub, it was home, it was my childhood, something I'd never even known that I'd lost, but that I'd been missing for so long and now here it was, a part of me again, that space filling in and me feeling . . .

Whole.

"Oh, honey," she said in my ear, "I can't believe it's you. I . . ." I felt her tears on my neck. "I saw you up there and I thought there was no way, it couldn't be possible that you were here, not to mention that you were"—she pulled back, gazing at me with gleaming eyes—"one of the Three! I—I can't even imagine."

I stared at her and I didn't know what to say. I felt myself vibrating inside, whirring on all frequencies, happy and also confused, relieved but also sort of lost. Again, that untethered feeling, like I was adrift in reality with no firm keel. Finally I found some words. I had no idea what to say first. What came out was "What are you doing here?"

Nina ran her hand down my face. "I've been living here. I—I'm sorry I never let you know that. I wanted to, just . . . finding the right way to say it, the right time . . ."

"But . . ." I wondered, *What would have been so hard about just telling me, Hey, Owen, I'm in Desenna?* I didn't see how that was so difficult at all. But I didn't say that.

"Owen . . ." I turned to find Victoria watching us carefully, making no attempt to hide her suspicion. "This is your mother?" she asked me, dead serious. And I had a weird thought: *Am I sure this is her?* I glanced at her again, taking this new image of her and trying to match it to the memories I had, but those had been made by a seven-year-old mind. . . . What memories did I even have in there? I searched around. There were glimpses from in our apartment at Hub, one where she was picking me up from school, walking me home through the caverns. The most vivid one was the night of the Three-Year Fire that I'd been reliving lately—

My head swam for a minute. I felt lost in time again, like I didn't know exactly where in my life I was. Was I here in Desenna? Was I back at Hub as a kid? Everything had already been too much. Now, this was more.

"Owen? Where'd you go, sweetie?" Mom reached to me. She cupped my chin in her hand, pressed her thumb against my cheek and began inscribing a clockwise circle.

And I knew, more than the smell or the sight of her, this touch . . .

"Yeah." I looked back at Mom, then to Victoria. "This is her. This is my mom."

"Fascinating," said Victoria. Mica handed Victoria a

small black folder, nodding as he did so. Victoria flipped it open. "Your paperwork all checks out. Seems you're a fine medic in our infirmary, Nina, and have been for some years, since arriving here from . . ."

"Yellowstone Hub," said Nina. "Well, by way of a medical caravan and then a Nomad pod."

"Of course," said Victoria. "And it says here that you live on Avenida de Rata?"

"Yes, that's"—Nina flashed a quick glance at me—"my partner's apartment. Emiliano. He's waiting outside."

"I'll go check his documentation," said Mica, stepping out.

Partner? Emiliano? This instantly bothered me.

"Mother, I . . ." Mom hesitated. "I know that Owen is your guest but we were wondering if he could come and stay with us?" She looked hopefully at me. "If that's okay. I know from our teachings that the Three won't be here long, and I'd like to make the most of the time."

Victoria's face remained inscrutable. "We would need to post guards by your house, given Owen's importance."

"Totally fine," said Mom.

"Then it's up to Owen," said Victoria.

I wondered what I wanted. Maybe to go with Mom, and yet at the same time I felt like I needed time to sort this out. There was so much new and crazy in my head that I had this urge to shut my brain down and just let everything settle. And also, why should I just go with her? Just because I'd magically shown up here didn't mean she got a big reunion out of it.

And yet I found myself saying, "Yeah."

"Well, then," said Victoria, "I guess this is another part of the will of the gods."

"Great, and thank you, Mother." Mom made a quick motion, moving two fingers from the bridge of her nose, to her lips, then down to tap over her heart.

Victoria nodded. "Owen, I'd like you back here tomorrow morning."

"Well, there goes all the fun *I* had planned for tonight," said Seven.

Seven's comment reminded me: "Where's Lilly? I want to see how she's doing."

"She's in the infirmary across the plaza," said Victoria.

"I'm taking Leech over there," said Seven, "if you want to join."

I turned to Mom and was almost going to ask for permission, but reminded myself that I didn't need to do that. "Where should I meet you?" I asked instead.

"There's a fountain out in the plaza. I'll wait there."

"Okay," I said, and was again held up, wondering what to do. Did I hug my mom for a good-bye, or . . .

Mom seemed to sense the moment, and she started out. "Go do your thing, I'll see you outside." She left, and I just stared at the door, almost doubting whether that had really just happened.

"Come on." Seven punched my shoulder, breaking my trance.

She held Leech's arm and led us through a series of corridors, then over a stone bridge that connected the temple with the infirmary.

"So that must be awkward," Seven said to me.

"More than awkward." I barely knew what to make of it.

"Is she like you remember?" asked Leech.

"Yeah, I mean, I think so. I feel like I really don't know anything right now."

We wound up a staircase, then down a long hallway. After all the talk of sacrifice and death, I was glad to see that, like on the *Solara*, this looked like a normal, if primitive hospital.

Lilly was alone in a room. The three of us stopped in the doorway, peering in. The room was dark. I stepped in and saw a fluid bag hanging beside her, and heard her hoarse breathing.

I went to her bed. "Lilly," I said quietly. There was no reply and I didn't want to wake her. I rubbed her arm, felt her breathing, and stepped back out to the door. She seemed okay, and safe, not about to be cut open or anything.

"So," said Seven looking in at her, "she's got gills. What does that mean—she's like . . . close to being one of us?"

"There were a bunch of kids who got gills at EdenWest," I said. "Doesn't anyone have them here?"

"Just me," said Seven. She ran her fingers over her neck. I saw the indentations there. "I'm the only one who's been down to the temple though."

"Our camp was right on top of a temple," said Leech. "We were thinking it's a proximity thing."

"Makes sense. EdenSouth is a couple kilometers away." Seven pointed to Lilly with her chin. "So . . . not to ask an awkward question, but . . . are you thinking she's going to be coming along with us on the journey? I mean, I like a party, and of course some friendly competition"—she gave me a little play punch—"but that's more of a three-person craft you've got, isn't it?"

"I'm sure we can fit," I said.

"Lilly's part of the team," said Leech.

"Relax, gents, I get it," said Seven. "I'm just thinking out loud here. . . . I heard that her gills got bad on your trip here, not to mention that someone poisoned her. I guess I'm wondering if it's best for the mission to have a non-god along. Could be . . . risky?"

I sighed.

"You have to have thought about it," said Seven. "Right?"

"Yeah," I admitted, and hoped Seven wouldn't take it any further.

She didn't. "Food for thought." She turned from the door. "Come on Leecher, let's put you to bed so Seven can still get out and have some goddess fun. Good night, flyboy."

"See ya." I took another look at Lilly's dark form, still hearing Seven's question and hating that I'd already had that same thought. I tried to push it out of my mind, and headed outside.

The plaza was still pulsing with people and the din of animated conversations. The edges of the vast cobblestoned space were lined with restaurants, the tables all outdoors. Aromas of cooked meats and smoke filled the air. It couldn't be more different from the closed quiet of Hub at night.

I found Mom by a central fountain lit by torches. She was sitting with a large man. They both stood when I arrived.

"There you are," said Mom. "This is Emiliano."

"Hey, Owen," he said. He was brown skinned and short, with a square face and broad shoulders. He had a bright smile full of white teeth that was no doubt considered attractive and that immediately annoyed me. "It's amazing to meet you." He put out his hand. "What a gift to have you arrive here."

I didn't want to shake it, but I did. I wasn't going to be the immature one who couldn't deal.

"Nina," said Emiliano, "I'm supposed to meet up with my cousins. I'm sure you guys have catching up to do?"

"Okay," Mom replied. "Have fun, Emil!"

Emiliano leaned over and they kissed. I looked away, annoyed by this, too, and also thinking, *Emil?* Here was my mother giving shortened nicknames like she was a girl at summer camp. Suddenly I wondered if that's what all this had been for her, since she'd left the difficulties of her family behind. Had everything just been carefree and fun? But then I felt the opposite, too, like, here she was! My mom! The feelings tugged in opposite directions.

We crossed the plaza, mostly not talking. I had no idea what to say. The more minutes went by, the more unbelievable and yet completely normal this seemed. I was walking with Mom, like we'd never been apart.

"You are looking big and strong," said Mom.

"I guess" was all I could think to answer.

"You must be hungry," said Mom. "Want to get something from one of the carts?"

"Sure."

We stopped at a little metal food cart, where a vendor was carving slices of meat off a leg on a spit and serving it inside soft wraps. "You've probably never heard of tapir but you have to try it. It's delicious."

"Um," I said, remembering the Walmart. "Okay."

Mom paid with some kind of wooden coin, and we moved on through the plaza. With my first bite of the sandwich, the tangy meat reminded me all too much of Gambler's Falls, but I managed to shake that off and keep eating.

As we walked, some people in the crowd recognized me. There was pointing and whispering, and every now and then people doing that two-finger motion like Mom had done to Victoria.

"You mean a lot to the people," said Mom.

"I've heard," I said. "It's hard to get used to."

"The Epics of the Three are kind of like our creation myth," said Mom. "It's the basis for so much of how we live here."

"You sound like you're really into it," I said. I didn't remember us being particularly religious at Hub. We certainly weren't after she was gone. Dad and I had never attended any of the churches, and I was pretty sure we never had with Mom either. In Hub, that was average. There were as many people who weren't religious as were. Here it seemed like believing in Heliad was required.

"I'm not an absolute believer," said Mom. "I don't think the lightning rain is actual god fire. But still, I think it's a beautiful way to live, given the state of the world."

I didn't reply, but I did think that made some sense.

"So, how have you been?" Mom asked. "I suppose that's kind of a silly-sounding question, all things considered."

I didn't know what to say. How had I been today? These last two weeks? The last eight years? But I could also tell that she was trying to connect. "Things at Hub were pretty much the same as when you left. Life was just kind of going along, until I went to Camp Eden, and then all this Atlantean stuff happened."

"Wow," said Mom. "Well, I'm glad to hear that things at Hub have been okay."

"I guess," I said, but then I couldn't help adding, "It

hasn't really been *okay*. I mean, it's always a struggle to have anything like a normal life, especially with Dad's lungs."

"They're still bad?" she asked.

"Yeah," I said, wondering what she'd expected—that he would just magically get better? "They're probably worse than when you left. I don't really remember what they were like back then."

Mom sighed. "They were bad. I suppose it's been hard for him."

Hard for him? I felt like saying, *Duh*. Instead I said, "You mean, raising me on his own?"

"I guess I mean that."

"I do a lot around the house," I said. *Stuff a mom should be doing.*

"You're not the little boy I remember," said Mom. "I probably should have expected that."

We were silent as we left the main plaza and started down a quieter street, the cobblestones more uneven. The shops here were closed for the night, bars down across their wooden doors.

I could feel my nerves spinning faster inside me. It was time to ask the question I knew I needed to ask. I finished my sandwich, and then waited another block before I finally did: "Why did you leave?"

Mom stopped. She looked up at the smoke-dampened night sky. "Well . . . I suppose I should have been more ready to answer this question. . . . I just . . ." She sighed. "I was unhappy, Owen. I needed to find out who I was. I needed to find someplace where I felt like I fit."

My next question was already lined up, almost like I'd been waiting for this moment. Maybe I had. "Was it us?"

"Oh god, no," she said, except she also looked away. "I wish there was some way to prove to you that it wasn't your fault at all. I used to look at you, at little you, and think to myself, dammit, Nina, how can you not be happy? He's so beautiful, he's so perfect. But it was like I was missing something inside. Not love for you, but . . . happiness for me. And that made me feel like a terrible failure. I felt like if I didn't find a way to be happy, then it would be worse for you to have me around than to not."

I wasn't sure if I thought that made sense. The topic still felt hot, stuffy like the air. "So," I said, "was it Dad?"

"Not really, no. I mean, he and I weren't getting along, but I think he was trying, in his own quiet way. We got married young, you know. And then, living at Hub was so hard, so dark and lonely. It was a struggle for me. I just couldn't . . ." She started to cry. "I couldn't make myself happy. I used to think I might end up like that girl tonight, up on the altar, just to end the pain . . ." She took a deep breath. "But after some time here, I finally started to feel better. Something about this place, the culture, the people, Emiliano, and the *sun*, I know that sounds silly but, oh, the sun . . . and something about me. I had to grow up. And only then did I feel like I was complete. A real person. That was a huge relief for me."

That answer felt heavy, like a locked trunk that I was going to have to let sink inside me and then swim down and rummage through. This whole conversation was starting to feel like it was deep underwater, and I was at the mercy of weird pressures and currents, sinking and floating at once, and gill-less, holding my breath, tight.

What she was saying reminded me of how I'd felt when I found Lilly and the CITs, how that world felt so right, like I could suddenly be my true self. Except for the part where Mom had to leave me to find that. "But so," I said, "once you found that happiness here, why didn't you . . . tell us? Let us know where you were?"

"Well, I don't know . . ." She wiped at her tears. "I meant to, but I was also so ashamed. I felt guilty and . . . I thought that since you'd gotten used to being without me, maybe it was better if I stayed gone."

This was all hurting me and angering me at the same time. I felt like I was on the verge of yelling, and I wondered if maybe I should. But I held back. "We never got used to not having you there, Mom."

Mom started to cry again. She nodded. "I can see that now."

She stopped walking. "Here's our place."

We were in front of a three-story apartment building. It had cement walls painted aqua and simple wood porches off the front. She started up the steps, but I stayed on the street.

"Owen?"

I was looking at the ground and I figured it looked like I was sulking, but I just felt like I was kind of stuck in place, my feelings all jumbled together. I hadn't thought about Mom for so long, and now here I was with her and I was realizing how much I had missed her, missed having a mom, but at the same time, her words and reasoning were filling me with a dark frustration. No matter what she said, there was still a truth in her words that I'd always feared: We were something she'd needed to get away from to be happy.

How was I supposed to feel about that? Was I supposed to be happy for her that she found this life here, to be happy that she was happy, when that life didn't include me or Dad? I didn't know if I could handle this. A part of me wished I hadn't found her at all.

"I know this is hard," said Mom. "I didn't mean for it to be hard. I . . . well, I didn't even know you'd be showing up here. But, seeing you, sweetie . . ."

I didn't want to look at her but then I did.

"Seeing you now makes me understand that I was wrong, all these years," she said. "I missed you so much, Owen, and I should have let you know about me. I'm so sorry, I see that now and I think I've been a big fool."

There it was. An apology. But did it help? I kept standing there.

"Will you please come in?"

I thought about leaving. Going back to the temple. If I went in, I was giving her what she wanted, I was saying that it was okay that she'd left us, that I was willing to forgive her . . . but I realized that while I *didn't* think it was okay, and while I wasn't sure at all if I was going to forgive her, if I was even capable of it . . . I did want to try having a mom again. At least to know what that felt like.

"Fine," I said. I started up the steps.

Their apartment was small, a narrow kitchen with electric appliances, a sitting area with pillows on the floor around a central table, and then a bathroom and two small bedrooms. A giant wooden carving of Chaac spread its wings across one entire wall.

Mom set me up in the second bedroom, on a little grass mattress on the floor. She gave me a pair of soft gray pants and a T-shirt that were Emiliano's and took my shorts, T-shirt, and sweatshirt to wash. I accepted the clothes, even though it was weird; but then, all of this felt weird. "Do you want some more food? Emil will be home in a bit."

"Nah," I said. "I think I want to go to bed. It's been a long day, week . . . everything."

"Okay, well, I can't wait to see you in the morning." She smiled hopefully at me.

I tried to return the smile. "Yeah."

I used the bathroom and lay down on the bed. Mom came in and knelt beside me, helping me spread out a white mesh mosquito net that was hanging down from the ceiling.

"There we go," she said, and she kissed my forehead. The feeling was so weird, like I'd time traveled back to Hub. "Good night, my boy," she said, and drew another circle on my cheek with her thumb. Then she left me in the dark.

There was an open-air window with wooden blinds. Yellow light from the street made slanted lines on me and the wall. Outside I could hear the din of city life, people walking and chatting.

I wondered if Seven was out there somewhere. Wondered for a second at how she seemed to be into me. Then I shook that thought away and wondered how Lilly was doing.

I wondered how my father was, far away, and what he would think if he knew I was with Mom. Would he be happy that I'd found her? Upset that I was with her? He always tried to hide how much he missed her, how much it hurt him that she'd left. . . . I wondered if he'd gotten the message that I'd tried to call, or what Eden might have told him.

I ended up lying awake for hours, long after Emiliano returned and I heard him and Mom go to bed, after the sounds of the street died down. I lay there and in my mind I was in Desenna; I was in EdenWest; I was in Hub; I was in the Atlantean city; I was in my ship, flying over the wastes, and none of these places felt like home, none of them felt like where I belonged. It was like I'd come unglued from the world, like I was drifting on a wind; and even here, in a room in my mom's apartment, I hadn't yet landed. If anything, I felt more untethered than ever.

19

I SLEPT AT SOME POINT, BUT IT WAS RESTLESS. I SAW the red-haired girl again in her frog pajamas, standing waist-deep in ash. This time, her skin had the gray translucence and dark veins that mine had in that dream on the *Solara*. Black blood, and she was sinking. Then the hospital room, Mom sitting beside me, Paul looking down. Only now he held the giant black blade, its serrated teeth glinting in the pale lab lighting, like the basement lab in Eden. "Have to get this out," he said, leaning over me and sawing. . . .

I woke to gauzy light. The mosquito net. Bright sun was splitting through the slatted window. The air smelled something like sweat and that fresh-cut grass back at camp, a kind of living smell. Birds called outside. There were hums and clangs of street activity. A sizzling sound came from the kitchen, along with a tangy, spicy scent.

I got up and found my clothes cleaned and folded at the foot of the bed. I didn't remember a time when my clothes had been folded. Back at Hub, my few outfits had just lived draped over the foot of my bed. Something like folding clothes had never been a detail that Dad or I would get to. There was too much else to do around the apartment.

I got dressed and went to the bathroom. I checked my shoulder. The wound had scabbed over. The red smudge of infection had mostly receded. It was still sore but not as bad.

I found Mom at the low wooden table, laying out forks and cups of whitish-green juice. She was wearing a long flower-patterned skirt and a light blue sleeveless shirt. Her hair was up, earrings on. This matched what I remembered about her, too—how she'd always dressed up, even at home, like she wanted to be ready at any moment for a special event.

"There he is," she said. "Well, someone got a good sleep."

"Did I?" I said, rubbing my eyes. It didn't feel like it.

"It's nearly eleven in the morning," said Mom. "You've become quite the teenager!"

"Guess," I said, thinking, *I slept so long because I've been running for my life for a week*. I thought about telling her that, but then noticed that as she laid out the forks, her fingers were shaking. I let the comment go and sat down cross-legged at the table.

Mom sat across from me. "I still can't believe you're here, and that you're . . . I mean, *the* Epics of the Three. You're part of that, Owen. That's . . . amazing."

"I've just been worried about surviving it," I said. "You

know, you're part of it, too. My Atlantean genes either came from you or Dad."

"Huh," said Mom. "Never thought of myself as having a purpose like that, raising a future world saver and all."

Another flash of annoyance: *You didn't exactly raise me.*

Maybe Mom realized how that sounded, too, because she changed the subject. "Emil's making an old pre-Rise dish from this region called *motuleños.*"

"Modified," Emiliano called from the stove. He wore a white apron over his black medic outfit.

He brought over two steaming plates. "Gull eggs, rice tortillas, no peas or cheese, but it's similar otherwise. We're pretty lucky here, foodwise, compared to most places."

Emiliano put the plate in front of me. I'd never had any kind of real egg. The dish was smothered in a red sauce. I took a bite and my mouth exploded with salt and spice. I sipped the juice, and puckered.

"Sour, right?" said Mom. "Those are real limes. We've developed a strain that does well here."

"It's good," I said. All of it tasted shockingly real compared to food up north, even in Eden.

Emiliano sat down. "You're a medic, too?" I asked him.

"Yeah," he said. "I work mostly in dermal care."

"Can't you tell?" Mom said, proudly leaning her shoulder toward me. "Look at how good that skin looks."

I didn't think it looked good. The surface was heavily tanned, with freckles like someone had scattered a handful of pebbles across her shoulder. Many of them were dark, black: the kind of spots that we were supposed to watch for, because they could lead to melanoma. "I heard you guys don't hide from the sun down here," I said.

"That's right," said Emiliano. "One of the main teachings in Heliad-Seven is to live a life in the open. That's why we left the false reality of the Eden dome, to live in the glory of the real light. It gives us life, after all."

"I've heard that," I said, glancing at Mom's shoulder again, "and so you're just going to be cool if you get Rad poisoning or whatever?"

"If that's what happens," said Mom, looking at Emiliano and smiling, "then so it shall be."

I felt myself tightening inside. I wasn't sure if it was the idea of my mom dying, or maybe the idea that she wouldn't bother to protect herself, or maybe just that all this sounded like something so foreign to how I'd grown up, and yet it seemed like she wanted me to approve.

"So," I said to Emiliano, "if you don't treat anybody's illnesses, what do you do as a medic?"

"Oh, there's plenty to do. We can splint broken limbs, treat people's cuts and abrasions and minor infections. But we have to leave the advanced care in Nature's hands."

"It's beautiful when you think about it," said Mom.

I *was* thinking about it, and I felt my pulse speeding up. "So," I said, "when somebody gets too ill, too broken, that's when you just kill them?"

Emiliano kind of winced at what I'd said. "It's not *killing*. It's very peaceful, the way we do it at the clinic. Everybody knows that it's selfish to prolong our lives and drain the resources of the people."

I turned to Mom. "So if those sun spots on your shoulders get bad, and you get sick, you'd kill—sorry, *liberate* yourself."

Mom sighed. "Owen . . ." She gave me another look that I remembered from so many years ago: like she was disappointed, the curve of her mouth suggesting that maybe she'd rather I wasn't here ruining her perfect breakfast in paradise with her boyfriend. Maybe she already wished I hadn't shown up, that she was still the free spirit who had abandoned me. "I remember Hub," she said. "All that hiding in the dark. It's better here in the light, living bright. It's worth the risk."

My next thought just shot out. "So, in *your* world, if my dad had all his complications from the cave molds and dust . . . he wouldn't get treatment. No rebreather, no nebulization shots. Right?"

Mom's face twisted further. I was definitely something awkward to have around now.

"Well," said Emiliano, "I mean, we can't even get some of that stuff here."

"So he'd be dead by now," I said. "My dad would have drowned in his own phlegm, or you would have liberated him."

"Probably," said Emiliano, "if his condition was severe."

I stood up and started for the door. "It *is* severe."

"Owen, wait . . ." Mom called.

I whirled. "And after you let my dad die, who would take care of his child? Not his mom, 'cause she took off to try to find her happy place!"

"That's not—"

But I was at the front door.

"Where are you going?"

I stopped. My feelings were like those waves in Houston, crashing against the debris of sunken memories inside me. I felt bad for saying what I had, and yet I felt like I'd had to. "I can't be here right now," I said. "I'm going to find my people."

"Okay . . . I'm sorry this is hard, I—I love you." Mom made a motion like she was pinching a kiss off her lips and then flung it toward me. "Catch it," she said.

Without even thinking, I moved my hand up and made a snatching motion near my face and something about that movement, if your muscles could have memories, triggered a deep, lost feeling inside. I had done that before, we had done this, so many years ago, a gesture of love that I had lived without for so long, and it made me want to either scream and leave or run and hug her.

But I just caught the kiss and grabbed the door. "Bye," I said.

Outside, the sun hit me straight on, like flames to my

face. I stopped on the steps, taking a deep breath. The two guards stationed outside glanced at me.

"Hey, flyboy."

Seven was sitting in the shade beside the stairs, leaning against the base of the wall, legs stretched out. She wore a white wrap dress with long sleeves. Lines of brightly colored flowers were woven at the hem, and rootlike curls wound up from the flowers to the center of her stomach, where they encircled an elaborate floral version of the Heliad-7 symbol. Her hair was up beneath a woven white hat that shaded her face. Her long legs were crossed and she had a small woven shoulder bag in her lap. Her face had that perfect makeup sheen to it, like she was glazed pottery. She had on these retro-looking sunglasses with gold rims, and was drinking purple soda from a weathered glass bottle that was beaded with condensation.

"Hey," I said. I hopped down the stairs and stepped over to her. "What are you doing here?"

She sipped her soda, then belched. "The Good Mother sent me to fetch you. Something's going down at Tactical that she wants us to see. Apparently, it's important." She held out her hand, like she wanted me to grab it. I did, and she pulled herself up. She got on her feet and her body bounced into me. I stepped back.

"Sorry," she said, not sounding it.

Then she rubbed at her head. "Ooh," she said. "I hate mornings." She took another sip of soda. "I wanted to get this down before I picked you up." She cocked her head toward the apartment. "How'd you sleep?"

"Not great," I said. "You?"

"Ha. I stayed out late with my friends. There's this place, Chaac's Cove, where we go dancing. It was fu-un, but I'm paying for it now. Such is a goddess's life. They're all expecting you to make an appearance tonight, by the way."

"I don't dance," I said, "I mean, I haven't, really . . ."

"You will," said Seven with a smile. We started up the street. "So, how's that all going in there? I heard your voice raised. Trouble in the big reunion?"

I shrugged. "I guess. It's weird. I lost it a little when we were talking about the liberation stuff here."

Seven smiled ruefully. "Live bright!" She raised her fist to the sky. "Yeah, it's a thing." She let her arm fall around my shoulder as we walked. I glanced at it, and my first thought was *That shouldn't be there*. Didn't I have a girlfriend? That's what Lilly was, right? Then again, friends could put arms around each other, and Seven and I were going to need to be friends, weren't we? Maybe to Seven, an arm around the shoulders was no big deal. So I let it stay there and tried to calm the sensor going off in my brain, the technicians sounding alarms.

I could feel people's eyes on us as we strolled up the narrow street, then over to the plaza. I also noticed that the two guards from Mom's place were following us at a distance.

Off the main square, a market was bustling with activity, people moving between rows of stands shaded by soft woven awnings. The people were old and young and a blend of skin tones and face shapes that was so much more diverse than what I'd seen back at Hub or at Eden. And all of them were out in the bright, searing eye of the sun, letting it irradiate their heads and shoulders and arms, seemingly without fear.

"It's hot," I said, looking at my own arms, covered in a sweatshirt. I felt tingling from my Rad burns.

"Scorching," said Seven. "You never totally get used to it." She pulled her arm off me, and adjusted the long sleeve of her dress, then her hat.

"How come you're not living bright?" I asked.

Seven smiled. "And melt my skin off? No thanks." She looked around. "Living bright and chopping off fingers and dying young might be good for the suckers," she said, "but not for me. I didn't choose this place. I'm just the fair maiden locked away in the tower."

"What do you mean?"

"I mean, I didn't ask to be woken up and turned into a great symbol of hope. Hell, I didn't even ask to be cryoed."

"Your parents?" I said.

Seven shook her head. "Not even. They were already dead."

"What happened?"

Seven was quiet for a second before she spoke. "We

were living in Buenos Aires during the Rise. My dad was in finance and I grew up in New York, but we traveled a lot. You probably read in school about what happened in Buenos Aires."

"I don't think so," I said.

"Well, things were already bad there, floods and storms, but then black blood hit, and conditions were so tight that it mutated and became supervirulent and twice as lethal. They set up a military quarantine. Nobody gets in. Nobody gets out. Five million people, and everybody died . . . my parents, my brothers. Everybody . . . except me."

"How did you survive?" I asked. "Wait, let me guess: EdenCorp found you."

"Yep," said Seven. "I was a match with their ice bodies. They were arranging to get my whole family out, but then the mutation happened and the quarantine. And we all got sick. So they came at night," said Seven. "We were in the group hospice. Whole families were getting rooms together to die in. It was late and my younger brother was dead and my dad was barely breathing. My mom was nearly gone . . . and this team of soldiers all in black with these gold visors, like robots, burst in. They asked me if I wanted to go. I didn't, but I also didn't want to die. So I said yes. I'm sure they would've just taken me anyway. They loaded me on a helicopter and I remember looking up at one of those visors and then . . ."

Seven looked around. "Then I'm waking up in a bed in

Desenna, and it's twenty-five years later, and I'm Heliad, daughter of the sun. Just like that."

"I'm sorry," I said. "Sounds tough."

"People have had it worse," said Seven.

"What was your name before?"

"Ha," she said, but she wasn't smiling. "Doesn't matter." She stopped walking abruptly. "You hungry? I am. And you want some of this." She pulled me across the street toward a market stall that had a trail of smoke wafting up from it.

A woman in a red dress and two young boys were grilling flat brown cakes on black skillets. Beneath, red tubes led to a solar battery.

Seven spoke to the woman in that version of Spanish I'd heard the night before. She smiled sweetly, her perfectly made-up face and sunglasses a goddess mask hiding the real person she'd let me see. The boys busily placed beans and some kind of orange vegetable on the center of the cakes and then folded them into triangular shapes. The woman picked them quickly off the skillets, placed them on squares of leaf, and held them out.

"Do we pay?" I asked.

"Never, that's rule number four," said Seven, taking the food. "It would be insulting for a god to pay for things. They think they're gaining our goodwill with their gifts."

The woman and the children saluted us with the two-finger motion. Seven nodded like she was used to it.

She handed me one of the triangles as we walked away. "Cocoa and eddo in masa," she said.

It was chalky but tasty, a blend of chocolate sweet and vegetable tang.

"So are you mad?" I asked as we continued across the plaza toward the pyramid. "Like, at Eden, at Victoria? That this hasn't been your choice?"

"I get cranky, sure," said Seven, "but, I mean, given a choice between dead and goddess, I think I'll take goddess."

"So then what did you mean last night when you said it makes you feel like you might die?"

Seven eyed me. "Ooh, see the boy remember key details, watch the ladies swoon."

"Seriously," I said, and yet also made a note of this apparent ability of mine.

Seven sighed. "I guess that sometimes I just wish there had been a third option available."

"Like what?"

"I don't know, maybe to be a girl in the Northern Federation. You know, live on Helsinki Island, and just have that life: school, graduation, university. After that, get an internship at an office, work for the bureaucracy, be a paper pusher in a sensible suit and awesome shoes, maybe meet a cute intern boy at the company party. Just be normal. Anonymous. No living bright. That would be nice."

"Maybe you can after we fulfill our Atlantean destiny," I said.

"Ha, maybe," said Seven. She didn't sound convinced. "I'd take just getting out of here. But in the meantime, I figure this is a free pass. I should be dead, but I'm not. I'm a goddess, and now, bonus." She wrapped her arm around mine. "I have a god to hang out with, too."

"You mean Leech?" I said, hoping that sounded like a joke and also wondering if this arm thing could still just be considered friendly.

"Yes, sexy Leech." Seven flashed a devious smile. Then she pulled her arm back.

We passed two older people slumped against a wall in the sun. Their skin was leathery and charred, black spots everywhere, some oozing yellow trails. One of them pointed to us and reached out, but the other grabbed his arm and pulled it down.

"Begging is forbidden," said Seven. She considered them for a second, then reached for the last few bites of my food. "You mind?" She darted over and gave our leftovers to the two. When she came back, she said, "Just doing the goddess's work. Those two will be gone soon, anyway. By the smell of their lesions, I'd say within the week."

"That was nice of you," I said.

Seven shrugged. "You have to do what you can, and at least pretend there's a point to all this."

We crossed the grand plaza. The main pyramid was maybe more impressive by daylight, because you could see its size compared to everything else, its crisp edges stepping up into the blue.

To our right, a team was building a new wall on the side of a building, hauling massive blocks up a long, slanted wooden platform. Others were working with spinning wheels and files to shape stones. I could see that some of them were carving faces.

"Looks just like it, huh?" said Seven.

"What?"

"The city where the Three died."

"You've seen that?"

"Yeah," said Seven, "the vision with the pyramid and the ash sky, and the three lined up and the throat slitting." She rubbed her neck. "I felt like I was that girl who died."

"For me it was the boy," I said, "but, yeah, I felt that, too."

"And those freaky priests with their knives . . . It must have been so sad, not just to die but to know your world was falling apart, that the people you loved were suffering. . . ."

"All by our hand," I said, remembering Lük's words inside the skull. "It's nice to finally have someone who knows that stuff," I admitted.

"I know," said Seven. "Everybody around here is like, *yay, Atlantis!* and I want to say, *shut up*, you have no idea what it was really like." She rubbed my arm. "I've been a lonely goddess."

"Ha," I said, and felt myself getting red. Because I

had to admit, the part of me that had at first found Seven annoying was pretty much gone. She understood what we were part of even better than Leech did. And then, when it came to finding her attractive . . . well, that part had definitely grown. Never mind the whole situation where Seven seemed to find *me* attractive . . .

All of it made me suddenly think that I *had* to see Lilly, talk to her, connect, before these new thoughts went any further . . . maybe after whatever it was that Victoria wanted us for.

We entered the pyramid and made our way through a series of corridors to a set of metal doors. Seven pressed a button beside the door, activating a little speaker. She identified herself and the doors swung open.

While all the hallways through the pyramid had been stone and softly lit, the room we entered now was bright and white. There were computer consoles along the walls, not to the same degree of technology as they had in Eden, but there were monitors showing views of the ocean, what seemed to be radar, and a bunch of other camera views.

The room was alive with commotion, people hurrying around.

"Come on," said Seven. She led me through the crowds and right up to one of the uniformed guards and threw her arms around his broad back.

"Nico!" said Seven affectionately. "High five!"

Nico was definitely one who girls would think was a

catch. He glanced at Seven but then also quickly around the room, like he was checking who noticed before turning around.

"Ooh, sorry," said Seven, pulling her arm back down but smiling devilishly. "I forgot, not in public."

"Hi, Seven," said Nico. He was quite a bit older, maybe twenty, and was crisply dressed in a navy blue officer's uniform. Most of the workers in the room had brown military-style uniforms. He gave her a glimpse of a smile but then returned to a computer in his hand. "Sorry," he said, "big doings."

"I heard," said Seven. "Any more details you can share?"

A queasy look came over Nico's face. "You know I shouldn't," he said. He looked at me for a second, seemed to frown, but then his eyes just darted away, as if I somehow outranked him.

Seven gave a pouty sigh. "Fine. What good are you, then?"

"I—"

She play punched his shoulder. "Just kidding. Can you point me to the Exalted Mother?"

"She's outside," said Nico.

"Thanks, sweetie," said Seven. She poked him on the nose, then turned to me. "Come on."

We walked through a set of sliding glass doors out onto a stone balcony that jutted over the cliff above the docks. The rainbow-slicked ocean stretched away toward the horizon, undulating in its rubbery way.

"Was that your boyfriend?" I asked, trying to make sure that I sounded indifferent. *You ARE indifferent, aren't you?* I wondered.

"Nah," said Seven. "He's a friend, and I'm a flirt. I like him, and he'd probably like more of me, but that's all it is." Seven eyed me. "Why, jealous?"

"Of course not." Except maybe I had sized him up when we'd met.

We found Victoria at the wall, gazing down at the sea.

"What's shaking, Mommy dearest?" asked Seven, leaning over and looking down.

"We have wounded incoming," said Victoria tightly.

Below, a rusty ship was pulling in beside the *Solara*, belching black smoke. Its gangway squealed down, and a ragged crowd began to shuffle off, followed by stretchers.

"This way." Victoria led us to a metal staircase that switched back and forth down the side of the cliff.

"Who are they?" I asked.

"Nomads," said Victoria over her shoulder. "They were part of a registered pod that we regularly trade with. Three nights ago they were hit by ACF forces in the Tennessee marshes. Seventy-five men, women, and children slaughtered. These few are the only ones who managed to escape."

"We saw something like that," I said, "up in Colorado. The Nomads were trying to tell the ACF that they weren't responsible for something, the um . . ."

"The raid on Cheyenne Depot," said Victoria.

"Yeah, that was it."

We reached the docks. The wounded were scattered in clumps around stretchers. Women and children, a couple men, everyone covered with cuts, abrasions, burns. I saw a leg that was mashed, a hand blown off. The children were either stunned silent or crying. Serena and the medics scurried around the wounded.

Victoria bent over an unconscious man on a stretcher. His face was mostly hidden in bandages, and the area around his temple and ear were soaked through with blood. She called to the closest medic. "If he has any family, offer them liberation. Tell them we'll free him from suffering, but that's all we can do."

She turned away and I saw a look of pain on her face. I wondered how the same woman who had watched a girl die the night before and placed her hand on a bloody heart could be so upset by these wounded.

"Bastard," said Victoria quietly.

"Who?" I asked.

"Your old friend Paul. He's behind this. These people just want to scrape out a living, but instead they've become sacrifices to his ambition."

I heard screaming. There were two children, around ten years old, who were kneeling beside a woman with massive injuries to her torso.

"Cheyenne Depot is a military base, or something, right?" I asked.

"It's North America's largest stockpile of decommissioned nuclear material," said Victoria.

"You mean bombs?"

"The warheads themselves were dismantled a hundred years ago," said Victoria. "The Northern Federation nations obviously still have nukes at their main bases, but the uranium at Cheyenne could easily be weaponized again. And last week, the depot was reportedly attacked by a Nomad strike force, which was able to subvert defenses, steal an undisclosed amount of nuclear material, and get out before ACF forces could arrive."

"Why would Nomads try to steal uranium?" I asked. "Are they trying to build a bomb?"

"That's just it," said Victoria. "There's no way it was actually Nomads. I think it was an EdenCorp force made to *look* like Nomads. And now the ACF has branded the Nomads a terrorist group. They're hunting down every pod they can find, looking for the stolen goods, and blowing them to hell in the process."

"Paul talked about mining uranium in that report we saw," I said. "He didn't say where, or what they were going to use it for."

"I think it's pretty obvious," Victoria muttered. She gazed over the sea of wounded bodies. "Listen, we'll have to postpone our trek to the temple until tomorrow morning.

I have to get back to this. Sorry we can't talk more now."

She turned away and moved back into the frenzy, talking to Serena as more wounded came off the ship.

I stood for a minute, looking for a way to help, but there was nothing to do. I found Seven kneeling beside the man with the bandaged face. His cheek had been marked with a V, for volunteer. A woman stood beside Seven, hugging a sobbing boy.

Seven looked up at me as I arrived. Her eyes were serious, shaken. "Want to help me administer the death rite?" she asked gravely.

My first instinct was no. I wanted to be away from all this death, but then I thought of my mom, who'd run from what upset her. The woman and boy were looking up at me, and I remembered that I was one of their gods. And I wasn't going to leave them when they needed me. "Sure." I knelt opposite Seven, the man's bruised and burned torso between us. Seven put out her hands and I grasped them.

She nodded to me and closed her eyes, then spoke:

"Be at peace. Let yourself glow unbridled.
"You have played your part; now we celebrate your release.
"And as we set you free, know that you will be divine,
"Divine in your freedom, a conqueror of fear."

Seven let go of my hands. She rummaged into her little shoulder bag and produced a tiny glass bottle. She removed a dropper filled with bright green fluid and squeezed it into the man's mouth. "Shine," she said to me, and looked to the woman. "This will ease his suffering in the final moments."

"Thank you," the woman whispered.

They knelt beside the man as Seven and I stood and backed away. Seven's face was stormy. She was biting her lip. And I saw the difference now. Death did bother Victoria and Seven, when it wasn't planned. When it was out of their control. These people weren't given a choice. Paul had taken it from them.

Seven and I performed three more death rites, kneeling over grizzly ends, holding hands, and by the last one I knew the rite and spoke it with her, our words feeling powerful in their rhythm and unity, in their ability to bring a moment of peace and silence for the crying families.

They thanked us, they hugged us, and I felt Seven's first two rules in effect. I was a god, and it was good, helpful; and yet the pain of this world, the weight of death, it crushed me inside. These were more people to add to the list of those who now lived on in our mission, if we could succeed.

"I get it," I said to Seven, watching the last of the wrecked bodies being carried up from the docks. "This matters. We matter to these people."

"It's new to you," said Seven. "Do a few thousand death rites, and the effect wears off."

"Fair enough. But it makes me feel like our mission is

even more important, like I'd do whatever it takes to stop Paul."

Seven was silent, gazing at the sea, arms wrapped around herself. "It makes me want to swim."

"What?"

Seven's eyes snapped up, goddess mask back on. "Victoria said we're not going to the skull, which means we have the day free. And I for one would like to spend the rest of it not thinking about anything like this."

"Okay," I said, but then added, "we should get the others, though."

Seven rolled her eyes. "Pout. Sure, let's round up the gang."

20

WE HEADED OVER TO THE INFIRMARY. "I'LL GET Leech," said Seven. "You can get your Lilly."

We split up in the hall. I reached Lilly's door and paused. There were voices coming from inside.

"We spent last weekend out at Banff." This was a man's voice. "There are still silt flats, up where the Columbia icefield used to be. You kind of sink in the muck. Those glacial minerals are good for your mother's joints."

A woman: "After a few hours in there, I almost have full movement."

Now a hissing silence, like of a video playing.

I peered in the door. Brilliant hazy sun streamed through a long window. Lilly was sitting up. She was in her same tank top and shorts we'd arrived in, though it looked like they'd been cleaned. There was a band of clear material around her neck. It held white pads over her gills.

She had the subnet pad. There was a tiny silver drive sticking out of the side.

"It's expensive though, getting over there," said the man's voice. "I'm not sure how many more trips we'll be able to make."

There was another quiet stretch.

"Hey," I said quietly.

Lilly looked up. Her face had been cleaned, her hair washed and brushed, but her eyes were freshly swollen and wet. "Hey," she said in a whisper.

I walked over to the side of the bed. "What are you doing?"

She pointed to the screen. There were two older adults, gray haired and wrinkly, gazing back out. The woman had almond-colored skin and soft features, so much like Lilly's. The man had Lilly's sky-blue eyes but with a lighter complexion and a squarish face.

"Walking's good, too, though," Lilly's mom said. "I can walk around the neighborhood. They're telling everyone to wear Rad protection all the time now. But I wonder what's the point in my case. . . ." She trailed off.

Dad's shoulder moved like he was rubbing her hand off camera.

Lilly held her breath, a fresh wave of sadness washing over her.

These must have been the vid chats that her parents had left her. "This is the first time you've watched them," I said, remembering what she'd told me back on Tiger Lilly Island.

Lilly nodded. "This one's from 2073, fifteen years after I was cryoed."

Lilly's parents were just staring slightly off center, like they didn't quite know where the camera was.

"They never know what to say," said Lilly. "They were never good at chats. I remember that from when I was kid." She laughed a little. "They look so old." Her hand reached out. Found mine. She pulled me slightly. "Sit."

I sat on the bed beside her. She shuffled over to make room.

"We, um," her dad began, "we finally got the box, from the People's Corporation. Just when we'd thought it would never arrive. . . ." He moved out of view.

"Oh, God . . ." Lilly whispered.

"There wasn't much," said her dad. Her mom was crying. "Some clothes, his watch, things like that. Oh, and there was this."

Her dad held up a photo. It showed a boy who looked to be about our age, tall and muscular, with his arm around a rail-thin girl with short black hair but Lilly's same giant eyes.

Lilly sobbed.

"Look at you two," said her mom, "so young and cute. We always wished he'd be with you, now, there in Eden, but . . ."

"He had his own mind," her father finished. He put away the photo.

They were quiet again, almost like they were waiting for Lilly to speak. The silence hissed from the speakers.

Lilly wiped at her nose.

"We hope when you get this," said her mom, "that you're happy and well. That life is good for you."

Lilly laughed darkly. "Yeah."

"We love you, Tiger Lilly," said her mom. "We love you so much."

"Okay . . ." said her dad. His eyes looked wet, too. "We'll chat more soon."

His hand reached out and flicked off the camera.

Lilly turned the computer pad facedown. "She'll be dead in a year. She's already halfway to dead, they just don't want to tell me."

"Plastics cancer," I said.

"Yeah. The next chat is just my dad. And it's so awful I couldn't even get through it. He'll be dead, too, in two more years." She sighed to herself. "It's not fair."

"I'm sorry," I said. "I'm sorry they're gone. There's too much death in this world."

"Thanks," said Lilly. "Leech told me your mom is here. How is that?"

"It's weird," I said. "I mean, it's good." I was glad to be able to tell her about this, except I felt bad about it, too. Out of all of us, I was the only one who had parents. "I'm lucky. But it's weird because she left, and so I don't know— I was kind of a jerk this morning."

I told her about the conversation. "It's weird to not only see her for the first time, after so long," I said, "but then to have her have this new boyfriend and be all into the Heliad thing. I don't know why."

"She's not like you remember," said Lilly.

"Actually she kinda is," I said. "She always liked a good show. And even as a kid I can remember her being kinda . . . flighty. Though I think that was her hiding her sadness or whatever she felt inside. But who knows? It was so long ago. I guess I blame her for leaving us. I think I've been mad at her for years. So, it's just coming out now."

"You guys can get through it," said Lilly. "It might just take a while." She looked back at the computer screen. "I never wanted to watch those. I always felt so guilty, like, why should I get to live when they died? Especially Anton. He was trying to make a difference when he drowned. And I got a free pass, a fantasy life inside Eden."

"Well, but that wasn't your fault," I said. "That's what they chose for you. And now you're out in the world making a difference." As it came out of my mouth, I realized something else, and felt like an idiot. "That's why you were mad at me back at the dry lake. You didn't just come along for me—you did it for you, for them."

Lilly nodded.

"Is that why you lied about the siren?" I asked.

"Yeah," she said. "I didn't really mean to. It was just that when I first met you, getting out was just as important as you. Something different was happening to you than to the rest of us, and I needed to know what."

"That makes it sound like you were using me."

Lilly rolled her eyes, but smiled. "No, I really liked you! It's just that . . . I've met guys before and it's been like 'wow' at first, but then gets disappointing the more I get to know them." I wondered if she meant Evan. "But it was different with you, and I so wish I could take that lie back."

"It's okay," I said. "It's really not a big deal. And out in the desert, I didn't mean to sound like it was all about me."

She half smiled. "You have to act like a typical guy *sometimes*."

"Yeah . . ." I smiled back, but suddenly it felt forced. Here we were, connecting like I'd been hoping we would, and yet now, a part of me was thinking about doing those death rites with Seven, how she'd held my arm, and how we were connected by the Atlantean visions. . . . I tried to push the thoughts of Seven away, to focus on Lilly. "I'm glad you're doing better," I said. "Last time I saw you, you were out of it, talking about hearing pretty music."

"It's been a strange couple of days," said Lilly. "I don't remember much after making the thermal balloon. Leech filled me in on what I missed. Sounds like it's been crazy." She looked at me seriously. "How are you holding up?"

"I'm okay." I felt a hum inside as our eyes met, and I felt like—no, forget Seven, this right here was what mattered. And I remembered those thoughts I'd had while we'd been flying through the night, and now they were rushing back, stampeding over the last twenty-four hours. Lilly. Sure, we didn't have a god-goddess connection, but maybe we had something more—

"I thought you'd stop by sooner than now."

The comment caught me off guard. My thoughts crashed to a halt. Lilly had looked away. "Oh . . ." I said. "Well, I was here last night, but you were asleep. I was gonna come by earlier this morning but Seven and I were—"

"Seven," said Lilly. "Ah."

"Well, yeah, we had to go to Tactical," I said. "There was this massacre, Nomads, and so we were doing death rites. It's a little ritual. It . . ." I hesitated, a little worried how what I was about to say would come across, but still said it: "It was actually pretty powerful. We mean a lot to these people . . . it's big."

"You mean you guys," said Lilly quietly. "The Three."

"I guess so, yeah."

"Leech said that she's a handful," said Lilly, "to put it mildly."

"I don't know about that," I replied. "She puts up a tough act, but I think there's more to her. She's had a hard life, just like the rest of us." I knew it sounded like I was defending Seven. Maybe I was.

Lilly's gaze was blank now, distant. "Sounds like you know her pretty well already."

"I feel like I do," I said. "I mean, that's one of the weird things. . . . We've had the same skull visions. I can relate to what she's been going through." I felt almost guilty saying it.

"That's some connection." This was the Lilly at a distance again, from the dry lake, from after my gills were gone.

"It's just—"

"Can I ask you something?"

"Sure."

Lilly's brow wrinkled. "Are you sure Seven's the Medium? Or is that part of the act, too?"

"Wow, whatever happened to a fair trial?"

Seven stood in the doorway.

"Oh, hey," I said, getting up off Lilly's bed but then wondering what signal that sent to Lilly, or what Seven thought of me being on the bed, and basically hating all this confusion.

Seven didn't seem fazed. "How you feeling there, Owen's Special Traveling Companion?" She stepped in. "Just kidding, no seriously, we haven't officially met. I'm Seven, daughter of the sun and third Atlantean. Owen's told me all about you: the hot chick from summer camp. How are you feeling, for real?"

Lilly gave Seven a look, not quite a glare but cold. "I know who you are."

Seven made a show of looking away awkwardly. "Okay then . . . Anyhoo, did flyboy tell you we're going swimming?"

Lilly raised an eyebrow at me. "Flyboy?"

"We're gonna go to the well," said Seven before I could reply. "It's really cool. Docs say it will be good for your gills, too. You'll heal up nice. No liberation required. Just kidding."

"Cute," said Lilly. She looked Seven up and down slowly. Then she looked at me. "I think I'll pass. I don't want to intrude on the bonding of the Three."

"Suit yourself," said Seven easily. "I'll be in Leech's room." She walked out.

"Come on," I said to Lilly. "You should come with us."

Lilly just sat there biting her lip. She closed her eyes and cocked her head toward the window, like something had distracted her.

"Hey . . . ," I said.

Her eyes opened. "Sorry." She looked at me strangely. "Did you . . . hear that just now?"

"Hear what?"

"Music," she said, staring into space.

"Um, I didn't hear anything except you saying you're not coming swimming."

Lilly shook her head, like she was returning from somewhere distant. "Yeah, no . . . I meant it—go have fun playing with the gods. I . . . I should rest and see about some things. Maybe I'll join you later." She gazed back out the window.

"What's going on with you?" I asked.

"Too soon to tell," she said.

I wondered what to say. This distance between us felt worse than ever. I tried, "Seven will be better once you get to know her."

Lilly laughed. "Owen, just go. I'm feeling tired."

"I—" I didn't believe her, hated hearing the excuses, and yet I knew Lilly well enough to know that there was no changing her mind. "Fine. See you later."

Lilly didn't respond. I left the room not knowing what to feel. One part frustrated, one part confused, and yet it seemed like this weirdness just kept building slowly between us, like layers of sediment, and there was no way to undo it.

"Trouble in paradise?" Seven asked as I walked into Leech's room.

"Where's Lilly?" Leech asked, emerging from the bathroom. His left eye was still bandaged, but his right was looking better. Still circles of black and red, but the swelling had gone down and you could actually see his eyeball. He was holding the sextant, and now placed it on the bedside table. It rattled as he put it down, a tremor running up his arm.

"She said she had stuff to do."

Leech frowned. "What did you do?"

"I didn't do anything, or . . . I don't even know! Just whatever. How's it going for you?"

"Better, worse, both," said Leech. "I can see now, at least a little. Getting out of here sounds good."

We headed back outside.

"Come on, boys," Seven said to the two guards standing by the doors, the ones who'd been shadowing us before.

We crossed the plaza. The midday heat was gaining

intensity, radiating back off the stones of the streets and walls.

Seven led us toward the outskirts of the city, through narrowing streets. The buildings became less frequent, patches of thick trees in between. I noticed that people were walking in both directions with towels, many in bathing suits. So much skin exposed in the daylight. And yet while there were many different skin tones and shades, along with discolorations and a few burns, nobody looked too bad. I wondered if that was because those who looked bad were already dead. Still, there was lots of laughing, smiles, relaxed expressions. People were at ease. Despite the sun and death . . . or maybe because of it. Either way, these were faces you rarely saw at Hub. Or even in Eden-West.

The air was muggy, cloth-like, even more than it had been the day before. We passed through a shadowy grove of tropical trees, their thick trunks knotted with vines, wide leaves bent this way and that. We reached a curve in the path, and found ourselves walking along the edge of a hole maybe thirty meters across, where the earth looked like it had sunk in on itself in a perfect circle, forming a deep hole. The soil and plants overhung the edges, thickening rings of large leaves, a kaleidoscope of triangles and shades of green. Beneath this rim, the hole was even bigger, partly covered by a lip of rock.

The hole dropped at least fifty meters. The rock sides

were colored in rings of brown and pale white, with small alcoves and smoothed outcroppings. Some areas of the walls were black with molds, some brilliant emerald with tufts of moss. At the bottom was a pool of water, a chocolate-and-blue color. The sun angled in and lit half the wall and half the water. Thin vines hung like wet brown hair down the length of the chasm from the trees and bushes at the top. Cool air floated up from the water, bringing with it a clean wet smell and the echoing voices of swimmers. Some had scaled the inner wall to various ledges. They dived in impossible arcs, disappearing into the water in bursts of bubbles, as if they'd pierced this reality and traveled into another.

"It's called a cenote," said Seven. "The Mayans used to toss people and babies into these things as offerings to the gods."

"Is that what everyone thinks the liberations are?" I asked. "Sacrifices to keep Chaac or whoever happy?"

"Nah," said Seven. "Everybody gets that cutting a heart out is not going to actually influence the weather or whatever. The Mayans were pretty crazy like that."

"Not crazy," said Leech. "I think just desperate, right? Nature messed with them all the time, and so they were doing what they felt like they had to do, to cope with what probably seemed like a brutal world that didn't care about them."

"Kinda like now," I said. Leech nodded in agreement.

"I try my best to just think happy thoughts about swimming," said Seven, "and not about the dead baby bones that might be at the bottom of this well."

She pointed to the waterfall. "Everything's real here except that. The Good Mother installed pipes. And she renamed it the Well of Terra. Where the earth provides, is what she was getting at. There's some whole thing about how if the water here ever dried up, it would signify that the Terra had left us and there would be eternal darkness and . . . yawn, yawn, yawn! Like I said, I just like the part about swimming."

We reached a staircase that tunneled down into the rock. People were coming and going. The steps were made with brown tiles and covered in a collage of wet footprints. We started down, the soft-seeming rock making a low and uneven arch over our heads, like someone had dug it out with a spoon. Occasional windows had been carved from the staircase tunnel to the cavern, to let in light.

The tunnel ended on a tiled platform built out from the side of the wall. Swimmers used three wide ladders made of thick wooden logs to climb in and out of the water. Others just jumped in, their splashes making big hollow thunks.

There was a group of older bathers in the corner who were being assisted by younger people, and they looked to be in pain, using the water to soothe the burning of their ruined skin, but they were quiet, and easy not to notice amid the laughter and children's shrieks scampering around the walls.

"So, shall we?" said Seven. She stepped to the edge, took off her hat, and started undoing her hair. Everyone else on the platform shuffled slightly, to give us space, the gods among them. Our bodyguards had taken up positions against the wall.

I moved to the edge and looked down. Shadows flicked beneath the surface, and I realized they were actually little fish. They reminded me of that idea I'd had in Eden, of finding an archipelago of clean water, with—but what good was that? Lilly wasn't here . . . again. I wondered if it might be time to start getting used to that.

"You coming, or what?" Seven asked. I looked over and was not prepared for the size, or, lack of size, of the bikini that she was wearing. She stood, hands on her hips, and the jade-green bathing suit looked more like tiny triangles stuck into place than an actual garment. The whole picture slammed into my brain and I reeled in my gaze as fast as I could.

"That's okay," said Seven. "You can look, as long as you come swimming!" She turned and made a show of raising her arms and arching her back as she stepped to the edge of the platform, clearly aware that she was the star of the show. I let my eyes follow her long, curving form, her extralong legs and her everything else as she proceeded to launch a graceful dive into the water.

A few people around us spontaneously burst into applause, as if anything Seven did was worthy of adoration.

"I hate your two working eyes," said Leech, taking off his shirt. He stepped to the ladder and carefully lowered himself in.

I pulled off my shirt, felt the tingle of sun cooking my shoulders and stepped up to the edge of the platform.

"Come on already, flyboy!" Seven was out in the center of the pool.

I thought about the sun, thought about my cramp, thought about Lilly . . . and I dove in anyway.

The water was a shocking glove of cold. I felt confused for a moment, had an urge to blow out my lungs and let my gills work, then remembered that would be bad. I pushed up to the surface and swam out to where Leech was treading water by some vines, thick cords that fell down into the water and then spread little starbursts of delicate tan hair beneath the surface.

"Where's Seven?" I asked.

"Somewhere under us," said Leech.

"How's your eye?"

"Fine. The bandages are solid. I think I'm going to try that. Live bright and all."

Leech paddled off toward the wall, where a group of kids a couple years younger than us were climbing up to dive off a high ledge. They shuffled their toes in an uneven groove in the limestone, grabbing little round hollows for handholds. The route led over a thick woven cord of gray roots that crawled down the wall. One of the boys slipped and fell off, crashing into the water to the chiding laughter of his mates.

I tilted and floated on my back, watching the white spray of the water falling down, and tracing the hanging roots all the way up to the green at the top of the well. Above that, a giant tree with smooth muscular limbs spread itself over most of the sky view. I wondered how long it took those roots to reach the water. And what made them know there was water down here? Why spend months or years on this impossibly long journey? Was it just faith? Or did something in its genes compel it to do so? Could the tree sense the water in a way that humans could never understand?

"Woo!" Leech was up on the rocky ledge. He put a hand over his bandaged eye and leaped off, crashing into the water. There was applause for his efforts, too.

I started to feel an ache in my side, my stupid cramp coming to life. I spied an outcropping of rock in the shadows along the edge of the wall and swam for it. I climbed out and sat. Leech joined me.

"This is cool," he said. "Not totally sure I want to fly out of here."

"Yeah," I said. I scanned the water and caught a blur, not unlike the shimmer of the siren, as Seven skimmed by down at the edge of the light. I felt a moment of longing, watching her, remembering the nights in Eden when water had briefly felt so free.

Seven shot up toward us and emerged, eyes on me, and for a moment her mouth was moving but making no sound, and I saw the red openings still fluttering, creaturelike. Then she blew out a little puff of air and breathed in deep.

"So, how come you guys don't have your gills anymore?" she asked. "It looks like you used to have them, flyboy."

"Mine came and went pretty fast," I said. "I think because I found my skull, so maybe yours will change soon. Just make sure you're not underwater when it happens."

"He's the only one that happened to," said Leech. "Mine took about two years to come and go. You said you haven't been near your skull very often."

"Just the one visit," said Seven. "The gills formed right after that."

"Maybe they'll change when we go tomorrow," said Leech.

"Yeah . . ." A shadow seemed to cross Seven's face. "They're fun, though . . . Plus, they really freak guys out when we're kissing and I do this . . ." She held her breath, puffed her cheeks, and made a little hitching motion. Her gills opened briefly, a flash of red.

"That would freak a guy out," I said, and was surprised to feel a little burst of jealousy toward these guys, whoever they were.

"Not you, though," said Seven. I found her eyes on me.

"You'd know exactly what they were."

"Well, yeah," I said, knowing there had to be a cooler response I could have found.

Seven pulled herself up out of the water and stood over the two of us. She shook her hair and sprayed us both. "Can you make room for little old me?" she said.

"We always make room for hot girls," said Leech, and again I wished I could be that quick.

We both scooted to the side and Seven sat between us, her hip bumping me. She leaned forward, gathering her hair and tying it up on her head.

"Cool tattoo," Leech said, looking at Seven's back.

"Why, thank you."

"Let me see," I said.

Seven turned, revealing a carved-looking Chaac with squarish eyes and beak. "I got it to hide my cryo scar," said Seven. "If you look close at the eyes and nose, you can see the white line."

"Oh yeah." I saw what she meant. There was a horizontal line of scar tissue, maybe ten centimeters long, between her shoulder blades. The black center line of each rectangular eye, and the top line of the square nose went right over it.

"Mine's like that," said Leech. He turned and pointed toward a similar faint line on his back.

Seven nodded to my midsection. "What's your scar from?"

"Oh," I said, looking down at the little line just above my shorts, "It's pretty lame. I had a hernia. Why do cryos have scars?"

"That's where they put in the tubes," said Leech, "to prep your organs and stuff."

"Ah." The lab beneath Eden flashed across my mind. "So why Chaac?"

"He's the meat collector," said Seven. "After a liberation, if a body's not needed for wall duty, we take the body out to sea and sink it, to return the energy to nature, so it becomes part of the cycle. The trash sharks love it. Mother wanted me to get a tattoo of Tona, since he's the one who takes the freed souls to the reed marshes of Tulana. That's supposed to be the sacred part, what the death rite helps accomplish, but I think we're all just meat, so Chaac's the one I want watching my back. A little rebellion from the goddess!"

"Is Tulana like Heaven?" Leech asked.

"Not really. It's not paradise. Souls go there to await reassignment. Like reincarnation. So it's more like a purgatory. Actually, a lot of artists make it look kinda like Cryoland."

"What's that?" I asked.

"Blank," said Leech, "a lot of white."

"And there's the dream," said Seven. She looked at Leech. "Do you remember your cryo dream?"

"Yeah," said Leech. "Strange."

"What's that?" I asked.

"When they cryo you," said Seven, "your brain freezes on kind of a single image or moment, like whatever you were dreaming about at the time you went under. And then, that's the only thing on your mind for the whole time. You're not actually thinking about it; it's more like an impression, like a burn.

"Mine was this day from the week before the plague outbreak," said Seven. "My whole family had gone to the beach. My two brothers and I played in the waves and the surf was high and Zane—that's my older brother—he was surfing and he wiped out pretty bad. He hit the reef rocks and got all messed up and we had to fish him out. I'm not sure why it's that image. Maybe because it was the last time we were together having fun, or because it was scary, or both. Who knows."

"Mine was strange, too," said Leech. He didn't elaborate.

"The weirdest thing though," said Seven, "is that I'm not even sure if that day at the beach actually happened, or if it's just a dream my mind made up. Everything back before Cryo is foggy, you know?"

"Yeah," said Leech.

"Dreams are weird," I said. "I've been having one lately that's totally freaky."

"Could be your brain trying to tell you something," said Seven. "I think our brains are kinda like this well." She pointed at the water with her chin. "There's the stuff on the surface where the light gets to, but then there's all the deeper stuff that we can't even see. I think dreams try to help us out sometimes by fishing up the things that have sunk too deep, that we've forgotten about, to show us, but they can't tell us what it all means, so it's like a collage, and we're supposed to figure it out."

"That's a cool thought," I said. I wondered about my own dream: Was the girl in the ash trying to tell me something? If my brain was collaging, what was it trying to get me to see?

"Whatever. Dream talk is dumb," said Leech. "I'm going back to the ledge." He slid into the water.

I sat there by Seven for a minute. She was quiet, knees to her chest, undoing and rebraiding her hair.

"What's up?" I asked her.

"Sorry," she said. She was staring at the water, its swells making her green irises ripple. "Talking about Cryo, about the past, just makes me sad."

"Because of your family?" I asked.

Seven shrugged. "There's nothing like being grabbed out of your time, out of your life, and plugged in forty years later to make you realize that you have no importance. That's one thing I think the Good Mother's got right. We're all just minute parts of nature. We're made to grow and spawn and die. We think we're the most important thing in the universe while we're alive, but really each of us is just a little spike on a heart monitor, one of a trillion beats, little fluttering bursts of energy, that's it." She waved her hand. "These are just the anthills and we're the ants and anybody who tells you otherwise is a liar." Her eyes stayed deep in the well. "Don't you ever feel that way?"

"Sometimes," I said, but I wasn't actually sure that I had. I could see what she was saying, and I'd considered it before—the idea that I was only one of billions of people who had lived and would live, and we were only one planet in a vast universe, but . . . I thought about this morning, about the death rites. "I don't know if that makes it pointless," I said. "I think there's still a point. I'm not sure exactly what it is, but I feel like there has to be one."

Seven shrugged. "Maybe for you. You have family. This is your time. It's where you're supposed to make your little blip on the monitor, the one that leads to the next blip and on and on. Not me, though."

"Come on," I said. "What about our Atlantean purpose?"

Seven laughed quietly. "Yeah, there's that. That *is* something, I guess."

"Something?" I said. "It's everything. I mean, think about it. You do have a purpose. Maybe *this* is actually your place, and you're supposed to make your blip on the monitor here. Maybe it's not an accident, and all the random things that seemed to lead to now are actually part of a design, a plan. . . ." These thoughts were kind of surprising me as I said them. But I felt like I really did believe it. "And like you said, it's better than the other options."

Seven finally reeled her gaze in from the depths and looked at me. "Listen to you, all inspirational. You sound almost . . . religious. Like being an Atlantean really is divine."

"I don't know about that," I said, "but I do know that I never felt like I mattered, or like anything I did would be important. But now . . . I'm feeling like maybe it will be. People believe in us, people are counting on you, me, and *that* guy." I cocked a thumb at Leech. "And now all we need to do is do it." I liked these thoughts. Maybe part of my job as the Aeronaut was to get everyone on board.

"I like it, flyboy," said Seven, and she sounded almost tired as she said it but she also smiled, and slipped her hand into mine. I wondered at the hand holding—another friend thing? But then I saw a tear slipping down her cheek. Her face didn't move as it happened, she just blinked.

"What's up?" I asked. I squeezed her hand.

"I was not expecting someone like you to come along," said Seven. "When I thought about Atlanteans arriving I pictured strapping mermen or something." She laughed.

"Thanks?" I said.

She looked at me. "That would have been a lot easier to deal with than this."

"Ha," I said, while thinking, *This? Like "us"?* I made a little show of flexing my completely unstrapping biceps, but then Seven's hand was pulling mine and when I looked up, she was leaning toward me, eyes growing, coming at my face. . . .

There was no time to move . . . or was there? But I didn't. And then she'd grabbed my face in both her hands. Her nose rubbed across my cheek and her lips pressed into mine. . . .

I pulled away, and it had only been a second and part of me wondered if that really counted as a kiss. Seven let me go, and smiled at me and I knew that, yes, it had counted, no matter how taken off guard I'd been. There had still been that second when I could have moved.

She smiled. "Sorry," she said.

"Oh, it's—" I stammered, "I mean, no, I—"

"Not for that," said Seven, her eyes narrowing. "For this."

She shoved me off the rock. My back slapped the water and then I was under. I heard a second splash and opened my eyes to see Seven knifing past me into the dark.

I hung there for a moment, suspended beneath the surface, kind of stunned, trying to wrap my brain around what had just happened, and how I felt about it: shocked, amazed . . . excited?

I kicked up to the surface, breaking back into air, and I held my face up to the sun. The heat of the bright, the chill of the water, and a swirling storm inside me, causing shivers and thoughts and no thoughts, too. I had a feeling like all of this was *a lot*, and confusing, and yet I also felt . . . alive.

My eyes adjusted to the bright from above and I saw heads peering down at us from an observation point at the top of the stairs. Had they seen the gods kiss? Did they approve?

There were faces of all ages up there, but I noticed one that was familiar—

Our gaze locked but then she turned and disappeared.

Lilly.

My insides sank, the stormy feelings all suddenly freezing, locking me up. How had it looked, from up there? Could she tell I'd been taken by surprise?

But had I? And it never would have happened if Lilly had been here. But she wasn't here. Hadn't wanted to be here, and someone had moved into that free space, created by the distance . . .

"Owen! You gotta try this!" I spied Leech up on the high ledge. He tossed himself off, plummeting into the water.

Seven was making her way up the ledges to the same spot. She looked down at me, smiling like nothing had happened. "Come on, flyboy!"

I could stay here, treading water and worrying about what Lilly had seen or what she was thinking, or I could go try to find her and explain or . . .

"Dude . . ." Leech was beside me. "Come on, have some fun."

"Yeah." I swam to the ledge and started climbing after Leech. I would find Lilly later, I decided. Right now, I just wanted to stay with my team.

I climbed, I jumped, at first clumsily, and then with more success. Eventually I even tried a dive. We applauded each other, and laughed, and there were no more deep conversations or surprise kisses, just careless hours as the afternoon passed, and I didn't think about what was ahead or behind us, or about Lilly or my mom or anything. I just had fun, being a god at play.

21

EVENTUALLY, WE LEFT THE WELL AND WANDERED THE market off the main plaza. Wherever we went, a bubble of awe and whispers formed around us, the Three, walking among the people. They saluted us, offered us things for free, our guards sometimes holding them back; and the more it happened, the more I felt at ease with it, like, yes, this was who we were.

Leech had no problem adjusting. He'd accepted a kiss from a really pretty girl in one of the market stalls, which caused the whole crowd to ooh and aah. Seven had entered the market in just her wrap dress, but by the time we'd emerged, she was adorned with silver earrings, a beaded hair band, hammered gold bracelets, all just given to her.

After, we hung out by the central fountain in the plaza. Seven told us about school, some of her friends, and I had a feeling like this was my team. I could picture us flying south together . . . and I'd thought about this for a few minutes before I realized that Lilly hadn't been part of my imaginings.

The sun was just beginning to descend, its rays still searing. "Ah." Leech had lain back on the stone wall of the fountain. "There's something to be said for this sun thing."

I still had my sweatshirt on and was burning up inside. Finally, I took it off and let the sun bathe my arms. It was a weird feeling, almost like I could feel the radiation seeping in through my T-shirt, through my skin, my Rad burns tingling, and yet it also felt like I was being lit up by energy, and the feeling was dangerous but also vital. "Live bright," I said.

Seven smiled. "He's a convert." She still had on her hat and long sleeves. She winked at me, but before I could come up with a reply there was a splashing of water and she flinched, arching her back.

"Oh!" Seven spun around. "Are you starting a splash fight that you are going to *lose*—"

But then we both saw that Leech had sat up and was clutching his one hand with the other. His arm was shaking violently. "Damn," he said, gritting his teeth and stomping his feet.

"What's wrong with you?" Seven asked.

"It's cryo sickness," I explained. "He was one of the first cryo subjects, before they'd really gotten the procedure perfected."

"It's fi-i-ne," said Leech. He'd wrapped his arms

around himself like he was cold. I hadn't heard his voice shake like that before. He drew in a deep, shuddering breath. "Fine."

"Man, Leecher," said Seven. "I'm sorry."

Leech nodded. "I'm gonna go back to the infirmary and lie down." He started to get up. "I'm supposed to get these bandages changed anyway." He slapped carelessly at his eye. It had to hurt, but he didn't seem to care.

"What about you, Owen?" Seven asked. "You gonna hang out with me tonight? My friends still want to meet the guy behind the legend."

"I—I should go home, probably," I said. "Have dinner with Mom. I left things kinda bad this morning." I felt like that was partly true but more like I'd had as much as I could handle for the day and needed some time to let things settle.

"Well, boo," said Seven. "That's no fun."

"Sorry," I said. I stood to go. "Will you be okay?" I asked Leech.

"Sure," he said, but I couldn't tell if he meant it or not.

I headed back to Mom and Emiliano's. On the way, I wondered where Lilly was, what she might be thinking. I felt the urge to go find her again, but also not to. Maybe letting a little time go by would be best. She could always find me.

Mom was on the back porch. She was sitting in a wicker chair, in the shade of a white umbrella, flipping through what looked like a little newspaper written in the local language.

"Hey," I said. "Didn't know if you'd be home."

"Oh hey," she said, smiling. "Yeah, I had a short shift at the clinic. I was hoping you'd come back. After this morning I was starting to worry that I wouldn't see you again until you left."

"Oh, nah," I said. "Sorry about that, I was just . . ." I tried to think of what to say. I didn't really know.

"It's okay, Owen, don't worry about it." She stood and motioned to the other chair beside hers. "Sit. I'll get you a drink."

"Sounds good."

I sat and put my feet up on the railing. The porch looked out on a series of alleys strung with clotheslines.

Mom came back with two frosty glasses of the lime drink. "Cheers," she said, holding hers out as she sat down. We clinked glasses.

"Listen," she said slowly, "I've been thinking about it. You have every right to be upset with me. I mean, furious, really. I haven't been a good mother to you. I haven't been a mother at all."

I shrugged at this. "I don't know." The tight feeling was returning, but I also had an urge to not end up shouting again. I found her looking at me. "I get how you like it here," I said, "and how you weren't happy. I know it wasn't my fault."

"It really wasn't," said Mom, "and, no, I wasn't happy and it's kind of you to say that, but I still made huge mistakes. You deserved so much more from me, Owen. All I can do now is hope that you'll give me another chance."

I wondered if I could. I felt like I still had a right to be mad, like I still was mad . . . and yet, maybe I could let that go. Or at least try. I wouldn't be here long, and who knew what would happen once I left. This might be the only time I got with her, and it seemed like a waste to spend it mad. "Okay," I said.

"Listen to you. You're a better person than I've ever been." Mom rubbed my shoulder. "You don't suppose . . ." she started. "Well, I have no right to ask this, but . . . You don't think you'd consider staying, do you?"

"You mean staying here?" I asked. "Like living in Desenna?"

"Maybe, yeah? I mean, it's better living than in Yellowstone. It might even be better for your father. His lungs would be better here." She flashed a look at me. "Not that he and I . . . but I mean, he could be here. You could live with him here, and I . . . I'd be near you. I'm sure Mother would allow it. You're a god, after all."

I felt my pulse picking up speed, knots forming inside. "You mean, when I'm back from the journey," I said.

"Sure," said Mom, "or even, I don't know . . . Owen, this journey you have to make, it's going to be dangerous, isn't it?"

"Yeah," I said.

"And you've nearly been killed just getting here. I know this is a typical mom thing to say, but I just hate the idea of letting you out of my sight after finally having you again. Isn't there some other way? Like, couldn't the Good Mother send a team after Atlantis and you could stay here and advise from Tactical or something?"

"I don't know," I said, and I felt like I was going to be torn apart inside by a storm of feelings—wanting to be with Mom but also feeling like, no, I was one of the Three, and what would Dad think of all this? And what about how Mom left us and how, as of two days ago, I hadn't seen her for more than half my life?

But at the same time I couldn't help thinking: Why couldn't Dad come here? It wasn't *that* crazy. And the air might be better for him. As a god, I could probably ask Victoria to give him a job. Would he want that? Would he do that for me? Mom wouldn't come back to Hub for me. But she'd been unhappy, and maybe that was just *life* and . . . Ugh! It was all impossible to figure out! But I couldn't deny that some part of me thought staying sounded good.

There were noises from in the kitchen. "Hello?" Emiliano.

Mom started to get up. She rubbed my head. "Thanks for talking, Owen. Thanks for being here. Thanks for even considering giving your mess of a mom a second chance."

"Sure," I said. I felt like I could no longer form sentences. Just mumbled words.

"I'll let you know when dinner's ready." She headed inside.

I sat on the porch for a while, watching the last rays of afternoon sun illuminate the hanging clothes, while the shadows deepened in the alleys. There were some kids playing with a ball down one alley. Tinny music echoing from another. Overhead, the sky was a liquid blue. Seagulls arced by. The easterly breeze carried salt and that faint tinge of oil.

I didn't know what to do. I didn't know how I *could* know what to do, about any of this.

I still wanted to be angry, to resist and resent, and yet, I couldn't deny the feeling that maybe, despite being one of the Three, being called home to protect the planet and all that big stuff, maybe I had just found my real home here. And if that was the case, what did I do with that feeling?

I had no idea.

I wanted to talk to Lilly, or maybe Seven, or even Leech, but instead, I followed another urge: I stayed and had dinner with Mom and Emiliano.

We talked about life in Desenna, I described life in Hub, and some of what had happened in Eden and since, leaving out the more dangerous parts.

Later, we laughed about Emiliano's crazy grandparents and about Mom's wacky cousin Paula, who I barely remembered but who'd been a professional cave diver, and they asked me if I had a girlfriend, and I said *I don't know,* and they asked me if I liked Seven, and I said *I don't know,* and instead of worrying about how complicated this all was, I just let the night be easy and fun. A night like a normal family somewhere, somewhen, might have had. Like I could maybe have again.

22

I FELT MYSELF WAKING, RISING THROUGH THE CHOC-
olate and blue water of the well, the eyeball of sky above,
emerging . . .

To find myself in a bed. I felt thick, hot fluid in my
lungs, burning my chest, drowning me. Not lake water. I
looked down to see my arms striped with black blood.

I was in a hospital again, a collage of Lilly's room and
the *Solara*.

An electric click. I looked down to see my abdomen
bubbling and stretching. Paul was there, his arm thrust into
my hernia scar. "Just need to make a few adjustments." His
eyes whirred and sparked.

He pulled out his arm, blood covering his blue-gloved
hand all the way up to the elbow of his white smock. He
was holding an organ. "We need to get this out of the way."

He passed the organ—it was dark red, a kidney?—to
my mom. She was standing beside him, also in a white
smock, her hair pulled back, and a clear plastic visor over

her face. She took the organ in both hands, smiled sweetly at me, and leaned over. "It going to be okay," she said. "We're almost done, and then you won't remember any of this." She reached out with her blood-spattered, blue-gloved hand. Her thumb touched my cheek and she made a gentle, clockwise motion, counting time. . . .

Yes, Mom, I thought, believing her. *I'll be okay. We're together now. Like you said.*

Something fluttered by the open door. The girl with the red hair. And somehow I left the hospital and was running after her. Through a hall, out into daylight and off the cliff.

I felt the sensation of flying again, and we were back in the ash below the caldera outlook. I bent over and dug desperately into the gray mush, like snow or quicksand. She seemed to be very deep, too deep, pinned in a chasm with black walls. I kept reaching for her hand, our fingers flicking off one another, hers this bony white but mine the gray translucent, the fingernails gone, crystalized skin like windows in their place. Everywhere my veins were swollen and black.

"Owen!" she screamed to me, and I kept reaching for her.

"Wait!" I shouted, but she was sinking deeper.

And there were other hands, digging at the side of the hole, which now seemed to be caving in, and I looked up and there was Seven. "Hey there, flyboy," she said, and her face was tattooed with the black veins, too; her lips puffy, cracked, black ooze dripping down her chin. Her eyes were ash gray and oil, the black consuming her.

She took my hands. Our hands together an indecipherable scribble of disease.

"We're kindred spirits," she said, "walking ghosts. You know it."

I tried to respond, but dream rules had suddenly changed and I couldn't make sound.

"Come on, we're gonna be late."

Shaking.

"Don't make me wake you up another way."

My eyes opened.

Seven kneeling beside me. She was leaning over, her face close, smiling. "Jeez, you sleep like the dead," she said, and then she smiled. "I could have done anything I wanted, and you probably wouldn't even have noticed. Well, you might have noticed *some* things."

"Hi." I smiled while also trying to make sure the covers were over me well enough.

Seven stood. She was wearing a white longsleeve shirt, brown pants rolled up to her calves, and hiking sandals. "The Mother sent me to get you. We're making for the temple. What were you dreaming about?"

I sat up. "I don't know. That weird stuff I was telling you about yesterday. I'm always back at Hub, and there's this girl, and then this time you were in it."

"Ooh, me . . . and another girl?" Seven smiled deviously. "You've got a naughty streak."

"It wasn't like that."

Seven laughed. "Let's pretend it was. I'll be outside." She left the room.

I dressed and headed out. Mom was in the living room.

"Hey," she said. "Good luck today. Let me know what happens, okay?" She blew me a kiss. I caught it, barely thinking, and pretended to stuff it in my shorts pocket.

"And be careful," she said.

"I will." Somewhere in the back of my head, I thought about how weird it was to have such a normal interaction with her, like that shouldn't be okay, and yet it felt fine. New, but fine.

Seven and I walked up the street. The day was hot, a bath of humidity, an alien feeling to me, the sky white with haze. I felt sweat breaking out all over me, my clothes sticking.

We grabbed fried masa in the plaza and then Seven turned toward the pyramid.

"I thought we were going to the temple?" I asked.

"Mom said to meet at Tactical, first," said Seven. "Something's going down."

"More Nomads?"

"Nope, something new."

There was a crowd inside Tactical. We found Leech not far inside. Everyone was watching a central screen showing the Northern News Network. It showed grainy, sun-bleached footage of a massive, rotting tangle of city: concrete buildings, many in ruin, sticking up from rippling layers of metal-roofed shanties. On a street in the foreground, people in ragged clothes ran back and forth, most with dark skin, many holding guns. Writing across the bottom identified the location as North Lagos Prefect, Coke-Sahel.

Gunshots rang out. The handheld camera flipped and darted, and now a trio of black helicopters swept across the skyline and hovered over a distant city block.

"This footage was shot this morning as what appear to be EdenCorp helicopters arrive over the slums of North Lagos."

Ropes dropped down from the copters, and then soldiers in gold visors.

"Details are scarce, but eyewitnesses say this Eden strike team kidnapped at least one if not more civilians before making its getaway."

"Bring up the other feed," Victoria instructed from the center of the room.

The screen flicked. This footage showed angry protestors marching up a narrow, mangled street lined with tin homes. Sewage canals full of brown water ran down either side of the street, crossed by thin wooden bridges. The peoples' faces were malnourished, skeletal, and yet behind them in the twilight, a giant Coke sign gleamed in proud neon.

They shouted in a myriad of languages, but all took care to point their fingers or weapons accusingly at the sky, jabbing at it as if to make sure the camera understood.

And I heard an English phrase among the chatter: "They will take him to the Ascending Stars!"

"The Ascending Stars!"

This video froze in place.

Victoria turned from her position, and all eyes naturally gravitated toward her.

"That's all the footage we've been able to capture so far. We know that at seven a.m. local time, this EdenCorp team executed a raid in Coke-Sahel. It has been confirmed that one male is missing. Approximately sixteen years old."

I remembered Paul's report to the board. Something about a lead in Coke-Sahel that they were looking into. . . . Was it another potential test subject? But why would they need any more, when the Three were right here?

Arlo spoke up from a nearby gamma link console. "We've heard more from the Nomads. ACF forces have been mobilizing, and there are reports of fighting over the Atlantic coast near the Philadelphia marshes. Air-to-air combat, maybe the ACF intercepting the Eden team."

"Well, at least that means the ACF might leave the Nomads alone for the moment," said Victoria.

"What was Eden after?" I wondered aloud.

"We're not sure," said Victoria, "but it sounds like Paul has his hands tied with this. Now's our chance, while he's busy fighting the ACF and quelling rumors, to get you safely off on your journey without him knowing."

"Do you want to move up the time line?" Arlo asked.

Victoria nodded. "Let's reschedule the departure for dawn after Nueva Luna."

"What's that?" I asked.

"It's our celebration of the new moon," said Victoria. "It would make the most sense to leave at dawn the next morning. The Three should depart with the sun at their backs, marking a new day, a new age." Victoria smiled. "That makes for the best theater, anyway."

"I'm not sure we should be basing it on your sense of theater, Mother," said Seven.

"It also gives us time to monitor Paul's actions," Victoria replied with an edge to her voice, "and to reprogram the drones to provide cover for you, lovely daughter."

"When's this Nueva Luna thing?" Leech asked quietly.

"Tomorrow night," said Seven.

"Okay, everyone," Victoria was saying, "I want as much detail as we can get about this Eden operation." She started across the room toward us. "Also, I want departure plans drawn up. And we need to get on with our trip to the temple. We'll meet out front in five minutes."

23

OUTSIDE, WE JOINED UP WITH ARLO AND VICTORIA
and four armed soldiers. Lilly was there, too.

"What's she doing here?" Seven asked. She didn't sound
like she really minded, but it made Lilly's eyes narrow. I
wondered if she'd turn that angry gaze at me, but she didn't
look at me at all.

"Lilly has been to the Atlantean temple at EdenWest,"
said Victoria. "I'd like every experienced pair of eyes along,
to make sure we've learned everything there is to learn in
there."

We crossed the plaza and proceeded through the city,
bystanders stopping to watch us pass.

I walked beside Seven. Lilly was a little way ahead with
Leech. I could tell they were talking, and I wondered what
about. Anything about yesterday? Or were they just chatting like friends. It almost seemed like they'd become closer
than we were at this point.

Seven was quiet. She had her gold sunglasses on.

"So," I said, "we're going to see your skull."

"Yep."

"What has it told you?" I asked.

"Well," said Seven, "I've only been down there one time, and it was brief. Mainly about that city in the ash, and about how there was this calamity, right? From the thing . . ."

"The Paintbrush of the Gods," I said.

"Right. That's about it so far. This time I figure I'll get the goods about how to actually be a Medium." She smiled. "I'd better, right? Before we ship off."

"All right," Victoria stopped the group. We'd reached a high gate with guard towers to either side. "I know we live bright here," she said, producing a metal container from her shoulder bag and twisting off the top, "but this particular group cannot afford to get the panresistant malaria, so please cover yourselves in this." She passed the jar around. Arlo circulated another.

"The mosquitoes are nasty out there," said Seven. I watched her rub the slick-looking orange goop onto her neck, face, and ankles. She passed it to me and I did the same. It smelled like citrus and burned rubber, strong enough to make my nose tingle.

"Okay," said Victoria. "Patrols have swept the area and we should be safe. Tactical has the drones on standby." She turned to the tower beside the gate. "We're ready."

There was a series of metallic clicks, and the heavy

metal door began to swing inward. Beyond it, a tire-track road led into thick jungle, all green leaves and blue-black shadows. I'd never seen so much tree life.

We stepped out beyond the threshold, and I caught a metallic smell and heard a buzzing din. There was a body hanging from the top of the door, the air around it thick with bugs. A multicolored bird was perched on its shoulder, pulling intently at a string of leathery flesh.

"I get that the bodies are warnings," I said to Seven, "but to who?"

"There are some tribes of people out in the jungle," said Seven, "some little settlements—and Mother would tell you that there's always the danger that some larger force might come after our food supplies—but I think they're mainly for the people inside. They make everybody feel safe, like it's a reminder of our power."

"Some of the followers believe it's an honor," said Victoria, overhearing us. "To have your flesh adorn a wall is to help keep your family safe after you're gone."

We walked in a close group. Unseen birds questioned and wondered in the trees, these beautiful looping notes with tiny chirps in between, like long queries and short answers. There was flapping in the wide leaves, shadows darting. A long-tailed bird, black with a jewel-blue belly, dropped down onto a broad leaf near me. It made me think of Eden, and I wondered if it had cameras in it, or mechanical wings, but then it left a splat of white droppings on the leaf and flew off.

Everybody was quiet. The air was stuffy, dense, daring us to speak. My sneakers were caked in the red soil. We began to climb a rise. The jeep track got steep, the ruts getting rocky. Blue sky appeared ahead, like we were about to reach a high point. We did. . . .

And there it was.

EdenSouth. Or what was left of it.

It sat on a wide flat expanse. The massive dome was streaked with soil red and burn black. Jungle crept up its sides, some vines reaching all the way to the top, where a giant hole gaped. The entire top of the dome, where the Eye would have been, was gone, and huge jagged fissures extended down one side.

"Impressive, isn't it?" said Victoria. I didn't know if she meant the size of the structure or the damage that she had apparently done to it. I remembered when I first saw EdenWest, how huge and fortresslike it had seemed. But EdenSouth was a ruin. It looked ancient, forgotten.

We followed the road down a long slope and onto the flats. The jungle was as thick as ever, but I began to notice geometric shapes in the shadows that glinted in the sun. Solar panels, like I'd seen in brilliant rings around Eden-West.

Victoria pointed to them. "We have to cut back the jungle almost weekly to keep them in operation. We only need about a third of the panels to power Desenna. Life is a lot simpler without a TruSky. Those things use tons of watts."

We came to the wall of the dome. The road ended at what had once been a heavy set of double doors, but they were blown apart, lying twisted and tangled in jungle to either side. A simple gate made of metal bars had been placed over this entrance. It was locked with enormous chains and thick padlocks.

Arlo unlocked them. The gates creaked open and we entered. As we were passing through, Victoria stopped by the wall. "I wanted to show you this," she said, calling us over.

We gathered as she pointed into the exposed cross section of the ten-meter-thick wall. "See here?" She pointed to a dark, solid-looking layer between what looked like some kind of foam insulation. "This inner layer is a lead composite."

"For keeping out solar radiation," said Leech.

"You would think. This has been on my mind since the news of the Eden raids on Cheyenne Depot. I always understood it to be for Rad protection, but after yesterday's news, I have begun to wonder if it has a different purpose. This is the same material that is often used in fallout shelters and nuclear laboratories in the Northern Federation."

"You think the uranium Eden stole is for weapons," I said.

"I do."

"But then what are they going to do . . ." said Seven, "nuke us?"

"Nuke everyone who's outside the domes and who wouldn't agree with their plan to set off the Paintbrush of the Gods."

"Yeah, but then what?" I asked.

"Then wait it out. The domes will fail under the sun's rays, but they are perfectly suited to survive a period of nuclear fallout, and the kind of cooling spike that the Paintbrush may cause. According to the geologic record, when the Atlanteans set off the Paintbrush, they caused catastrophic volcanic activity, followed by a miniature ice age. The domes would be the safest place to be for all of those scenarios. And when it was over, they would emerge as the lone rulers of the planet."

"But the domes use solar energy for power," said Leech.

"Actually," said Victoria, "they have significant battery backups and natural gas generators. If power were rationed enough, it could last years."

"That's . . ." I started to say, but then I met Leech's gaze. I looked to Lilly, but she wasn't even with the group. She was a few paces away, staring off into EdenSouth. "That's so very like Paul," I said. "I mean, it's crazy, but . . . he could do it."

"But what about the selectees?" asked Leech. "We heard that Eden has an exodus plan for leaving the domes. To go to EdenHome."

"I don't know," said Victoria, "EdenHome is a new development since I . . . resigned from their employment. Maybe it's a back up plan, in case they don't find the Paintbrush."

I wondered about that. Paul's report had made it sound like EdenHome was a definite part of the plan.

"So, if when we find the Paintbrush first, then what?" asked Leech. "Don't activate it? Destroy it? Isn't it still a chance for humanity to recover?"

"I don't know that answer either," said Victoria. "The teachings of Heliad-Seven would say that it would be wrong to set it off. It's humans that need to change, not the earth."

"Paul thinks we are the earth, or we're all nature," said Leech. "And so activating the Paintbrush is the 'natural' thing to do."

"Yes, Paul would say that," said Victoria. "Ultimately, all of this is older than my religion, and I am not one of the Three. The more I get to know you, the more I feel that you can be trusted to make that choice. It's why you were chosen." Then she glanced at Seven. "Well, I'm not sure I can trust you."

Seven glared at her. "Thanks."

We walked down a short tunnel and emerged into the dome. I expected something that looked like Camp Eden or the Preserve, but around us were the remains of the Eden-South city. The buildings were largely intact, a crumbled wall here and there. Most were in gray shadows, but some glinted in the hazy white beams of sun that shone through the hole in the dome ceiling.

The structures were made of greenish glass and sleek metal beams in trapezoidal shapes, but unlike the polished perfection of the EdenWest city, these were coated in a film of red dust and cloaked in green and black molds. Waterfalls of vines cascaded through the cracks in the ceiling and braided their way down buildings, fanning out across the streets, and climbing other buildings. Trees had sprouted on rooftops and in clefts and cracks. Some whole sides of buildings were furry with colonies of moss, which in turn were sprouting leafy plants and more vines.

There was a strange quality to the silence, a hollow echo of the dome that made it seem somehow claustrophobic, even though the place was enormous. Without any TruSky to obscure the ceiling with haze, the place looked even more astoundingly big but also somehow confining, its rusty girders and burned panels like a prison.

We walked up a main avenue picking our way through debris. Our feet crunched on cracked hexagonal panels of dark glass. "Is this a SensaStreet?" I asked Leech.

"Yeah. Each block used to talk to you as you walked, respond to your moods based on the force of your step, body temperature—stuff like that. I never quite got the hang of it." He spoke quietly with his head down.

"You okay?" I asked.

"Sure," he said, and then pointedly turned away.

Birds called, their wings fluttering in the cavernous space. I saw a long iguana sunning itself on a piece of debris at the side of the road. Doorways were cloaked with dark folds of spiderwebs. It was amazing how quickly the jungle had worked to reclaim this place. I thought of the towns on our flight from EdenWest, out in the desert, preserved like museums. This place, it seemed, would be gone in a few years, digested by nature.

After ten minutes we reached the lake. Like in Eden-West, there was a long body of water stretching toward the far side of the dome, only this one was greenish and choked with plant life. Far out in the water, a giant white shard of the ceiling stuck out at an angle. In its center were the broken remains of the Eye, a sphere half-submerged in the water. It had sprouted its own island of plants and trees on its top. Some kind of large bird was sitting on the very tip of the fallen piece. The Aquinara stood silent to our left.

We followed the edge of the lake. Ahead I saw a pyramid made of stone. It was like the one in Desenna but clearly older; and for a moment I thought it was Atlantean, like from my skull memories, but it wasn't quite the same. It was made of flat layers, like stacked blocks of decreasing size. It had a square top and staircases leading up the sides. There were other buildings around it, crumbled remains mostly consumed by jungle. The scene had a weird time-loop quality, with these ancient structures encased by a giant dome from far in their future.

"Victoria?" Leech called. He pointed down a city street. "Is that it?"

A few blocks in, there was a strangely shaped building, about ten stories high, with smooth, curved sides. Unlike every other building in the empty city, soft pale light glowed from its windows. I realized what the shape was. It was the outline of a double helix, the shape of DNA.

"The cryo facility," said Victoria. "Why?"

Now I knew why Leech had been quiet. "I think my brother is in there," he said.

"Really?" said Victoria, sounding surprised.

"I'm not totally sure," said Leech softly. "It's what Paul told me."

"It could be," said Victoria. "We have the records back at Tactical."

"And you said . . ." Leech spoke slowly. "They're still alive in there, right?"

Victoria put a hand on his shoulder. "They are, but . . ."

"I see lights on," said Leech.

Victoria sighed. "Yes, I left the power on to Cryo so I could keep our lovely Seven alive. I could have kept only her pod operating and shut off the rest, but . . . It's funny, during the violence of the revolt and the coup, I had to make many hard choices about people's lives. I've built a religion based on accepting death, but . . . I couldn't pull the plug on those people."

"Why not?" I asked.

"Everyone should have a choice," said Victoria. "It's

one thing to help volunteers free themselves from this world, but it's another to just unplug five hundred people who thought they were going to be woken up."

I thought back to the lab beneath Eden. I'd unplugged those kids . . . but Anna had asked me to. And the others, weren't they beyond choice? It had seemed like it, like I was doing the right thing, but where was that line? Had I played God, thinking I knew best?

"So why haven't you woken them up?" asked Lilly. For once, she sounded like her old self. "You woke up Seven."

"Don't sound so glad," Seven said sarcastically.

Lilly didn't look over.

"That's the problem," said Victoria. "About two years ago, we had a brutal hurricane. They're always bad here, but this one—we named it Atlacamani, Aztec goddess of storms. All of Desenna lost power, including Cryo. They were without power for over five hours, which drained the battery backups. It wasn't enough time to thaw the bodies, but it was long enough for the brains to lose their stimulative charge."

"Are you saying they're all brain-dead?" asked Leech.

"Yes, that's mostly what I'm saying."

"How can it be mostly?" he asked.

"Well," said Victoria, "I'm not sure how much you know about the cryo process. When a subject is put into Cryo, a complete brain wave simulation is created, like a map of exactly how that brain works. The idea is that this is a backup of all the thoughts and memories and how the person thinks. And it can be reloaded if there's a complication."

"Tell them the other thing you can do with those," said Seven.

Victoria shot a look at her. "What our lovely goddess is referring to is that, though it was strictly forbidden in the contracts that cryo subjects signed, some Eden technicians did learn how to perform selective manipulation of the brain wave maps."

"What does that mean?" I asked.

"It means they could change your memories, alter them to suit their needs," said Seven. "Mother *guarantees* she didn't do that to me, though."

"I certainly didn't," Victoria snapped. "That is a line I am not willing to cross. Identity is sacred. We're nothing without it. But others didn't feel that way."

"When did they cross the line?" Lilly asked.

"I don't really know the specifics," said Victoria. "But I do know that there were certain cases of Cryos who did not volunteer, people the project deemed to be vital but who would not agree to work with them. And yet those people awoke from Cryo with memories as if they had chosen it willingly, and as if their families were fine with the decisions."

"So you're saying our memories could be lies," said Leech darkly. "I might never even have wanted to be a Cryo . . ."

Victoria frowned. "I am saying that it is possible. But I have no idea if that was done in your cases. Then again, there's not much I would put past Paul."

"So," asked Leech, "what about reloading the brain wave maps?"

Victoria smiled sadly. "After Atlacamani, when we restored power and rebooted the system, we found that the security systems had reset. We have the brain wave maps in storage, but we are locked out of the programs that would allow us to reload them."

"You don't have a password?" Leech asked.

"There are multiple layers of security, and, no, I don't. Paul does, as do certain key members of the project programming teams, but—well, I can't very well ask them, can I? Arlo has had a team working on it, but it's been almost two years and we haven't been able to circumvent the encryption yet. So for now, the cryo facility is a room full of frozen bodies, only nobody's home."

"But you could tell me," said Leech, "if he's in there."

Victoria nodded. "Yes. We'll check the moment we get back, okay?"

"Thanks," said Leech.

Victoria continued on. "The temple is this way."

Leech kept staring at the distant building. He looked small, standing there, the same kid with sloping shoulders and scrawny arms who used to make me so angry. I stepped up beside him. "Hey," I said. "Sorry."

He had his arms across his chest, holding his biceps, and shaking, cryo sickness making him look like he was cold in this muggy air. "It's okay," he muttered. "He's in there, I think."

"I'm sure Paul didn't mess with your memories," I said, not knowing but thinking that Leech's story of meeting Paul had sounded true. How could you be sure, though? I couldn't imagine that, the idea of having your very memories, your very identity in doubt.

Leech shook his head. "Don't worry about me," he said. He turned and looked at me seriously, his good eye seeming to glare almost like he was mad, but I had finally learned that this was also his trusting face. "Will you come with me, when I go in there?"

"Oh," I said. I hadn't expected that question. Did this mean that we were, like, real friends now? But I knew my answer. "Yeah. Definitely."

He nodded and we started after the group.

We passed Lilly, who was standing at the lake's edge, staring out across the water. A breeze swirling down through the broken dome fanned her hair back off her shoulders. I heard a rustle, and saw that below a small wall, waves lapped against thick black plastic, the lake's false bottom revealed.

My first instinct was not to say anything. She seemed to be spacing out. In fact, it sounded like she was singing to herself. But I saw that the group was getting ahead of us.

"Hey," I said. "Are you coming—"

She turned and her eyes reeled in like she was returning from some distant daydream. But when she saw me, her gaze hardened. "You don't need to worry about me. You've got other things on your mind. And so do I." She started catching up.

"Lilly . . . Yesterday wasn't what it looked like," I tried.

She didn't stop. "That depends on what you think it looked like."

I felt a sinking inside, and also that distance again. Was it even possible to make amends at this point? Was it even worth it?

I walked a ways behind her, as we crossed a wide, flat stretch of overgrown grass and shrubs toward the pyramid. It seemed like it had once been a park. There were benches and statues buried in the overgrowth.

We reached the base of the giant structure, gathering beside one of the wide staircases that led to the summit. It was made of huge gray stones, all interlocking with precise seams. The side of the stairs was decorated with a giant serpent, ending at a carved stone head at the base, its tongue curling out to the ground.

Arlo stood in a recessed doorway cut into the wall beside the stairs. There was a modern-looking steel door there with a keypad lock, another behind-the-curtain Eden moment, only this door was splotched with rust.

"This was the central pyramid of Chichén Itzá, a late

classic Mayan city," said Victoria. "The Mayans were master astronomers. This pyramid is perfectly aligned to the equinoxes. It is over a thousand years old, but this is not the first pyramid to exist in this location. It is built on the ruins of a prior structure, and beneath that one lies even another: the original Atlantean temple that marked this spot, ten thousand years ago."

Victoria pointed across the field, to where two large walls made a kind of wide aisle. "The Maya used that structure for a ball game, but its original design was for a different purpose they never guessed at. Owen knows what it is."

I felt eyes turning to me. I didn't know what Victoria meant . . . but as I studied the ball court, I saw how the angle fit the probable wind currents, how the hoops for the ball would likely line up. . . . "It was a landing area. For Atlantean craft. Ships a lot bigger than mine."

Arlo typed in a code and there was a grinding sound as locks opened. He pushed the door inward on creaking hinges and led us in.

The passageway was cool and dank, narrow, with a flat concrete floor and a curved ceiling. It seemed like something Eden had dug. Arlo, Victoria, and the soldiers lit headlamps.

It led straight in toward the center of the pyramid, then intersected with another tunnel running perpendicular. This passage had stone walls like the exterior. A Mayan passage. We followed it, having to hunch over. The air was heavier, dense with mold and dust. We turned left, again and again, making a square spiral inward, until we arrived in a cramped room. It was barely wide enough for us all to stand shoulder to shoulder. Its ceiling stretched up into darkness as if we were at the bottom of a well. The walls were decorated with more looming faces, sinister and square.

"Step to the walls," said Victoria.

We all crowded back, and when the headlamps aimed at the floor, we saw that there was a round stone in the center with notches in its edges. Arlo and another man bent and began to lift, straining. The stone scraped, and they had to twist it back and forth. It was a half-meter thick, and when they finally removed it, it thudded so heavily that I felt the walls tremble.

"In we go," said Victoria. She sat down and scooted herself into the hole. Her headlamp illuminated a series of carved depressions in the rounded side, making a ladder. She descended out of sight.

We followed, me climbing down after Seven. I lost count of how many steps there were. Maybe we'd gone down ten meters, maybe more, when I reached out with my foot and found space.

"It's a short drop," I heard Victoria say.

I let my feet hang and let go. I fell for a second and landed on an uneven floor, sloping steeply downward. My ankle buckled and I started to fall, but Leech caught me.

"Thanks," I said.

"Sure."

I looked around and saw that we were standing on a kind of mound, made of crumbled rock. This mound was entombed in a large square room, like the basement of the Mayan pyramid. We were standing on the exterior of the older pyramid, as if we were climbing down through one of those nesting dolls that get smaller and smaller.

"The entrance is at the base," said Victoria.

The ceiling was just above our heads, huge stone blocks. I had no idea how they were suspended up there and suddenly I had this overwhelming sense of depth and even more so of weight, pressing down, massive weight that could crush us, *would* crush us. Even the air felt compressed. It was hard to pull in a full breath. There was dust in our eyes, a sour smell, and the sound of feet scuffling over loose stone as everyone skidded down the side of the ancient structure.

We reached a soft clay floor and edged along the Mayan wall facing the ancient structure, until Victoria's light shone on a squat, narrow entrance.

She peered inside. "A minute of hell," she said, "and there's a room on the other side." She took a deep breath and went in.

"God, I hate this part," muttered Seven, following Arlo and his men.

"After you," I said, motioning to Lilly.

She followed without replying, not even making eye

contact with me. I felt what had been guilt souring into frustration. How was I even going to talk to her if she wouldn't give me a chance?

The tunnel was tight, clutching at our heads and the backs of our necks. My shoulders scraped on the rough sides, and the feeling of tightness and compression became unbearable. I had this sudden urge to spread my arms, to kick at everything, to try to stand up and bash myself against this rock and make space. I would've taken the danger of being thousands of feet up in the air, any day, over this.

"Hey, keep moving," Leech snapped from behind me.

"Owen." Victoria's light shone from up ahead. "You're almost there."

I held my breath and scuttled forward and finally made it through into a small, circular room.

"Okay," Victoria whispered, almost like she was afraid even her voice could bring the earth down on us. "Time for Seven to do her thing."

I saw that there was a triangular space in the far wall, with a handprint.

The key is inside you. The siren's voice took me by surprise. I looked around, but there was no blue light. Weird. It had felt like her.

"And I hate this part even more," said Seven. She stepped to the pedestal, placed her hand on the spikes, scowled at Victoria, and pushed. Her breaths quickened, and then she hissed and snatched her hand away. In headlamp light we watched the trickles of blood slip down the spikes.

The room rumbled. Waterfalls of dust sprouted from the ceiling. The floor began to shift and turn, lowering and arranging itself into spiral stairs like the ones to my temple in EdenWest.

We followed them down. The pedestal was actually the top of a long spine, and the stairs spiraled around this, down into a wide-open space. As we descended, I felt that tremor starting up inside me, the magnetic hum of a presence. We were close to the skull. I hadn't been expecting this feeling, since it wasn't my skull, but it felt good. I hadn't realized how much I'd missed it.

We found ourselves in a cavernous hall, stretching in both directions. On one side was a long line of enormous stone columns, a wall behind them. The floor was covered with a thin layer of salt water. Drops plinked, the sound echoing.

Victoria led us down the hall, our footsteps splashing, and stopped at a section of wall between two columns. We gathered, and I saw that there were lines of carved symbols, pictograms and curly shapes that seemed to resemble letters.

"Whoa," said Lilly, staring at the wall wide-eyed.

"Is that writing?" I asked.

"Atlantean writing," said Victoria. "I can translate it with a few steps, but Seven can just read it. Would you please?"

"See the dog do tricks," said Seven. She stepped to the wall and ran her fingers over the symbols.

"'After the fracture and the flood,'" she read, "'the masters and their magic consumed by the ravenous earth, there was a journey through aeons of dark as the world healed, the refugees seeking their heart but lost, so lost. And when the seas calmed and the land quieted and the stars could bear to watch once more, the memory descended in ships of blue light, to begin the rise, hoping to reach the heights of the masters, without resurrecting their horrors.'"

I thought of what the siren had said to me. "What does it mean by the horrors?" I asked.

"I think the Atlantean refugees believed that the Paintbrush was a horror," said Victoria, "one that they never wanted to repeat. I have come to believe that the Three are actually a defense constructed by the Atlantean people in secret, to insure that their masters, or any future leaders, would never be able to repeat their mistakes."

I pictured the priests on that pyramid top, Lük and his partners preparing to die . . . for a cause. It was different to think of them like that, a secret band, going to desperate ends to save the future.

"Why not just destroy the Paintbrush?" Leech wondered.

"I don't think they could get to it," said Victoria. "The masters were like the king who dies clutching his treasure, or that Pre-Rise story of Gollum who can't give up the ring even as he falls to his end. Even with the world crumbling around them, they couldn't relinquish their technology. To do so would be unthinkable. It is not so different from during the Rise . . . and so the people had to come up with another way."

"So we're kind of like rebels," said Leech.

"I like it," said Seven.

"Is there more there?" Lilly was peering at the wall, almost like she was doubting Seven's translation.

"No," said Seven. "What, that wasn't enough?"

"Just wondering," asked Lilly. She bent down, looking at a series of dull etchings beneath the main writing.

"I don't think that's anything," said Seven doubtfully.

"Guess you don't," said Lilly. She shrugged and turned away.

"It was after deciphering this message," said Victoria, "and considering the roles of the Three and the masters, that I realized I needed to rebel, too, against Eden's plans. The horrors all over again. It couldn't be more clear that what Paul is doing will lead to tragedy. I felt, too, that there must be some better way to live in this world. And so Heliad was born."

She turned. "The navigation room is this way."

Everyone followed except Seven. She was still looking at the wall. "What's up?" I asked her.

"Your friend there is acting pretty weird." We both watched Lilly wandering away from the group, gazing around. "Any idea what her deal is?"

"No," I said, "less than ever."

We caught up, reaching an arched entryway at the far end of the wide hall. We stepped through it and found another navigation room, larger than what we'd seen in the Anasazi city, more like the one in EdenWest. A curved dome with an obsidian ball perched in the center.

"Finally," said Leech. He placed his hands on the ball. Light ignited from inside, and stars burst to life on the walls. Leech put the sextant to his good eye. "Swelling is down just enough." He turned slowly around, hovering on a spot, then lowering the sextant and sliding the jewel dials on it, then looking again. "This would have made the room in EdenWest make a lot more sense." He reached to his back pocket and pulled out his notebook. "Can I get a light?"

Leech sat down cross-legged on the floor and started sketching. Arlo shone his light over his shoulder. I saw Leech's hand shaking around his pen. "This is going to take a while," he said, "but I think I can do it."

"The rest of you," said Victoria, "let's go to the skull."

We walked back into the large hall. On the wall opposite the columns, Victoria's light uncovered a narrow entryway. As we squeezed through the tight back-and-forth passage, I could already see the brilliant white, the skull anticipating Seven's arrival.

We crowded into the tiny chamber and there it was, dead and yet so alive, tuned to our frequencies and glowing.

Looking at it, I had that same magnetic feeling of warmth and certainty that I'd had around my own skull.

"Okay," said Seven. "Here goes." She closed her eyes and placed her hands on the crystal. Light jumped around her fingers and then seemed to crawl up her arms, illuminating her. This must have been how I looked when it had happened to me. Her eyelids fluttered, and her body seemed to freeze in place. She had uploaded.

Come home, Rana.

The voice spoke in my head. I looked around, looking for the siren, but, no, this voice was different. It had come from the skull, from the brilliant light behind those hollow eyes.

That voice wouldn't be for me, and yet . . . I felt a strange urge, the magnet heating up. I stepped toward the skull.

"Owen?" asked Victoria.

I didn't answer. I couldn't be sure, but I placed my hands on the cool white stone.

The light leaped over me, too, and I dissolved into the white.

24

"HELLO."

There is no time inside the crystal skull. There is before, and there will be after, but within the crystal electric medium there is only a sense of now and that all things are and have been and will be. Qi-An. The harmony of nature and all the beings within it.

I am standing in a wide room. The floor is tiled with large polished stones. Fires burn in copper bowls hanging by chains from the high ceiling, casting warm light. To my left are other rooms and halls stretching as far as I can see. There are columns to my right, similar to the columns outside the skull chamber, only here they lead into the night. A warm breeze rushes in, curving around the columns, carrying the whisper of the sea.

A girl sits before me, kneeling on a pillow. She is in white, with flowing ebony hair. I have seen her before. In the first vision I had of the skull, where I saw the Three having their throats slit. I remember her sad eyes, terrified but resolved, just before her consciousness was transferred. She has features like Lük: ancient, but also like she could almost be a sister of mine, and yet a gulf of time yawns between us.

But she is not the only one here. There is another girl, sitting in the same position, on a pillow to her left. That girl is not looking at me. She is looking straight ahead, and now I see that Seven is standing beside me. Seven's eyes are closed, her hands clasped at her waist.

I look from one Atlantean girl to the other. They are identical. Except that the girl in front of Seven is silent and still. And the one in front of me is speaking.

"You are inside the skull," she says.

"What am I doing in here?" I ask. "Are you Rana?"

"Yes."

I look at her still twin. "Who's that?"

Rana glances around the chamber. "There is only you and me."

I turn and touch Seven's shoulder, saying, "hey," only my fingers go right through her. She stands unaffected, eyes still closed. Maybe we have each made our own connection to the skull, and in her mind, Rana is speaking to her as well. But still I wonder: Why is this happening to *me*? I'm not the Medium. When Leech was hooked up to my skull, Lük didn't speak to him. . . .

"This way." Rana stands. Her sandaled feet click on the stones. "You are the memory of the Qi-An, of the First People."

"Yes," I say.

"You are the Atlantean Medium," she says to me.

"No I'm not," I say, but she doesn't seem to listen. Just walks toward the columns. It is as if she is a program, and she is running for me even though she's really meant for Seven. Maybe she has mistaken me for Seven, but how is that possible? My skull was so precise.

Rana holds her hand out toward me. "You must hear the song of the Heart, so that you may sing to it. Come, I will show you."

I wonder if I should try to leave. But then I feel drawn to her, compelled to learn from her, so I take her hand. It feels like an exposed wire, hot and sizzling with electricity.

She leads me across the wide floor and between the thick columns.

We step into a cool, starry night, ten thousand years in the past. We are in a vast courtyard. I find that I am barefoot. The grass is supple between my toes. Tan stone buildings, ornately carved with figures and symbols, make a square around us. This is not Lük's city.

"Where are we?" I ask.

"This is Tulana, grand city to the south," says Rana. She moves like a breeze to the center of the courtyard, where there is a statue of a jaguar sitting atop a turtle.

"Is this where the Heart of the Terra is located?" I ask.

"No," says Rana. Moonlight falls on her shoulders. "This is before," she says, "before the masters tried to force the Terra to obey, before they unleashed the ash and fire."

"The horrors," I say.

"The Paintbrush of the Gods," says Rana, and I feel her ghost fingers flicking through my mind. "This is what you call it."

There is a peal of laughter, and now a group of children appear in the courtyard, running out to its center.

They form a circle, their hands making a chain around the oldest girl. Her skin is nearly ebony, her eyes lavender. While the younger kids spin around her, she becomes still, palms out, and something blue begins to glow in each. A pale turquoise, similar to the vortex engine, and yet also like the siren.

The girl begins to rise from the grass. Her toes point downward as she leaves the ground, lifting to ten meters, where she does a somersault to the cheers of her friends. Then she arcs her body into a dive and swoops down over the others. They squeal and duck. The girl spins, but then falters and tumbles to the grass. The others laugh and run to her. She laughs, too.

"Once, we heard the Terra's song, her whisper in every branch of our being," says Rana. "We were in balance, Qi-An, and the Terra allowed us to know the more intricate harmonies of the universe, the deeper spiritual frequencies of her soul."

"You could fly?" I asked. "Like, literally?"

"We could play with gravity and space same as you

might play with wind and water. It was informal, it was spiritual, personal. Games in a courtyard . . ."

Rana's tone darkened. "But the masters wanted more control. And with control come laws, and with laws come right and wrong, the concepts of *more* and *better*, and from there begins the journey to the horrors. Qi and An separate, fractured. Science and ambition split from magic and being. The masters went so far as to imprison the Terra in a crystal cage. But the Terra did not take kindly to this. And when they tried to use her full power to remake the earth, she revolted, and the horrors were unleashed."

Rana reaches down and rubs her palm on the turtle's head. The turtle and the jaguar gaze east, toward the sound of the sea.

"The turtle is the balance, the support, floating safely, so that the jaguar may leap. The jaguar will leap because the turtle cannot reach. Qi and An. The turtle is aware that it cannot leap. The jaguar is aware that it cannot float. This is balance. This is truth. Qi and An. One cannot be without the other. So you must be."

Rana turns and walks away. I am about to follow her when something catches my eye. A shadow. I turn, and I feel certain that I saw something, a dark shape back among the columns where we came from. Seven? The siren? But I watch for a few more seconds and don't see anything.

"This way." Rana is leaving through an archway. I hurry to catch up and we walk down a tree-lined path to the base of a pyramid. Rana starts up the steps. She seems to float. I follow. Each step is almost a meter high, and we rise quickly over the trees, over the other buildings, up into the moonlight and stars.

We reach the top of the pyramid, a flat plateau. There are no lights. Beyond is the sea. It rolls in the nighttime breeze, thunders on the cliffs below this temple. Rana faces it, the damp breeze ruffling her hair. I stand beside her.

"In order to speak to the Terra," she says, "you must sing your soul."

Rana opens her mouth and an ethereal note emerges; and it sounds too pure, as if it's not being made by her vocal cords, but instead by some energy inside. The note seems to engage with the breeze, to tangle with it and spiral off in all directions. It becomes everywhere. And there is a song to it, lilting and sad, and it nearly makes me cry, a feeling normally so foreign to me, as if it's being unlocked from somewhere deep inside me.

Then a second note begins to hum in my ears, a different tone, higher, in perfect harmony with Rana's.

And there is a light. Growing from a spark to a blue corona, somewhere below the horizon. The Terra is singing back.

Rana pauses. "In between the two notes you will hear her dialogue, and you will speak with her. It is not merely language. The Terra is *feeling*." She begins to sing again. The Terra responds. The horizon glows with blue fire.

I wonder if I should tell her that I don't hear any speaking right now. After all, I'm not the Medium—

Only you can free me.

Wait, I do hear that. Was that the Terra? Speaking to me? How could that be?

Rana pauses. "Do you hear the voice? Do you feel how to sing your soul?"

I think to say no.

Only you, Owen.

"Yes," I say, because though I don't understand why, I do hear the voice.

Rana smiles. My answer seems to satisfy her. She stops singing, and, as the horizon goes dark, she turns back to me and touches my sternum. "Good," she says.

White begins to flutter on the borders of my vision. The program is ending.

But there is another sound, a scraping of feet, somewhere nearby. I try to turn my head. There is a figure in the shadows down the pyramid steps . . . but white is overwhelming everything.

"Are you sure there's no one else here?" I ask.

Rana is fading. "There can only be us," she says.

Only you, says the Terra, and then I think that the voice is familiar, but I am still certain that something else lurks nearby, somewhere behind me . . .

Before I can turn, everything dissolves to white.

25

I FELT THE WORLD AGAINST MY SKIN AND OPENED
my eyes. I was back in the skull chamber. My hands were
still on the skull. I pulled them off, and noticed that everyone was looking at me.

"What just happened to you?" It was Seven. She was
peering at me through the glow of the skull, like I was
something alien.

"I, um, I was in there," I said, shaking away the cob-
webs of light. "I saw you. I guess because I have similar
genes, the skull did its thing for me. You know, about Rana
and the Terra and how you sing to it. You saw that, too,
right?"

"Yeah." Seven was still looking at me warily. "Of course
I saw it, but . . . I don't understand why you did. I thought
you already found your skull."

I shrugged. "I did." But then I remembered the voice of
the Terra. It said I was the only one. The same thing Paul
had said a few days ago . . . What was that all about? It

made me wonder if there was something different about me. Different even from Seven and Leech. Would that explain why I could see the siren when they couldn't?

"What did you say about singing?" Victoria asked me.

"The Medium," I said, then I looked at Seven. "You can tell them."

"No, go for it." She sounded kind of annoyed that I had heard the message, too.

"Well, that's how she talks to the Terra," I said to Victoria, "through this song. And the Terra sings back."

"What do you sing?" Victoria asked. I could hear that pure curiosity in her voice. I remembered when Paul had gotten that tone, too. "Is it words?"

"Not really . . ." I looked to Seven.

She looked up into her brow, like she was searching for how to explain it. "It's not really music like we think of it," she said. "I feel like it's just . . . in here, now. In my head. And I'll know what to do when we get close."

"Fascinating," said Victoria. "We'll bring the skull up. You'll need it on the journey." She motioned to two of the soldiers, who wrapped a sheet of foam around it and slipped it carefully into a padded bag. "Let's see what Leech found."

As we all started out, I looked around. "Where's Lilly?"

"She took off while you two were in the skull," said Victoria. "She was muttering to herself. Something about . . . well, I couldn't begin to understand emotions at your age but I suspect you know."

"Jealous," said Seven seriously, wrapping her arm around mine. "Sorry."

I found her half smiling but I didn't return it. "Whatever," I said, feeling exhausted from the time in the skull.

And yet I also felt revived. That connection had been electric. Energy coursed through me, like when I met Lük for the first time. "Do you feel that buzz?" I asked Seven.

"I do," said Seven. "What's it like for you?"

"Like humming," I said. "Like we're a note that's sounding in some kind of amazing chord."

Seven nodded, but didn't add anything.

We returned to the navigation room. Leech was busy sketching, stopping frequently to shake out his hand and flex his fingers.

"How's it going?" I asked.

"I've got it," he said. "At least . . . I think. I'm cross-referencing the star positions on this map with what we found in the sextant room. I'm close."

"We have some fairly current satellite imagery back at Tactical," said Victoria. "We can probably check your maps against those."

Leech got up. "Sounds good."

We stood there in the dark of the cave, and suddenly it became real what was going to happen next. "So then," I said to Leech, "that means we're ready to go."

"The Three, to depart and defend the Heart," said

Victoria. "A momentous event for my people. And an even bigger undertaking for you."

"Sure," I said, feeling a ripple of nerves. Leaving Desenna meant going back out into the wilds. I never would have believed, just a few days ago, that this place would feel like safe haven.

As we headed back to the spiral staircase, we passed Lilly standing in front of the inscription on the wall. She didn't move, just stood there humming, like she had been up at the lake. I thought to say something to her, but it just felt awkward, so I kept going.

"Hey," I heard Leech say to her. "You coming?"

"Yeah," said Lilly. "Just checking this out. It was better than watching the show back in there."

"Yikes," Seven said to me, "watch the claws."

As we made our way out of the temple, I found myself feeling more annoyed with Lilly than ever. Was it my fault that the skull had spoken to me? It was part of my destiny, Seven's, too, and I had to wonder: Could Lilly really understand what that was like, what any of this was like?

By the time we got out of EdenSouth and were on the jungle trail back to Desenna, it was midafternoon. Leech was walking up ahead with Arlo, pointing out various aspects of his sketches. Arlo seemed genuinely interested in the cartography. I could hear them talking about longitudes and latitudes. Lilly was near the front, between soldiers, and didn't seem to be talking to anyone.

"You know those kids who got their throats slit?" Seven asked me.

"You mean our Atlanteans?"

"Yeah. Do you think we, maybe, *were* those people? I mean, long ago. And now we're, like, reincarnated or something?"

"I don't know," I said, thinking. "In a way, yeah."

"Maybe that's why we feel a connection with each other." I found her looking at me. "Why it's so *easy* to be around you. Because we've known each other before. Because we died together, and now here we are again. Jeez, flyboy, do you think we might have been . . . you know . . . a thing, back then?"

"Ha," I said, and felt myself burning up at the thought. Seven was right, though. Everything did feel easy with her.

As we passed back through the gate. Leech found me. "I'm gonna get my bandages changed, then probably work on the maps a bit. You?"

"He's coming out to Chaac's Cove with me later," said Seven, eyeing me. "Aren't you? Last free night before the big mission. You can't say no again."

"Right." I glanced ahead at Lilly without even meaning to, maybe to see if she was looking or not. She wasn't.

"You can invite Lilly," said Seven, noticing, "but she'll probably say no."

"Probably," I said.

"You in?" Seven said to Leech. "I have cute friends."

Leech made his slopey grin. "They're fitting me for an eye patch tonight. Do your friends like pirates?"

"I think they could get into that," said Seven. She started backing up, gazing at me. "Say yes."

"Okay," I said. "I'm going to head home for dinner now, though."

"That will give me time to put on something sparkly. Eight o'clock, plaza fountain."

"See you then," I said.

Seven grinned. She looked genuinely happy. "It's a date."

26

AS I WALKED DOWN THE AVENUE TO THE APARTMENT, I realized that I'd been referring to Mom's place as home all day. The thought bothered me but also didn't.

Mom wasn't there when I got in. She'd left me a note that she and Emiliano would be at the clinic until dinner.

I sat out on the back deck, watching the clouds, reading the breezes. I thought about leaving. It would feel good to fly again. I thought about that view inside Seven's skull. That distant light on the horizon, the light of the Terra, and the sense of some end place that we had to go. It excited me to imagine heading toward that light. I had this sense that there would be something there, some big answer, to what I didn't even know.

Mom and Emiliano came home and we ate and mainly talked about their Nomad years. At first, hearing about it made me grumpy, but I told myself to relax, to just be here in this now, that the moment was all that mattered. Qi-An. We had a good time, eating and laughing, and I decided I could worry about sorting out my feelings for Mom once we were gone. For the rest of the time here, I would just let it be good.

"So it sounds like you have a date tonight," Mom said as we were cleaning up.

I realized that part of me having fun with them over dinner had been a way to avoid thinking or talking about tonight. "We're friends," I said. "Leech will be there." I knew how both those things sounded.

"That doesn't make it not a date," Emiliano added.

"I don't know," I said.

"I'd say have fun," said Mom. "Just go with it."

Just go with it. Someone had said that to me before, and the idea had been on my mind lately, like, when did you go with it, and when did you not? Then I remembered who said it. . . .

"I'm actually going to head out now," I said.

Outside the air was cool, the sun mercifully folded in the misty horizon. I had an hour before I was supposed to meet Seven, and so I skirted the side of the plaza to the infirmary.

"She's not here," a nurse informed me. "I think she went to the well. We told her she didn't need to go there anymore but she went anyway."

I headed back out of town, remembering another time when I'd gone looking for Lilly. That night, she'd been mad at Evan. Tonight, if she was mad at someone, it was probably me. Part of me wanted to just leave her to do her thing, to let the distance that had formed between us cement into place. But another part of me wanted to find her and at least invite her along tonight, even though she'd probably say no. Maybe I needed to try talking to her again about the kiss, too.

The twilight world was pierced by birds, making their looping spiral sounds, asking me, *Why?* Why everything. Especially when it came to Lilly and Seven. There were chirps and shrieks in reply, but I had none.

I reached the well and peered down into the deep shadows, the dark water. A last pair of older ladies were climbing out.

And there was Lilly, alone, floating on her back, wearing her teal bathing suit, her hair fanned out around her face. I asked my two guards, trailing behind me, to wait at the top. I walked quietly down the stairs and peered around the corner. She was out beyond the center, by the waterfall and the thickest clusters of vines. Her arms waved slowly, her feet sticking up, and her face, lashes and nose, lips . . . and I thought, my God, gods, Terra, everybody listening, she's so beautiful, and then I wondered, hadn't I already known that?

I felt a crush of memories riding on a wave of adrenaline: dawn, back in Eden, emerging from the water after being up all night together, feet swishing in the wet grass, Lilly smushing brownie in my mouth, exploring the shipwreck— How had we gotten so far from those moments? How was I standing here twenty meters from her and yet feeling a world away? Right then, more than anything, I wanted to rewind time, to figure out how the distance had started and avoid it somehow, fix the awkward moments, figure out if it had been me, and if it had, scream at myself to stop being an idiot. There didn't need to be distance—

"What are you doing here?" Lilly called.

But there was distance. Clear as her echoing voice.

"I came to see how you were doing," I said.

"I thought you had big plans tonight? Leech told me you guys are all going out."

"Yeah, we . . . You could—"

"If you want to talk to me, you're going to have to come out here. I need to stay in for a while longer." She didn't sound like she cared one way or another.

I thought about leaving. I hated how this felt. But I took off my shirt and climbed down the ladder. The water took frigid bites at my limbs. I dunked under, opening my eyes in the chocolate blue and spied a few of the tiny black fish blurring by. I lifted to the surface and started making my way out toward Lilly. I could feel my stupid cramp beginning to awaken, like a prodded spider about to knot up in its hole.

"How are you?" I asked as I reached her.

"Just listening to the music," she said, still gazing up, eyes reflecting the hazy sky.

"You keep saying that. Are you ever going to tell me what you mean?"

Her mouth paused half-open, but then she just said, "It's nothing."

When she didn't add anything further, I asked, "Are your gills getting better?" I noticed her bandages were gone.

"Much better," she said.

Another pause. I didn't know what to say next. Lilly kept staring up, her eyes flicking slightly back and forth, almost in a rhythm.

"What are you doing?" I asked.

"You have to float on your back to see. Look at the waterfall."

"Okay." I pushed my legs out and let the back of my head dip into the cool. Just below the rough oval entrance to the well, a small trickle of water slid in a smooth sheen over a patch of moss. Then it became a little spout falling free.

"I'm watching the drops," said Lilly. "You have to follow one at a time, and watch what happens halfway down."

I tried to pick out a single drop. It took a second to get the focus right and then I had them. Each would appear as a little silver speck, and travel down less like it was falling than like it was sliding on a string.

Then, there was this moment, in the middle of the descent, when it seemed like the drops slowed, and you could focus on their crystal shapes. Like time had slowed for them. And they would kind of float instead of fall, little round spheres in space, and then they would speed back up in time again, blurring; and it was impossible to tell which landed where with all the other plinks on the water's surface. "You mean how they kinda slow down along the way?" I asked.

I heard Lilly sigh. "Yeah," she said quietly. "That's the very coolest part."

I wondered why she sounded sad. But I probably knew. Because we saw the same detail. And I thought, *man,* because that was so Lilly. She would notice the time-warp drops. She would show me. We would see it together.

I picked out another drop. Followed it down. Watched it defy time and hover gracefully, before joining the infinite pool.

I turned to Lilly. "Look, I know you saw that kiss yesterday, but I—"

"Save it, O. I get it. I know how Seven is. It's not hard to see her sinking her claws in. And I get that you guys are connected by deeper things."

"Well, yeah," I said. "But also, I've been feeling all this distance between you and me and wondering—"

"I heard you the other night."

"What?" I said, but I knew, I knew completely and utterly what she meant the second she said it, like somewhere deep inside my guilt at having uttered that word in Lilly's room two nights ago had been coiled, ready to strike. "You mean," I said slowly, "when I told Seven I'd thought about you not coming along."

"Yeah," said Lilly. "And you know what? You're right."

"Wait, Lilly—"

"No, Owen, it makes sense. Besides just the basic fact that there's not enough room in the ship for four of us, or, side note, that I can't stand *her*, Seven's made it pretty clear how she feels about me. But the bottom line is you can't have someone along who's not part of the team and you can't keep having to save me. That's not the role I want to play."

"What are you saying?" I asked, hating hearing this, hating most of all that I'd already thought it.

"I'm saying that I'm not going with you," Lilly said quietly.

"But . . ." I felt like only now that I was actually considering this, did I realize how much I didn't want it. "You wanted to help. For your family, for the kids in Eden. That's why you came along."

"I'll find my own way."

"Lilly . . ." I felt a knot forming inside. "But I need y—"

"Stop." Lilly righted herself, and finally looked at me directly. Her eyes were huge and dazzling as ever, the fading light reflected in rims of tears. "I'm glad you came here tonight because I wanted to say thank you. You got me here alive, across deserts and mountains, when you should have left me behind. I never thanked you for that."

"Come on, you don't have to—"

"*Thank* you," said Lilly. "There. Now, look. You go have your night with your Atlanteans. And tomorrow, you'll get ready to go and then you'll fly off and you won't have to worry about me, and you'll get this done."

I wanted to argue with her. And yet, I knew there was no arguing with her. "Of course I'm going to think about you."

"Try not to."

"Why are you saying this? Why are you doing this?"

"Because it's best for the mission. For everyone, including me. I need some time to figure out my next move, anyway, and I don't want to do that in the shadow of the Three."

"Lilly, no . . ."

She leaned forward and kissed me softly. "In case there's not a chance to do that later. For luck. Now, go, and I'm serious—don't worry about me."

I didn't know what to say, and I hated that feeling like I'd known this was coming, in a way, ever since Gambler's Falls, when we'd first heard about Seven, maybe even since Lilly admitted that she'd lied about seeing the siren . . .

"Okay," I said, and I wondered again how something like we'd had could have faded.

But, no, this didn't totally make sense. I thought about the strange way she'd been acting lately, and a suspicion formed in my mind. "Is there anything you're not telling me?" Because there had to be something. Something that explained this.

Lilly nodded. "So much," she said, and she kind of hitched, a smile and a cry at once. "So much, Owen. I'll tell you later. After. When you come back, maybe."

"*If* we come back. Lilly, I don't want to do this without you."

Lilly nodded. "I know, but there's what we want and there's how things are. So, I want you to go. This is . . . this is me letting you go. It's what's best. It's what we both need."

"Can't I at least say good-bye to you when I leave, I—"

"That's the part I don't want!" Lilly's voice tightened with frustration. "I'm saying this now so that we can be past all that."

"But why?" I said uselessly.

"Because I don't know if I could survive it. And because we both need to get on with what we need to do. The fate of the world does not have time for our little heartache."

"It should," I said. "I . . ." My heart was pounding. Looking at her, I felt my breaths dashing in and out, my arteries vibrating and everything rushing out of control. This was it, then. How could this really be it? And how was I ever going to survive, knowing I'd somehow screwed this up?

Lilly lay back in the water. "Go, please."

"I . . ." I felt my cramp knotting tighter, almost like an alarm going off. Our time was up. "Okay, but maybe, like you said, when it's over . . ."

"Worry about it after you save the world," said Lilly.

I didn't know what to do. There, beneath the gentle splashing of the drops into the well, the hollow seashell echo around the walls, the darting swallow chirps, within the cool pressure of the water, and its lightly sugared taste . . .

I felt myself sinking like a stone inside, dropping into the depths as Lilly, now a few meters away, resumed her position floating, staring upward.

I wanted to do something. I wanted to say something. But . . .

"See ya," I said quietly, and I turned and swam away.

"See ya," she called after me. "And, Owen . . ." I turned around, feeling my heart jump with what she might say next, hoping it would undo what had just happened. "You can use my towel."

"Um, thanks." I climbed up the ladder, dried off, and grabbed my shirt. I took a last look back, to the girl floating in the water, Lilly, my Lilly . . .

And I did as she wanted. I left.

At the top of the well, I looked back down. The water was completely in shadow now, but I could still see the flicker of fish beneath the surface, a perfect place, like a fantasy I'd once had, a place for Lilly and me.

Only, I had just left that place, maybe forever. And I saw now that the water was empty. Lilly had left, too. As if she'd never been.

27

I WALKED BACK TO THE FOUNTAIN IN A DAZE. SEVEN and Leech were waiting. Leech's bandages had been replaced with a black eye patch, and Seven was . . . well, shimmering.

"Hey, flyboy," she said, with that tone like she knew exactly how good she looked. She wore a sheer, skintight dress that was a kind of midnight green, or possibly blue, yet it sparkled as if the fabric was woven with some kind of diamond thread or metal. There was a strap over her right shoulder, and then the neckline swooped down low and under her left arm, leaving that shoulder bare. The dress slid down over her hips to not very far down her legs. She wore high bronze boots that reached over her knees. Under her left arm there was a series of horizontal openings, like a very orderly creature had clawed her there. These stretched around from her spine to her stomach. Her hair was up, piled in some kind of vortex on her head. Her eyes and lips were painted in dark green, too, and all of her skin seemed to be dusted with a crystal powder that gave her an ethereal glow.

"I'm not really dressed for the part," I said, because I was just in my usual shorts, damp from swimming, and T-shirt.

"Nah," said Seven, "that's your look, plus you're a god. You can wear whatever you want."

"T-shirt god," I said. Seven raised an eyebrow at me . . . and then she laughed.

"I can't believe that joke just worked," said Leech.

"The patch looks good," I said to him.

"Yar," he replied.

Seven grabbed my arm. "Come on, boys. Time's slipping into the infinite."

We crossed the plaza. The sky was inked black, yet luminescent, with a general glow of the city in the humid air. There were smells of spicy food, the tang of crushed limes. Tables had been spread out across the cobblestones and people sat in amber light from torches and lamps, their conversation mingling with the clinking of glasses and plates. Behind them, entryways invited secret conversations. The din blended with the moisture, and you felt like you were in it, afloat.

"I was gonna ask Lilly to come," Leech said, walking on one side of me while Seven was on the other, "but I couldn't find her."

"I saw her. She's not coming tonight. And not when we leave, either."

"She's not?" Seven asked. She sounded genuinely surprised. "Ah, she'll come around. I'll talk to her."

"I don't think that's going to work," I said. I thought Seven would have been glad to not have Lilly along. Maybe she didn't really mean it.

"What did she say?" Leech asked.

"That she wasn't one of us. And she wanted to find her own way."

"That sounds like her," said Leech with a shrug.

"She hasn't said anything to you, has she," I asked, "about anything weird that's been going on with her?"

"I don't think so," said Leech. "She's asked me a lot of questions about what we're up to, and about"—Leech indicated Seven—"but she didn't really tell me anything else."

"Here we are," said Seven, stepping ahead of us.

We followed her through an area of tables to a low, rounded doorway. I saw eyes turning to us as we passed. This crowd was all quite a bit older than we were, old enough to be out at cafés among the bottles of wine and triangular glasses of neon-colored concoctions. There were dresses that matched Seven's in shine and sheerness, and men with sun-darkened faces and hair swept back, wearing open-collared shirts. Leathery smells of cologne mixed with floral essences. Compared to them, I felt too young, like, what were we doing here? Even Seven looked too young for this, but she didn't seem to feel it, or let on that she felt it.

Inside was dark. A trio of musicians made concussions of sound from the corner: a heavy hollow bass guitar, a small metal instrument with high-pitched, tinny strings, and some sort of electric console, making square, synthetic tones. The result was something both new and old, with the thump of wood and the buzz of electricity.

Seven led the way through a crowd and we reached a chipped wooden bar with a pink glass top.

"Hey, Stefan!" she called. The bartender turned around.

"Seven." He smiled.

She flashed her most disarming grin. "Is tonight the night?"

Stefan, who was at least ten years older than us, laughed to himself. "I'm sure you could handle it," he said, "but, no, this is not the night I get you a drink. The Good Mother would cut my throat." As he said this, he leaned over the bar and his hands slid out to meet Seven's. Their fingers intertwined for just a moment, and I saw something was passing between their hands. A little parcel. Seven slipped it into one of the claw slits in the side of her dress.

She shrugged. "You are not wrong about the Overprotective Mother. Have you seen my people?"

"Not yet," said Stefan. "Have a good night, and be safe."

"Not a chance," said Seven. She turned to me. "You won't make me be safe, will you?"

I tried to smile like I was carefree, easy. "We'll see."

"He won't," said Leech, punching my arm. "Will he? Now where are these friends of yours?" He scanned the crowd.

"I thought you had a girlfriend," I said to him.

"Paige?" Leech asked. "That was another life. You know where we are now? Here."

"There they are!" said Seven.

Three people our age arrived: a guy and two girls. Seven introduced us to Kellen: brown-skinned with solid muscles and a kind of goofy grin, his hair spiked and green. He had spiraling tattoos down his bare arms. Marina was beside him. She had shiny red hair and wore a black strappy dress.

"And this is Oro," Seven said, specifically to Leech. "And this is the Atlantean L—"

"Carey," said Leech, gazing at Oro. "How's it going?"

"Hey." Oro had dark features and a coating of shimmer similar to Seven. Her night-black hair was gathered in multiple ties and twisted like a serpent around in front of her neck and over her shoulder.

"What's up?" said Kellen. We shook hands and then Oro leaned in and gave me a hug. Her cheek hit mine like I was supposed to kiss it and I managed to pull it off.

"So, Chaac's Cove," said Seven.

"Are we shining?" Kellen asked.

Seven nodded. She tapped the side of her dress. "Got a fresh batch."

"Nice," said Marina.

Seven turned to me. "Let's do it."

I smiled back, but inside I couldn't help worrying how far in over my head I was about to get.

We left the club, crossed the plaza, then headed down side streets, our guards trailing behind us. Leech and Oro were talking, and he'd already made her laugh twice. Seven chatted with Kellen and Marina about friends and school. They all went to what sounded like a small academy, maybe for the kids of important people.

The air began to smell of salt. We turned down a narrow street, where alcoves to either side led to quieter, more anonymous looking cafés and bars, the kind of places where adults kept shadows as company.

Up ahead there were spinning white lights and the deep thump of drums. Bundles of torches framed a guarded entryway. A sign stretched overhead reading CHAAC'S COVE. There was a line of teens waiting to get in, but Seven marched us up to the front, where we were given wristbands and ushered through.

The sand-covered path was lined with flickering torches and twisted through thick trees. We emerged on a rocky bluff. The main pyramid was just up the coastline. A staircase made of logs zigzagged down the craggy black cliff to a half-moon of white beach tucked among rock overhangs. There were three bonfires raging, a band playing on a small stage at the far end, and teens everywhere, dancing to the band, around the fires sitting in clusters, and swimming in the white-capped waves, their bobbing heads looking disembodied.

"This is the only clean water in the whole area," said Seven as we descended the steps. "Just a lucky break that a current wells up here and keeps the sludge line offshore. You'll swim with me, right?"

"Yeah," I said, feeling the vortex pull of her eyes again.

We reached the beach, submerging in the wash of the music and the wild dancing of firelight. Kellen and Marina headed immediately to a table of drinks. They came back with six cups, passing them around. I started to sip mine, a sweet, fruity punch with lime and papaya, when I noticed that the others weren't drinking.

Seven fiddled into her dress, and produced the small square package. She flicked it open and dumped green pills into her palm.

"Time to take your vitamins!" she called over the pulsing music. She popped one in her mouth and slugged it down with her punch.

Leech was beside me. "You sure I won't end up with someone cutting my heart out if I take this?" He was smiling as he said it.

"Relax," said Seven. "We're gods! We're immortal! Besides, this is a small dose, not even close to what we use for liberation."

"Right," said Leech. I thought he sounded a little

nervous. He caught me looking at him. "Yeah . . ." he said like he was reading my thoughts, "but you know where we'll be in two days?"

"You mean on the journey?" I asked.

"Exactly," he said, "Me neither." He took the pill and washed it down. "Live bright!"

One pill remained in Seven's hand, and her eyes were on me. I had a feeling of ropes pulling tighter inside me.

"You don't really have to," said Seven.

I nodded. "Right."

"Here." Seven held my pill up to her mouth and bit down on it. There was a crunch. She held half the pill out to me and swallowed the rest. "You'll barely feel it, except in a good way."

Everyone's eyes were on me. "Sure." I took the pill and tossed it in my mouth and washed it down.

"To the sacrificial ledges!" Kellen called, and he and Marina broke into a run away from us. I saw a line of people navigating a treacherous climb up the jagged rocks to an outcropping where they were flinging themselves off into the sea.

Seven took my arm. "Shall we?"

"Yeah." Her eyes were already flickering, slightly similar to what I'd seen in the eyes of Aralene, the sacrificial girl.

We started toward the cliffs, trudging in the sand and after a few steps I felt it. My sense of where the world was around me had shifted. The ground seemed farther away, and like I wasn't completely connected to it. When I looked around, the fringes of my vision blurred like billowing curtains. I felt like I was more floating than walking.

We reached the base of the cliff and Seven started peeling off her dress, firelight flickering off it. Beneath it she had on black skintight shorts and a straplike top. "Am I ready for action?" She struck a pose, fists on her hips.

"Definitely," I replied.

Oro and Marina were wearing similar things beneath their dresses. Kellen had stripped off his shirt and shoes, down to just shorts. Leech did the same, and so did I.

We climbed up the black rock, its surface pocked with little scooped-out holes and ridged with sharp spines. Other kids were climbing up behind and ahead of us.

We reached the small ledge at the top. Kellen and Marina jumped almost immediately, Kellen pinwheeling his arms, Marina pulling off a graceful dive. They both disappeared into the abyss below, a swirl of black water and white foam. Oro jumped, followed by Leech. I watched as their heads popped up and they joined the others swimming around the rocks toward shore.

"Okay," said Seven. "Ooh, you look worried."

I gazed down at the turbulent sea. "I get these cramps," I said, hating to admit it. "I drowned back at camp in less serious water than this."

"But you never swam with a shark like me," said Seven.

Lilly's eyes were sharklike when we swam together, when we kissed. "No," I said. "Good point."

"So don't worry. You're a god of the air, not the water. Let me take care of getting you to shore."

I still felt like I wanted to say no but I also felt like my thoughts were slippery, like the channels in my brain had been greased by Shine. "Okay," I said.

"Come on, we'll jump together," said Seven.

Tandem. "Okay."

She took my hand. I stared down into the dark sea, so much more wild than the lake.

"On three! One!" Seven's eyes danced in the bonfire light. I was starting to see faint trails of light around movements. Sound seemed more distant, like I was in a wide room inside my head. I found a fleeting thought there. *Bye, Lilly . . .*

"Two!"

Seven tugged and we leaped from the spiny lava cliff. We fell, speeding up, arms wheeling and I thought we were falling too far, the jump had been too high—

We slammed into the water. I pitched forward and water barreled up my nose, forced open my mouth, crushed against my chest; and there was foam, and salt, stinging, no sense of up and down in the dark with the waves rocking me around, the Shine making everything looser. I flailed, sure I'd be dashed on the rocks, bloodied and crushed.

Then Seven's hand found my arm and she pulled me

along, and I righted myself and kicked and we burst up through the surface.

Seven's gills tucked away. "Woo! Nice!" Her face was joyous, an expression that, Shine or not, seemed so free, a pure version of her, no mask and no weight of her past or future. Just *now*.

I liked seeing that, and wanted to feel that way too. Like Leech had said, this was where we were, here and now. "That was great!" I shouted. We swam toward shore, and were gathered up by a swelling wave that tossed us to the beach. We tumbled forward and my feet hit sandy bottom and I lurched to my feet in waist-high water.

The bonfires seemed to have grown taller. Their flames like waving hands, the tips inexplicably green, leaving echoes in my vision. Above, the stars spun.

I saw Leech and Oro joking and laughing with each other. They climbed out of the surf and headed back over toward the cliff again. I looked around but didn't see Seven.

Something slipped past my legs, and hands yanked me down. I dunked under and crashed against the sand. Ocean and light blurred and I lost track of my senses again. Seven slipped over me and our legs and arms intertwined, and then she grabbed my wrist and we staggered to shore.

"Gotcha," she said, jumping up and smiling wickedly.

"No fair," I said, getting to my feet.

"Oh yeah? Let's make it fair." Her hand flashed out of

the water and a fistful of wet sand strafed my chest, stinging on impact.

"Ow!" I shouted, but I smiled. She giggled and started
bounding out of the surf.

I ran after her, tripping over the breakwater, the world
swimming around me.

She raced up the sand, between two of the bonfires and
into a wide gap between two tall spears of rock. I sprinted
after her into a narrow sand alley shrouded in dark shadows.

The music became just a muted thump of bass. The rush
of the waves echoed back at me from the rocks, along with
the sound of my own breath. Firelight danced on the cliff
above, casting the shadows of the other kids like a primeval
tribe.

The path rounded a corner and came to an end. I looked
around the small space, struggling now to keep my balance, the ground feeling not quite connected to my feet, my
vision getting foggy. I spun around, where was—

"Gotcha." Seven. Right there and she slammed into
me and her hands found my shoulders and she pushed me
backward against the spiny stone. My back cried out in
pain but then her soaked body was against me, pressing,
and her lips crashed into mine.

They were desperate, grasping, her tongue darting and
licking the edges of my mouth, my chin. She was wearing some kind of papaya-flavored lip balm, sweet, tangy. I
kissed back, feeling too slow, thinking that I didn't know

how to do this, I wasn't ready for this. It was so different from the careful kiss with Lilly. This was some kind of chaos, like the goal was to get a lethal hold on each other, and it was overwhelming and yet it was so intense, creating an overpowering wave of craving inside me. My hands landed on her shoulders and ran slowly down her long, dripping back.

"Mmm." She ran her hands over my torso, then grabbed her black top. Moving . . . Oh no . . . She pulled it over her head, off completely, and tossed it aside and then she threw herself back against me.

I couldn't breathe. It was all sensation and movement and I wished I hadn't taken Shine, wanted to feel everything more acutely. *You have to remember every millisecond of this*, I thought, and yet it also felt like too much already. My insides were a tornado.

Our skin made a warm, wet seal, our hearts leaping toward one another, darting and jabbing. I let my hands slide to her waist, around to her stomach, then slowly up to her neck again.

She grabbed my wrists. Her eyes got enormous, swimming with phosphorescent edges. The firelight danced eagerly on the rocks behind her. "I want you."

I gazed back at her unable to find words. So I just started kissing her again. Meanwhile, her hands dropped to my waist, started undoing the button on my shorts. . . .

And some part of me felt like I'd known this was coming

and yet I hadn't really ever considered it. And as her hands moved, I couldn't help thinking, *Wait! Too fast!* Wasn't there supposed to be more lead up to all this? Even though I knew her, I also barely knew her. And parts of me felt more than ready, and were screaming at the rest of me like *what is wrong with you? Stop thinking!*

But . . . I paused. Pulled back from our kiss.

Seven looked up at me. "What's wrong?" she asked, breathless, her fingers still moving. I looked into her eyes, her pupils darting, like flies trapped against windows, and I felt my own head still swimming, like my skull was a pool and my brain was doing somersaults. And, oh no, *oh no!* I felt things falling away inside because I suddenly knew, despite how right this felt . . .

That Seven wasn't . . .

Lilly.

No! The ready part of me screamed. *Who cares about Lilly? She's gone. She's the past and you weren't even a god then, and you and Seven are connected by ancient power! You've known it from the moment you saw her and she is RIGHT HERE—*

But I needed more time. Because Lilly was still in my head, too. And the feelings I'd had for her . . . they weren't far enough away yet.

I felt myself starting to move, and as the movement began, I felt a bunch of things at once: frustration, disappointment, all of my nerves and adrenaline and desires whipping into a final vortex . . . but also something like relief. My hands fell over Seven's. And moved them away.

"I gotta slow down," I said, breathless. "We should slow down."

Even as I said it, I was trying to tell myself that this would just be a pause, just until another time, until I had some perspective and we'd hung out more . . . or maybe just until the Shine wore off.

"Don't slow down," Seven was saying. Her hands fought against mine, reaching for me again. "Just keep going, Owen. Slowing down is death. Just be here now, go with this moment . . ." She pushed harder, almost clawing at me, her breaths fast, and I saw this contorted look on her face, like she'd become some kind of desperate creature. It was more than I could handle. I didn't know, I couldn't be sure—

Except of one thing. I couldn't just go with it. I'd lost the moment, and I hated that I felt that way, but it was like I'd been tossed ashore from wherever we'd just been.

And a little voice in my mind, whose shouts had been distant, was now echoing and booming, a voice that kept repeating: *Lilly*. I wanted to shout back. *What good does this do?* Lilly was gone, she . . . but it didn't matter. The voice, my heart, whatever it was, just kept on shouting.

"Let's just hold on for a sec," I said, pushing her gently.

"No, Owen, don't—"

"Seven, let's—"

"Let's *what*?" She jerked away, glaring at me. "Wait until we're dead? Take it slow and die? You can't live in this world like you're going to have another chance at anything!"

"No, I know, I just—"

"No, you don't! You don't know!" Seven yanked her hands free, glaring at me. "Come on!" she shouted and slammed me in the chest.

"What's with you?" I shouted back, knocking her hands aside. "Can't we just take it slower?"

"NO!" she shouted, and it was so lethal and so wounded. Tears had started to fall from her loose-spinning eyes. Was I really being some kind of big jerk without realizing it? "You really don't get it," she mumbled, "do you?" She spun and stumbled away. Then she dropped to the sand, head in her hands. "No, you don't."

I stood there frozen, leaning against the rocks. I watched her cry and thought of Lilly and wondered if it was possible for me to screw things up any more.

Finally, I moved. I knelt and picked up her top and held it out to her. "Here," I said.

She looked up, fierce, and hissed, "Am I even real to you?"

"What's that supposed to mean?"

She looked at her hands. "What am I, even? What the hell is all this?"

"Of course you're real . . ."

"You don't know," she said. "If you really knew . . ."

"I know you," I said, wondering if I did.

"Don't just say stuff to say it," said Seven. She sniffed hard, grabbed her top, and slipped it on.

She stood up and when she looked at me it was cold like maybe she hated me now, but then she softened a little. "Dammit, flyboy." She leaned forward and pressed herself against me, but lightly this time, and I considered again what I'd just missed, and I thought to myself, *You are some kind of idiot.*

Seven wrapped me in a hug but all the electricity was gone. Then she pulled away. Smiled, but sadly. "You're a worthy god."

I smiled, too, but inside my heart was wringing itself out. Whatever this was, it was the worst. "So are you. Really."

Seven laughed and looked away. "Right." A shadow passed over her face. But then she sighed and seemed to return to herself. "I'm going back swimming. You coming? I promise, I'll be more gentle."

"I'll be there soon," I said.

Seven turned and walked back out to the sea, her stunning, beautiful form leaving my sight. Girls. They were quite possibly harder to figure out than gills, ancient DNA, or secretive plots. Leech would be bashing me with his boccie ball right now if he knew what had just happened.

I leaned against the rock, feeling drained, looking up

at the stars and watching them wobble, flaring in strange bursts from the Shine. Eventually, I walked back out to the beach. I spotted Seven, Kellen, and Marina playing around in the waves. I got my shirt from the sand and saw Leech and Oro making out by the rocks.

I tugged my shirt over my wet shoulders and sat by one of the bonfires. The flames flickered in liquid movements, Shine green. I watched people dance and leap off the ledge and, as the night got later, fall all over each other. When a couple rolled into me while sloppily making out, I got up and headed for the stairs.

I'd lost track of Seven and her friends. They were maybe over dancing to the band. There was a frenzy there of bouncing bodies. I thought about joining them, felt a wave of loneliness, but I started up the stairs anyway.

I wandered back through the dark streets. The only people still out were little cackling groups, drunks, spinning and dancing and falling on one another and I thought their movements suggested Shine. Lots of it. Maybe that was the real key to living bright.

Mine was wearing off, and a deep headache was setting in, along with a weird numb tingle in my fingers and toes. My thoughts felt like mush, and yet when I reached the plaza, I didn't continue home. There was somewhere else I needed to go.

But Lilly's room was empty.

"She hasn't been back since you were here before," said

a nurse emerging from a nearby room.

I stared at the neatly made bed, and then noticed that Lilly's red bag was gone, too.

I'll find my own way, she'd said.

And now that it was too late, I wondered how I would find mine, without her.

PART III

And when the Three have been truly revealed
They will return, to defend against the masters,
And yet has not this journey been made before?
Over and again the cycle repeats,
And so we must be wary of the Terra's patience,
For if we fail her too often,
She may make plans of her own.

28

I STUMBLED HOME, FEELING HOLLOW, SCRAPED OUT, and fell into bed. Slept dreamless and blank until well into the afternoon. When I got up, my head ached even more. My eyes felt like they'd been toasted, and though I was thirsty, my stomach didn't feel up to anything.

There was a note from Mom; she and Emil were working the full day. I dressed and headed to the infirmary. As I crossed the main plaza, I saw decorations being put up for Nueva Luna. Groups were constructing giant moons made of wood and paper, moons with ghoulish faces, with symbols and streamers hanging off them.

I found Mom on a different hallway from any I'd been on. The rooms were narrow, each with only a bed and a large pot of flowering vines that crept up the wall and spread over the ceiling. Many had patients. They were mostly sleeping or talking quietly with family. There was little medical equipment to be seen. The floral scent was overwhelming, and yet, beneath it there was an unmistakable smell of death.

Mom knelt beside a man dressed in white. It was hard to tell how old he was, maybe forty, but his body was a wreck. His hair was gone. His chest sagged, like it had caved into the bed. He had a long, black lesion down the left side of his face. He breathed with difficulty, a rasping wheeze. And yet there was a lovely flower wreath around his neck. A bag of lime-green fluid hung beside him.

Mom pressed on his inner wrist with her stethoscope and the man moaned softly. "Sorry, William," said Mom. "I know it hurts."

As she let go, I saw the rippling of his flesh, the tiny white lines burrowing around. Heat worm.

"How much longer?" William wheezed, his tongue flicking out to try and moisten his cracked lips.

Mom checked her watch. "Soon. We'll administer the Shine as soon as you've had a chance to see your family."

"Now," he moaned softly. "Please."

Mom was dabbing William's head with a cloth. "Shhh," she said to him. "Try to rest."

As her hand was drawing away, she pressed her thumb against his cheek and made a circular motion. I could almost feel the echo of that touch, tugging gently at my skin, and I worried. Was I really going to leave the mom I'd just found?

"Hey, Owen." Mom stood and started writing some notes at the counter. Her eyes were red and wet.

"Hey," I said. "How's it going?"

"Oh, not so good for William, but it's almost over." She wiped at her eyes. "These are always hard for me," she said. "To sit idly by. I mean, there's nothing else to be done, even if we wanted to." She shook her head. "But it's still hard."

"Sorry," I said.

"Ah, don't worry. It's just an emotional day. Things are getting to me that shouldn't, you know, with your big trip starting tomorrow."

"Yeah." I didn't know what to say. I walked over and hugged her.

She wrapped her arms around me, and it felt maybe safe, and it was a good feeling. Except that it complicated things.

"I don't suppose you've thought any more about what we talked about yesterday," she whispered softly.

I could barely remember yesterday, and yet I knew she meant asking me to stay. "Mom," I said.

"I'm sorry for bringing it up," she said. "I just can't help it. I spent all night thinking about how to get word to your father, how to apologize to him. And even about how maybe Victoria would agree that you leaving here is too dangerous. I—I know it's not fair of me, especially since so much is my fault, but after all the time we've missed, I just can't bear the thought of being without you again."

I listened and hated hearing this as much I wanted it. I was still angry that she'd run off, and yet also I felt willing to forget that, just to have a real family. It sounded better than flying off into the wilds. But turning my back on destiny, my team, on all the people who'd sacrificed to make this possible . . .

"I have to go," I said. "My team needs me."

Mom sighed. "I figured you'd say that." She pulled back, holding my shoulders. "Okay. Well, don't blame a mother for trying. We'll just pick up when you get back. If . . ."

"What?" I asked, but then I didn't want to hear her say it.

"Just . . . what if you don't make it back?" she said, her voice small. "To find you now, if it's only to lose you . . . while knowing how badly I messed up the past . . . I don't know if I could ever recover."

"Mom . . ." I didn't know what to say. Part of me felt like, How was this fair? I never got a say when she left. And wasn't she supposed to be the strong one, here? But that meant I needed to be.

"I'll make it back," I said. "Promise."

She looked like she might say more, but I really didn't want her to. I couldn't deal with this anymore. Luckily, maybe she sensed that, too. "Okay. Will I see you after the ceremony tonight?"

"Yeah," I said. I didn't think I'd be heading out on the town with Seven again.

"Okay, good." Mom smiled.

There was a knock at the door. A woman and three

children stood there. Teenage kids, two girls and a boy. William's family.

"Oh, come in," said Mom. She moved to the mother and guided her inside. The mother's eyes were wide, while staring resolutely at her husband.

They gathered around the bed. I stood back against the wall. Everyone seemed afraid to speak.

"Hey, okay, showtime." I turned to find Seven at the door. She was in her white dress with the flower embroidery. She looked exhausted, wearing her sunglasses even though the room was dark.

"Hey, flyboy," she said as she passed, "wanna help?" She knelt beside William.

"Sure," I said. I knelt across from her and we joined hands. Seven took off her glasses. She gave me one quick glance, then kept her eyes on William. We repeated the rite, our words in rhythm, and I thought again about the night before, wondering what I'd missed and how things would be between us on the journey.

We finished the rite, and Seven said, "Ready?"

"Yes," said William faintly. His family began to weep.

Mom turned the valve on the bag of Shine. Liquid leaped into the thin clear tube, rushing in loops down into William's chest.

He closed his eyes. There was a moment of stillness. And then he smiled.

"I will be the divine," he said softly. When his eyes

opened, his pupils were dilated and darting around, as if each corner of the room was some new discovery to him. I imagined the auras and spin that he was seeing, his last glimpses of the world coated in magic.

"I'll be back to prepare him for tonight," Mom said to the family.

"My work here is done," said Seven flatly. "You coming over to Tactical?" she asked me. "Leecher is figuring out the map stuff."

"Yeah," I said. "Mom, I'm gonna go."

"Okay," she said, "I'll see you later. And Owen, sorry to let all those thoughts out. You do your thing, okay? Don't worry about me."

"Okay," I said, thinking that, like Lilly, Mom should have known better than to think I wouldn't worry.

"Mom putting the guilt trip on you?" Seven asked once we were back out in the plaza.

"Kinda," I said. "She's sad about me leaving. Wishes I could stay."

Seven punched me in the shoulder. "Just stay strong, partner. Twelve hours from now we will be home free."

"I guess," I said. I noticed her yawning. "Did you get any sleep?"

"A little. Wouldn't want to get too much. Hey." She stopped me. We were by the fountain. "Look, I hope I didn't freak you out last night."

I looked away. "I wish I didn't get freaked out."

Seven smiled. "Yeah, well, you wouldn't be you if you

didn't. Besides, it would've been weird anyway, right? We're like, first cousins a hundred times removed or something." She laughed and I was glad to laugh too. "The other thing about last night," Seven said, "was just the anticipation of finally getting out of this place. You don't know what it's like to be so close."

"Victoria's not giving you a guilt trip about coming back when we're done?"

"I wouldn't listen if she was, but, no way. Victoria could care less what happens to me after we fly out of here tomorrow."

"Really?" I asked. "I would bet she has some feelings about you leaving, maybe?"

"Hah." Seven slapped me on the back. "I've learned that it's a mistake to assume that the Benevolent Mother has feelings. We're just a means to an end for her. But that's fine with me."

I thought of Victoria on the dock with the injured Nomads. She'd seemed to have feelings then. "So," I said, "you wouldn't come back here after we're done?"

"Beyond no," said Seven. "I have performed my last death rite. It makes me sick to see those people giving up, drugging themselves, and then walking into oblivion."

"How is that different from you taking Shine?" The question had come out before I'd really thought about it, but now that it was in the air, I realized that this had been bugging me.

Seven flinched. "It's totally different. Taking the dirty

edge off this world is completely different than running from it. It's like I said at the dock: Do a few thousand of these death rites before you judge. Shine just makes the time in prison pass a little faster. But pretty soon we'll be out of here, and then, problem solved."

I thought of the dark side of her I'd seen last night, after I'd stopped her, and wondered if just getting out of here would be enough.

The plaza was filling quickly. The moons were being raised on ropes that spanned the area. I saw a giant jaguar on a turtle being erected out of branches and flowers.

We got to Tactical and found Leech and Victoria and Arlo standing at a flat, circular table. It had a monitor top and Arlo was swiping a satellite map back and forth.

Leech was looking from his sketches to the map. "Okay, then south, forty degrees. The mountains should be starting to the east."

"Yes, the northeastern reach of the Andes," Arlo confirmed.

"Hey," I said.

Leech glanced up. "Hey. We've almost got it."

"Cool." Seven and I gathered around the table. Victoria joined us.

"Where's Lilly?" Seven asked. "Still saying she's not coming?"

"Her stuff's out of her room," said Leech. He looked at me.

I just shrugged. "I don't know where she went."

"Well," said Seven, "did you look for her?" She sounded almost bothered by this.

"Why would I do that?" Why would Seven want me to do that? Had I been reading all the girl signals in the wrong language, or what? "Lilly didn't want me to look for her. She made that pretty clear."

"Oh man, flyboy." Seven rolled her eyes. "You have a lot to learn about women."

"Well, broken hearts aside," said Victoria, "it does simplify things somewhat."

"Maybe she'll turn up," said Leech. He sounded disappointed but quickly turned back to his map. "Okay, so check it out: We fly south until we hit the Andes . . ."

As Leech was talking I noticed Seven slip away from the circle. She faded back, directly behind Victoria, until she was in the center of the room. Then she headed for the doors to the balcony. Nico was holding one open for her. As they stepped outside, I saw that his face looked tight, serious.

"And then follow them southwest," Leech was going on, "and there should be a series of lakes. . . ."

Arlo moved the map. "These?"

"Yeah . . ." said Leech. "And then . . ." He put his hand on the screen and slowly dragged the map to the right. "There."

He pointed to a high mountain peak. It almost resembled

a chair, with a high jagged back and sloping sides around a bowl. On the back side was a sheer cliff that dropped hundreds of meters. There was actual snow in the chair's seat, possibly a remnant glacier. "Can we zoom in?"

Arlo tapped buttons on the edge of the table. The picture clicked, enlarging, and stopped.

Now the craggy peak was almost filling the screen. You could see the uneven flanks of the bowl, the sheer granite drop behind it, and, nestled in the crook of the highest edge, a faint impression of geometric shapes. Buildings. A large round dome, a smaller structure that was maybe a tower, and some other curves that seemed to be built into the wall.

"That's at four thousand meters elevation," said Arlo. "You're going to be some kind of light-headed."

Leech exhaled slowly. "That's it, though. That's where we're going." He looked up at me. "Think you can fly us up there?"

"Definitely," I said. Flying again sounded like a dream compared to all this emotional business.

"What's there?" Seven was back. She was staring at the map, but she looked worried about something. I wondered what she and Nico had talked about.

"Not sure," said Leech. "Maybe my skull."

"It's about three thousand kilometers from here," said Arlo.

I ran the numbers in my brain. "If we can keep the

vortex charged, that should take us about three days," I said, "with stops to rest."

"We should be able to give you a recharge along the way with the drones," said Arlo. "Their range is about half that distance, but we can cover you for a little while."

"Excellent," said Victoria. "Okay, I need to get ready for the ceremony. Seven—" she started, but then looked around. Seven was gone. She sighed. "Arlo, you and Leech should have time now to make your trip, if you hurry." She rubbed Leech's shoulder. "You're sure you still want to go."

"Yeah," said Leech. "I do." He looked at me, his eyes wide and serious. "We're going over to Cryo. He's there. You can come along, right?"

"Yeah, sure," I said. "Now?"

"Now." Leech closed his sketchbook and started shoving it into his pocket. I could see his limbs shaking, and I wondered if it was the sickness, or what we were about to find.

29

WE LEFT TACTICAL AND CROSSED THE PLAZA IN HAZY dusk light. Arlo led the way, and an armed guard joined us. The moons were strung high, and all the café tables and chairs had been cleared. Torches had been lit and people were crowding in.

Leech had been quiet as we walked. Now he said, "I wish I was armed." He reached toward his belt. He had the sextant around his neck, but . . .

"Where's your boccie ball?" I asked.

"Can't find it," said Leech. "It was gone from my room this afternoon."

"Huh," I said.

"Owen!"

Mom and Emiliano were heading toward the pyramid, guiding William, the volunteer, between them. They were both dressed in long, crimson ceremonial robes.

"Where are you going?" Mom called, looking at me quizzically.

"Just a sec," I said to Leech, and started toward them.

"Wait—" Leech called, but I was already on my way over to them.

"Hey, guys," I said.

"Hello," William said dreamily, his eyes darting around.

Mom glanced over my shoulder at Leech and Arlo. "Shouldn't you guys be sticking around for the ceremony?"

"Yeah, we'll be back in time," I said. "We're just making a quick trip first."

"Oh, where?" asked Mom. "I don't need to be worried, do I?"

"Nah," I said, "it's gonna sound weird, but we're heading over to EdenSouth."

"EdenSouth?" Mom's face grew serious. "Why?"

"Leech has a brother in the cryo facility here. He wants to see him."

"Well," said Mom, sounding very parentlike with disapproval, "but he knows that those people are all, essentially . . . gone, doesn't he?"

"Yeah," I said, "but he just wants to see him, just to know for sure, I guess. And he wants me along, as a friend."

Mom nodded seriously. "I don't love the idea of you going out there in the wilds on your own." It almost sounded like she was weighing whether or not I could go, and I felt I didn't need her permission, and yet I still found myself wondering what she would say. "But it's good of you to be there for your friend." She rubbed my head and her smile returned. "See you in a little bit. Be careful!"

"Yeah, I will." I turned and rejoined Leech and Arlo.

"Sorry," I said.

"Did you tell them where we were going?" Leech asked as we continued walking.

"Yeah," I said. "Why?"

Leech seemed to sigh. "Let's just get out there."

I wondered why that would bother him. Maybe he didn't like the idea of any more people knowing what he was going through.

Outside the gate, the jungle was shrouded in deep shadows. The sky had shaded to lavender and pale blue. We walked quietly along the tire track road. Our footfalls seemed louder in the fading light, and I felt like we were more exposed, aliens in a strange land, at the mercy of hidden eyes.

We crested the rise and the dome sat giant and broken against a blood-and-pink wash of sunset. In the distance, tall clouds rose high in the sky. There was a flash in one's belly. I saw a faint glow in the dome, light from Cryo illuminating the inner walls, but once we descended the rise, all we could see was the looming, dark exterior.

The daylight faded, and color bled out of the world. Arlo and the guard ignited headlamps.

The birds became quiet. The sounds of animals became more infrequent, lonely searching little voices, and the occasional crash of something in the brush.

We reached the entrance. Arlo unlocked the gate and it squealed open. We walked through the tunnel and into the silent city. Through the torn ceiling, the sky had cooled to deep purple. The buildings were dark, cloaked in shadows. Things scurried out of sight, startled by our presence. An owl hooted, the sound echoing in the cavernous space.

The distant glow of Cryo reminded me of approaching the skull. We wove through the empty streets, rounded a corner, and there it was: a solitary tower of soft light, like some alien spaceship from the future had landed among ancient ruins.

We reached the glass doors and Arlo produced a keycard. Very official lettering was stenciled in frosted letters across the glass.

EdenSouth Cryogenics and Extension Services

There was a hiss as the doors unlocked.

We entered a clean hallway with white walls and a sky-blue carpeted floor. There was a little stone fountain, turned off, and art on the walls, paintings made of soothing bands of color.

We walked down the hall, our footfalls quiet on the plush carpet, the space so still that our breaths seemed loud. The hall ended at a reception area with a monitor-topped desk and sleek black couches. The wall behind the desk was one giant window, and through it, we could see the pods.

The light was soft and blue-white. The walls of the giant central room curved in the sweeps of the helix shape, two wide ovals with a narrow center, like a figure eight. At the middle, catwalks spanned the levels. There were ten floors, six above us, the rest burrowed underground. Each floor was open in the center, with a wide platform stretching around its perimeter. Circular pod doors were inset into the walls. The edge of each pod door was illuminated by a collar of soft blue lights. Every ten pods, a little workstation stuck out from the wall, with a monitor screen and an angled touch pad. The workstations were dark.

At various points on the platforms, skeletal elevator shafts and metal staircases connected the floors. Carts were parked on the central catwalks, with seats in front and a curved bed in the back for transporting a pod. Claws on steel wires hung down from the metal ceiling beams that ran between giant triangular skylights.

Leech put his hands on the glass. He breathed, making a cloud of fog. His fingers were trembling. "He's on the sixth floor."

"Wait here," Arlo said to our guard.

There were glass double doors to our left. They hissed open and a burst of cold air washed over us, making me shiver. We walked out onto the platform of level four. There was a vacant sound of moving air and humming machinery. It sounded like a giant version of when I'd open the little refrigerator back in our apartment at Hub. The blue pods stretched away on the wall to either side of us, and on the opposite wall, across the central space. Leech headed for the nearest silver-doored elevator.

"We gotta take the stairs," said Arlo. "Power's off to nonessential features."

There was a metal staircase at the corner where the catwalk met the platform. We climbed up two floors, our steps echoing in the hollow space.

"He's on the far side." Leech's voice came out in a tight whisper. He led the way across the catwalk to the far wall.

There were little silver plates with numbers above each pod door. Leech walked slowly, reading them. I saw now that the doors were slightly translucent, just enough that you could make out the shadow of the top of a head and, dimly, shoulders. It was unsettling to think of someone in there, either a cryo kid or some terminally ill person who'd chosen Extension Services in hopes of a future cure, all of them placing their trust in Eden. They had no idea what had happened since. There would be no cures, no waking up to a better place. Instead, they were all frozen in a ruin.

As we walked, I gazed around the space, at all the blue rings of light and silhouettes above and below. I found myself stepping lightly, nearly tiptoeing, like I was trying not to awaken ghosts.

Leech slowed, and stopped. He pointed to a door. A shadow of a body inside. "This is it," he said.

"Okay, one sec." Arlo moved to the wall. He knelt

beneath the pod door and flipped open a little metal panel. Inside was a red rectangular latch. "We have to use the manual opener." He twisted the latch. The blue lights around the edges of the pod door began to blink off, one at a time, like a countdown. When they'd all gone dark, there was a sharp hiss and the door unsealed. A faint cloud of cold sprang free.

Leech took hold of the door's edge and swung it open. It seemed heavy. Behind this was a circular panel of clear plastic with a steel handle in the center. On the other side we could clearly see a head of brown hair. The inside of the pod was softly lit in a whitish lavender.

Arlo unfastened three red latches around the edge of the clear panel. "Okay," he said.

Leech gripped the handle with both hands and pulled. The pod slid out, rumbling on smooth rollers, a long, clear cylinder. Leech moved around to the side and put his trembling hands against the surface.

"Isaac," he said quietly.

I stepped to the opposite side and saw the delicate face inside, a young boy with brown hair and freckles like Leech's. His eyes closed, lashes and lips dusted with frost, his skin pale gray. He wore a white hospital-type gown, and lay on a contoured plastic surface with a small white pillow beneath his head. He had a peaceful sleeping expression on his face.

I heard a heavy sniffle from Leech. He slid his hands

down the sides of the pod. He turned to us, and I saw the tears beneath his good eye. "Can you guys give me a minute?"

"Yeah," I said. Arlo and I moved back out to the catwalk.

"Poor kid," said Arlo. "Listen, Victoria wants me to take the readings from the power meters, so just meet me back in the reception area when he's done, okay?"

"Sure," I said.

Arlo checked his watch. "Don't rush him, but we should start back in about ten minutes." He headed down the stairs.

I could hear Leech talking quietly to Isaac. I leaned against the railing, peering up and down at all the pods. It was unsettling being in here. I felt my pulse jogging along. And it was sad, pointless. These people had tried to run from death, only to end up stuck here, paused. I wondered if this was any better a fate than living bright.

"Owen, come here."

I turned to Leech. He was just gazing at me, but even though his mouth wasn't moving, I still heard his voice, speaking softly.

I walked over, confused. He pointed down to the side of the pod. There was a little console there, and a small drive was stuck into a port.

"I'm playing my journal entries for him," said Leech. "They used to say in EdenWest that Cryos can perceive sounds on a subconscious level." Leech looked down at Isaac's small face. "I just want him to know what I've been up to." His recorded voice reverberated in muffled tones inside the pod.

A shudder wracked Leech's body. He sighed, shoulders slumping. "This sucks," he said, his voice choked. "This really sucks."

I stood next to him. "I'm sorry," I said.

Leech nodded. "Thanks, but . . ." He glanced over his shoulder. "Did Arlo go back to reception?"

"Yeah."

Then Leech said quietly, "There's something else we have to do here."

"What?" I asked.

Leech bit his lip. "Arlo doesn't know. Nobody does . . . except me."

I felt a little burst of nerves, and another uptick of my pulse. "What are you talking about?" Leech's gaze at me was dead serious. "What?"

He took a deep breath. "Be right back," he said quietly to Isaac, then he turned, leaving his journal entries playing. "Follow me."

Leech started down the platform, past the catwalk, reading the numbers above the pods. He stopped in front of another one, and bent down. He opened the panel, and flipped the red latch. The pod lights began to blink off.

"What are you doing?" I asked. And yet, inside, I felt

myself tightening, everything starting to race.

"You'll see," said Leech.

The blue lights extinguished. The pod hissed. Leech hauled open the door. Slid the clear pod out.

He stepped around to the opposite side of the pod and turned back to me. "Look," he said.

I didn't move. "What is this?" I asked, but my heart was galloping, I barely knew why. Maybe because of the way that Leech was looking at me—it was so weird, like he was scared or sorry or something . . . but also because I had this terrible growing feeling. An apprehension of something, something coming at me as if through a fog.

"Look," said Leech. "Now."

I stepped over, holding my breath.

Inside the pod was a child. A girl.

She had straight, deep red hair, pale features, the white gown. She looked a few years younger than us. Maybe twelve . . . yeah, twelve . . . and her body was striped in black, the veins discolored. Some had burst in inky puddles beneath translucent skin.

"Her name is Elissa," said Leech.

Elissa. "She's a Cryo?" I asked. My voice had gotten hoarse. Fingers shaking. I knew something. There was something . . .

"Sort of. She died of the black blood. Paul wasn't able to save her in time, but when he identified her DNA as being a potential match to the Atlantean genome, he ordered her cryoed, in case they needed her for future study."

"How do you know this?" I asked.

"Part of it I read in the rosters that Victoria has. Part of it I knew from back in EdenWest."

I kept looking at her, the black veins, the small nose, the flat base of her chin. *Elissa* . . .

"Do you remember her?"

I looked up. Leech's eye was boring into me.

Did I— "What?" My heart was slamming, trying to break free and run.

Like it knew, it already knew . . .

"When Paul and his team found her, there was some initial hope that she could survive the plague, but then they learned that Elissa's lungs had been too badly damaged. She'd always had weak lungs, from an accident when she was younger. From severe smoke inhalation."

I leaned my hands against the cool pod. Felt my balance swim. This girl . . . "Smoke?" I said weakly.

"Listen, Owen," said Leech. "I'm going to say a couple things, and I want you to just think about it all for a minute, and try not to freak out—"

"What things?" I whispered. *The smoke, the ash, plague, it* . . .

"Victoria doesn't know about this," Leech was saying "Nobody does and I don't think we should tell anyone, either."

But I had to cut him off. "Tell me what this is." I

swallowed. It tasted metal. Her red hair, the lines of disease . . . "Do I . . . do I know this girl?"

Leech was still staring at me. He nodded. "Yeah. She lived at Hub. She died when the black blood plague hit in 2061."

"Wait . . . 2061? That's wrong, the plague was—"

"No. It's not wrong. There's more, Owen. Her lungs had been bad since the Three-Year Fire. The Three-Year Fire that was nine years before the plague. In 2052."

"No," I said, but inside, I felt things starting to crumble, the world outside my head and inside, none of it was stable, it was all falling apart . . . "The Three-Year Fire was when I was a kid. It . . . it was just a few years ago."

"It was when you were a kid, but that wasn't a few years ago. It's 2086. The Three-Year Fire was thirty-four years ago."

"What are you saying? It was just . . . I was six, it was—" I stopped.

Leech kept staring at me. "Stay with me, Owen. Try to put it together in your head. Some of this has probably been floating around in there. You've said some things about dreams . . ."

"Who is she?" I shouted. I looked down at the girl in the pod. *Elissa.* Died of the plague, smoke inhalation—

When I lost track of her.

Oh no.

The thought had yanked itself free of the swirl in my

head. And now more.

I was supposed to be watching her, but she ran off. She loved to run off. She . . .

I looked at Leech. I didn't want to, couldn't . . .

But suddenly it was there.

"She's my sister."

30

MOM HAS TAKEN US TO SEE THE AFTERMATH.

The dream washed over me, no, the *memory*, the one that had been sticking in my head the whole time, the one that had been turning itself over and over in my dreams . . . taking other information and wrapping it together, collaging, trying to show me this, the truth, and now it wiped out the world and I lost track of myself and everything as the storm of understanding raged.

Mom takes us up to the ledges the morning after the Three-Year Fire, to see the smoking caldera, to see the oceans of ash and the charred trees that look like dark guardians. The sky is a swirl of turbulent clouds, and the ash and the sky seem to be one. It is so different from the night before, when the flames and the dark scared me. Mom thought it might be scary and that's why we didn't wake up Elissa, Elissa who is only three. But today it is safe and so she has come along because Dad is at work.

We are up there, and Mom spies a friend. Elissa is just

playing with some pebbles, sitting peacefully, and Mom tells me to keep an eye on her. She goes over to talk. Elissa is busy drawing happy faces in the ash with her finger, the faces with little S-curves of hair off each side. She always draws herself. I can't help gazing out over the ashscape and I catch a glimpse of something moving down on the gray. It's a little vole, padding along, leaving a faint trail of footprints and tail in the soft gray-white blanket, and I think that it's amazing that this creature has survived the night, and now here it is surveying its new home, not oohing and aahing or moaning for the loss of what it once knew like we humans always do, but getting down to the business of what is now.

I watch its nose swishing along—

But then my mom is screaming OWEN! and I see her running toward me, her face wild with panic, and I spin, because I know in an instant. Elissa is gone.

Where?

The trail, the one that zigzags in switchbacks from the ledge down to the flats. And I look down it and there is a flash of white pajamas, the ones with the little frogs that she would not change out of this morning, putting up a huge fight until Mom finally gave in and just put her boots on with the PJs, and all I see is a glimpse of them because Elissa has fallen into the ash, into what we'd later call a sucker hole, where the ash blanketed a crosshatch of burned logs, concealing a hollow space beneath.

We run down. Elissa's shoulder and arm are visible. She is wedged sideways between logs, and some of the black cinders still have glowing red underbellies. They crackle and hiss, and down here the world is blurred by updrafts of heat. This hole that Elissa has opened is a chamber of leftover anger. The black smoke plumes up and there is no way she has air in there. No way.

Mom lunges for her but her step crushes into the hole, too, and she sinks up to her waist and she will have bands of burn around her leg that don't heal, even years later.

—She never left—

Memories flashed in concussions.

Adults swarm and drag Mom out and then a chain of people are able to grab Elissa by the arm and when they pull her out, we see the singe marks on her pajamas, the ash streaks on her face, and the puffy awfulness of her eyes and nose and throat, all locked up in desperate defense. We can't get her free because her arm is stuck, and finally it gives and something pops free and we see that Elissa's hand is still gripping her plush crocodile. Mr. Teeth, she called it, and it has lost a leg to the sucker hole, and is singed black, too, but what is important is that she has survived . . .

Mostly. We will learn in the next few days that her lungs are scalded and will never be normal again. She will need nebulizer packs and a rebreather, just like her father—

—Not just your father sitting on the couch during the

Federation soccer games, Elissa is there, too, both of them coughing, all of you eating pizza. Mom is there as well, Mom who never actually left—

Mom and Elissa filling back into my memories, as if they had been erased, the images I thought were real actually scrubbed, made incomplete. *Elissa, Mom . . .*

"There, there, honey," a voice said from somewhere far out on the surface.

Mom . . .

Elissa does okay and most days are fine, but when the black blood plague comes nine years later, she succumbs early and severely. Her lungs are too weak. I can fight it, I am older, and I survive long enough for the World Health team to arrive. Arriving, too, is a team from EdenCorp. All attempts to save Elissa are too late. And I have it bad, too, very bad, in a bed, wracked with fever, Mom bending beside me, comforting me.

I felt the thumb press against my cheek. I looked up. Mom was standing beside me and she began to inscribe the clockwise circle.

But still more . . .

The circle being inscribed, by my mother. She sits beside my bed. I look down and see that I am in a gown, and all my veins are clogged with the black sludge of plague. All efforts have been exhausted—

—your scar is not from a hernia, it's from removing your spleen, because of the plague, and since you were

already open there, the incision could be used again to install the cryo monitors and tubing, you know it, you know it—

I am dying, they tell me. It is only a matter of time, but there is a possible solution. I have been offered an opportunity, to sleep for now, to be cured later, and I have been assured by the man at the foot of the bed that I will wake up intact. His name is Paul, a man with kind eyes—before his circuits and glasses. "You will still be YOU," he says, "only better. Cured. And there is a special future that awaits you."

By the door my dad still doesn't understand quite why they are offering to do this and Paul says, "Because Owen is special, and it is either this or death." A terrible choice, Dad will lose his son either way. He has already lost his daughter, but at least I will live.

And so Dad leans over my bed and rubs a hand on my sweaty forehead and back through my hair, and he coughs because the emotions are making him well up and that is making his breathing bad. In a hoarse whisper he says, "Good-bye, Owen. I love you, Son. You'll be okay."

I nod but can't speak—my lungs drowned.

And Mom presses the circle inscription in my cheek and says it will be okay. Sitting there beside me, she smiles through teary eyes and says, "Don't worry, Owen. Don't worry."

"Don't worry."

Beside me now.

"Mom's here."

I blinked and swam out of it, out of the storm of memories, back to the pod and the girl, the black-veined girl, my sister Elissa lying dead and preserved, in a bed of white.

The circle completed on my cheek, Mom's hand moved and rubbed my back. "I'm sure this is hard. But I want you to know it was never our intention."

"What?" I whispered. Looking at the curves of eyelids and lashes, dusted with glowing frost. Elissa. Elissa who hated when I stole the Spam slices from her pizza . . .

"You were never supposed to see this."

I wrenched my eyes free of Elissa. I looked across the pod to where Leech was staring hard at me.

I caught a glimpse of metal. Turned left.

To see the gun pointing at Leech.

To see my mother holding the gun.

But the memories in my mind, the re-formed, unerased truths had shown me something more.

"You're not my mother," I said weakly, "are you?"

31

"AREN'T I?" SAID MOM.

But, no.

She wasn't. Whoever she was, she'd learned my history, learned my mother's mannerisms, and I'd believed that she was, but . . . no. I could see my old mother now, my real mother, sitting by my bedside long ago, who'd been replaced in some memories and removed from others. Another woman from another time . . .

Another time.

The gaps were filling in, memories unlost: afternoons at school, nights when Dad worked late, and the truths that I had believed, taken as fact: *You never had a sister, your mom left when you were seven. . . .* They fluttered in the rafters of my mind like ghosts that had been exorcised and were still shrieking but powerless. I had a sister. I had a mom. I lived a life in Hub and they had been there, too.

And even more. All these memories, real or fake or somewhere in between, they had all occurred not just a few years ago, but—What did Leech say?—the dates. The fire, in 2052, the black blood in 2061, and since then, for twenty-five years . . .

I'd been in Cryo. Which meant my dad . . . my real mom . . . what had become of them? Were they even still alive? And all my memories of them . . . were they real or fake?

Victoria had called it selective manipulation.

They could change your memories, alter them to suit their needs, Seven had said.

But not all my memories had yielded. The one terrible scene of Elissa falling into the sucker hole had lingered, stapled to my consciousness as . . . my cryo dream. The last thing I'd been thinking about, way back then, knowing my sister had died but that I would be saved, the guilt, the sense of failure, it made an unerasable mark that no manipulation could fully remove. And it had maybe even made me: the camp Owen who was weak, tentative, unsure of himself . . . How much of that was the effect of decades in Cryo seeing that devastating dream over and over?

"Who are you?" I asked the woman beside me. She was dressed all in black now, with thick boots.

"Her name is Francine." The voice boomed throughout the cryo complex.

Paul's voice.

"Sounds like Emiliano has uploaded the new operating system," said Francine, glancing back toward the reception area where we'd entered.

Behind Leech, the screen on the nearest control terminal flickered to life. All of them were turning on throughout the complex. Paul's face appeared on every one, a hundred Pauls in all directions. He was smiling, and he'd taken his glasses off, his electric eyes sparking. One was still brilliant blue, but the other, where Lilly had hit him with the skull, was now flickering in pale white. He wore a headset and seemed to be sitting in a cockpit. One of the copters.

"Hello, Owen, Carey. This wasn't quite the plan," said Paul. "We were going to get you at tonight's festival, but here we are and as it turns out, I like this much better. Carey, I'm impressed. You picked up on much more than I thought you had these last couple years."

Leech was looking at me. "I'm sorry," he said. "I didn't think you'd believe me before now. You didn't trust me, so I wanted to have some proof before I told you. . . ."

I almost screamed at him, but I fought the urge because he was right. If he'd tried to tell me this without showing me, I never would have believed him. I barely knew if I believed him now. Except I did.

"And, Owen," said Paul, "Francine may not technically be your mother, but she did spend many, many hours with you while you were in Cryo in EdenWest. She was one of my lead team doctors. We'd float you up to near consciousness every now and then so you could get to know her, hear her voice and feel her touch, so that she could imprint on you." I saw vague memories of this, now, of Francine beside me in a white coat as other doctors fluttered around, monitoring me and running tests. My technicians . . . had that idea come from the cryo lab workers? All these things . . .

"Naturally, to do this, we had to remove your more recent memories of your mother, and then build an emotional barrier to them coming back: That's why we implanted the idea that she left you. Then we replaced your real mom with Francine in your younger memories. That was all relatively easy tinkering.

"As for Elissa," said Paul, "the thing about selective manipulation is that the brain can be very stubborn. It holds on to certain keys, like the locks to rooms of memory. You can't remember everything all the time, after all. We found that there was no way to effectively replace your mother without also removing your sister. She was your key, the central thought to your whole batch of childhood memories. She colored everything, likely because of the guilt you felt for her condition and her eventual death. So removing her was essential for scrubbing away the other things that we needed to remove. And we freed you of some terrible heartache in the process.

"It took a lot of trial and error, but we had plenty of time to get it just right, before we woke you up and placed you on the Mag Train heading to Camp. Do you remember waking from a nap just before arriving at EdenWest? That was a very long nap."

I couldn't listen to this. Couldn't . . . All my ideas about my mom . . . how I saw my life as before and after she left, the idea like some jagged, snaking wall through my mind . . . It had all been fake.

"Why did you do this to me?" I managed to ask.

"You mean save your life?" said Paul. "Obviously so that you could fulfill your destiny. As to altering your memories, well . . . You remember what I said back in Eden: You have to have a *vision* for how things will go. All this work I did on your mind was really for this very moment. It was an insurance policy. I'd learned from working with Carey that it might be helpful to have a card I could play to get you in line, rein you back in, if at some point you became resistant to our plans. After all, I knew you'd be changing so much, acquiring so much skill and power, and teens can be so *moody*. I wanted to be sure I could still get through to you, if I had to.

"I sent Francine to infiltrate Desenna right after you escaped from EdenWest. Emiliano is one of our operatives there, one of the many who prefer our way of thinking to Victoria's. We'd arranged an identity and job for her to assume. And now here we all are, together again. This was clever forethought by me, I must admit, especially since at the time I didn't yet know the full extent of your importance."

I couldn't hear this. My sister, dead—*I had a sister*—and my parents. I almost wanted to ask Paul what had happened to them. He would know, and he probably knew that I knew this. Maybe he was waiting for me to start asking, but nothing he said could be trusted.

A thought suddenly occurred to me, another memory, so ridiculous it almost made me laugh. "You said you never lied to me."

"I know." Paul shrugged. "Kinda lousy of me."

"You're a bastard!" Leech yelled.

"Carey, language," said Paul.

"We're not going with you!" Leech went on, his face boiling.

Paul made a face I remembered from Eden, a kind of displeased wince, as if someone's defiance were an off-key note. "No, that's true," he said. "You're not." He made a small nod.

"Sorry," said Francine.

There was a terrible explosion of sound as she pulled the trigger, and Leech spasmed back, sprawling to the floor.

32

"WHAT ARE YOU DOING?" I SCREAMED, MY VOICE A tattered rag. I fell forward against the cryo tube, over my sister, my found sister, to see Leech splayed out on the floor. His chest was convulsing, thumping up and down. He coughed out wet, choking sounds. Blood spread across his shirt.

"Carey is no longer necessary," said Paul, again with as much concern as if he were delivering a report to the campers back at flagpole. "You on the other hand, Owen. Well, it's like I said, you are the key."

My legs buckled. It was all too much. I slid off the pod, down to my knees, shaking.

"We'll be at the rendezvous in ten," I heard Paul say. "Do you have the item?"

Mom—no, Francine *Not My Mother!*—turned toward the screen. I noticed now that she carried a heavy backpack, which she was showing to Paul. As she turned it toward me, a faint pale light glowed from inside.

Seven's skull.

"Got it. Do you still want us to deliver the present to Victoria?"

Paul suddenly grinned more widely than I'd ever seen, his bionic eyes flaring. "I *do*. I want to show her what living bright can really be."

The screens flicked off.

"Ready?" The distant shout came from Emiliano. Footsteps clanged up the stairs.

I gazed under the cryo pod and saw Leech twitching. Blood spreading. I saw Emiliano arrive and reach down to pluck the sextant from around Leech's neck, then roll him over and yank his sketchbook from his pocket.

"I need you to get up now, Owen," said Francine.

"No." I moaned softly. I wasn't getting up. I wasn't doing anything.

Hands scooped under me, and Emiliano's muscular arms hoisted me into the air. He slung me over his shoulder. I wanted to fight him, but everything was off, spinning but out of gear. I felt like I was beyond broken, more nothing than something, a hollow shell, falling in on myself. I wanted to die. Dying would be better. It had to be better.

"Did you deploy the code?" asked Francine.

"Yeah," said Emiliano. "It's going to start anytime now."

We crossed the catwalk. With all the strength I could find, I craned my neck up and saw the back of my sister's head, Elissa, the cryo pod . . . and then I lost sight of her. Leech was still lying there, one hand clawing at the ground. "You can't just leave him," I said to no reply. Then he bobbed out of my sight, too.

A huge sound erupted through the entire facility. A giant horn. It lasted a couple of seconds, and then there was a rush of air.

"I wish we could stick around to see it," said Francine. "I put a ton of time into that cognition substitution software. I really want to know if it's going to work."

I felt us descending the staircase. I thudded against Emiliano's back, a useless sack of meat. A lie, my life, all a lie . . .

The hissing sound flooded everything, and there was a gathering whir of machinery cycling to life. What had they done? What was the present for Victoria? But it didn't matter. None of it mattered.

Mom, Elissa, Dad . . .

Back through the glass doors, into the reception area. An upside-down view of two more bodies. Arlo, a black pool seeping into the soft carpet around him, and the guard, leaning against the wall, his neck twisted unnaturally. Also a set of feet in sandals. I craned my neck.

"Hey, flyboy." Seven was standing there. Her hands were bound behind her, and she'd been tied to the desk. The side of her face was red, puffy from being struck, but I saw that her eyes were loose, darting around. She'd been taking Shine again. She'd left Tactical seeming angry. Had she taken it to cope? It had probably made her easy to catch.

As Francine neared Seven, the skull glow from her backpack increased. Francine untied her from the desk and grabbed her shoulder, pressing the gun into her back. "Let's go."

Seven stumbled forward, her movements rubbery. Any thought I might have had that we could try to escape was useless. Seven would be no help.

And what was the point, anyway? How could there be a point?

"I found a boat," said Emiliano as we moved down the hall. "Should shorten our trip to the west hatch."

Francine pushed Seven along beside me. She tripped, almost fell. "You are useless," said Francine. The affectations of my mother were gone. Now she was just a scientist and a spy.

Behind us, the whirring and thumping of machinery increased. The walls and floor began to shake.

We reached the front doors and pushed out into the moist night, dark except for the soft glow of the skull, and silent save an occasional bird call. There was a rumble from somewhere distant. Thunder. I thought of my mother counting. Not this mother . . .

"Lake's this way," said Emiliano. He took a step to the right. But a sound made him pause.

There was a strange gathering, like a giant breath

inhaling, all around us . . .

It was the wind. The wind speaking . . .

"QiiFarr-eeschhh . . ."

The words were unintelligible, and for a second I wondered if it was some kind of trick of the breeze between broken windows or just my broken mind making things up. But there was no mistaking the clutching swirl of wind that had begun to spiral around us.

Wind that seemed to have intent.

The skull erupted with light so bright it rendered the backpack transparent.

"Damn!" Francine twisted away, frantically tossing the pack off her shoulders as if the light had burned her. "What's with that thing?"

The light grew, blinding us in white, washing out everything.

I tried to look at Seven through the glare. Was she doing this? But the light was reflecting in her busy eyes and she was just kind of smiling dumbly at it. If this wasn't her . . .

"QiiFarr-eeschhh . . ."

The white was everywhere, as if the world were being erased around us. I could barely make out the outline of Francine, shielding her eyes and whirling back and forth.

Then I saw a new silhouette emerging from the side of the building, walking swiftly.

Within the rippling haze of light, I could just make out the form, a woman . . .

The siren?

Or maybe Rana, somehow made real . . .

She raised something over her head. Spun. Swung. It slammed Francine in the back of the head.

"Guh!" Francine crumpled to the ground.

The figure moved in a blur.

Emiliano turned. He saw the figure and dropped me. I landed on my back and looked up and in the ocean of light, I saw her strike again with the swinging weapon. Emiliano pirouetted and sprawled to the ground, a tooth flying free in a spray of blood.

The figure swam over me. All glow.

Then the light dimmed. My vision became a smudge of green.

A hand wrapped around my wrist.

"Owen. Come on."

Not Rana.

"Get up."

Lilly.

Lilly bathed in skull light.

She dragged me to my feet. In her other hand, she held Leech's boccie ball weapon.

I just stared at her, my brain overloaded.

"Where's Leech?" she asked.

"Inside," I mumbled, wobbling, almost falling.

"Let's go," she said, catching me. She pulled me to her shoulder, then tied the boccie ball onto a belt loop of her shorts. She grabbed Francine's backpack. The skull's glow increased—

"Quiet," she said to it.

The light went out.

"How did you do that?" I asked.

Lilly made an almost embarrassed smile. "Well, that's easy. It's mine."

"Yours?"

"Yeah," said Lilly. "I'm the Medium."

33

"YOU," SAID SEVEN. SHE WAS STANDING A FEW meters away, kind of bobbing from one foot to the other. She sighed. "Figures."

I looked from one to the other. "What do you mean?"

"She knew," said Lilly, eyeing Seven coldly.

Seven shook her head, Shine exaggerating the movement. "No, not *knew*, but . . . worried, yeah. I always worried. When Victoria woke me up, she told me I was a match to within a hundredth of a percent of the Atlantean DNA. . . ." She snapped her fingers. "So close."

"But you said you saw the world inside the skull," I said, "and felt it."

"I thought I did," said Seven. "I saw that vision from the pyramid top, of the Three being sacrificed. And I thought that was everything, but then you came out of the skull yesterday and started talking about singing to the Terra and all that . . . I never saw that."

I remember how she appeared inside the skull, standing

there, but with eyes closed.

"Figures it would be you," Seven said, scowling at Lilly. "I had a feeling, after the way you were acting down in the temple. Boo for me." She dropped to the ground, sitting on her heels.

"What are you doing?" Lilly snapped at her.

"What does it matter, now?" Seven muttered.

More pieces fell into place: Seven's strange worry back at Tactical, when she heard Lilly wasn't coming, how that seemed to bother her. And how she'd let me do the talking after the skull.

"Why didn't you tell me any of this?" I said.

Seven shrugged. "I kept hoping it would change." Her words were slurred at the edges. "I mean, I was close enough to be woken up and get gills and be treated like a god, close enough to open blood locks and see visions of death. I thought that was enough. I mean, how could it not be? And I figured maybe more would happen, like once we were out of here, and, if not, well . . . at least I'd be out of here."

"So, was all that stuff with me just an act?" I asked her.

She looked at me, and even with the blur of Shine in her eyes, it was a sad look. "It wasn't an act, flyboy. Not how I felt about you. I mean, sure, the part where we were going to fly out of here as gods made it more exciting, but . . . Well, you can believe me or not." She stared at the ground, shaking her head. "It doesn't matter now. I'm just a ghost. We're all ghosts."

"Oh, please. You—" Lilly bit her lip and turned back to me. "Where is Leech?"

"Back at the cryo pods," I said. "My—" I looked down at Francine. "Sorry, she's not my mom. She works for Paul."

"Oh no," said Lilly. "Owen . . ."

"Later," I said. "Paul said they don't need Leech anymore, and they shot him."

Seven started to laugh. She smiled at the sky. "There's more." She kind of sung the words. "Guess who doesn't need who?"

"What are you talking about?" I snapped at her.

Seven's head kept moving to whatever music her Shine-bathed mind was playing, but she didn't answer.

"Ugh." Lilly looked like she might explode. "We'll figure it out later." She bent, grabbed the gun from Francine's hand, and held the handle right in front of Seven's face. "Can you handle this without doing anything stupid?"

Seven's eyes tracked to the weapon. "Can I shoot them?"

Lilly rolled her eyes. "I don't even care. Just don't let them leave."

"Okay," Seven said quietly.

Lilly pulled out her Nomad knife and cut Seven's ropes. then handed her the gun. "We'll be right out."

Thunder boomed, echoing through the dome. There was a pattering sound: rain on the roof, high above.

Lilly and I headed back through the doors, into the

thrumming facility. I could barely keep my body moving. I had to hold back everything that I now knew, all the thoughts coming at me, wanting to tear me apart, had to just focus on what came next, had to get to Leech . . .

And yet here now was Lilly. More confusion. More that didn't make sense. I stopped running. Stood there unsteady in the hall, its walls groaning with activity. "Wait," I said. "You told me to leave you."

"Owen, come on, later—"

"No! Everyone's been lying to me . . . forever! And that includes you."

Lilly paused, gazing at me seriously. "Look, I wasn't sure. To be honest, I didn't know for absolute certain until a few minutes ago. I mean, I'd been feeling something since the moment we arrived here, hearing that music, but there was Seven, and she seemed like the real, if annoying, deal. But then we went into the temple . . ."

"You were there," I said. "You were that shadow in the skull with me, weren't you?"

"Yeah. But even after that happened, I thought it might be just something weird about that skull. After all, it sucked you in and you're not the Medium."

"True."

"So I said good-bye to you in case I was wrong, but also because I needed to be left alone, by everyone, so I could figure it out. Honestly, I didn't think you'd listen to me about Seven without proof. And she'd already mentioned cutting my heart out once . . ." Lilly sighed. "I meant the part, too, where I wasn't going to be able to stand saying good-bye to you. So, if I was wrong, you needed to just leave anyway, and if I was right, well, I figured I could surprise you with evidence if I found it. So . . ." Lilly shrugged at me. "Ta-da." She motioned to her neck. "Plus, no more gills. They disappeared this morning."

I just looked at her and felt woozy. My thoughts were like a hive of bees, and there was no way to focus on each one. I couldn't decide if I wanted to scream at her or hug her or maybe both.

She could see it on my face. "What happened in here?"

"I'll show you," I said, and a great tremor shook me as I considered that going to get Leech meant going near that cryo pod again. . . .

Things started to swim. "Whoa." Lilly caught me by the shoulder. "Here." She draped my arm over her shoulders and continued into the glass-walled reception area.

We ran out onto the platform. There was steam everywhere, billowing clouds. Moisture dripped from the railings, made the floor slick, puddles starting to form. The temperature was getting warmer, fast. Yellow lights flashed on every level, and the workstations were flickering, columns of data flashing across them.

"What's going on?" Lilly asked as we climbed the stairs.

"They set off some kind of program."

"Are they killing everyone?"

"I don't know. Paul was in a copter. . . ." I worked to reassemble what I'd heard. "They were going to rendezvous nearby, something about a surprise, but, the point is, they're coming." We started across the catwalk. "Over here."

Leech was still there, lying on the floor. He'd rolled over on his side in a pool of blood. We heard him cough as we approached. At least we hadn't lost him yet. Through the din, I could just barely hear his tapes, still playing to Isaac.

The cryo tube was still open above him. There were lights blinking inside the glass. As we rushed over, I felt more waves in my brain. I didn't want to look in there again, didn't want to know what I now knew, what I had to face about everything.

Lilly dropped to her knees beside Leech. I stood on the other side of him. My eyes strayed from Leech to the profile of Elissa—*No*—back to Leech.

"Oh man," said Lilly. There was blood everywhere. A slick around him. The source seemed to be his chest or shoulder, maybe abdomen—his whole shirt was soaked, and it was impossible to tell. "Carey," she said. "Can you hear me?"

His eyes were closed, his face slack. "We have to get him back to Desenna." Lilly hopped up and peered into the cryo tube. "I thought you came here to see Leech's brother?"

I stepped to the tube again. Put my hands on the glass. It was warm now, the inside fogged with condensation. Looked back inside. Orange lights were flashing in sequence up and down the insides of the pod, and the blue frost was gone, but Elissa was still there, little Elissa.

More memories.

We like to play hide-and-go-seek in the apartment, but it's so small. There are only four rooms with barely a place to hide in each. Elissa's favorite is under the dining room table, and I can see her immediately but I pretend not to and we play until her cough kicks in. . . .

"Owen?"

"This is my . . . sister," I said, choking on the words. "I'm a Cryo, Lilly. Paul lied to me. Set it all up."

"Oh, God," said Lilly. "Leech told me one time that he was worried about you . . . about what you thought about the world. He wouldn't tell me what he meant. But . . . oh, Owen."

"It's all been a lie, everything." The thoughts started crashing in now. "I had black blood, and they cryoed me. It killed her. Elissa. My sister. Only Paul changed my memories, set me up. He called it an insurance policy. Nothing I've been thinking this whole time has been real. Nothing I've wanted has been true. I'm not even who I am, or . . ." I fought the tides in my head, but the waves rushed over me. I slumped against the tube, arms draped over it. Lilly's hand rubbed my back.

"I'm so sorry," she said quietly. "I'm so, so sorry."

I rested my cheek on the warm glass.

And I cried.

The feeling hitched up out of me in little spasms, making my eyes hot, my throat tight. I looked down at Elissa's still face, a face like mine, like my real mom's, a match, a lost genetic code, restored in me now. . . . They'd both returned to their rightful places, back into the memories from which they'd been removed, filling the distance on the couch between my father and me as we watched soccer, long ago. . . . My vision blurred with tears.

"Owen," said Lilly beneath the din of machinery. Her hand still on my back. "We have to go. I know it's hard but we need to keep moving."

I listened to the humming and whirring of the cryo facility through the glass of Elissa's pod, her coffin. I heard Lilly, but I didn't move. The tears were like energy seeping from me, some release, the last bit that I had left, draining out of me. This shell that had been scraped out, changed—what even was I?

She tugged at my shirt. "We have to get Leech and get out of here. Paul will come. We have to move."

"I—" I started, but I couldn't get up from the tube. More thoughts, battering around. If Paul had erased all this and hadn't told me, what else had he changed? What more was he waiting to reveal when the moment suited him? Was I even from Yellowstone Hub? Was my name even Owen? Or were the old memories real and these new ones fake? Had there never even been an Elissa—was *this* girl a fake and my sisterless past real? Had Paul planted her to be revealed now? What was the truth? Was any of it real? "I can't." I sobbed more. "I can't."

"Owen . . ."

But, no. No. I slumped down. Fell to my knees. Caught my head in my hands. I couldn't do anything. There was no going forward. No more.

You are Owen from Hub. You had a sister and you were cryoed—

She likes to jump on me when I'm reading in bed, but Dad says stop because it shakes the walls too much and isn't polite to the neighbors—

No, empty beds, just you and Dad, a hollow center, they weren't there, they were never there—

They were there.

Far away, outside my closed eyes, there was a great hissing sound.

"Owen." Lilly sounded more serious than ever. "We need to go. Now." She tugged on my arm. "Hey!"

"I can't," I mumbled. It was all too much.

More wicked hissing sounds all around us. Massive clouds of steam.

"Don't do this." Lilly grabbed my shoulder. "We need to go—"

But I swatted her away and scrambled back, flipping over onto my butt and elbows. "No, I can't!" Tears were surging out of me and I had no idea how to stop them. "I don't even know who I am or what I was or anything!"

Lilly's face darkened. "Yes, you do!" She lunged forward and landed on me, legs straddling my waist. She looked furious, her face bloodred.

"I can't tell, I—" Everything inside felt like shelves tumbling, their contents flung free and shattering on the floor, like when we'd have an earthquake back at Hub—

There was no Hub—was—

Lilly smacked me. My cheek stung numb. "Stop it! Listen to me!" she shouted over the din around us. "You're Owen!" She stabbed my chest with her finger. "This is YOU! And I *know* you and you have to get up and *run* with me! You need to DO it!"

"I can't, just . . ." More thoughts in all directions. "How do I even know that you're real?"

Lilly unleashed a clenched, animal-like scream. Her head thrashed down and her lips crushed against me. Our teeth collided. I felt her forehead, slick with sweat, sliding across mine. Our noses squished against each other. When she finally pulled away, she tugged on my lip so hard with her teeth that I felt a tear of skin. "NOW do you think I'm real? Did you FEEL that?"

I just nodded.

"That is you! And that is *me*. Now you get up with me, Owen, and you help me carry Leech and we are going to get out of here or we are going to die because I will *kill* you before I leave you behind! Do you understand me?"

Her eyes were black in the shadows, storms erasing their

normal blue skies. Her entire torso heaved with her panting breaths. And the glow of the skull from her backpack had created a corona of light around her.

And for just a moment, the cyclone inside my hollow center, the empty gale winds of questions, ceased; and out of all of it, I understood something so clear, so true, like I'd opened a kind of gate into some view of infinite space and I was nothing and we were everything and through all of it, there was one thing I knew:

"I love you," I whispered.

Lilly just glared at me. Her eyelids trembled. Tears started to slip down her cheeks. Her face grimaced in a look like she hated me so much right then, like she wanted to kill me. And I wondered if she really would—I had no idea anymore—as she slowly leaned down, her desperate breaths splashing on my already-wet face, until the tip of her nose touched mine and her eyes blurred into one, and she spoke in a livid whisper:

"If you really love me, then run with me. Get out of here alive. Because if you want to just stay here and die, then what you just said to me is a lie and I will hate you for all eternity." She stared at me, a mountain lion assessing its prey. Her eyes dared me to disobey. Then she leaped back up to her feet.

I felt the words. I drank them. Let them tear me open and pin my insides in place and make me still . . .

"Okay." And I got up.

I shook my head. And then I noticed what had happened all around us. The cryo doors had all swung open, and all the tubes, the hundreds of tubes, had slid out. Lines of clear coffins, of bodies.

"Help me get Leech," said Lilly.

I was about to when there was another deafening series of hisses and clicks.

The top of Elissa's cryo tube yawned open. All the tops throughout the complex, opening to the elements, so that the bodies could rot in the humid air and invite the flies and vultures, I guessed. Maybe this was what Paul had in mind. To punish Victoria by showing her how easy it was for him to kill these people that she'd tried to keep alive.

"I don't want to leave her like this," I said, stepping over to . . . yes, she was my sister. I knew that. Solid fact, pinned in place. There was her face.

We both like jelly and groundnut sandwiches, but she is weird. She eats the crusts and leaves the middles.

"Owen . . ." Lilly sounded worried.

"I know we need to go," I said. And I knew what I had to do.

I tell her that's the best part, but she says that the middles are too squishy, too full.

I reached down and pressed my thumb against her cheek. It was still cold, kind of half-thawed.

On the way to school we walk together, Mom a few paces behind, and Elissa likes to follow me, walking on the narrow concrete edge of the sewer aqueduct, and it annoys me, always so annoying because she is too little and it slows me down but mostly because I cannot stand the idea of her falling in, of her getting hurt.

I drew a clockwise circle.

Asleep before me each night, her little face in green generator light, her cheeks deactivated, and all I hope is that she'll make it through the night without any coughing fits. They wake me up and break my heart. I love her. My sister. I always have.

I leaned over and closed my eyes and kissed her forehead. It was damp. Smelled like soap and mildew, like the Camp Eden bathroom. Like the caves at Hub during a mold bloom, in the spring, so long ago.

"Good-bye, sister," I whispered.

"Oh no," I heard Lilly breathe behind me.

I lifted my head and opened my eyes and—

Elissa's eyes had opened, too.

3 4

SHE'S ALIVE. MY FIRST THOUGHT. *SHE'S BACK.*

Her lovely brown eyes—

But her eyes were dark, the whites clouded over in a filmy charcoal gray, congealed fluid, a mix of the black blood crusted and dried. Her lids blinking, the cloudy eyes flicking back and forth . . . Twitches began to ignite up and down her arms and legs. Spasms. Movement.

There was more movement. I glanced up. A head rose out of the next cryo pod over. A woman, matted blond hair and a pale face, moving disjointedly, still thawing, but waking up . . .

No. Rising.

Another head, another body, all of them, every one above and below. In all directions, hundreds of bodies were rising from their frozen sleep.

"What has he done?" Lilly asked hoarsely.

"It's a program," I said. Francine had said *software.* Cognition substitution.

Elissa began to sit up.

I stared dumbly at her, unbelieving. Her chest didn't move. She made no sound except for a rubbery stretching as still-cold limbs and tissue began to move.

All around us, Cryos sitting. Necks creaking around.

Her head jolted toward me. The gray milky eyes. A tremor and her brow worked, her mouth twitched, like systems coming back online, technicians inside throwing switches.

Her arms rose. She reached for me with long fingernails and hands striped in black, the squiggles of black veins up her arms like a tattoo of tree branches. Her fingers touched my cheek.

And began to scrape. To dig in. The other hand locked on my arm. Yanked me close.

I couldn't fight, I didn't know . . . was she alive? But, no, she'd been dead. This was operation, function, but not life.

Hands to my neck. Closing. Tightening. And now she leaned over with her mouth opening and there was a strange kind of guttural sucking sound as air ran down her throat, rushing into spaces that had been closed for so long, not a breath but just simple physics, and yet it sounded like a deep, hungry inhale.

Teeth toward my throat. My sister. Back in Yellowstone, I let her out of my sight. She fell in that sucker hole. Now breathing into ruined lungs that were my fault, back to even the score . . .

No! I had to keep reality straight. I closed my eyes and shoved her back. Her claws tore the collar of my shirt as I jerked away from her. She snapped her teeth at me, snatched at the air where I'd been. Some of the thawed black blood began to leak out the corners of her mouth now, to dribble onto her perfect white gown. *That's not my sister,* I told myself. *That's a machine and it's programmed to kill.* I wanted to unsee her, to never know this, but I knew already that this image would haunt me forever.

Her twitching arms grabbed the side of the pod, and she started to pull herself out.

They were all getting out. Victoria could free people through death. But now Paul could raise the dead.

"We have to go," I said. I spun, bent down, and grabbed Leech's arm. Lilly got the other. Luckily he was small, and we got him between us, one limp arm over each shoulder, and we sprinted for the stairs.

There were thuds and smacking sounds from every direction. In the humid clouds of steam, pierced by the flashing orange lights, silhouettes of bodies stepped out of their pods, many stumbling on unsteady limbs and collapsing to the ground, making flat sounds like pieces of cold meat dropped on a table. Half-thawed bodies reanimated and unleashed. And despite the slipping and sliding, the staggering into walls, I could see them all slowly orienting their blank gazes toward the staircases. Each inefficient on its own, but as a collective they were like a wave, coming from all directions, and we were barely ahead of it.

We reached the stairs. "I got him," I said, pulling Leech away from Lilly. She dashed in front of me. I turned back to see a mob lurching across the catwalk toward us, and in the front, small and frail and oozing with disease, was Elissa. *Not Elissa,* I told myself again, trying desperately to believe it, even as more memories returned to my mind, more beautiful visions of the sister I'd forgotten.

I hoisted Leech down the stairs. Lilly grabbed his arm again and we raced to the glass doors.

Sliding and scraping of thawing feet, slapping of hands on walls. And those weird guttural intakes, air sucking in, the dead bodies breathing.

We were through the doors. Pulled them shut.

"Is there a lock?" Lilly inspected them.

Thwack! The first Cryo walked right into the glass like she didn't even know it was there. A middle-aged woman, bony beneath the hospital gown hanging cockeyed off her, vacant red-stained eyes and the echo of boils all over her skin. She bounced back, walked into it again, then started banging her head against it. Harder, harder.

"A lock isn't going to help," I said.

More were reaching the glass. Hitting it. Trying to walk right through. A thundering succession of thuds, creating red blotches on the glass.

As we sprinted down the hall, I heard the first splintering crack. Then a crash as the windows gave way.

We burst outside. There was a roar echoing around us.

Rain was cascading through the hole in the roof. Waterfalls everywhere.

"Damn," said Lilly. I followed her gaze. Francine and Emiliano were gone. Seven was gone. "They got her. I should have known she was useless!"

"Doesn't matter," I said. "We have to get back to the city. Warn Victoria. They have no idea."

"Yeah." Lilly hurried to the side of the building, and returned with her red bag. "Can you carry this?"

"Got it."

We jumped at a crash from behind us. I turned to see them hitting the doors. A tall old man covered in lesions, a young boy, a teen girl, all just backing up and walking straight into the glass, their skin still blue in spots and their eyes vacant yet targeting us.

We ran back through the city and out into the inky jungle. The rain was torrential, soaking us instantly. We stumbled along the undulating, dark trail, a blur of water, a slick of mud. Even with Leech, we were faster than the staggering, thawing horde, and soon their shuffling, mud-splattering pursuit was lost to our ears. For a time there was just the rain beating on jungle leaves, and soon the growing rumble of the drums in the plaza, as the festival's beginnings proceeded unaware.

I felt dampness on my chest. I looked down to see that Leech's blood was soaking through my shirt.

"You're gonna be okay," I said to him.

"Nnn," he moaned faintly.

We crested the rise between EdenSouth and Desenna. I looked back at the dome, and through the cracked ceiling I saw the ominous orange light of Cryo flickering on the inner walls.

Ahead, we could see the rainswept skyline of the city, lit in flashing lights and flickering torches. The drums were loud, thumping along with tinny echoes of music—

And then it all exploded.

A huge wipe of fire across our vision . . .

One . . . two . . . Mom says, counting down the thunder. It scares Elissa when she does this. . . .

The force of the blasts reached us and knocked us flat.

I felt a moment of loss, no sound, no breath, but then things filtered back in and I scrambled to my feet just in time to see a line of white lights swoop up over the back of the now-smoldering central complex. Copters. They arced overhead. Lightning rains flashed, taking out two copters, but there were at least five others.

"New plan," I said. "Get to the ship. Get out of here."

"Is it still on the pyramid?" Lilly asked. "The one that just got hit by rockets?"

"Yeah." I peered ahead. The pyramid was choked in smoke and flames. "We have to try for it." There was one thing I still felt certain of in my head, and that was how to fly. If the ship was gone, then . . . I didn't want to think about that.

"Okay," said Lilly. She glanced behind us. I heard it, too. The dragging and squishing of feet.

We ran on toward the city. The music had been replaced by screaming, shouts of confusion.

The copters came around for another pass, dodging lightning rain and firing again, streaks of light that arced into the heart of Desenna and caused more plumes of smoke and fire, more chest-thumping blast waves.

The copters veered off and disappeared over the trees. No more lightning rains followed them.

We pressed on through the damp dark, now thick with waves of acrid smoke. We reached the gate. It was in tatters, piles of rubble and twisted metal.

"Looks like they cleared an entrance for their cryo army," said Lilly.

We made our way over the soaked wreckage, slow with Leech. In the jungle he'd been sort of moving his feet along with us, but now his legs hung limp. I saw that his face had turned a frightening white.

"You still with us?"

He coughed weakly.

"Let's hoist him up," said Lilly, getting her arms under his shoulders. I took his legs and we moved awkwardly over the rubble. It was tough going. I slipped, jammed my ankle in a crevice, scraped my forearm on a broken slab of stone. By the time we were through the wreckage, my cramp had started to knot up—

Not from a hernia. From spleen surgery. My life is all a lie—

I shook away the thoughts. Later. I would deal with

them later, and it would be terrible, but now—

"Here they come," said Lilly, glancing behind us.

I turned and saw the first forms, gray skin, soaked hair, and white gowns now smeared with mud, lurching from the shadows. We got Leech's arms back around our shoulders and raced through the streets toward the plaza, fighting a tide of panicked people who were heading for their homes. I wanted to warn them about what was coming, but I didn't have the voice, the strength. They would have to find out on their own.

The central plaza was in chaos. Buildings to either side had been hit in the rocket attack, and the café areas were scenes of carnage and flames. People were rushing in all directions like frenzied molecules, many in ceremonial robes, their faces painted in the emeralds and cobalts and whites, painted for a joyous celebration of living bright but now streaked with blood and dust.

"The Three!" someone shouted as we passed, as if we were returning with hope instead of leading an onslaught of horror.

I looked to the sky. "No more copters."

Lilly glanced back toward the gate. "They're just waiting now," she said breathlessly. "Just sit back and watch the show."

We rounded a collapsed spill of bricks, people pinned, screaming, medics on the scene—

My mother was a medic. NO, that wasn't her! Was my

real mom one? Ever?

We made it to the doors into the pyramid. There were guards there, wide-eyed, watching the sky.

"Watch the plaza!" Lilly shouted at them. "And get ready. They're coming from Cryo!"

The guards looked at us, confusion on their already shaken faces, but we hurried by them, ducking inside and up the wide stairs. At the top, we were halted by soldiers digging at a pile of rubble. The hall leading to Tactical was blocked. Black smoke billowed from the seams.

"Did they get hit?" I asked.

A soldier turned to me. "Direct hit on the second pass. We can't get in there from any side. And there's been no word . . ."

Lilly looked past me. The stairway up to the pyramid top was clear. I nodded to her, and we hurried up.

My legs were screaming from the extra weight of carrying Leech. We reached the open-roofed hallway, passed all the bloody handprints, up the final staircase, and out to the platform.

The city unfolded below us, a hell of fire and smoke and rain. Clouds buffeted our backs, blown in by a salty sea breeze, making us cough. Thunder cracked overhead. The masses were scrambling below, a tide of shouts pierced by screams.

The left corner of the platform was gone, as if a bite had been taken out of it. The crater extended to the sacrificial stone, half of which was blasted away.

The other side of the platform, where my ship was . . .

Was okay. It was just sitting there, its blue light glowing serenely. There were bags of supplies stored in its front, all ready for our morning departure. The collapsed section of roof ended less than a meter from its bow.

"I wouldn't want to say we're lucky," said Lilly, "but . . . that's pretty lucky." Her voice hitched as if now, after everything else, she might cry at the sight of it.

We laid Leech down in the craft, along with our bags. Then we heard a new sound, a ripple of shocked screams from below. I peered over the edge of the remaining platform. The Cryos were swarming into the plaza, moving faster now, their bodies warm and attacking without hesitation, without fear, without thinking. Every once in a while my eye was able to see a specific moment of the chaos, and there was blood and tearing and struggle and I wished I hadn't seen it. But there was no denying that the wave of Cryos were treating the bystanders merely as obstacles. Their tide was clearly headed this way. Paul had aimed them right at Victoria.

"Time to fly." I checked the craft. There were puddles on the floor, but the mast looked true, the vortex was at full charge, and I finally felt like my feet had landed on a concrete sense of *yes*, this was what I was. I could fly. We could make it.

The screams were getting worse from below. Shots rang

out from the guards at the pyramid entrance, followed by the smashing of glass.

I checked the sails and found they'd been patched up. "Everything's good to go. Thank you, Victoria."

"Don't thank me yet."

We turned to see Victoria being helped up the steps by Mica. She was in her costume: the crimson robes, the jade-green face, golden sun corona on her head. She was limping, and her free hand was clutching at her chest. Mica guided her across the platform to where the large ceremonial chair lay overturned. He let go of her for a moment. She wobbled in place as he righted the chair, then eased her into it.

She sat there gathering her breath, her eyes tracking slowly over the fire and smoke, the ruins.

There were muffled gunshots from inside the pyramid halls. Mica moved back to the top of the stairs, pulled a rifle off his shoulder, and watched the doors warily.

"Paul did this, didn't he?" Victoria said weakly.

"Yeah," I said.

Victoria nodded slowly. "Fitting weather." Then she kind of laughed, but it hitched into a thick, wet cough. "He thinks he is making a point, showing how much control is possible if you *just have vision*. That's what he would say." She coughed again, tearing at her insides. "He probably thinks I'm lamenting the loss of my kingdom, sitting here crying as I watch it all end in blood and fire."

"I'm sorry," I said. And I found that I really did feel bad

for her. Compared to Paul, she was infinitely more human.

"Don't be," said Victoria. "This was always how it would end. Every civilization is just an attempt, a best guess, given the moment, the ecology, the weather. And they're all imperfect, shots in the dark, and they all end in a flood. The tide that swallows a people is born of its own darkest desires. This one is no different." She sighed. "We can only hope that our little step helps the next attempt get closer to divine. That someday humanity becomes something better than itself."

Victoria's eyes tracked to me. Raindrops dabbed at her green paint. "Your mother found me in my chamber. She took the skull, and left a knife in my back. Very clever. Paul was always the most clever. Mica found me shortly before the attack. I suppose if I'd been down in Tactical I'd already be dead." She coughed, covered her mouth with her hand, then looked at it. She held her palm out toward us, coated in red. "Funny," she said. Water washed the blood in streaks down her arm.

"We got the skull back," I said.

More shots from behind. The smashing of glass close by.

"Mother," Mica warned. "We need to go."

Victoria ignored him. "You have the skull," said Victoria. She coughed. More fluid. "That's fortunate. And do we know what happened to dear Seven? Last I saw her she was sulking around Tactical after you left and drowning her angst in Shine."

"I'm here, Mother." Seven came sauntering up the steps. I saw that her face was badly bruised, probably from Francine and Emiliano, and there seemed to be long cuts on her arms and a dark patch by her neck, maybe from the claws of Cryos, yet somehow she'd changed into her white Heliad dress. She'd put a tiara on her head, and even dusted herself in sparkling powder so that she glimmered in the firelight like a star fallen to earth. She scooted around Mica and crossed the platform, her steps wobbly, her legs like rubber.

"Look," she said. "I dressed for the big event! Even though I'm not part of it. All that work just to get cut from the grand finale." I caught a glimpse of her eyes and could see the free spin, worse now than before, like she'd taken even more.

And somehow it made my heart break for her, despite the storm in my head. I remembered Seven's story, of being plucked out of life, of having no place in time. A feeling I now knew all too well. Maybe we could get her in the craft, anyway. Lilly would object. And she might be right. But still . . .

Seven swooned, and as her hands went out against the air to steady herself, I saw that she was holding the giant obsidian knife. She righted herself, and started making little circles with it in the air in front of her. The blood and water trickling down her pale arms and neck collected glitter dust in shimmering rivulets.

We stared at her, strangely rapt, as she moved to the

very edge of the blast crater, and it seemed for sure like she was just going to walk right off. Leaning . . . "There's a lot of divine on display down there tonight," she said darkly. Then, she turned and stepped over behind Victoria's ceremonial chair, leaning on it woozily, and stood there almost like she and Victoria were a team.

"I'm glad you're here, Seven," said Victoria.

"I know you are, Beloved Mommy, but I have a surprise for you."

Victoria coughed, and even in pain, when she spoke she sounded exasperated. "What's that?"

Seven lifted the knife, its point wavering, flicking water drops, and for a moment Victoria flinched and Mica tensed, but then Seven wagged it at us. "She's the Medium."

Victoria didn't move, but her eyes seemed to register real surprise. "Really." She tried to glance up at Seven, the motion clearly hurting her. "You—"

"Am just a girl who died a long time ago," said Seven. She giggled lightly. "I was never even here." She swayed, looking like she might fall over. The knife traced unstable arcs.

Banging now. Close. Mica shouted down the handprint hallway. "Hold that position!" Screams and more shots muffled, but close. "Mother," Mica said. "Quickly."

Victoria ignored him again. She was looking at us. "So, you three, right there, *you're* the Three."

"Yeah," I said. "Listen, I can fly you all out, at least far enough from those copters—"

"That won't be necessary," said Victoria.

"Why—"

"She's going to kill you," Seven suddenly blurted. "Don't you get it?" She laughed, high and shrill. "She's been planning to kill us all along. Haven't you, O Benevolent Mother?"

Victoria's gaze stayed on us. Then she sort of shrugged. "Well, not until you'd flown away and were well out of my people's sight. I was going to wait until you were about fifty kilometers south before I had the drones shoot you down."

"Wait, what?" I said. "Why?"

"It's so *obvious*," said Seven. "Mother, the great director at work."

"I suppose that boy told you," said Victoria, glancing up at Seven. "You wrapped him around your finger and he was able to get you that information."

"Nico," said Seven. She drew a little heart in the air with the tip of the knife. "Darling Nico."

"He's dead, I'm sure," said Victoria, "down in Tactical."

Seven stopped drawing. "Oh well." She aimed her gyrating eyes at me. "Rule number six: no gods equals no Paul finding Atlantis."

Don't think you know what Mother is thinking, she'd said.

"Sad, but true," said Victoria. "You would've flown out

of my story, satisfied my people, and then I would have ended your threat to the world. Without you, Paul can never find the Paintbrush."

I felt myself draining to empty. After all this . . . We'd been dead all along.

"But I don't know if he needs us," said Lilly. I saw that she was slowly rotating the backpack off her shoulder. To get to the skull, and fire its light, talking to stall . . . "They shot Leech, even though he's one of us."

There was a loud succession of thumps and now the smashing of glass. Screams that had been muffled now became immediate. Shots rang out. Mica fired three rounds back down the hall. "We need to go, Mother!" he shouted.

"Okay, okay. Owen, Lilly, I'm sorry but it's time for you to volunteer, for the good of everyone else." She nodded to Mica.

His gun swung around toward us—

"Lilly!" She didn't have the skull out yet, and I dove and pulled her into the craft.

As I fell I heard Seven scream. "Live bright!"

There was a sound—a tearing crunch followed by a choked gasp—and then the crack of bullets. I tensed, expecting them to hit the craft, but they didn't.

Lilly and I looked up to see Mica aiming across the platform, and Seven staggering back from the ceremonial chair, her hands empty and held high. Red blossomed on her dress.

The ceremonial knife was buried in Victoria's chest.

Seven stumbled toward the edge.

"Seven!" I shouted, but out of the corner of my eye I saw Mica spinning his gun toward us.

"Get her," said Lilly. She had the gleaming skull in her hands and jumped up, whispering in ancient tones. *"Qii-Farr-saaan . . ."*

White light burst from the skull and Lilly at once, seeming to pour out of her eyes and mouth. Wind buffeted Mica as he fired, and the bullets sailed wide. Lilly stepped out of the craft and walked toward him, her hair flaring around her. Mica stumbled back, the wind vicious, the light blinding.

I turned to see that Seven had reached the very edge of the platform, her toes over the abyss.

"Careful!" I shouted, starting toward her.

She wobbled in place, looking at her chest, at the blood seeping into her soaked dress, then down at the plaza, far below. She turned to me. "Claire."

"What?"

"That was my non-god name. Just Claire." She smiled at me. "Time to fly."

I stepped closer, holding out my hand. "It is. Let's go."

Seven shook her head sadly. "Not with you. Third option."

"Third—" I didn't know—but then I did.

Her smile faded and her eyes locked on mine. "So long,

flyboy." She spread her arms.

"Wait!" I lunged for her. My fingers grazed her dress, but she stepped off the edge and plummeted out of sight.

I stared at the space where she'd just been. Distantly, I heard the heavy sound of impact.

"Get back!"

I turned. Mica was shouting from somewhere down the steps. Lilly was aiming her light down there. There were gunshots, snarls, and now a terrified scream.

"They're here!" Lilly called. "We need to go!"

I started toward the craft, but glanced at Victoria, slumped in her chair. Her hands were flailing at her neck. Her eyes were wide and staring at me and her mouth was moving like she was trying to say something, but only making choking sounds. . . .

I checked Lilly. She seemed to be holding them back. I ran over to Victoria. She had managed to pull a chain out from around her neck. A necklace with an antique metal locket at the end. I reached around the hilt of the giant knife, pulled the locket from her fingers, and flicked it open. Inside were two capsules of Shine. I found her looking at me. I tapped the capsules into my hand.

But we needed information first. "What do you know about the Ascending Stars?" I shouted at her. "What is Paul doing?"

"I . . ." she croaked. Her mouth kept moving, but blood dribbled out of the corners, and no sound came out. She looked up toward the sky. Coughed up more blood.

"Owen!" Lilly was backing up toward the craft. "Hurry!"

I saw the bodies jerking their way up the staircase. Women, men, children, old and young, some with blood around their mouths, some with bullet holes that hadn't worked. They fought against the wind and light, relentless.

I looked back to find Victoria reaching for me, her fingers pawing at my hands, at the Shine. Her fingers . . .

I pressed the Shine against her bloody lips. "There's one more thing we need," I said. I grasped the wet handle of the ceremonial knife with both hands and pulled. It tore free with a crunch. Victoria gasped. Then she looked at the knife and at me.

"Time to volunteer," I said. I grabbed her right hand and pressed it down against the armrest.

As I lowered the knife, it shook in my hand, and I thought there was no way I could do this, but I remembered what Leech had said: Paul would never hesitate, to kill us, to take my memories, erase my sister, then raise her from the dead and send her after me. Victoria wouldn't hesitate to shoot us down to save her people. . . .

And after everything we'd been through . . . I wouldn't either.

I lowered the knife against the base of Victoria's pinkie, the heavy serrated teeth denting the skin. I glanced back at Victoria. Her eyes were wide, the pupils just starting to spin, but I felt her arm stop fighting. She closed her eyes.

I pressed down and sawed back and forth. There was a wet, tearing sound. A faint, high moan escaped Victoria's lips.

I finished and threw the knife away, holding back the urge to vomit. The finger lay there, slightly curled, dotted with rain and leaking blood, its hidden bar code something we might need. I grabbed it, warm in my hand, lurched to my feet, and shoved it in my pocket.

I looked Victoria in the eye one more time. "Live bright," I said, and ran for the craft.

"Okay, let's go!" I shouted. Lilly had backed up nearly to the craft. She slumped her shoulders, the light and wind extinguishing. She jumped in. I hit the pedals. As the Cryos streamed up onto the platform, we started to rise.

But they were fast, much faster than they'd been. Hands clutched at the side of the craft, yanking us to the side. Tattered hands, the skin shredded from tearing through glass and bodies.

I grabbed the wet sail lines, stabbed at the pedals, and we banked hard right, out away from the pyramid edge. The craft bucked and we were dragged back left. It was a boy, maybe twelve, his elbows on the edge of the craft, hanging on. His eyes were filmy but blue, and he had once had a delicate face with wavy black hair. His bloodstained teeth gnashed at me. His hand reached out, grabbed my shirt.

I flinched away and kicked as hard as I could, crushing his face. He toppled free. I wondered as he fell, had he been a candidate? Did he have the cursed genes like me? Had he been promised that he would wake up to a better future, that he would help save the world?

There was a tattered scream. I looked back at the platform and saw the horde swarming over Victoria.

More bodies were coming up the steps, reaching what was maybe their final destination. Their programming seemed to run out at this point, and aside from the ones crowded around Victoria, the rest were just milling around dumbly, bumping into each other.

I rose higher, buffeted by rain and wind. Banks of smoke began to obscure our view, but I got one more glimpse and there, in the fray, lit by the fires of the burning city, I saw a little face on the pyramid roof, one last time: Elissa.

My sister, blank and plague filled, dead but risen—into my mind and also into a dark world full of horrors, the horrors of gods like Paul.

A gust reeking of fire and death caught the sails and we began to accelerate away. I craned my neck, squinting in the rain, watching Elissa fade from view, lost among the shuffling bodies and smoke, lost to me, again.

We arced out over the city walls, through the swirling storm, away from Desenna, over the black jungle. I guided us out of the thunderstorm, and sped over the coastline. Below, waves made beautiful foam brushstrokes on the luminous sand. Above, a universe of stars glittered.

"Hey." Lilly's hand landed on my shoulder and I finally felt myself start to collapse.

"Like this," I said, demonstrating how to move the pedals and the sail lines.

"I've been watching," she said. "I'll get the hang of it. South, right?"

"Right. And if the copters come—"

"I'll tell you."

It was time now. For everything I had seen, everything I now knew, to sink in. I collapsed into the hull, and let it all pull me under.

35

MOM AND SISTER DON'T LIKE SOCCER LIKE DAD AND I do, *but they know it's part of the Tuesday night ritual. Dad will be late from the plant, Mom, too, from the clothing redistributor, so it is up to Elissa and me to get the pizza ready. We quarrel over who gets to knead the dough, but I'm older so I win. There's not a lot of room in the apartment kitchen, so I roll it on the floor.*

As I work, I feel something falling on me, and I look up and sly Elissa is dripping millet flour down on my head. "You look like an old man!" She laughs, but then she starts to cough.

I know to pause our fun, to get her inhaler. I hurry to the table, bring it back, and sit her on the step stool, her face dusted in flour. I help her squeeze and breathe. I rub her back.

"Breathe in . . ." *I say,* "and out."

"Breathe."

"Come on, breathe."

I shifted, hearing Lilly's voice. I was half-awake, eyes closed, letting the memories stitch themselves back into place in my brain. There were gaps—these pieces I was getting back were like single cans of food on otherwise empty shelves—but they were something.

I sat up. Everything hurt, my body stiff. Rectangles of faint gray light painted brown walls. We were in a room. It was sometime close to dawn. The light was coming in through an empty space that used to be sliding glass balcony doors.

We'd landed on the roof of the abandoned hotel in the predawn. We climbed down onto the balcony of this room on the top floor. It had been some kind of suite, a hundred years ago. There was an impossibly wide bed, a giant bath, ornate furniture. None of the plumbing worked, chunks of plaster had fallen off the walls, and the bed looked damp and infested.

So we slept on the floor, which was covered with enough sand from years of storms that it was nearly like sleeping on a beach. We slept well, for a little while.

But now Lilly was with Leech, on the balcony. I got up slowly. The night before seemed distant, hazy, and there was more work to do in my head. I felt like I was going to need weeks, years, maybe the rest of my life, to put myself back together. Right now, though, Leech needed our help.

I stepped through the windowless door. It was hard to say what floor we were on—the rest of the building was underwater. There was a gentle sound as waves plunked around in the room below ours. Our balcony hung out over the sea. The coast was a few hundred meters behind us. It was amazing that this building had even stayed standing.

Leech was lying on a recliner chair. There had been two overturned and heaped in the corner of the deck, held there by a rusted chain and padlock, and the foam cushions of one had been pinned behind them. As we'd been coming in the night before, Leech had asked us to put him there, so he could watch the stars.

We didn't argue. There was nothing more we could do for him. We all knew it.

We'd flipped over the chair, wrung out the cushion, and laid Leech there. We wrapped him in the fuzzy pink blanket we'd gotten at the Walmart. He had been shaking all over, arms, legs—blood loss or cryo sickness, probably both. And then he told us to get some rest and so we did.

He was still shaking now, and his breathing was paper thin.

Lilly had her hands on Leech's chest. "Go slow," she said. "Just try to get a breath in."

He seemed to nod, and closed his eyes to try. There was a sound like wind whistling through a crack in a door.

"It's gonna be okay," I said to him, knowing it was a lie, wondering why people always lied at times like this. I tried to pull the blanket up higher over his shoulders, but it was stuck in place by dried blood. There was a sand-speckled puddle of it on the floor.

Leech's hand reached out and grabbed mine. His cold fingers gripped my wrist. I met his eyes, his squinty brown eyes, bloodshot now, his freckles so dark against his pale skin. "D—did Paul say why?" he asked.

Why had they shot him? How could they no longer need him when he was one of the Three? I shook my head. Hating it. "No," I said. "They took your sextant and your sketches, but . . . no."

Another wicked shudder wracked Leech, and he seemed to nod. "Wouldn't have mattered," he said. "Cryo sickness was going to get me anyway. It was only a matter of time . . . I'm glad I found Isaac. In my cryo dream we were playing Monopoly. We played for hours when we wanted to stay out of Dad's way."

I remembered him leading games in our cabin. "I'm sorry," I said uselessly, "about everything."

"No," said Leech, "don't be. I should have told you more, told you everything, from the start at camp. We didn't have to be enemies, could have been a team, could have gotten out sooner and made it farther and . . ."

"We were a team," I said to him. "You saved me last night."

"You saved me first," said Leech.

"Then we're even." I reached out and gripped his fist. "Friends?"

Leech kind of laughed. It looked like it hurt. "Sure."

His other hand slapped on top of mine. Our eyes met. "You have to stop them," he said.

"We will," I said, a lump growing in my throat, "but we need to know where to go. Where the next marker is."

Leech nodded. "South," he said. "If you . . . paper . . ." He was shaking too much, his mouth still moving but the words lost.

"I'll look," said Lilly. She went inside.

Leech started tapping his leg. "Pen . . ."

I fished his pen out of his pocket and pressed it against his palm.

"Here." Lilly returned with some damp, stained stationary. It said *La Tortuga de Oro* at the top in gold lettering, with a script sketch of a turtle among waves.

I held the pad out for Leech. He took a deep, pained breath and then, he tried to draw. He made what looked like a coastline, but then his hand devolved into shaking, and the pen made erratic black strokes.

"Damn!" he shouted. He tried again, more shaking. Scribbles where he'd once been able to make such intricate art. He slapped the paper away and hurled the pen off the balcony. He stared desperately up at the sky, blinking tears, looking betrayed. "I—"

He seemed to freeze midbreath. His eyes slipped back in his head. He slumped down. I put a hand over his chest. All was still.

"No," I said quietly. It wasn't fair. Leech didn't deserve

this fate. How did he deserve any of what had happened to him? And now that he was gone, what chance did we have?

Lilly leaned over him, tears falling, and kissed his forehead. When she stood back, she took a deep breath and started to sing. Her voice sprang to life in the pure note that I had heard inside her skull, the song of the Medium, this high, lilting tone, only Lilly knew more of it than I'd heard, loops and darts, a melody of the ancients, of the sea, of the wind—

And of light.

The white glow began to light the horizon, illuminating the folds of haze. I looked up and watched it grow. The horizon brightening with the eerie white . . .

And then she appeared.

The siren dissolved into being beside us, hovering just beyond the balcony. Lilly was still singing, eyes closed and swaying.

Owen, said the siren. She reached out her hand, like she wanted mine.

But I didn't respond. So much reality had been undone for me, I'd already considered that the siren had never even been real, that she was just a part of the damage done to my mind. The fact that she was back now only made me wonder again . . .

You asked me what I am, said the siren.

I had.

But you know what I am, in your heart.

Did I? I considered the song, the light on the horizon. *You're . . . the Terra. Aren't you?*

Yes. I am the living earth. I am the nexus of Qi and An.

So, I said, *you're like . . . a god?*

The Terra almost seemed to smile. *I am before the gods. There will be time for questions. Now, I need you to take my hand, before the Mariner is gone.*

I reached out and placed my hand in hers. I didn't expect it to even feel like anything, but it was solid, her grip tight. With her other hand, she reached over to Leech, and touched two fingers to his forehead.

And I felt a strange opening in myself, a widening of knowledge, as if information was being given to me, uploaded. I saw maps. I saw two coastlines where there was one, I saw compass directions overlaying one another . . . I was seeing Leech's thoughts, the Terra giving them to me.

And I saw the way to the marker, high in the Andes.

The Terra moved her hand away. *There. You can make the journey now. I will see you when you arrive.*

Arrive? I asked. *Where?*

In the white realm. The Terra winked out. Lilly had stopped singing. She was gazing at me. "I saw her. The siren. That was her, wasn't it?"

"Yeah," I said. "She's the Terra. She helped me see how to get to the marker. She gave me Leech's knowledge of it."

Lilly's eyebrow cocked. "The Terra. And she *spoke* to you? Gave you Leech's Mariner knowledge? I didn't hear her say anything . . . and you've also been inside my skull, even though you're technically the Aeronaut. Can you explain all that?"

"Not yet," I said. Lilly was still looking at me, worried. "What?"

"There was something else down in the temple," she said. "Another part of the inscription. Seven could read some of it but not all. Remember those other symbols?"

"Yeah." I said. "You could read them?" Lilly nodded. "What did it say?"

Lilly pulled a piece of paper from her pocket. "I wrote it down as soon as I got back." She unfolded the paper. "It said: 'And when the Three have been truly revealed, they will return, to defend against the masters. And yet has not this journey been made before? Over and again the cycle repeats, and so we must be wary of the Terra's patience. For if we fail her too often, she may make plans of her own.'" Lilly looked at me. "What do you think that means?"

I just shook my head. "I don't know . . . do you think I'm part of the Terra's plan?"

"Maybe. It seems like everyone has a plan of their own."

"Great," I said.

"Yeah." Lilly looked back at Leech. "Good-bye, Carey," she said. She put her hand on his, lying on his stomach.

I put mine on hers. I wanted to say something, but I couldn't think of anything. Maybe there was nothing to say.

Around us, seagulls called. The wind kicked up frothy waves that started to smack the building, misting us with salty spray that smelled like oil. The first rays of sun speared through the mist, and when the waves crashed against the building, the sun and the oil made brilliant rainbows. It was a beautiful day on the ruined earth.

After a minute, Lilly asked, "Do we leave him here?"

"No," I said. I wasn't sure what we should do, but then I remembered something Seven had said.

"Let's give him to the sea," I said. "To Chaac, or whatever."

Lilly nodded. She looked at the rusted lock on the chains around the chair legs. "Bet I can pop that with my knife." She went inside.

I looked at Leech. All his shaking still, his features plastic somehow, without the energy of life behind them. I half-expected him to move again, to reanimate like a horror of the cryo lab, but this wasn't something Paul had done. This was natural. Just death. Sad, and yet merciful compared to what we'd seen.

Lilly got the lock off. We used one length of chain to tie Leech in place. We lugged the chair up over the railing, leaning it down until his feet touched the water, then we slid him in. The chair thunked into the water. For a moment it floated, bobbing out over the waves, and then it began to sink, down into the gray water. First Leech's torso, then his head slipped under, and finally his feet.

There was a shadow of him, like a creature of the deep, and then he was gone.

We watched the waves for a minute and held hands. I heard Lilly crying. Then she turned and left. She came back holding the small silver drive, the messages from her parents. "I don't want to see these again. My memories are enough." She flicked it into the sea. The flash attracted a seagull, who swooped overhead.

I held up my arm and looked at the leather bracelet, the one I'd made for my dad. When I hadn't known . . . I wondered if I'd ever know whether my parents were alive, or when and where they'd died.

I unsnapped it. Thought I'd bury it here, too. But then I stopped.

"Um," I said. I fiddled with the bracelet and then held it out to Lilly. "There's no romantic story behind this. I made it for my dad. I was going to throw it in the water because it just reminds me of what I didn't know. But . . . it would be different if you wore it."

"I'm interested to see where you go with this," said Lilly, but she took the bracelet, turning it over in her fingers.

"Well, like, maybe you could be my memory. You're everything good that I want to remember, everything I've got that isn't broken. I'm not ready to let go of my parents, my sister, but . . . could you just take it?"

Lilly smiled. She turned the bracelet over, then snapped it onto her wrist. "I'll be your memory, Owen Parker," she said, and kissed me left of my mouth. She pointed to the symbol, the mark of Atlantis I'd etched in the leather. "And I'll be your partner getting here, too. And if you promise not to let anymore leggy blondes get between us, I'll promise to tell you when I hear weird music from skulls and stuff."

"It's a deal," I said.

We hugged, letting our breaths align. It felt safe, being in each other's close space. Then we pulled away and watched the sea for a while.

As the sun began its daily burn, we rose from the sunken building top. At first, the ship felt light, and I had to adjust my flying. It was quiet, too, without our third, Carey from Inland Haven—*That's bloodsucker to you, mammal!*—another who would live on in our journey, the list growing longer. Leech, who'd freed me from a life of lies, and who I could only repay by finishing this.

I checked his maps in my head, wondering again why I could, what I really was, what the Terra meant by what she said . . . but we would find out.

"Any sign of Eden?" Lilly asked.

I scanned the sky. "Not yet. But I'm sure there will be."

I caught the wind and we started south, over jungle shadow and purple sea. Once the sun was high, we stopped in the shade of a cluster of palm trees that had sprung up among the coastal wreckage, and in the evening we set off again, on until Venus appeared and shepherded her flock of stars out to play in the night sky.

We flew, and flew, Lilly and I trading turns flying and sleeping, and we stopped to eat and hide from the sun, and we even played cat and mouse with the moonlit wave tops at times.

Night became day, became night, and we barely spoke, silent with memory, silent with fear, but there was no distance. Only us, heading south, always south, toward the Andes, and the beginning of the end.